Acclaim for **AMIT CHAUDHURI**'s

Freedom Song

"Chaudhuri is a lush prose stylist; whether he is writing about a boy's first encounter with death during a visit to Calcutta or an indecisive lover at Oxford, he effortlessly creates what one man calls . . . 'a silent composition of loved details.'"
—*The New Yorker*

"Chaudhuri's languorous, elliptical, beautiful prose is impressively impossible to place in any category at all."
—Salman Rushdie

"Every fiction . . . must create an illusion of reality; and Chaudhuri's novels succeed in doing so to an impressive degree. He has such a tender intimacy with the world and the people who inhabit it." —*The New York Review of Books*

"Chaudhuri evokes the sweet decorousness of a way of life. . . . [He has] an exquisite gift for imagery."
—*Los Angeles Times Book Review*

"The three books of *Freedom Song* are beautifully evocative compositions, each rich with fascinating improvisations on the themes of family life, memory, and dreams."
—*The Philadelphia Inquirer*

"To read Chaudhuri is to offer yourself the unmitigated pleasure of being in the company of the absolutely first rate, to see again the possibilities of the novel as an art form."

AMIT CHAUDHURI

Freedom Song

Amit Chaudhuri was born in Calcutta in 1962 and brought up in Bombay. He is a graduate of University College, London, and was a research student at Balliol College, Oxford. He was Creative Arts Fellow at Wolfson College, Oxford, and most recently a Leverhulme Fellow at Cambridge. He has contributed fiction, poetry, and criticism to numerous publications including *Granta, The New Yorker, The New Republic, The London Review of Books, The Times Literary Supplement,* and *London Magazine.* His first novel, *A Strange and Sublime Address,* won first prize in the 1991 Betty Trask Awards, the Commonwealth Writers Prize for Best First Book (Eurasia) 1992, and a runner-up award in the 1991 Guardian Fiction Prize. And his second novel, *Afternoon Raag,* won the 1993 Southern Arts Literature Prize and the Encore Award. He lives in Calcutta.

Freedom Song

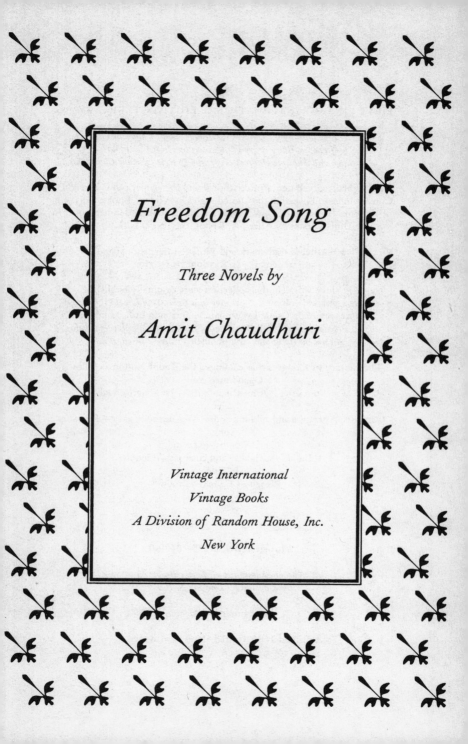

Freedom Song

Three Novels by

Amit Chaudhuri

Vintage International
Vintage Books
A Division of Random House, Inc.
New York

FIRST VINTAGE INTERNATIONAL EDITION, FEBRUARY 2000

Freedom Song copyright © 1998 by Amit Chaudhuri
Afternoon Raag copyright © 1993 by Amit Chaudhuri
A Strange and Sublime Address copyright © 1991 by Amit Chaudhuri

The three works in this collection were originally published
as three separate volumes: *A Strange and Sublime Address* (1991) and
Afternoon Raag (1993) by William Heinemann Ltd., London;
and *Freedom Song* (1998) by Picador, London. Chapter Four of
Afternoon Raag was first published in *New Writing 2*.

The Library of Congress has cataloged the Knopf edition as follows:
Chaudhuri, Amit.
Freedom song / Amit Chaudhuri.—1st American ed.
p. cm.
Contents: A strange and sublime address—Afternoon raag—Freedom
song.
ISBN 0-375-40427-9
I. India—Social life and customs—Fiction.
I. Title.
PR9499.3.C4678F74 1999
823—dc21
98-35260
CIP

Vintage ISBN: 0-375-70400-0

Author photograph © *James Brabazon*
Book design by Dorothy S. Baker

www.vintagebooks.com

Printed in the United States of America
10 9 8 7 6 5 4 3 2 1

Contents

A Strange and Sublime Address

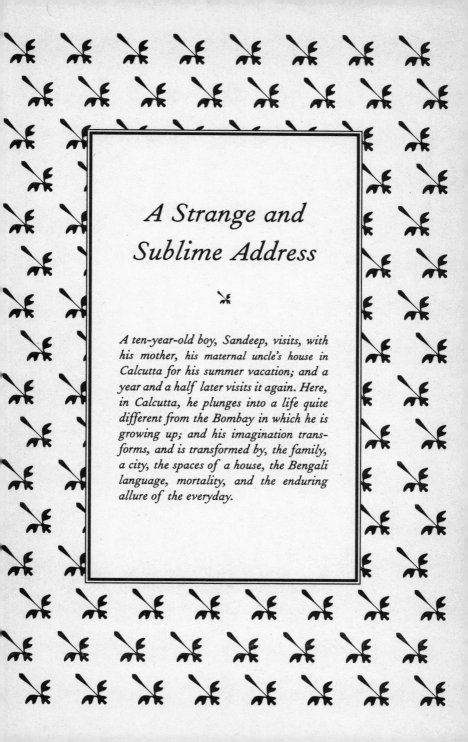

A ten-year-old boy, Sandeep, visits, with his mother, his maternal uncle's house in Calcutta for his summer vacation; and a year and a half later visits it again. Here, in Calcutta, he plunges into a life quite different from the Bombay in which he is growing up; and his imagination transforms, and is transformed by, the family, a city, the spaces of a house, the Bengali language, mortality, and the enduring allure of the everyday.

To my parents

Acknowledgements

I should like to thank Karl Miller for his early encouragement, and the *London Review of Books*, in which Chapter Seven of *A Strange and Sublime Address* first appeared; I am also grateful to Alan Ross and the *London Magazine* for publishing "Lakshmi Poornima Night." Thanks are also due to Dan Jacobson for the generosity of his interest and the helpfulness of comments during my days in University College; to Imogen Parker, my agent; and most of all to my editor, Nadia Lawrence, without whom this book would not have been possible.

Note

The word "mama," in Bengali, and presumably any other North Indian language, means "maternal uncle." Different prefixes may be attached to this word to describe and categorise the different types of maternal uncles that exist in this world. For instance, *chhoto* means "small" or "young"; therefore, "Chhotomama" in the story means "Junior Uncle." Chhotomama's wife is called "Mamima" in the story; this may be roughly translated as "Motherly Maternal Aunt." Children are usually addressed by their nicknames; these may or may not have a meaning. All in all, the Bengali family is a tangled web, an echoing cave, of names and appellations, too complicated to explain individually. Their meaning, hopefully, is brought out in context.

Chapter One

H E S A W the lane. Small houses, unlovely and unremarkable, stood face to face with each other. Chhotomama's house had a pomelo tree in its tiny courtyard and madhavi creepers by its windows. A boy stood clinging to the rusting iron gate, while another boy pushed it backward and forward. As he did so, the first boy travelled in a small arc through space. When the taxi stopped in front of the house, they stared at it with great dignity for a few moments, then ran off in terror, leaving the gate swinging mildly and illegally. A window opened above (it was so silent for a second that Sandeep could hear someone unlocking it) and Babla's face appeared behind the mullions.

Chhotomama and Saraswati, the maidservant, came down and helped them with their bags. Sandeep ran up the stairs with his cousins, not looking back. There was a thrilled impatience about his movements, as if he either wanted to finish or begin something quickly. His aunt, by contrast, stood at the head of the stairs, in a place that was half sunlit and half shadowy, with immaculate serenity, seemingly not having moved from where she had said goodbye to him about a year ago; she said:

"How have you been, Mona?"

When she saw Sandeep's mother, she went down the stairs and grasped her hand in a relaxed way; all the excitement shone in her eyes.

"Didi . . . ," she said.

They went up in a procession, Abhi, Babla, Sandeep, his mother, his uncle, his aunt, as if they were going up to a shrine on pilgrimage. Later, they sat on a wide bed beneath an ancient fan which, as it rotated, moved unreliably from side to side, like a great bird trying to fly. The holiday mood transported them with its poetry; they could have been anywhere—on a hillside on the Western Ghats or in a cave in Kanheri. Sandeep's mother now opened a suitcase and distributed gifts she had brought from Bombay.

Gleaming objects, clothes, perfumes, emerged from the suitcase.

"And here are saris for you," she said to Sandeep's aunt. "Though Calcutta saris are the loveliest."

"Oh but these are beautiful," replied Mamima, unravelling a sari, which broke out into a galaxy of hand-woven stars, a cosmos of streaking comets and symbolic blue horizons.

"She's right," said Chhotomama. "Calcutta saris *are* the loveliest. Though this is nice," he said grudgingly, touching the cloth.

Near them, Sandeep and Abhi silently wrestled with each other, looking vaguely like the two angry, rumpled pillows at the head of the bed. The grown-ups, who made a little shifting arena around their bodies, paid them scarcely more attention than they paid the pillows. Both arms pinned down, Abhi stared into Sandeep's eyes in mock exhaustion and with a distant affection.

"Give up?" cried Sandeep.

"No," whispered Abhi. "No I don't give up."

Irreconcilable as two conflicting principles, they fell to struggling again. It was, actually, an excuse for embracing, touching, exploring each other's presence; not having met for a year, they, great friends, wanted to do these things, and fighting seemed the only acceptable way towards intimacy. Babla, meanwhile, sat listening to the adults talking; his eyes darted from one face to the other, then back again, as if he were following a game of tennis, as if he could see questions and answers, like white balls being tossed from one end of the court to another.

The morning passed in a wave of words. Sandeep's mother talked about Bombay, about Sandeep's father's responsibilities in "the company," about how he worked too hard, and how he never had time to go anywhere. Chhotomama, whose problems were more ordinary and also more difficult to solve, loved listening to the remote complaints of his sister's life, objecting to or agreeing with, now and then, a phrase. Sandeep, an only child, felt the shared background of brother and brother, and brother and sister, throw upon him a shade as that of the cool, expansive branches of a rooted banyan tree. He wandered in the shade, forgetting it was temporary. Mamima brought his mother and Chhotomama cups of tea, which they stirred thoughtfully in the middle of a discussion; Saraswati went to the market and returned with a large, dark boal fish for lunch. The grown-ups never fell short of subjects for discussion; in the kitchen, as Saraswati worked, the pots and pans also held a different, but no less urgent, dialogue. Sandeep, doing something or the other with his cousins, gradually adjusted his senses to Chhotomama's house, to the pale walls, the spider-webs in the corners, the tranquil bedsheets on the old beds, the portraits of grandfathers and grandmothers, the fans that swung drunkenly from side to side—all so different from the quiet and perfected apartment he lived in in Bombay.

. . .

AFTER they had exhausted all their games, they had a bath. They stood naked in front of the bathroom; their clothes lay in a heap at their feet; their testicles hung silently and insignificantly like small, unplucked fruit. Babla's penis was hardly visible, a sleeping beetle everyone had forgotten to notice. He wasn't aware that anything unusual had happened; having spent only six years on this planet, clothes were still a relatively puzzling and uncomfortable phenomenon to him.

Mamima now kneaded Abhi's and Babla's bodies with mustard oil. She twisted them, took them apart, put them together; they surrendered to her as plasticene surrenders its infinite forms to a child's fingers. When she rubbed an arm or a leg, it appeared to detach itself from the body, with a wonderful absence of pain, and come into her skillful hands, a live, grotesque appendage. She would oil it till it shone, and then fix it, with a grim, satisfied smile, where it belonged.

A sharp aura of mustard oil flowered, giving Sandeep's nostrils a faraway sentient pleasure—it wasn't a sweet smell, but there was a harsh unexpectedness about it he liked. It reminded him of sunlight. In Bengal, both tamarind and babies are soaked in mustard oil, and then left upon a mat on the terrace to absorb the morning sun. The tamarind is left out till it dries up and shrivels into an inimitable flavour and a ripe old age; but the babies are brought in before it gets too hot, and then bathed in cool water. With their frantic miniature limbs and their brown, shining bodies, they look like little koi fish caught from the Hooghly River, struggling into life.

The bathroom was a small square room, with a basin on one side, and a window on the right. The window-sill was cluttered with shampoos and soaps and unguents. On the other side of the closed window, pigeons sat through their afternoons with

a serene lack of urgency, and sometimes shifted to look in un-curiously at a nude bather. One could hear mynahs and shaliks singing outside, though one could hear their fragmentary chorus more clearly from the toilet, which was next to the bath. An obsessive, busy music repeated itself behind the frosted glass. Sometimes, one heard the shrill cries of their young, and felt surrounded and safe.

There was a tap in the middle; at the top, a round eye sprinkled with orifices protruded from a pipe that was bent downward like the neck of a tired giraffe; this was the shower. There was no hot water and no bathtub, but no one seemed to miss what was not there. Sometimes, in the afternoon, Saraswati would wash saris and sheets, tedious yards of cloth, beneath the running tap, sitting fixedly on her haunches, rubbing the clothes, banging them repeatedly with a loud watery "pluff" on the floor. As she banged them, the bathroom echoed with a strange rhythm. Later, she would wring the saris into long, exhausted pythons of cloth. She would notice the boys observing her with dark, inquisitive eyes from behind the door, and she would say:

"What are you looking at, you hooligans?"

WHEN they had had their bath, they trooped out like naked ruffians on an island, spattering the floor with their wet footprints. Later they went down to have lunch in the dining-room; they dangled their feet ferociously from chairs round a large, shabby table with pots thronging in the centre.

Pieces of boal fish, cooked in turmeric, red chilli paste, onions, and garlic, lay in a red, fiery sauce in a flat pan; rice, packed into an even white cake, had a spade-like spoon embedded in it; slices of fried aubergine were arranged on a white dish; dal was served from another pan with a drooping ladle;

long, complex filaments of banana flower, exotic, botanical, lay in yet another pan in a dark sauce; each plate had a heap of salt on one side, a green chilli, and a slice of sweet-smelling lemon. The grown-ups snapped the chillies (each made a sound terse as a satirical retort), and scattered the tiny, deadly seeds in their food. If any of the boys was ever brave or foolish enough to bite a chilli, their eyes filled tragically with tears, and they longed to drown in a cool, clear lake. Though Chhotomama was far from affluent, they ate well, especially on Sundays, caressing the rice and the sauces on their plates with attentive, sensuous fingers, fingers which performed a practised and graceful ballet on the plate till it was quite empty.

Chapter Two

LATER, after washing their hands, they went up to the second and topmost storey of the house. Sandeep's mother and Mamima reclined on the large bed. Their conversation was a transparent stream that occasionally trickled into desert patches of silence. Chhotomama turned on the radio, which began to babble immediately like the local idiot:

"Both grandson and grandfather love eating Thin Arrowroot Biscuits."

"Nothing's as kind to your skin as Boroline Antiseptic Cream."

He lay back on the small bed, secure as a soldier in his trench, with the newspaper in his hands; he folded it several ways and made it crackle festively. His face and his arms drowned in the black-and-white ocean of the newspaper, surfacing intermittently. Sighing regretfully, Chhotomama fell asleep, the newspaper covering his face. When the breath came up from his nostrils, the newspaper rose and fell lightly, as if it were breathing as well. On the big bed, Mamima and Sandeep's mother began to dream, sprawled in vivid crab-like postures.

His aunt lay on her stomach, her arms bent as if she were swimming to the edge of a lake; his mother lay on her back, her feet (one of which had a scar on it) arranged in the joyous pose of a dancer.

A mournful song now came on the radio. It was an old radio, a wedding gift, shaped like a box, with outdated knobs and dials. When Sandeep was younger, he had thought there were little men, talented homunculi, inside the box of the radio, who performed those songs. But that seemed long ago. Beside the radio, there was a clock with a white face which always ran ten minutes fast. Every night, the time was readjusted, and every morning, with great accuracy, it had gained ten minutes. At about half-past four, when the clock said twenty to five, the grown-ups woke and stretched their arms like reluctant children. The Sunday lunch, then the Sunday nap—and the thought of Monday, that difficult day, was aborted. The radio crackled with the nervous, breathless sound of football commentary; dust had settled on the floor and furniture of the house.

Calcutta is a city of dust. If one walks down the street, one sees mounds of dust like sand dunes on the pavements, on which children and dogs sit doing nothing, while sweating labourers dig into the macadam with spades and drills. The roads are always being dug up, partly to construct the new underground railway system, or perhaps for some other obscure reason, such as replacing a pipe that doesn't work with another pipe that doesn't work. At such times, Calcutta is like a work of modern art that neither makes sense nor has utility, but exists for some esoteric aesthetic reason. Trenches and mounds of dust everywhere give the city a strange bombed-out look. The old houses, with their reposeful walls, are crumbling to slow dust, their once-gleaming gates are rusting. Dust flakes off the ceilings in offices; the buildings are becoming dust, the

roads are becoming dust. At the same time, dust is constantly raised into startling new shapes and unexpected forms by the arbitrary workings of the wind, forms on which dogs and children sit doing nothing. Daily, Calcutta disintegrates, unwhispering, into dust, and daily it rises from dust again.

A house in Calcutta must be swept and scrubbed at least twice a day. Once, in the morning, Saraswati polished the floor with a moist rag, and Mamima religiously dusted the tables and chairs. The dust rose in the air in breathless clouds and seemed to evaporate and disappear. But by evening, it would condense, like moisture, and resettle on the surfaces of things. A little before sunset, a woman called Chhaya came to clean the house a second time, smiling at the boys as they waited impatiently for her to finish. She had a serious cultured face with a serious smile, the face of a kindly and understanding teacher; it was hard to believe she lived across the railway lines, in the clump of huts called the basti, from which whiffs of excrement rose on windy days.

She would sweep the floor—unending expanses, acres and acres of floor—with a short broom called the jhadu, swiping away the dust in an arc with its long tail, which reminded one of the drooping tail of some nameless, exotic bird. She would collect the dust in a corner, and here there would be an accumulation of unlikely treasure that had blown in from outside or had gathered, unnoticed, inside: a single elegant pigeon's feather, a page lost from a book, a dead spider which ants had forgotten to carry off, the long, black, tender loops of Mamima's and Sandeep's mother's hair.

Then she would dip a grey rag into a pail, and sit on her haunches at one end of the room, and swish the rag around the floor. Carefully, deliberately, she would begin to advance to the other end of the room, swiping the floor with the moist rag, her right arm moving regularly and automatically, like a fin, till she

had reached the other end. Her odd movement forward on her haunches had an amphibian quality, half human and half of another world. It was laborious, and yet had the simplicity and poise of a tortoise's amble; when she finished, hardly a speck remained; the floor was bright as a mirror or a lake on a calm day. Then, at last, she would unbend her body and straighten her back. Most of the time she worked, her body was slightly bent, as if in obeisance to an invisible god.

THERE are several ways of spending a Sunday evening. You could drive to Outram Ghat, and then stroll with your family by the River Hooghly, watching balloons floating volitionlessly in the air, the steamers in the water, the smoky outline of the Howrah Bridge, like an altar on the horizon. You could stay at home and listen to plays on the radio once the football commentary was over: comedies, melodramas, whodunits. The heroine's voice would quiver like a note on the violin; the star-crossed lovers would frequently cry "Never!" and "Forever!"; the murderer would murder accompanied by drums and cymbals; the funny man would mispronounce words and fall in love with the heroine. It was like Shakespeare, and yet it was not like Shakespeare.

Sometimes Chhaya would come in and say excitedly:

"They're showing a seenema in the field!"

"Seenema! What seenema?" Mamima would ask.

"*Street-Singer,*" she would reply, or the name of some other such film made forty years ago in the New Theatres.

The boys would run up to the terrace and lean out to look at the field that lay beyond the professor's house. This surprising piece of empty land, which builders and contractors had somehow overlooked, was usually a meeting place for fireflies; at night, wandering with their small lights, their miniature

green hurricane lamps, they turned the silent field into a lighted marketplace of activity. Servants and their children, rickshawallas, people from the basti, had now gathered in the field to watch the seenema; a great piece of white cloth had been hung between two poles at one end. After some time, giant black-and-white figures came alive on the piece of cloth, and a white funnel of light ran from the projector to the screen; the audience sat dwarfed by the indistinct majesty of the figures moving before them. Voices, loud and elemental as thunder, boomed from a scratchy soundtrack. Sandeep tried to follow the story, but all he comprehended was the sound of thunder and the darkness of evening and the dance of black-and-white phantoms.

When they came down, their eyes smarting, Chhotomama looked up from the newspaper and said:

"Let's go for a drive."

And Mamima, who had been sewing a button onto trousers, bit the thread and asked:

"Where to?"

"Anywhere," said Chhotomama, with child-like conviction.

"But won't you be tired driving? You have work tomorrow."

"The roads will be deserted today. The roads are always deserted on Sunday."

They went down; Chhotomama backed the car out of the small garage that was attached to the house. It was an old, grey Ambassador; its faded, mottled colour did not seem to be its natural colour, but a complexion attained with age and unrewarded industry. It was battered like an old cardboard box, and the needles on the dials on its dashboard never changed direction, like futile compasses always pointing north. When it ran, the engine and the ramshackle body of the car combined to make a grating, earthy noise, like a drunk man cracking an

obscene joke in a guttural dialect and laughing at it at the same time.

Chhotomama sat at the steering wheel with superior confidence; Mamima and Sandeep's mother huddled in womanly league at the back; the three boys were crammed together in the front, Sandeep by the window, Abhi next to him, and Babla inside, between his father and his brother, where it was hottest. The best place, by the open window, was graciously afforded to Sandeep by his two cousins, and Sandeep accepted it graciously, a tyrant condescending to please his subjects. Babla, the youngest, had to be content to squeeze into the worst place. It seemed there was no democracy among children—always an aristocracy based on strength, intellect, and seniority. But seniority counted most, because a boy of ten is bound to be stronger and cleverer than a boy of nine, having spent an extra year in the world, at a time when each year is like a precious deposit in a newly opened bank account. Among boys of the same age, there would be a silent tussle, a clean, honourable contest. Once a leader emerged, however, no elections were held.

They went past the bridge in Dhakuria, past Gol Park, where a statue of Swami Vivekananda, with arms folded in fierce serenity, stood staring unflinchingly at an advertisement for biscuits; past Gariahat Market; past Rashbehari Avenue, which would be lit with rows and rows of shops on a weekday, and which was distinguished by having the largest number of underwear shops in the world; then into Chowringhee with its colonial buildings, vacant and proud, looking on Sunday evening like a black-and-white photograph of another era.

A swift, streamlined breeze, such as only blows on summer nights, came in through the window. Sandeep, who envied birds and fish because they could float in their chosen element, the fish by moving with the tide and the bird by opening its

wings and allowing the wind to carry it, transport it, loved going for drives because it seemed to him the only human equivalent of floating, of letting one's legs rest and setting one's body adrift. As the car turned right into Park Street, he felt at peace as effortless images of shops and restaurants passed by him as coral and anemones pass by a fish's life. A sports shop—the red letters said CASTLEWOOD (INDIA)—had its glass doors closed, but its lights were on, and he could see two tennis racquets crossed diagonally behind the shop window. Still and surreal, they had the finality of a religious symbol. The car passed Flury's, tea-shop, cake-shop, and idler's den in one, where young clerks came with their newly married wives, wives they had never spoken to before marriage and whom they were still shy and unfamiliar with, and with whom they tried to make halting conversation across the table, where clever young men from St. Xavier's College came to glance sideways at the young, unassuming wives, who glanced sideways at them, together with the Anglo-Indians and the Chinese from Free School Street—here they congregated, like votaries belonging to a single religious order, each morning, afternoon, and evening, drinking tea and eating sausage rolls and nodding at each other. Around the giant letters, FLURY'S, were sprinkled small, absurd, many-coloured stars, a parody and tender caricature of the stars of the universe. MONDAYS CLOSED said a melancholy sign. As the battered car drifted homeward, the rear window, in a wide-eyed ignorance, recorded the last images— empty pavements, a drunk leaving a bar, a dog at a zebra crossing—of Park Street.

Chapter Three

MONDAY morning came like a fever. Chhotomama would be at the dining-table, eating a rapid meal of dal, fish, and rice, trying to avoid chewing as much of it as possible, before he rushed to work. Then he would run upstairs, where a pair of polished black shoes would be waiting for him like a long-promised gift. He would spend five minutes persuading his feet to enter the shoes, or the shoes to swallow his feet. When this was done, he would knot the shoelaces and stand up straight, returning the stare of the world with a look of schoolboyish triumph; in a white shirt and grey trousers, he would look like a different person. He would become an archetype of that familiar figure who is not often described in literature—the ordinary breadwinner in his moment of unlikely glory, transformed into the centre of his universe and his home. Over and over again, he would shout, "I'm late!" in the classic manner of the man crying "Fire!" or "Timber!" or "Eureka!" while Saraswati and Mamima scuttled around him like frightened birds.

Then he would rush downstairs and start the car, which would make angry, reproachful noises. At last he would back it

out of the garage and drive it down the lane, while a group of ragged urchins ran behind it cheerfully, shouting and waving their arms, looking like a school of tiny ancillary fish in the wake of a whale. Not until the last sputter of its engine had died away, and the last grey clouds of its exhaust fumes blended with the atmosphere, did peace reign once more resignedly over the household. These mornings would have been intolerable if they had not possessed the ring and obstinate fanfare of a Hindu festival or wedding ceremony, which distracted everyone and kept them from thinking or analysing too deeply; they would have been unbearable if it hadn't been known that the chaos never lasted more than twenty-five minutes.

SOMETIMES, late in the morning, a young man—any young man, useless and unambitious, perhaps distantly related to the family—would arrive at Chhotomama's house on his way to or from somewhere, patches of sweat darkening his colourless shirt, a white layer of prickly-heat powder around his neck.

"Didi," he would say to Sandeep's aunt, with excessive politeness, "did you remind Dadabhai about my job?"

"What's the use?" Mamima would say, bringing him a glass of water. "Does he listen to what I say? Does he have time to listen?"

"But you must remind him," he would reply, rebuking her gently. "Again and again and again."

There would be an oily smile on his face, and his features and facial muscles, lubricated by a desperate, greasy willingness to please, would become extremely, marvellously, mobile. He would glance at Sandeep and whisper confidentially to Abhi:

"Who's this?"

"My cousin-brother Sandeep."

"Sandeep . . ." he would murmur. "Where do you live, Sandeep?"

"Bombay."

"Bombay . . ." he would repeat, as if betrayed, a mixture of distrust and tragic reverence for the unattainable in his voice. "Bombay is a nice city . . . " He would pause. "Though some prefer Calcutta." He would pause again. "Calcutta has charm." With every pause, this perspiring, jobless man would grow smaller and smaller on the divan, and Sandeep bigger and bigger, like a trick of animation in a cat and mouse cartoon.

After another thoughtful pause, he would ask, as if this would decide everything:

"Do you play football?"

"No," Sandeep would say.

Abashed and hurt, but trying to recover, he would ask:

"What will you be when you grow up?"

It was Sandeep's turn to hesitate, and he would say:

"A writer."

"A *writer?*"

"He writes in English," Abhi would reveal.

Once more, the man would diminish and Sandeep grow several feet in this endless, terrifying cartoon.

"*English?* And what will you write when you grow up?"

"Horror stories."

The man would become more relaxed now, and ask patronisingly:

"Oh horror stories . . . How old are you?"

"Ten."

"How many brothers do you have?"

"None."

"How many sisters, then?"

"None."

"None?"

It would go on like this for some time. The man did not seem to like Sandeep, which was a pity, because Sandeep liked the man.

IN THE evenings, people came out on the balconies in the lane: widows in white saris, housewives with children in their arms. The men returned home, slowly. Sandeep and his cousins sat on cane stools on the verandah, watching the balconies on the opposite side, each with its own characters, its own episodes.

In a house further down the lane, three sisters leaned against the railings in freshly pressed saris, one holding a bamboo fan. They murmured to each other and covered their mouths with their hands when they laughed. They were known as Cinderella's Ugly Sisters, but the analogy ended there, because there was no Cinderella in the family. Disappointingly, the ugly sisters were not even ugly. But they were more than twenty-five years old, and still unmarried, which is why people had begun to think there was something physically wrong with them. No woman above twenty-five and single at the same time was beautiful.

A teacher and his wife lived in the house exactly opposite. They had a twelve-year-old son whom Sandeep and his cousins disliked because he always came first in class, and batted and bowled at cricket matches. He belonged to that despicable species called the "all-rounder." His father wanted him to be a success in life: a manager in a large company, perhaps. Everywhere in the lane, fathers prayed their sons would be successes. One would be a doctor because his father had once wanted to be doctor. Another would be an engineer. Another would go to America and be a famous scientist. No effort

would be spared; "future" and "career" had become Bengali words, incorporated unconsciously but feverishly into daily Bengali parlance.

The teacher also had a ten-year-old daughter, who was being taught how to dance and paint and sing, besides how to talk and read and write, so that, when she was twenty-one, she could be married to a success in life: a manager in a large company, perhaps. The urge to do well, which existed behind closed windows like libido, was sad and strangely obscene, because no one would admit to it. Meanwhile, children, like Egyptian slaves, dragged huge blocks of frustrating study all day to build that impressive but nonexistent pyramid of success.

On certain evenings, when Chhotomama was home, he would call out across the lane to the teacher's ten-year-old daughter:

"Chandrima, give us a dance!"

The girl, standing on the balcony with both her hands on the railings, and her face resting on her hands, would shake her head elaborately from side to side. She would open her lips to print a silent "No" on the air, and dangle her body shyly. So Sandeep's uncle and his aunt would both cry out:

"Come on Chandrima, give us a dance. You know we love your dancing!"

After some coaxing and persuasion, Chandrima would begin to dance on the balcony, and the balcony would become a stage. She would embroider funny gestures with her small hands, so that they looked now like an absurd bird, and now like a doe's head, and now like barely visible wings. All the time, she would be singing to herself and swaying from side to side, beating a rhythm on the floor with her foot, and never managing to do it in perfect measure. Scornfully, Sandeep looked away, talking to his cousins; yet he could not resist

glancing, too frequently, at that swaying figure from the corner of his eyes. When the performance was over, the girl ran inside with a sharp, involuntary shyness, while Chhotomama shouted, "Wonderful! Amazing!"; for some reason, Sandeep's heart shouted within him, but he did not say a word.

Untidy but regular activity continued on the pavement. Girls played hopscotch; three boys sat on the ground, shooting marbles; a child was practising how to walk—each time it took a careful, tentative step forward, a step taken with huge, melo-dramatic conviction, its other leg forgot it was a leg, and the child, bewildered by its own body, collapsed in a soft heap. It began to cry and its tears made its elder sister smile; stooping, she lifted it with thin, lovely arms.

With a loaded tray in her hands, Sandeep's aunt came into the verandah. There were cups of tea on the tray, and three tumblers of milk for the boys. There was also a small, earthen pot with dark, fried sweetmeats, each an orb, dipped in syrup.

She set the tray on the floor of the verandah, which had just been swept clean by Chhaya; then she bent her knees, slowly lowering her body, and sat down on the floor herself. She was most comfortable on the newly cleaned floor, her bright red-and-blue sari thickening around her, crumpling into several folds, her hands moving carefully through the minor storm of her garments as she served the sweetmeats. Her legs, like two romantic, indefinite paths on a mountainside, were lost in her sari's vast landscape.

Chapter Four

LATER, when they came inside, Sandeep found his uncle sitting with a friend at the dining-table. They were talking enthusiastically about something, and banging their fists on the table, making one or two old pots tremble—the table was used as much for banging (a kind of drumroll to indicate the significance of what was being said) as it was for eating. It was old and weathered; stains from teacups and gravies and dirty fingers had multiplied on it like signatures. But it was clean; each afternoon, each night, Saraswati wiped it with a wet, dirty-looking rag, which, in spite of its appearance, was actually clean too, clean like the soul of a wronged criminal.

In the kitchen, Sandeep's aunt had gathered black jaams onto a plate. Every May, around this time, jaams came into the markets and houses of Calcutta, dark and shiny as grapes or berries. His aunt put them into a small pan, added mustard oil and sugar, and then put the lid on. Solemnly but fiercely, she began to shake the pan up and down, holding it tightly in her hands.

"Now," she said between clenched teeth, her voice shaking with her shaking body, "now we turn the jaam into pulp, and

mix it thoroughly with the mustard oil and sugar." She sounded like a woman on a cooking programme on the radio. Politely, Sandeep enquired if he could have the opportunity of shaking the pan. With his aunt's permission, he took it in his hands and shook it vigorously, a mildly spiteful expression on his face. No mercy, no restraint, was to be shown towards the jaam. One by one, they took turns—his aunt, Sandeep, Abhi, even Babla—abandoning their civilized facades and letting themselves go the moment they held the pan, like prophets on the verge of a vision or epileptics surrendering to a seizure. In the end, the jaam became soft and moist and pulpy, purplish in colour, both sweet and tangy, delicious.

It was served in bowls to Chhotomama and his friend, who ate the rich, battered flesh and spat out the thick seeds onto a platter after sucking them dry. Sandeep sat down casually at the table. He liked listening to his uncle talk about business. He liked it because his uncle's account of the small-business world always seemed like a suspense story or a myth or a fairy-tale, full of evocative characters that worked themselves slowly into his imagination: cheats, sophisticated two-timers, astringent moralists, clever strategists, heroic fighters, risk takers, and explorers. Each new business venture sounded like a new military onslaught, each new product like a never-before weapon capable of conquering the world added to a nameless arsenal. And Sandeep believed every word of it, that is, the tone of the words rather than the words themselves, because they were said with such confidence, such superior conviction. Only the other grown-ups seemed unpardonably cynical about Chhotomama's abilities. They said things like: "Anindo doesn't have a head for business. If he'd stuck to a proper job, he would be leading a better life."

But the children had boundless faith in him. Abhi had told Sandeep that the latest machine his father's factory had made

was an agricultural device that could gather rice from the fields, separate the chaff from the grain, and then bundle it, all at once.

"It's the only one of its kind in the world," Abhi said gravely. Sandeep nodded, equally grave, and wondered about this magical implement, this work of genius. Surely this amazing machine should have silenced all the grown-ups? Were they jealous? Though, granted, Chhotomama had led an unpredictable life. When he had been a student, he had believed he was a Communist, and had planned his part in the coming revolution with great passion and earnestness. History would take care of everything; no more would the square pegs have to be fitted into round holes and the round pegs into square ones. When the coming revolution failed to come, he had begun to believe he was a businessman, and had invested all his savings, with a few friends, into starting a small company. He still had that passionate temperament, and he now planned his new transactions and ventures with the involved enthusiasm with which he had once planned revolutions. Whenever he had doubts, his friends convinced him not to have any, and he agreed with the air of a man who enjoys being convinced. There were times when it seemed a wonderful "pretend" game, not real or dangerous at all, like the games Sandeep and Abhi played in the afternoons. Figures of expected earnings—half a million, one million, two million—expanded and contracted in the air, the endless zeros rose and burst like balloons, the huge sums were lost in an imaginary world of numbers . . .

IT WAS unbearably hot the next afternoon. The sun had come closer to the earth; the hours seemed trapped in an unending midday. Exhausted, they took frantic baths, the children drenching each other in a circus of water, and then they sat,

their blue-black hair combed and shining beneath the dervishing fan.

Shonamama rang the doorbell. He was a bachelor, Sandeep's mother's eldest brother, and he lived a twenty-minute bus ride away from Chhotomama's house. A pensioner, he walked through the lanes of Calcutta with a black umbrella in his hand which threw a dark island of shadow around him. Now he climbed up the staircase slowly, enjoying the shadows and the cold touch of the banister on his hand. The stone stairs seemed to exhale a coolness as the roads outside radiated trembling, enervating gasps of heat. Entering the room, he closed his black umbrella delicately, and called out:

"Saraswati, a glass of cold water." Then, turning to the boys, "Now we *really* know that the Tropic of Cancer runs through Calcutta."

"Does it really?" asked Sandeep. "Does it really, Shonamama?"

"Of course it does," he said peremptorily, and proceeded to drink the cold water from the glass in a single draught, pausing neither for breath nor thought. He made a strange gurgling sound as he drank, and his Adam's apple bobbed up and down. The glass had been covered on all sides in a cold, vapoury sweat, a fine, chilled dew trickling from top to bottom, and Sandeep brushed his fingers against it and, taking the dew, smeared its moisture on his forehead and his neck.

"Aaaah," said Sandeep and Shonamama at the same time.

THEY had shut all the windows and closed the shutters so that the room was a large box covered by a lid, cool and dark and spacious inside. And they were like tiny insects living in the darkness of the box, breathing in the air of the world through invisible perforations. Whenever there was a power-cut, they

fanned themselves meditatively with newspapers or bamboo fans, and the children deserted the bed and lay down or sat down on the floor, because the floor was a stone slab of coolness, an expanse of warm ice that would not melt. Sandeep's aunt and mother lay on the bed, murmuring to each other, and each time they turned, there was a shy and subtle clink of bangles. And whenever the power returned, the fan whirred at full speed, and the silent room filled with its gentle, understated hum. Shonamama was sitting on the stool in the far side of the room, reading a book by the light of a single lamp. It seemed strange, that lamp shining in the daytime, and the room so dark, as if night had fallen inside it.

Sometimes, Sandeep and Abhi would walk up quietly to a window and open a single shutter, slanting it so that as little light entered the room as possible. Then they both peered through it; it was like peering into the narrow slit of a letterbox. They were momentarily blinded; outside, everything dazzled intolerably; a few people walked on the pavement like survivors, vanquished by the heat. It was possible, at certain moments, for Abhi and Sandeep to call out to a dazed passer by, "Eh, stupid!" or "Faster, fat man!" and close the shutter and become invisible. Then they would break into loud hiccups of laughter; they felt they had the dangerous power to unsettle the world outside, and then fade innocently into thin air, like spirits. The heat outside and the coolness inside made them feel inviolable and reckless.

Once or twice, Sandeep remembered Bombay and felt oddly unhappy without knowing why. Alone in the big apartment on the twenty-third floor, he was like Adam in charge of paradise, given dominion over the birds and fishes; he was too much in the foreground. He hated being in the foreground; he wanted a housefly's anonymity. At school, he was Adam expelled, at large among the alien and the unforgiving. But

here, in Chhotomama's house, he pulsed into life and passed into extinction according to his choice; he had liberty.

During these alternating bouts of happiness and unhappiness, when Sandeep felt his equilibrium disturbed, his thoughts would run something like this: I wish it were the first day of the holidays, and I had just come back from school, and I had just entered my room, and I had just heard we were going to Calcutta. His mind went back to that moment, which had never really existed in quite that way, and savoured it.

To regain his composure, all he had to do was take a second look through the shutter. A bhelpuri vendor was wandering past, his prop under his arm, the basket of bhelpuri balanced almost stylishly, like a Malaysian fedora, on his head. Later, the key man went by, with a cluster of keys around a large ring, the metal shimmering against the sun, the keys jangling. The vendor had called out in a loud voice, "*Bhel*puri!" but the key man had said nothing; he had simply shaken the ring and let the jangling keys speak for him. The strange metallic whisper of the keys could be heard, immaterial and ghostly, even when the man had disappeared, seemingly evaporated by the heat.

Chapter Five

SANDEEP woke in the sharp light of morning to shouts coming vague and muffled from the distance. He rubbed his eyes, knelt upon the pillow, then jumped sideways from the bed to the window. His cousins were already there, watching something with deep patience and interest. It was their father. He was late as usual. He was sitting at the steering wheel of the old Ambassador, one arm casually hanging outside, one arm on the wheel, glancing backward enquiringly, as if he were checking some crucial point no one else could see. A few idle men had gathered around the decrepit car.

"Okay boys, start pushing," Chhotomama commanded without turning his head, looking keenly at a private landmark on the horizon.

The idlers were quite unexpectedly altered into purposeful, energetic men, as if someone had turned a key in their backs. They took position, like a small battalion—two by the window, two at the back, and another reserve, who would do the indispensable work of shouting from the rear. At Chhotomama's words, the team strained forward, and the recalcitrant car, after some stolid silent thought, decided to concede a few

feet into the road. People had come out on the balconies, and were watching with sympathetic curiosity. Their eyes followed the car's reluctant progress; their lips parted to pass a few well-considered comments; husbands and wives who had quarrelled the previous night were reunited in their avid appreciation of the spectacle; brothers who could never agree about a single point reached a brief consensus about the condition of the vehicle; astonished children who had never spoken anything but thickly meditative nonsense uttered, to the delight of their mothers, their first word as the car belched twice into motion and then stopped again.

Sandeep and his cousins stared out in embarrassed silence. As they watched, their heads turned together in exactly the same way, tilted at an identical angle; their necks craned with painful tension as the disgruntled car moved beyond view. There was an apprehensive hush, then a faint rumble, then excitement as they saw the car returning, this time facing the other side of the road.

"Harder, boys, harder!" persuaded his uncle.

He looked almost heroic and serene, in complete control of the troubled situation. Sandeep's aunt, who had been in the verandah on the first storey, surreptitiously entered the room. She glanced shyly out of the window, then turned away, covering her eyes.

"Why don't we stick to horse carriages?" she whispered.

Chhotomama had passed out of view again. Sandeep tried to insinuate his head between the gaps of the mullions, but failed. Then there was a sudden throbbing in the distance, culminating in a long, drawn-out roar, an affirmative crescendo at the end of a tiresome musical. The engine had come to life. The five men returned, sweating, talking loudly and rapidly, showing off, playing to the gallery.

"Boudi!" they called. "Boudi!"

"Yes?" said Sandeep's aunt, hesitantly approaching the window.

"We sent Dada off, finally!" announced the reserve, who had shouted the most because he was gifted with an impressive voice. "The car's all right!"

Sandeep's aunt nodded and smiled. She knew that this kind of thing occurred too frequently in the mornings, and the derelict, geriatric car changed into a difficult, obstinate animal. It was one of those beasts that the people of Calcutta had been unable to domesticate—better, perhaps, to go back to the horse and the horse carriage. On bad days like this, when the fans stopped turning because of a power-cut, when the telephone went dead because of a cable-fault, when the taps became dry because there was no power to pump the water, and, finally, when the car engine curtly refused to start, it seemed a better idea to return to a primitive, unpretentious means of subsistence—to buy a horse and a plough, to dig a well in one's backyard, to plant one's own trees and grow one's own fruit and vegetables. Calcutta, in spite of its fetid industrialisation, was really part of that primitive, terracotta landscape of Bengal, Tagore's and the wandering Vaishnav poet's Bengal—the Bengal of the bullock-cart and the earthen lamp. It had pretended to be otherwise, but now it had grown old and was returning to that original darkness: in time, people would forget that electricity had ever existed, and earthen lamps would burn again in the houses.

THERE were two rooms on the second and topmost storey. The first was the large one facing the road; here, Sandeep and his cousins slept and woke, and here they wrote and rewrote themselves into their imaginary expeditions and adventures.

There were two beds, one big and one small, on which they voyaged daily into nowhere. The cupboards rose like ugly reefs from a fictional ocean, casting long, rectangular shadows in the evening. At one end of the room, there was a mirror and a dressing-table; the mirror imaged the room and gave it a sense of extra space. Next to it, there was a wooden clothes-horse, with several horizontal bars running parallel to, and on top of, each other. One would have expected to find it in a gymnasium, but here it was—it was called an alna, and all kinds of clothes and garments hung from its ribs. A lizard lived behind it.

The other room, facing the backyard, a few palm trees, a field, and a professor's house, was much smaller, with one double bed in it. Near the window, there was an ungainly study-table, with Abhi's textbooks on it and metal boxes that contained pencils, rulers, and erasers. But no one who studied at this table would ever read more than a page because, just by the open window, almost at arm's length, was a palm tree wearing its rings of coconuts like jewellery, balancing a crow on its broad, fan-tail leaf, and behind the palm tree was the professor's house, with two daughters always getting in each other's way, a rooster, an educated-looking dog and a cat without a conscience, and the professor's son, who performed such enviably intricate exercises in the morning. You just had to watch that window.

Within this room there was another room, hidden away in the corner. Three steps rose to it; it was a world within a world; a world, in fact, more richly inhabited than the sparse outer husk in which it was enclosed. If you sat at the study-table, it was just on your left. It was the prayer-room. Different gods and goddesses reclined or stood in various postures within. Krishna was there with his flute, his peacock plume, and his

mildly flirtatious smile; Saraswati sat thoughtfully upon her swan, playing her veena endlessly and attentively; Lakshmi was accompanied by her mascot, the white owl; Ganesh, with his humorous elephant head, had been afforded a place as well, with his unlikely mascot, the giant rodent. Durga, the mother-goddess, had been given a slightly more prominent place than the rest. Elegant and self-contained, she rode a fierce lion. Of all the gods, Sandeep liked Ganesh the best, because he seemed so content with his own appearance.

After her bath, Sandeep's aunt would wrap a sari around herself, not wearing the blouse as yet, so that her bare shoulders showed above the borders of her sari, gleaming, a little moist. She would not approach the gods until she had bathed; then she must rub Jabakusum oil vigorously into her hair, till the black hair reflected the sunlight and turned almost silvery. It was a sweet-smelling oil, dark red and rich, like wine.

She entered the prayer-room and lit two incense sticks, then stuck them, like slim pencils, into a perforated brass stand. She arranged slices of cucumber and oranges and sweet white batashas on three brass plates and placed them in front of the gods. The gods too are hungry, she said. They too need nourishment. Sandeep smiled politely but contemptuously when he heard this. But when do they eat? he enquired patiently. She muttered something incoherently—not an answer, but a mantra she had begun to repeat to herself as soon as she sat upon the shatranji on the floor.

Sometimes it was a mantra; sometimes it was a long incantation about the exploits of a god or a goddess—how, for instance, a demon had been outwitted, or a demon's sister had been embarrassed. Or it was a description of a divine wedding: how a god had won an earthmaiden, or how a goddess had been won by a mortal king after a prolonged and wasteful courtship. They were an irresponsible lot, jealous of each other, doing

silly, petty things at times and silly, spectacular things at others—not unlike Sandeep and his cousins.

Sandeep himself did not believe in God, much less in gods. Like most children, he was the opposite of innocent: he was skeptical but tolerant of other creeds. What he enjoyed about the act of worship had little to do with belief or disbelief in divinity; it was the smell of sandalwood incense, the low hum of his aunt's voice, the bell ringing at the end of the ceremony, the white batashas, clean as washed pebbles, taken out of a bottle hidden in a small cupboard, the cool taste of the offerings that were distributed after the prayer, in fact, the general, dignified uselessness of the whole enterprise. And he liked the sight of his aunt surrounded by her gods in that tiny room, like a child in a great dollhouse, blowing the conch eloquently; it was a strange sight, to watch a grown-up at play. Prayer-time was when adults became children again.

AT LUNCHTIME, at the dining-table, Sandeep asked his aunt:

"Mamima, what did you pray for today?"

Separating some tiny and particularly persistent bones from the fish, she replied:

"Oh I prayed the car would start in the mornings."

"Didn't you pray for a new car?" asked Abhi, a high-pitched inflection of disappointment in his voice.

They went on eating, inspecting the fish, searching for the fishbones, the tiny, tiny fishbones. Babla sat with his mouth open, into which his mother put little balls of fish and rice. What you prayed for mattered least in the prayer-room; all that mattered was the vivid entertainment of the instant. The gods, in their supreme, all-seeing inadvertence, forgot to answer the prayers, and the devotees didn't care. All that was important to the gods and the mortals was the creation of that rich and

endlessly diverting moment in the small chamber, that moment of secret, almost illicit, communion, when both the one who prayed and the one who was prayed to were released from the irksome responsibility of the world. Oranges, white batashas, cucumbers.

Chapter Six

IN THE morning, the sweeper came equipped with brooms and rags to wash the toilets and the bathrooms. He was tall and ugly, and his eyes were always bloodshot. He had an angry look about him, but he wasn't an angry person at all; simply a dirty and a surprisingly clumsy one. He made an awful noise as he worked, banging things here and there; perhaps it soothed his nerves in some way. The only time he usually spoke was at the end of the month, when he demanded, in a loud, half-joking voice, as if he were amused at something, his wages.

He had a son who accompanied him at times, who was around thirteen years old. He had stopped going to school four years ago, and had begun to help his father. When he came to Chhotomama's house, he carried a bucket half full of water in one hand and a rag in the other, with a mixture of aplomb and hesitation that reminded Sandeep of a soldier crossing a minefield. He was called Nimai, after the wandering, saffron-clothed saint who preached love to the people of Bengal. The sweeper was a religious man, and, deep down, he believed in the all-pervasive power of love.

One morning, the sweeper came to give his excuse for not

having turned up to clean the toilets the last two days. He had brought his excuse with him. It was a baby, its face a fist, its eyes crinkled, and when a hand brushed the tiny strip of cloth that covered it, its naked thighs and buttocks were revealed, and also, in a flash of humorous candour, the fact that its sex was female.

"It's only two days old," he said with some surprise in his voice, as if he were taken aback each time he tried to understand it. Nimai, meanwhile, was distributing dry, yellow sweets from a cardboard box, an important smile on his face.

"We thought *she* would die this time, it was so difficult," said the sweeper, tenderly emphasizing the pronoun that referred to his wife. "Nothing bad happened, thank God." He smiled broadly, revealing bad teeth. "Anyway, it's got *her* complexion." The baby was dark as a tree trunk. "Didimoni, perhaps you don't know, but it's her fourth child," he said, as if it were not his.

Sandeep's mother replied severely, "Four children are enough, Ganesh. You'll send this one to school, hopefully."

"Oh yes!" said the sweeper, a look of great responsibility in his eyes, mingled with sly enthusiasm. "An English-medium school I'll send this one to, Didimoni!"

"Bengali-medium or English-medium, you must stop having children now if you want to raise these three properly. Poor Nimai has already lost his chance of an education."

Poor Nimai, still distributing sweets and eating some of them himself, did not look as if he minded unduly.

The time came when the baby was to be passed from person to person. All the three boys wanted to hold it, but there was the delicate question of weight. There is an episode in the *Ramayan* in which princes from various kingdoms file into King Janak's court and try their hand at lifting his great, ponderous bow, in order to win his virtuous and beautiful daugh-

ter, Sita. Everyone fails except Ram, who lifts the bow with a powerful flourish, and pulls the string till it resonates and breaks. Sandeep and Abhi and Babla discovered that, unfortunately, they did not have a Ram among them, and the dangerous precariousness with which they tried to hold the baby made it apparent that the baby was far heavier for them than King Janak's bow was for Ram. What was to be done? Humiliated, with sheepish smiles on their faces, they saw the baby transported into the arms of the women. Later, it was laid on the large double bed, where it waited on its back, like a helpless tortoise on its shell, remarkably tolerant and unprotesting. There, Saraswati, the maidservant, and Chhaya, the floor cleaner, found it when they came into the room. "The baby! Ganesh's baby!" They squeezed it into a ball. They rolled it like dough. They tossed it in the air like a bag of cotton wool. When they kissed it, they blew into it like a balloon. Chhaya leaned secretively toward it and said, "Ablablablablabla." Sandeep, listening, enjoyed the comically incantatory sound of baby talk. The nonsensical words re-created a world of pure elemental feeling. The syllables came out, shapeless, formless. It was a caricature of language, and the baby liked it.

IN THE afternoon, drugged by an alternation of soporific heat and coolness, light and shade, Sandeep's aunt and his mother fell asleep. The magazines they had been reading lay open— one on the recipe page, and one on a story of unrequited love—on their faces; there, they fluttered like wings with every exhalation of breath. A small transistor radio lay in Sandeep's mother's hand, vibrating eerily with music; from afar, it looked like a singing book. One could hear muted thumps from the terrace, like a heartbeat, as Saraswati washed clothes and banged them against the floor.

The boys, in a rare, unenergetic moment, were sprawled by the window, looking at pigeons. The pigeons, red eyes and rainbows around their violet-black necks, were moving about on the parapet studiously. Copulation and some scatological considerations were all that preoccupied them. The furthest extent of their aesthetic contribution to life was the intricate manner in which they arranged their excrement on the parapet, so that it came to resemble a mosaic or an abstract graphic on stone. Defecation was a purely inspirational act with them, arbitrary and spontaneous as the Romantic's conception of his poem.

At present, one pigeon in particular was entertaining himself by bullying other pigeons near him. Wheeling in mock anger, strutting up and down like a rich businessman in a small town, nodding his insufferable little head continually, making loud gurgling noises in his beautiful throat, he made himself a majestic nuisance to those around him. At first, the others ignored him politely, till a rebel pecked him critically on the head. The pigeon did not like being criticised. A fight ensued, more sound and fury than anything else. The flap-flap-flap-crack-flap-flap-flap pattern of the pigeons' beating wings seemed to have lulled Sandeep's mother into an even deeper serenity, for she sighed with pleasure in her sleep. Midway through the fight, one of the pigeons flew off hurriedly, and the other remained, adjusting the wrinkles on his feathers. Then he flew off as well. Their companions, heads like bits of stone, appeared not to have noticed.

On the far side of the parapet, while the rest dreamed, two pigeons began to kiss each other in a solemnly painful manner, beaks locked together, heads moving up and down simultaneously as if they were trying to release themselves from the mysterious lock. It was a strange kind of passion; it was the only way birds could embrace, or come close to embracing—

locking their beaks in that funny, tortured way. Finally, the male climbed on the female's back and proceeded to flap its wings in an abstracted fashion. The female waited, bending its head in a world-weary manner.

"What are they doing?" asked Babla, noting the nuances of the scene in fascination.

Sandeep did not know.

"I think they're fighting," he said, not sure of the validity of his own superior knowledge.

"If they're fighting," said Abhi, "why doesn't the other one struggle?"

"It's lost," said Sandeep. "It knows it's defeated."

The entire spectacle, from courtship to climax to possible marital bliss or discord, lasted around ten minutes. God had apparently created these birds with the sole purpose of amusing slothful boys, and probably Himself, on unpleasantly humid afternoons.

THE next morning, Mamima and Sandeep's mother went shopping. They bathed early, and wore weightless saris and outsized goggles to keep the sun out from their minds. They were possessed by the curious joy of buying things, a temporary lust which left them refreshed, exhausted, later.

Mamima's midday prayer was postponed to a later date. The gods were not fussy about punctuality; after all, they had all eternity at their disposal. The boys, forever unemployed, went with their mothers. They took a taxi to the vegetable market at Gariahat. The taxi was on the verge of collapse: only the dust and grease and grime and rust between the arthritic joints kept it from falling into a desultory heap. The driver was a Sikh; he had kept a picture of Guru Nanak by the steering wheel; while the driver looked at the road, the guru, with a

sun-like halo round his head, looked at the driver. Beneath the dashboard, in a place that was painted black, were a few painted flowers, now a faded yellow, and in white letters, the name of the kind-hearted bank on whose loan the taxi had been bought.

The Sikh spoke a courteous Bengali to the women, made still more courteous and comically elaborate by the fact that it was spoken in a broad Hindustani accent and according to the rules of Hindustani grammar. This gave the gentle, rounded sounds of the Bengali language a masculine openheartedness; it even made the language smell of onions and chappatis. Flattered and impressed, Mamima and Sandeep's mother giggled like schoolgirls.

He was a garrulous man, and he spoke, in a manner both broken and eloquent, about Calcutta. He had come here as a young man about fifteen years ago. He had first caught a glimpse of Calcutta in a black-and-white film called *Pyaasa*: it was the quay scene showing the barges on the River Hooghly that he liked best, he said. He spoke of Calcutta with a mixture of disgust and reverence. But he no longer wanted to return to Punjab. The city, or the idea of the city given to him years ago by the black-and-white film, had absorbed him without his ever knowing it.

They got off at the market. Walking in through a deceptively simple doorway, they found themselves wading through the beginning of an ocean of vegetables. On parallel rows of raised platforms, the vendors sat and harangued and cajoled and lovingly seduced the customers who passed critically through the little lanes in between. The ground was strewn with soiled cabbage leaves, which cats nibbled at. On the wall behind the vendors were pinned pictures of gods and goddesses from calendar cuttings or cheap prints. Incense sticks burned before them, filling odd corners of the market with transcen-

dental smells of sandalwood. Near the pictures of the gods were large glossy photos and posters of film stars and cricketers, neither wholly mortal nor wholly divine. The eye rested on no empty spaces: wherever one gazed, there was a fruit, or a vegetable, or a basket, or a dog, or a god. Tiresome, fat ladies stood haggling with the vendors, stolid and immovable as pillars. One could spot a haggle from a distance: the customer and the vendor preaching endlessly to each other, like two devout and convinced priests on Judgment Day, one a mullah and the other a clergyman, trying to convert the other to his religion. The market echoed with questions and replies; fingers slyly tested the smoothness and coolness of a tomato, or the exact shade of purple of an aubergine. One assertion was repeated like a mantra through the whole market: "Yes sir, they're fresh. No question about it, they're fresh. See for yourself, brother, touch it, it's fresh."

The vendors' children had turned the market's alternation of raised platforms into a playground. Between these platforms, they played hide-and-seek and lost and found and lost and found each other. Sandeep watched them from the sidelines. Two boys used an old, blighted onion for a ball, and a discarded brown-paper bag was turned into a mask. Near them, a girl of about twelve or thirteen was sitting alone behind a brown hill of potatoes. Her dress was dirty, and she had an unclean look about her; she was evidently not selling the potatoes, and, in fact, had nothing to do with the business of selling whatsoever. But she sat there, this cross-eyed girl, the squint in her eye making her look just a little deranged. The vendors and their children ignored her. She seemed quite far away and contented, however, eating bits of raw cauliflower by herself, stalks and all—until she felt Sandeep's eyes on her, which made her self-conscious, and eat the raw pieces of cauliflower in a

defiant way. Sandeep thought he was falling in love with her. Later, when his mother and aunt had finished shopping and he was leaving, he glanced back to find that she was looking at him; he could not be sure; the squint in her eye made it difficult to be sure. At any rate, one eye was looking at him, and the other one was looking at the rest of the world.

Chapter Seven

ON SUNDAYS, the streets of Calcutta were vacant and quiet, and the shops and offices closed, looking mysterious and even a little beautiful with their doors and windows shut, such shabby, reposeful doors and windows, the large signs—DATTA BROS., K. SINGH AND SONS—reflecting the sunlight. The house would reverberate with familiar voices. Chhotomama was at home. Chhordimoni, Sandeep's great-aunt, and Shonamama, his eldest uncle, had also decided to spend the day here. If you overheard them from a distance—Sandeep's uncle, his mother, his aunt, Chhordimoni, and Shonamama, all managing to speak at the top of their voices without ever making a moment of sense—you would think they were having a violent brawl, or quarrelling vehemently about the inheritance of some tract of land which they were not prepared to share. And, indeed, they *were* engaged in an endless argument (about what, they did not know) beneath which ran a glowing undercurrent of agreement in which they silently said "Yes" to each other.

Much of the talk concerned relatives scattered all over India and all over the world. Much of it was about money and the cost of living. Chhotomama's business ran in fits and starts, like

his car. It had to be pushed before it worked; it was unreliable. There was no demand for this and no demand for that; this supplier had let him down; that partner was unscrupulous and lazy; the times were not conducive to . . . In short, money was short. "Today the palm of my left hand's itching," said Mamima. "God, God, I wonder—it means I'll have to spend more money—on what, I wonder." If the right hand itched, it meant one was going to get money—but it seldom itched, and when it did, money seldom followed. Someone was not playing the game.

The subject would switch from money to people "who need money more than we do," and these people were usually poor relations, or, to be more accurate, poorer relations, old men and widows whose sons were too young to earn or who themselves had lost interest in working for a pittance. The second case was more frequent among men: there seemed to be something masculine about giving up one's job and dignifying one's idle hours by speculating about existence. So they had to be helped and supported, while constantly being assured that they were not being helped and supported, to which they would reply, with different degrees of sincerity, that of course they were and how could they forget it? They were helped and supported, not necessarily because they deserved it, but because money was meant to flow from the hands of one member of the family to another.

This kind of talk, whether at the dinner-table or in the bedroom, did not become too oppressive: it was too full of metaphors, paradoxes, wise jokes, and reminiscences to be so. It was, at bottom, a criticism of life. And there were unpredictable breaks, when Sandeep's mother and Mamima would begin to murmur conspiratorially about the colour of a sari. And there were unpremeditated instants when everyone would suddenly stop talking, perhaps to think, each one about some-

thing different, and there would be a gap of hushed clarity, in which a crow cawed outside. And the children would be arrested in whatever they were doing at that point of time: one swinging by the window, one lying on his stomach reading a comic, and one sitting on the ground, listening and comprehending nothing. And then they would resume their argument, very loudly, as if they were early-twentieth-century actors in some green, neglected village in Bengal, where there were no mikes and no electricity, and every actor had to bellow his speech melodramatically before the large village audience would hear and applaud what he was saying. One would have almost expected Sandeep's uncles and aunts to have been attired in the splendid, vibrant costumes that folk artistes wore in keeping with the dramatic excessiveness of their gestures. Yet his uncles wore white pyjamas and nothing else, and the women were draped in faded, hand-woven cotton saris—their bodies cool even in the cumulative heat of conversation.

Sometime during the day, probably not too late, or too early, as on weekdays, Chhotomama would take a bowl of water and other equipment to the verandah, place them on a chair, perch himself on a stool, and shave. This was one of Sunday's simpleminded pleasures and self-indulgences: to shave at what time one pleased, and as long as one pleased, with the children nearby, watching, convincing one that a morning stubble was an amazing thing, and that the shaving instruments were holy tools, and that the act of sprinkling water on the face was somehow profound. When he would look up from the mirror, he would sense the stillness of the street around him, the endless, enduring world of pigeons and crows, the perpetual movement of pariahs, beggars, and vendors, and he would feel, simultaneously, the warmth of the sunlight and the coolness of the brush on his cheek. The boys would stand around, noting his movements the way passersby in Calcutta break their

journey to work to stare at acrobats or a monkey show on the pavement. With curiosity and envy, they followed the determined attentiveness with which he put the cream on his brush, and then swished the lather with a flourish on his face, white and frothy, till it gained a rich uniformity that looked both ornamental and delicious, and then carefully ploughed it with his razor in primitive agricultural fashion.

Later, he would enter the toilet, armed with an ashtray, a newspaper, and a pair of reading glasses. The toilet was his study. Here, filling the room with cigarette smoke, he read the significant news of the day; he pondered on "world affairs" and "home affairs"; he pontificated to himself on the "current situation" from a Marxist angle. He was a water-closet thinker.

This part of the daily ceremonies over, he would enter the bathroom to have his preluncheon bath, humming a small tune to himself. He would turn on the old, ineffectual shower and, suddenly elated, begin singing aloud to himself. He had a resonant tenor voice, a voice both strong and delicate. When he sang in the bath, the notes echoed in the four enclosing walls like rays of trapped light darting this way and that in a crystal, a diamond. He usually sang old, half-remembered compositions that had been popular thirty or forty years ago in a Bengal where the radio and the windup gramophone were still new and incredible machines breaking the millennial silence of the towns and villages:

> *Godhulir chhaya pathe*
> *Je gelo chini go tare.*

Roughly translated, this meant

> *In the hour of cow dust, on the shadowy path,*
> *Who passed by me? I felt I knew her.*

Knocking on the bathroom door, Sandeep made a pest of himself by asking: "Chhotomama, what does *godhuli* mean?"

Lost in the general well-being of cleansing himself, his uncle replied patiently: "The word *go* means 'cow,' and the word *dhuli* means 'dust.' In the villages, evening's the time the cowherds bring the cattle home. The herd returns, raising clouds of dust from the road. *Godhuli* is that hour of cow dust. So it means 'dusk' or 'evening.' "

As Chhotomama explained, his voice emerging from behind the steady sound of water, Sandeep saw it in his mind like a film being shown from a projector—the slow-moving, indolent cows, their nostrils and their shining eyes, the faint white outline of the cowherd, the sense of the expectant village (a group of scattered huts), and the dust, yes the dust, rising unwillingly from the cows' hooves and blurring everything. The mental picture was set in the greyish-red colour of twilight. It was strange how one word could contain a world within it. Quite unexpectedly, Chhotomama now began a song by Tagore:

> *Bahe nirantar ananta anandadhara.*
> *Baaje ashima nabhamajhe anaadiraba.*

In an unsatisfactory translation, this meant

> *Endless and unbroken flows the stream of joy.*
> *Its timeless sound resonates beneath the great sky.*

It was a song of praise, a prayer-song. Sandeep did not understand a single word of it, but he thought that the tune and especially the sound of the difficult words communicated with him in an obscure way, and he was aware that the repetitive sound of the language had mingled with the sound of the water

falling in the bath, till they became one glimmering sound without meaning. Whether the bath ended first, or the song, Sandeep could not tell. A cool spell of remote, waterfall-like music was woven and broken at the same time, as if the words of the song could not endure existing a hundredth of a second after they had been uttered. Chhotomama unlocked the door noisily and came out, smiling, a towel wrapped around his loins and thighs. Pottering about for his new pyjamas and vest, he looked like the chieftain of some undiscovered, happy African tribe. His wet hair stuck out in all directions from his head, like a black, untidy porcupine. The bath, the inner temple where he had performed his last sacrosanct ritual and offered his songs for the day, was now empty and without music, except the sound of a single drop of water falling on the floor with a tone and perfect pitch of its own. Every few seconds, it seemed to repeat that exact pitch without alteration or variation.

At about six o'clock in the evening, the lights went out. The power-cuts had got more frequent with the heat, and the two servant girls and their little brother who had come downstairs and plopped shyly on the floor to watch the Sunday film on television had to be disappointed and sent home.

"I'm sure they'll show us a better film next Sunday," assured Sandeep's mother.

"It's not me," said the girl with the unwashed hair and incredibly clean hands. "It's Syed," nodding at the boy, who had worn an imbecilic, puzzled expression ever since the lights had gone off. "He's never seen a film." The girl's name was Runa. She was a Muslim janitor's daughter. Sandeep was sorry to see her leave: he had often fantasised about marrying her one day. He noticed, from the corner of his eye, how her bright and ragged body ran impulsively down the stairs, and listened to her slightly hoarse, illiterate voice calling to her brother and sister to follow. The stairs were dark, and a gulf seemed to

separate her from him. Then, two minutes later, he forgot she ever existed.

Saraswati brought lanterns into the room, each with a strong, yellow yolk of flame. Then she bent to light the candles, and used the dripping wax to stick them onto chipped tea saucers.

"Doesn't Saraswati look like a witch?" whispered Sandeep to Abhi. Indeed, wavering shadows from the candle flame falling and shifting on her face gave her ordinary features a preternatural fluidity. Her cheekbones and jaw seemed to flow and change with the changing light, as if she were shedding her old face for a new one.

"Saraswati, you look like a witch," said Abhi.

"Be quiet, you little monsters," she replied.

She had set down the candles in their saucers at intervals on the floor: one in the room, one in the corridor, one near the staircase. It looked like there was a festival being celebrated, some esoteric myth in the process of being retold by symbols. As Abhi leaned forward perfunctorily to blow a candle out, and Saraswati rushed towards him—her intention, she said, was to drag him out of the room by his hair—Chhotomama called from the corridor: "Enough mischief, boys. Come on, let's go out for a walk."

So they went out for a walk. They went through narrow, lightless lanes, where houses that were silent but gave out smells of fish and boiled rice stood on either side of the road. There was not a single tree in sight; no breeze and no sound but the vaguely musical humming of mosquitoes. Once, an ancient taxi wheezed past, taking a shortcut through the lane into the main road, like a comic vintage car passing through a film set showing the twenties into the film set of the present, passing from black-and-white into colour. But why did these houses— for instance, that one with the tall, ornate iron gates and a

watchman dozing on a stool, which gave the impression that the family had valuables locked away inside, or that other one with the small porch and the painted door, which gave the impression that whenever there was a feast or a wedding all the relatives would be invited, and there would be so many relatives that some of them, probably the young men and women, would be sitting bunched together on the cramped porch because there would be no more space inside, talking eloquently about something that didn't really require eloquence, laughing uproariously at a joke that wasn't really very funny, or this next house with an old man relaxing in his easy-chair on the verandah, fanning himself with a local Sunday newspaper, or this small, shabby house with the girl Sandeep glimpsed through a window, sitting in a bare, ill-furnished room, memorising a text by candlelight, repeating suffixes and prefixes from a Bengali grammar over and over to herself—why did these houses seem to suggest that an infinitely interesting story might be woven around them? And yet the story would never be a satisfying one, because the writer, like Sandeep, would be too caught up in jotting down the irrelevances and digressions that make up lives, and the life of a city, rather than a good story—till the reader would shout "Come to the point!"—and there would be no point, except the girl memorising the rules of grammar, the old man in the easy-chair fanning himself, and the house with the small, empty porch that was crowded, paradoxically, with many memories and possibilities. The "real" story, with its beginning, middle, and conclusion, would never be told, because it did not exist.

The road ended, and it branched off, on one side, to a larger road, and on the other side to two narrower ones that led to a great field, a maidan, with a pair of poles at either end which were supposed to be goalposts. As they came closer, they

noticed that the field was full of people whom they had not been able to discern at first in the darkness: now they came slowly into focus in the moonlight, like a negative becoming clearer and clearer as it was developed in a darkroom. There were all kinds and classes of people—college boys, schoolboys, couples, unemployed men, families, hawkers, groups of girls. The clammy heat had made them leave their houses or hovels in search of a breeze. It was a strange scene because, in spite of the number of people who had congregated together, there was scarcely any noise. The shadowiness of the place made them speak in low voices, as if they were in a theatre or an auditorium where the lights had been dimmed meaningfully, and a film or a play was just about to begin. If there had been no power-cut, or if it had still been light, the maidan, needless to say, would have throbbed with its own din and activity. But the darkness had brought a strange lethargy and even peace to these otherwise highly strung men and women, and there was a perceptible sense of release, as if time was oozing by, and the world happening elsewhere.

Just as Chhotomama and the boys were preparing to join the others in the maidan, to settle on the cool grass and pull the grass out luxuriously with their fingers, the lights came back. It was a dramatic instant, like a photographer's flash going off, which recorded the people sprawled in various postures and attitudes, smiles of relief and wonder on their faces. Each day there would be a power-cut, and each day there would be the unexpected, irrational thrill when the lights returned; it was as if people would never get used to it; day after day, at that precise, privileged moment when the power-cut ended without warning as it had begun, giving off a radiance that was confusing and breathtaking, there was an uncontrollable sensation of delight, as if it were happening for the first time. With what

appeared to be an instinct for timing, the rows of fluorescent lamps glittered to life simultaneously. The effect was the opposite of blowing out candles on a birthday cake: it was as if someone had blown on a set of unlit candles, and the magic exhalation had brought a flame to every wick at once.

Chapter Eight

ONE Friday evening, Mamima and Sandeep's mother sat in front of the dressing-table and applied a tracing of kaajal to their eyes, a faint gloss of lipstick to their lips, a line of kumkum powder in the parting of their hair, and pressed a red kumkum dot in the centre of their foreheads. They took gold bangles out of a cupboard and slipped them onto their slender wrists (the gold did not dazzle, as gold never does, but blended with the lustre and colour of their skin), and they wore firmly pressed, shimmering saris around their bodies, like bright wrapping paper around a lozenge. They gazed into the mirror and at each other with vague, approving looks, and sometimes bent down to help each other with their hair. Like lilypads, they floated on a surface of images. They dabbed themselves with perfume; each drop of strong perfume could spread like a rumour around the room and then the house. If Mamima or Sandeep's mother had been somewhere, you could tell by the fragrance they left behind; they became strange creatures; the house became a strange forest.

They were preparing to visit relatives—an old couple who lived far away on the southern tip of Calcutta, somewhere near

the road leading out from the city. It was difficult to understand why they were fussing so much about this simple visit to these simple people, unless they were using it as a pretext or an excuse to devote their passionate ardour to themselves. Devotion—that was the word: the immemorial tradition of applying kaajal and kumkum, and other ancient cosmetics like sandalwood paste and mehndi, belonged more to the world of intricate, systematic ritual than to the world of fashion; in fact, the craftsman-like way in which the women made themselves up ("making oneself up"—the same, after all, as creating oneself) reminded one of the Bengali artisans who decorate and lay the immeasurably delicate finishing touches on their idols on the day before the festival. Looking critically into the mirror, they appraised their faces and hands with a detached aesthetic interest, as if they were someone else's face and hands waiting to be adorned from simplicity to a complexity that was oddly, unmistakably feminine. And deep down, the women also knew that the old couple living in the darkness of the suburbs would be disappointed if it were otherwise: for them, the younger relatives dressing up with such extravagance was a form of entertainment which they would talk about for days; it would be a welcome distraction in their small, clear lives; the old lady would finger the texture of their saris and ask questions; the old man would inhale the perfume without appearing to do so and sit with a pleased expression on his face.

THE car broke down once on the way. Chhotomama cursed and muttered. Later, they were caught in a traffic jam. At one point, they halted at Ganguram's at Gol Park to buy sweetmeats and a pot of sweetened pink yoghurt for the old couple. The sweetmeats and the yoghurt came in pots of red earth. All around them, people were eating from these pots and from

plates made of leaves. The pots and plates would have to be discarded, sadly, once the meal was over. (Sandeep remembered the civilisation of Mohenjo-daro, which he had learnt about at school; there, too, people had eaten from rudimentary but graceful utensils which they had thrown away after use.) In the car, Sandeep balanced the two pots in his hands to keep the syrup from spilling, as if they were bombs that might explode. By the time they reached the place, it was very dark. It was off the main road; as the car turned into a narrow lane with cramped shops and rickshawallas smoking dimly incandescent beedis, lounging in the corners, they moved forward in space and backward in time simultaneously. Calcutta grew remote and unrecognisable; the city was no longer clearly demarcated from the folk-tale Bengal that surrounded it so thickly. Myths and ghosts and Bengal tigers roamed beyond an unclear boundary; the sputtering car passed a temple and a tank where buffaloes and children bathed in the daytime. The place was a little colony or village tied by a network of faint lanes; there were few electric lights to illuminate the area. One's eye got reluctantly used to moonlight, and one saw houses, each some distance away from the other, and ponds in which spores settled and multiplied, on which weeds formed an almost firm, palpable surface, where the lotus rose and opened with a shy passion in the darkness. So lives multiplied and opened in the cool houses and settlements of the area, or closed and remained hidden, according to conditions and circumstances. Sandeep saw hundreds of insects in the twin funnels of the car's headlights, rushing forward in an obsessive stream, an agitated Milky Way of tiny, mindless, winged life. The place made Sandeep remember what Shonamama had once told him: "When we were young, the world was made of small islands of consciousness. Miles separated one village, sometimes one house, from another. Letter-writing was the only means of

communication—there were no telephones. A mountain or a river formed the border to our world. Our world was small, and things loomed large and astonishing for us: you wouldn't understand."

"Where was this?" Sandeep had asked, wondering if it was a real place, or something Shonamama had dreamed up.

"In Sylhet," replied Shonamama. "Sylhet is now in Bangladesh."

"Sylhet . . ." murmured Sandeep.

"When India was one big piece, and the British ruled us. When our father died, we moved to Shillong. In Shillong," Shonamama said, "there are mountains and waterfalls."

As the car moved forward with difficulty through the narrow paths, Sandeep returned to Shonamama's childhood. Nothing had changed. The headlights of the car made twin stars in the darkness.

Two boys were playing carrom on the steps of a small, painted shed which had the following words on its wall in large, black letters: NATIONAL ASSOCIATION OF SPORTSMEN. A single table-tennis table inside the shed could be glimpsed through the window. The boys interrupted their game to give Chhotomama directions to the house in a series of sporadic, enthusiastic gestures. Oh yes, they knew the old couple. And yes, their son and daughter-in-law had arrived last night with their first child.

"Is it a girl or a boy?" asked Mamima, rolling down the window.

"A girl," said the boy.

Mamima rolled up her window before the mosquitoes came in. The two boys vanished behind them. When they reached the house, they found that the old man was waiting on the verandah with a lantern in his hand. Moths were shuddering

round and round the lantern, though the old man was oblivious to them. He had come out because he had heard the throbbing of the engine in the distance. The night had been silent except for the questioning cry of an owl and the continual orchestral sound of crickets in the bushes. The throbbing of the engine had, therefore, travelled through the silence to the old man's listening ear, and to his wife's ear, even when the car was relatively far away and beyond their range of vision. They had pondered over the sound, and finally, he had lit the lantern and shuffled out. "I told her," he said, referring to his wife. "I told her that I heard the car, I knew it was the car, I told her you were coming."

Once they were inside, Mamima gave the pot of yoghurt and the pot of sweetmeats to the old lady. "There was no need," she said. "Oh really," she said. "This is too much," she insisted, with the air of one who has just received the Kohinoor diamond as a birthday present. "Come, come, come," said Chhotomama, with the air of someone who has just given the Kohinoor diamond as a birthday present, and refuses to be overawed by his own generosity. "It's nothing." It *was* nothing, of course, only Ganguram's sweets and yoghurt, but they fussed and fussed and created the illusion that it was something, something unique and untasted and unencountered.

The son and the daughter-in-law emerged shyly from the anteroom. They both stooped gently to touch Chhotomama's feet, and Sandeep's aunt's and his mother's feet, a traditional greeting and a mark of obeisance towards one's elders.

"Oh no no no," said Chhotomama, struggling to keep the son's hand away from his feet. "There's no need for all this." This was half a token gesture towards modesty, and half towards the new, "modern" India—Nehru's secular India, free of ritual and religion.

"I have not met you for two years, Dada," said the son,

struggling to get his hands near Chhotomama's toes. "You must not stop me." This was half a token gesture towards modesty, and half towards the old, "traditional" India—Gandhi's India of ceremony and custom.

Sandeep, meanwhile, had come to the conclusion that the grown-ups were mad, each after his or her own fashion. Simple situations were turned into complex, dramatic ones; not until then did everyone feel important and happy. Will they never grow up? thought Sandeep irately. He glanced around him. A single blue, fluorescent tube was burning on the wall. It was not a big room. Despite its bareness, the impression it gave was of austerity rather than poverty. It made one remember that poverty meant displacement as well as lack, while austerity meant being poor in a rooted way, within a tradition and culture of sparseness, which transformed even the lack, the paucity, into a kind of being. There was a wooden table in the centre of the room and a divan on one side; there was a series of shelves, carved into the wall, that had a picture of Ramakrishna and a statuette of Shiv next to incense sticks on a stand whose sandalwood fragrance brought a faint, subconscious aura of devotion to the room; there was a book of Ramakrishna's anecdotes and parables, wedding photographs, one in black and white and one of the son and daughter-in-law in colour, a peacock feather, and a jar of spices. In one corner, there was a money-plant in a pot, and against the wall, beneath the window which opened into the branches and sweet-smelling foliage of a mango tree, there was a harmonium, and a tanpura laid horizontally. On the floor, two cane shatranjis were rolled out to sit on. The objects in the room were numerous enough to be noticed and a few enough to be counted and remembered. The short stretches of empty space in between seemed to have been deliberately created by the congruence of the walls and the balance between light and shadow. Space gave

the little room its strange composure and a cool, accommodating presence.

On one of the shatranjis rested what looked like a dark bundle.

"Have you seen the baby?" asked the young man, picking the bundle up.

"Ooooh," said the women. "What's it called?"

"Annapurna," said the father, his voice becoming thick with affection and pride. "My wife chose the name."

"It's a lovely name," said Chhotomama.

Anna means "rice" or "food," and *purna* means "full" or "complete"; joined together, the two halves give birth (just as the two parents had given birth to the child) to the word "Annapurna"—Annapurna, which means "Provider of Food or Sustenance," and is one of the many names of the mothergoddess, Durga.

The bundle called Annapurna stirred. She had been aroused from deep slumber, yet she smiled with toothless good humour. Maybe she didn't realise she had woken up, maybe she thought she was having yet another one of her sundry manycoloured dreams. But no, she had just urinated on her father's shirt with an engrossed look on her face. By doing so, she proclaimed her return to reality. The father grumbled as a wet patch on his shirt spread and grew larger. No one was embarrassed. How could one be embarrassed about a baby urinating? The *baby* was not embarrassed. Nor did she seem to have done it with anything but the best of intentions. Besides, there was a rumour that baby's urine is particularly innocuous, even pure, like spring water.

The man hurried inside to change his shirt, and the old man took charge of his grandchild. Smiling, they all settled down to talk. The baby proceeded to play with her grandfather's spectacles, and make critical comments about the conversation.

"Oog," she said. "Oog."

She thought spectacles were made to be eaten and chewed and probably digested. When Sandeep borrowed Chhoto-mama's wristwatch to reflect a miraculous dot of light on the wall, she gaped respectfully. Once, when she began to cry, Sandeep held a tumbler of water against the light, and showed her the rays of light that darted in the water like tiny fish; the baby became silent, and leaned forward peculiarly, as if she were ready to change her religion. The baby was an imbecile; she could be made to believe in anything she saw. Spittle drib-bled from the side of her mouth. Great cobwebs of saliva hung from her lips. This was Annapurna, a moist, unctuous thing.

The old man began to croon in her ear in a feeble voice:

Sway, sway, swaying, a comb in your bright hair,
Now the bridegroom'll come, now he'll take you
* away . . .*

Annapurna tried to move; her grandfather's arms surrounded her like the Wall of China. The spectacles fell from her nerve-less fingers to her grandfather's lap; her fingers became slug-gish and greedy.

The daughter-in-law and the old lady had made a dinner consisting of dal, aubergines, cottage cheese, and two kinds of fish. There was koi fish and there was rohu fish. The baby fell asleep again. What a strange life, thought Sandeep, sleep-ing and waking. The old man was still singing the rhyme in her ear. The old lady took pains to see that everyone ate well. Plates had been arranged on a small, clean table. "You must taste the koi," she said. "Our bou made it." The daughter-in-law smiled. "Won't you eat?" asked Mamima. "Later," they said. They watched them eat. Sandeep fell asleep, so did Abhi and Babla. "I'll remember this koi for many days," said Chho-

tomama. The daughter-in-law had vanished, but her smile remained. Sandeep woke for a lucid moment to find he was back in Chhotomama's house, the creased warmth of the double bed, lying next to his cousins. He had not been conscious of the homeward journey. A firefly had floated in through the window, a wandering, free light. "What's its name?" asked someone and someone replied, "Annapurna," and a third voice said, "It's a lovely name."

Chapter Nine

ON SATURDAY, a cool breeze surprised them. It smelled of wet earth, sodden leaves. It had rained somewhere in the villages, in groves and fields, and the breeze had travelled to this lane, bringing news of rain from the far-off place of its beginnings. They had congregated after lunch on the double bed on the second storey, when it ran its fingers down their backs, making them break out in goose-flesh. There was something erotic about the first breeze that brought the monsoons.

"Did you feel that?" asked Mamima.

"Yes," said Sandeep's mother.

"And that smell . . . ," said Chhotomama, breathing in deeply.

He had never known any smell like that of wet earth, her own sweet odour, earth-musk. The most natural and unpretentious fragrance.

A few days later, there was the first kal-baisakhi storm. A layer of grey clouds covered the sky, inverting it like a bowl, shutting out sunlight. Dead leaves and old newspapers

streamed through the lane like a procession of protest-marchers. Someone cried out from a balcony. A woman's voice. "Ratna! Ratna, come in this instant!" The wind blew silent and straight. A woman walking alone on the road was teased by the wind; the loose end of her sari, the aanchal, flew helplessly, a lost fragment of colour; it was the most beautiful movement seen on this rainy day. Crows hopped alertly. They sensed a presence, powerful and dangerous, though they could see nothing and no one. The nervous, toy-like city was set against the dignified advance of the clouds, as if two worlds were colliding. There was an end-of-the-world atmosphere. Then, lightning, sometimes a single, bright scar that flashed on a cloud's black face and was gone, and sometimes filling the grey space with light. A moment's heavy silence; then the thunder spoke—

guruguruguru

In obedience, the leaves began to tremble, and the branches moved uniformly, disciplined as a battalion doing exercises—Bend! Rise! Bend! Rise! And, slam! a door or a window banged shut without warning; ghosts and spirits were abroad, making mischief, distracting the servants, knocking at the windows. Only the children had time to investigate or smile at the spirits, because the grown-ups were busy, panicky. Saraswati bundled the clothes left to dry on the terrace, and brought them in before they got wet—with the wrinkled clothes in her arms, she looked like Mother Teresa carrying the light, wispy bodies of dying children. Mamima rushed to shut the windows, which were banging their wooden heads in a religious frenzy. She just managed to lock the last one in time. As if by common consent, it began to rain with a steady sibilant sound. They sat in the

room with the windows closed, listening to the sound of the rain beating against the windows and falling on the tin roof of the next house. The children talked to each other, but sometimes they stopped and became attentive, listening, for no apparent reason, to that sound. The room became cool; the beds and floors became cool. When they opened the taps, the water sparkled. They rinsed their mouths with the water. Sometimes, Sandeep and Abhi opened a shutter and stared out into a world where arrows of rain fell continually. They stretched out their hands. They allowed the round, orb-like raindrops to settle on the back of their hands like dewy insects, though the drops lost shape as soon as they touched the flesh. Running to the smaller room at the back, Sandeep glanced out of the window and saw the palm tree dancing by itself, to itself. A silent wave of delight passed over him as he watched it dance.

SO ANOTHER season had come. In another corner of the world lay the great continent called Australia, an immense unwieldy mass of land floating on the ocean like a giant makeshift raft on water. Who had been set afloat on that raft? Kangaroos, aborigines, and cricketers. And India was touring Australia, and there was a test match being played between the two teams at Sydney. So Chhotomama would wake up at five o'clock in the morning and try to catch Sydney on the radio. He would spin the rapid knobs, and after an incoherent period of time, when the radio cackled in an evil witch-like way, the voice of the Australian commentator would come through, loud and urgent one moment, weak and distant the other, as if a few words were being carried off, on their passage towards India, by a cormorant crossing the ocean.

The room would echo with a strange Australian accent, and an odd and vivid pronunciation of vowels. Everyone would be sleeping, of course, muffled heads and breathing bundles of bodies, because the rains had made the nights cool and relaxed. Abhi, Babla, and Sandeep slept like primeval creatures huddled on the island of the bed, close to the horizon, outwaiting the dawn that would bring the first thought to their heads. Their bodies slept with a pure detached love for every moment of sleep.

Into the midst of this delicate surface world of slumber, which could be burst like a bubble so easily, and yet miraculously escaped being burst for around eight hours, Chhotomama trod heavily at five o'clock in the morning.

Twiddling the radio knobs, fiddling with this, dislodging that, coughing, laughing, yawning, he disgusted everyone with his obstreperousness, his clumsiness. The amazing thing was, *he* did not think he was making any noise; he thought that as long as he did not actually utter a word, he disturbed no one. Whatever mischief his hands and legs did, as far as he was concerned, was not his responsibility. Anyway, Sandeep and Abhi had decided that one had to simply and unquestioningly tolerate the grown-ups. One had constantly to see the comic aspects of their characters to remain sane.

THE test match came to an end. India did the one honourable thing: it lost. How could Gandhi's country bear to win? With the test match, the sense of expectation died out temporarily. For a few days, the rains fell heavily—continuous white screens blotted out landscapes and landmarks: the main road with its tramlines, its lampposts, its old medicine shop, and then the park; these melted before Sandeep's

eyes, while he watched, a little amazed that he too did not melt away.

The gutters in the lane overflowed with an odd, languid grace. Water filled the lane; rose from ankle-deep to knee-deep. Insects swam in circles. Urchins splashed about haphazardly, while Saraswati returned from the market with a shopping bag in her hands; insects swam away to avoid this clumsy giant. Her wet footprints printing the floor of the house were as rich with possibility as the first footprint Crusoe found on his island.

Chhotomama had not gone to work; his car had failed him. The car usually became temperamental during the monsoons. It was also temperamental in the winter and the spring and the summer, but Chhotomama said it was especially temperamental in the monsoons. He did not blame the car; he blamed its maker, whoever he was.

He did some work at home, rummaging through files. Then he scanned the newspaper *The Statesman*, reading the editorial four times, shaking his head and laughing abrasively. "The man is a fool," he said quietly. "I must write to the paper . . ." He took a foolscap sheet and began to write. He scribbled "Dear Sir," and paused and then crossed out "Dear." The letter began "Sir . . ." He was very angry with the editor.

After the letter was written, he relaxed on the bed, lying on his stomach. Whenever he relaxed, he remembered he had a terrible backache.

"Abhi!" he called. "Come and press my back."

Abhi came and put his fingers, gentle as a faith healer's, on his father's vertebrae.

"Oooh . . . oooh . . ." said Chhotomama, a noise like a wind blowing through an aperture. It conveyed, at once, pain and pleasure.

"A little above," he said, navigating Abhi's fingers.

The fingers moved a little above.

"A little—a fraction—to the left."

The fingers shifted a fraction to the left.

"Another fraction left."

Another fraction.

Searching for that exact spot of pain was a delicate matter, a life or several lives might depend on it; it was like trying to detect a mine in a minefield, or a vein of oil in a desert.

"Yes, yes!" said Chhotomama. "*There.* Press it *there.*"

"Baba . . ." said Abhi, his fingers poised, a master pianist about to embark on the opening phrase of his sonata, while the audience waits, breathless.

"*Press!*" said Chhotomama, drowning, his voice a choked bubble. "Oh *what* is it, Abhi?"

"Baba, the cricket bat we had talked about . . ."

"It's yours," cried Chhotomama, giving in to blackmail and letting the world know about it. "It's yours! Now, press *there.*"

Smiling, Abhi began to play his sonata. The notes rose, lovely and exultant. Chhotomama closed his eyes and sighed, intoxicated by music no one else could hear.

FIFTEEN minutes later, Chhotomama asked Babla to stand on his back. He was small and would be able to balance himself; he was light enough to stamp out the pain without hurting him.

"I'll fall, Baba," said Babla, who was not a brave boy.

"Of course you won't," said Chhotomama. "Come, only for a few minutes."

Babla climbed on the bed. He put one leg on his father's back. It was like the picture of Edmund Hillary on Mount Everest. All that was needed was a flag. Then he put both his feet on his father's back.

"Walk," said Chhotomama. "Stay in the same place, but walk."

It was a contradictory demand. Babla tried it. He smiled; he seemed to like the idea of staying in one place and walking at the same time. He did not know legs could do such things. It looked like the reverse of the Shiv Tandav. (The Shiv Tandav: in the last phase of the universe, when the world is old and corrupt, Shiv wakes from his trance, and sets about destroying everything. With giant strides, he stamps out life. This is the Tandav, the terrifying, cosmological dance of destruction. The sculptors traditionally represent this with Shiv dancing, arms gracefully apart, one leg raised, the other foot on a helpless child lying on his stomach: the latter probably symbolises the innocent life which is crushed as a part of the dance. And the Shiv Tandav was reversed when Babla, the child, danced on Chhotomama's back, while the latter lay on his stomach and made noises.)

MAMIMA was about to enter a competition held by a famous coffee-making company. She was filling out the entry form with an intent face. "Mona," she said to Sandeep, "give me a good English slogan about coffee." Sandeep, the boy from Bombay, who wrote poems and stories, was supposed to have a good vocabulary in this idiotic foreign language which no one, especially coffee companies, could apparently do without. Already, he used words like "tentative" and "gingerly" and "enthusiastic." Would he help his aunt, whose command over English was imperfect, and who cared little about this, with a dignified nonchalance some Indian women have, would he help her win two air tickets to Kashmir? "I'll think about it, Mamima," he said indifferently. Yet he was moved, watching

her on the bed, hunched and cutting out the entry coupon meticulously with her scissors.

Till it was lunchtime, the boys played their energetic "pretend" games. It was good that it was raining, because they discovered they had stopped sweating. Chhotomama, out of bed, found them in the corridor.

"What are you playing?" he asked, smiling indulgently.

"We're playing freedom-fighters," said Abhi. "We're killing the British. We're cutting the British to pieces."

"And who are you?" asked Chhotomama tenderly, bending low to Babla. "Are you cutting the British to pieces as well?"

"I'm Subhas Chandra Bose," said Babla, standing at attention and looking undauntedly into his father's eyes.

"No, I'm Subhas Chandra Bose," said Abhi. "Babla, shut up."

"Abhi, shut up," replied Babla, still at attention.

"What did you say?" asked Abhi in a mafioso voice. "Repeat that."

"And you?" Chhotomama asked, turning finally to Sandeep. "Who are you?"

"I'm Mahatma Gandhi," he said, and realised he had made a mistake.

Chhotomama was taken aback momentarily. A contemptuous smile asserted itself on his face.

"Gandhi! Gandhi was no freedom-fighter! He was a sham yogi who knew no economics!"

Sandeep did not know what "economics" meant; he knew that the girls in his school had a class called Home Economics. "He's the Father of the Nation," he replied naively, repeating what he had learnt at school; he saw that, once more, he had committed an error.

Eyes burning, Chhotomama began to lecture them on

preindependence Indian history, quoting several historians of several nationalities. As he spoke to the children, he behaved like a scholar at a seminar addressing a group of inimical scholars who had views hostile to his own. By a magical suspension of disbelief, he forgot he was talking to Sandeep and Abhi and Babla; he saw, in front of him, three conservative, pro-Congress intellectuals.

He began to revile Gandhi, the Father of the Nation, the bald anorexic with the grandmother's smile.

"That man!" he said. "That man in his obscene loincloth, his ribs sticking out!"

He began to deify Subhas Bose, the brilliant, sidetracked Bengali. He radiated with irritable energy, argumentativeness, obstinacy, a remarkable unwillingness to give in. He spoke with true pride of Subhas Bose, pride shone in his eyes, the pride a son feels when he remembers a calumniated father. The boys, following him as he lectured excitedly and paced from room to room, forgot to finish their game, which remained at a promising, preliminary stage; the British would live to fight another day.

IN THE afternoon, it stopped raining. It was cloudy, humid, and hot. Chhordimoni, Sandeep's great-aunt, who had come early that morning, and had stayed back, had spent the morning making little pyramids out of betel leaves, stuffing them with betel nuts (the betel nuts were round as planets and hard as rocks; she broke them into halves and quarters with a sharp and dangerous implement), smearing them with choona. She chewed on one for hours, her jaws moving imperceptibly. It was a strong and hardy jaw; it was never exhausted. In the afternoon, everyone slept, and nothing moved in the world but

Chhordimoni's jaws, with a stubborn, grinding motion that defied logic, with a subtle rhythm, taking utmost pleasure in the betel leaf.

Chhotomama was asleep, with a half-open book by his side. Sandeep glanced through its pages; it was a novel by Sarat Chandra Chatterjee. Chhotomama's shelves were full of these books: Sarat Chandra, Bibhuti Bhushan, Tarashanker, Rabindranath; like the names of wines, the names of these authors; an entire generation had been drunk with these names.

Sandeep could hardly read Bengali. He could hardly write it. Brought up in Bombay, away from his own province, Bengal, he was one of the innumerable language orphans of modern India. He was as illiterate in his language as . . . as Chhaya and Saraswati. But he liked opening these classics and looking at the letters while, outside, new rain-bearing clouds moved in the sky. He saw the letters as characters, "characters" in both senses of the word: এ was a fat man standing straight with his belly sticking out; ঞ was the fat man scratching his back; ী was an adolescent, lately grown tall and awkward, his head bent forward shyly; শ was a dancer, his right leg forever lifted in a self-consciously statuesque pose. The letters were intimate, quirky, ancient, graceful, comic, just as he imagined the people of Bengal to be.

IT WAS a time of many insects. The skies were prolific with tiny, beating creatures. In the evening, there would be a tribe of insects of arbitrary sizes and origins by the fluorescent lamp on the wall. This made the lizard happy. When it saw an insect minding its own business by a corner of the wall, its body ticked urgently and accurately, like the hand of a clock that never runs faster or slower than the exact time. It would

turn and stop and advance with staccato, Morse-code-like movements—dot-dot-dash-dot-dot—glide forward in a way that was both jerky and streamlined, and seize and swallow the little insect if it was lucky: if the lizard was lucky, that is. One could never manage to see that precise instant, that half instant, when it actually grasped the insect with its mouth and swallowed it. Now the insect was here, part of the world of creation, and now it was gone, into the underworld of the lizard's belly.

Once, an insect wandered into Babla's ear. Babla, who had dozed off at seven o'clock in the evening, woke with a start and began to cry loudly. The cry turned into the high-pitched wail of the tragedian trying his best to move his audience. Upon anxious interrogation, he refused to answer, but cried and pointed to his left ear, but not too noticeably, as if he were afraid the insect might take offence and enter his brain.

"It makes a noise," he wept. "It crackles."

Mamima made him lie down. Wave after wave of tears followed; something sad and irreversible seemed to have happened in the house, and only Babla, the youngest child, gave it a voice and expression. Saraswati heated a bowl of oil, Mamima dipped her little finger in it, and holding it an inch away from the ear hole, let a drop of oil fall into the dark tunnel. Then another, and another.

"Close your eyes," she said. "Don't be a little coward. The insect is more afraid than you are."

Babla was not convinced. He could not bear the thought of a living creature wandering inside another living creature, himself. He lived alone inside his body; he did not want to share it with an insect. A short while later, a flying ant came out from the darkness of the tunnel into the dazzling, lit space of

the room. Its wing were sticky with oil, and it stumbled onto the pillow. It seemed overwhelmed by what it had seen in Babla's ear. Mamima killed it swiftly with a magazine, and it appeared quite ready to die, as if its mission in life were now complete.

Chapter Ten

SOMETIME during the rains, Abhi's and Babla's school started again. The last week of Sandeep's summer holidays was spent alone in the daytime, with the house and its uninhabited spaces all to himself. Of course, his mother and his aunt were present, but they were more like the furniture in the house that would always be there and which comforted by their presence— they were more like beds to lie in or chairs to sit safely in rather than companions to conspire with; they would always be there.

With the coming of the rains, Saraswati caught a cold, and her coughs got worse and worse. Without Abhi and Babla around, Sandeep began to see Saraswati as an individual rather than a mythical figure, which was a mildly disturbing experience. When she got fever, she went up to the terrace and lay upon a mattress beneath the sun. When it rained, she came in. "Hai hai! O misery!" she exclaimed. She wanted to work, but Mamima had commanded her to rest. "O misery, misery!" she said. Why did she want to work? Shivering at the same time? It was not because she was good or wonderful (imagine Saraswati being good or wonderful), but because she was frightened of

not being needed. Sandeep pitied her, and it hurt him to feel an emotion as elevated as pity for such a crumpled, ugly woman, who could not even talk proper Bengali, who only spoke in a crude village dialect which was a huge source of amusement to the children, and who ate puffed rice soaked in water in the afternoon. Once, when asked to write her name, her fingers, shy and tortured, had scrawled something painful on a piece of paper. There was a fixed smile on Saraswati's face as, far away, her fingers took several minutes to accomplish their task. "What is this?" they asked mockingly, pointing to the stillborn, deformed word on the paper. "Who knows?" she replied. "I could never write. Besides, an old woman can't write." "How old are you, Saraswati?" they asked her. "Forty or fifty," she said. "I'm not sure." Forty years for her was a long time, as was fifty years; they were both nearly an eternity but a little less than a lifetime, and she liked both numbers equally. The sense of time had bypassed her, like a gentle breeze, without disturbing her. What an ignorant woman! Pratap, who got the lowest marks in class, was less ignorant. And now that she was ill, Sandeep pitied her, albeit with difficulty, for he usually reserved emotions like pity for beautiful orphan girls in stories or films. "Hai hai!" she said. She would not take medicines. Stubborn, pig-headed, stupid woman. Instead, she ate the bitter tulsi leaves of the tulsi plants that grew in pots on the terrace. Bitter, bitter leaves. She too was like the furniture in the house; many, many people had rested in her without knowing it. Old, decaying piece of furniture, never to be removed, giving rest again and again.

At four o'clock each day, the magic moment, Abhi and Babla came back home from school. Sandeep watched them silently from the upper window, his face pressed against the mullions, his hands clutching the long, cold mullions. He felt a light twinge of envy as he watched the porter help them off the

school bus. When they glanced up and saw him, they waved, and he waved back. This was his way of welcoming them back to the shadowy world of the holidays.

But when they came up, they were full of what they had done at school, what this or that teacher had said, what mischief a friend had been up to. They flung their bags onto the bed. The bags, made of khaki cloth, were stuffed with textbooks and ragged exercise books that had names and classes written neatly on their brown-paper covers. In some of Abhi's books, Sandeep found the following written on the first page:

> Abhijit Das
> 17 Vivekananda Road
> Calcutta (South)
> West Bengal
> India
> Asia
> Earth
> The Solar System
> The Universe

It was a strange and sublime address.

Now, ripping the shoes off their feet, they roared to Saraswati for food, and began talking about the school play. Sandeep told them in hushed tones, as if he knew what he was about to say was inconceivable:

"Saraswati's not well."

"Ooof!" said Abhi. "Why did she have to fall ill *now*?"

Their faces glowed with sweat and the radiance of another excitement. It gave Sandeep a sense of the other world to which they belonged and in which he played no part; it made his after-

noon games with them seem small and temporary. He felt the shadowy, secret life of the holidays, the vivid underground existence during those long afternoons in the house while their parents slept calmly, slip out of his grasp. Yet the three of them, Abhi, Babla, and Sandeep, sprawled on the great bed together, and talked and talked, reliving the illusion of togetherness. By simply talking, by simply never ceasing these long, meaningless conversations, Sandeep felt he could buy time and keep the holidays from ending.

It rained during the day, and the old, mysterious sound of thunder rang in the sky. With Abhi and Babla at school, Sandeep lounged in the upper room, lying on his stomach upon the bed, haltingly reading Bengali sentences in a children's magazine, cautiously looking at the pictures. He sometimes found, to his surprise, that it took him a minute to read a single short line of Bengali. He would stare at a difficult word uncomprehendingly for what seemed like hours. How slowly time passed in the last, empty moments of the holidays! The thunder echoed in the sky again, and he was impatient for Abhi to return, so that he could discuss the sound of the thunder with him. He peered at the magazine, and found that it gave him a strange comfort to read these Bengali riddles, limericks, jokes; to hear, through the riddles, limericks, and jokes, the language speaking to him. A fly settled near his hand. Looking up, he saw the lizard motionless upon the wall. By accident, he saw himself in the mirror, lying on the bed, his body relaxed and his face serious. He heard his aunt blowing the conch and ringing the bell in the prayer-room. He wished he could live in the mirror, always, the way he saw himself now, a lazy, motionless image, with the fly and the lizard, the sound of the conch and the rain, the jokes and rhymes in his mother-tongue upon his lips.

IN THESE last days, he grew used to the company of women. He eavesdropped on their conversations; he asked them questions to which only a woman would know the answer. He wandered at large among these slow, motherly figures, these timeless busybodies and humorous Samaritans, who went around the world in their long, flowing saris like priests in their robes. To be in this old house in the daytime with his aunt, his mother, Chhordimoni, and Saraswati was to see women assume life with an unimpedable vegetable dignity.

When Chhordimoni spent a few days with them, it was a great pleasure for Sandeep to watch her briskly and fiercely ordering the rest of the world about, for she was convinced of its insignificance, as she got a special meal prepared for the evening. "Duffer!" she would say to his aunt. "Is that the way to peel a banana flower? Give it to me!" She would proceed with trembling hands to peel it, and fail, because she was so old and unsure of her own movements, though her intellect was clear and frustrated with the aging body it lived in. Often, Sandeep's mother had told him what Chhordimoni was like in her younger days, a portrait of a majestic and imperious woman, whom servants and children were afraid of, grudgingly taken by men as an equal, one of the first women graduates. And now this. "Here! Take it! Do you think I have time for these things?" she would say, roughly pushing the vegetable back. She would call the washerwoman a fool for putting too much starch in her sari; she would call the vegetable seller an ass for bringing such sickly looking aubergines; she would call Saraswati an imbecile for refusing to take medicine. The air rang out with expletives, intense names as untranslatable as poetry: "Duffer! Crow face! Retarded child! She-goat! Cow-

eyed imbecile!" Sometimes, in a fit of calculated irony and sar-
casm, she produced the opposite range of words: "O genius!
O wonder-worker! O helpless child!" When she fell silent, the
inspiration seemed to go out of the air, and a great calm settled
upon everything.

In one of these serene and silent moments in the afternoon,
Sandeep asked her:

"Chhordimoni, how old were you when you got married?"

She was lying on the bed, scarcely listening. From the well
of her subconscious, a voice replied:

"I was twenty."

"Was that a long time ago, Chhordimoni?"

"Yes. Fifty years." She counted silently to herself. "Fifty-
two years ago."

"That's a long time," said Sandeep.

"Yes."

He paused to think. Then he asked:

"Did you see the Romans, Chhordimoni?"

"No."

"Did people say 'thee' and 'thou.' Chhordimoni? Did you
ever hear them say that?"

"I don't think I did, Mona."

There was a brief, thoughtful silence. Then:

"When did Chhordamoni die, Chhordimoni?"

"When I was twenty-five, I think."

"Why did he die, Chhordimoni?"

"He was not well, Mona."

"Not well like Saraswati?"

"More not well than Saraswati, Mona."

Sandeep paused. He could not picture his not-well
grand-uncle.

"Did Chhordamoni have a moustache, Chhordimoni?"

"He had a big moustache."

"Did you have Rabimama and Jatinmama after Chhorda-moni died or before he died, Chhordimoni?"

His great-aunt stared thoughtfully at him for a moment.

"Before he died, Mona."

"Did he play with Rabimama and Jatinmama?"

"There was not much time, Mona. But he did play with them, and he took them out on the horse carriage . . . though he had a bad temper, sometimes."

"As bad as yours, Chhordimoni?"

She stared at him with tragic, bewildered eyes.

"I don't have a bad temper, Mona."

"But sometimes you do, Chhordimoni. Not always, but just sometimes-sometimes."

"It's only when people are stupid. Now go and bother your aunt and let me sleep."

She turned over on her side, cracked all her knuckles meticulously, and began to snore almost instantaneously. After regarding the wrinkles on her face and hands for a while, Sandeep crawled over her body to the other side of the bed, where his aunt lay reading the health page of a magazine. He loved crawling like a clumsy, four-legged beast across and over the bodies of the grown-ups, these warm figures in cool saris, and then curl up between them like a mountain-cat among huge, sheltering boulders.

He nudged his aunt, who lifted an arm and placed it on her forehead, making her bangles sing as she did so.

"Mamima," he asked, "when were you married?"

"Why are you interested in our marriages today?" she said without turning her head.

"No, tell me, Mamima, tell me when you got married."

"I've forgotten."

"You've not forgotten, Mamima! How can you forget?"

"I tell you I've forgotten."

"All right, then tell me *where* you got married."

"I was married here in Calcutta. Your Chhotomama came in a car. He was wearing a white dhuti and a silk panjabi with gold buttons, and a topor on his head. I, of course, didn't see him till later. But my cousin, Beena, saw them coming and she rushed into our room and told me. She said: 'The bridegroom's come.' "

"What did you say?"

"I couldn't say anything, because they were putting chandan and sindoor on my face, and kaajal around my eyes. I wasn't allowed to move."

"Not even talk?"

"Well, I could talk, but since they were drawing such beautiful patterns on my forehead, I didn't want to spoil it by talking about the bridegroom. Who wants to know about the bridegroom?"

"Weren't you interested?"

"Not in the bridegroom."

"Had you ever seen him before?" In Sandeep's mind, it was no longer Chhotomama, but some other man who was about to get married to Mamima, who was no longer Mamima, but some other woman.

"Only in a photograph."

"Did you like him?"

"Not a bit. He had much too big a nose for me. Also, Shampa, my little cousin, who was the only one from our family who had come with them in the car—she was a small, lively girl then, and she wore a blue frock that day—told me that he had argued with the driver all the way about which was the shorter route to Boubazaar."

"Why did you marry him, then, Mamima?"

"Oh I liked your mother and Chhordimoni. When I met them, I thought, They're nice people. So, because I wanted to know your mother and Chhordimoni better, I married him."

"Do you like him now?"

She wrinkled her nose: "Not at all. He's such a busybody."

"Why didn't you . . ." He paused emphatically.

"Why didn't I what?"

"Why didn't you have a love-marriage?"

She wrinkled her nose a little more.

"Of course not. How boring!" She was silent, and then said, "Not knowing the person makes it so much more exciting! It's such a great adventure . . ."

IN THE course of the conversation, it was divulged that, on the first night, he had asked whether she liked cricket, to which she had replied no. They had both agreed that they loved Tagore songs and Sachin Deb Burman's voice. He had asked her if she could sing, and she had said no again. So it was he who had sung a song for her, which she had found very funny because of the seriousness of his face, though she had to admit that he sang very well. First she had Abhi, the dark one with large eyes, and they named him Abhijit, another name for Vega, the bright star, and called him Abhi for short. Then they had Babla, the fair one, who looked more like his father, and they named him Surajit, which means the "One Who Has Mastered Music," partly because it rhymed with Abhijit, and partly because Chhotomama wanted a son who could sing. Abhijit and Surajit, two brothers, rhyming names, always arguing with each other. O I remember when Babla was born, said Sandeep. I remember going in the car, which was not so old and rundown then, with Saraswati and Abhi and Ma. I remember

the nurses and the doctors with masks on their faces. Do you? asked Mamima, surprised. Yes, I often remember that scene, though I didn't know it was Babla's birth until now. Saraswati loved the child, said Mamima, and then she said conspiratorially, she even nursed him to keep him quiet. Sandeep thought of Saraswati's small, wrinkled breasts. They talked until his aunt was tired and wanted to sleep.

"But what shall I do, Mamima?" Sandeep asked.

"Well, go to the terrace," she said in a sleep-heavy voice. "I planted some chilli plants in a pot. See if the chillies are growing, and guard them from bulbuls and parrots."

So he went upstairs to the terrace to watch the chillies growing.

SARASWATI was sleeping on the terrace, a small, huddled figure. The sun was high and scorching, and it was uncomfortably hot, as it always is between rains. Next to her there was a potted tulsi plant and, next to that, two chilli plants. The chilli blossoms were like little lavender stars; the chillies grew from their centre, fierce pointed clots of purple, each a tiny phallus. Sandeep shooed away two crows that were hopping around the plants with a sly and tactful curiosity; they flew to the terrace of the neighbouring house, and from there to the next house, and then to the next. At each house, they paused like burglars and darted around guiltily, as if they were perpetually on the verge of breaking some law, perpetual trespassers in God's world. Then, quite suddenly, in a fit of candour, they hoarsely declared "Ka! Ka!" in the reverie of the afternoon. No one woke.

Between two and four o'clock, a golden stupor descended upon the city. Sandeep loved these two hours when it was too hot to move, when the eddying waves of people disappeared

and a low tide came upon everything, leaving lane after lane like gullies in the sand and house after house like sandcastles upon an empty beach, when the splendid arguments in the tea-shops came to a brief conclusion, and everyone agreed with everyone and fell silent.

Clothes hung from clothes-lines in the terrace, and undulated like many-coloured waves, all at once, when a breeze blew from the direction of the railway lines. They were happy, cheerful flags that signified life in a house. There were trousers, shirts, petticoats, blouses, and magnificent lengths of saris, each with a different and striking motif, each a small waterfall of life and colour, unravelled to dry. Sandeep had often seen Saraswati unfolding these sinuous boa constrictors of cloth (how wrinkled they looked, then, bad tempered and wrinkled, and how rejuvenated they would look tomorrow, when they were ironed and given their customary face-lift), beating them against the air with a single electric movement to rid them of the last drops of water, then clipping them, her arms wide apart, as if outstretched in a deep and satisfying yawn.

A mist of drowsiness hung over the lanes. In the still houses, families had eaten their lunch of rice, dal, and fish and fallen asleep. Afternoon was a time of digestion, a time of full-ness and contentment, full bellies and closed eyes. In all the shadowy houses of Calcutta at this moment, the gastric juices were solemnly at work. There was not a movement in the cor-ridors, no noise; yet if you put an ear against the belly of one of these sleepers, you would probably hear a rich gurgling sound.

Not everyone was asleep. People who had had a meal less substantial dotted the lane perfunctorily. Sometimes, a girl came to a terrace, ostensibly to hang, let us say, a sari on a clothes-line; at the same time, a young man appeared on the

terrace three houses away, apparently to inspect a water tank. They glanced at each other, then fumbled with their work, then glanced at each other, then fumbled, then glanced—such shy, piercing glances exchanged in the heat of the afternoon! How straight and undeflected the man's glance travelled, how swift and disguised the woman's answering glance! What rhythm the moment possessed!

Near a derelict tea-shop, a rickshawalla lay slouched in the shade of his rickshaw. Idly, he clapped his hands in the air. After a moment, Sandeep realised he was killing mosquitoes. Clap . . . clap . . . clap . . . clap . . . Four mosquitoes. Clap . . . clap . . . Two more mosquitoes. One was reminded of the joke in which a man whose neck was aching stopped for a minute on the street and turned his head up to ease the pain. People who had been walking past noticed him, and thought that he was watching something terribly interesting and important in the sky. One by one, they stopped beside him and stared up with deep attention. Meanwhile, the first man, feeling somewhat better, continued his journey, leaving everyone else still gazing thoughtfully at the sky. This is what must have happened to Calcutta in the afternoon; the first man had casually walked away; the rest of Calcutta was still staring at that fascinating, nonexistent point in the emptiness, waiting for the revelation.

HE HEARD car horns blowing in the distance. He heard shouts—a taxi driver must be insulting a bus driver. It was the first traffic jam of the evening, punctual, ceremonial, and glorious. The two hours of golden stillness had ended. The cars and crowded buses were on the roads again; Abhi and Babla would come back home from school; pigeons flapped their wings and

rose above rooftops, a clean universe of rooftops and terraces. Tomorrow, Sandeep remembered, he would return with his mother to Bombay. He saw Chhaya at the turning of the lane, walking in the direction of the house. It was time—it must be—to sweep the dust from the floors.

Chapter Eleven

A YEAR and a half passed before Sandeep came to Calcutta
again. In Bombay, his father had been promoted to an even
higher position in his company. They had moved from their big
apartment to an even bigger one; from the twenty-third storey,
they had moved to the twenty-fifth storey of a twenty-five-
storey building. Standing in one of the balconies or looking
out from the windows in the hall, one could see almost all
of Bombay, the swarms of lights in the evening, the hoods
of tiny cars shining and vanishing in the sunlight during the
daytime—a view marginally more breathtaking and margin-
ally more unreal than the one seen from the balcony of the
twenty-third floor. No sounds, no smells, only a pure, perpetu-
ally moving picture.

One and a half years after the last holidays, Sandeep and his
parents visited Calcutta in the winter. Sandeep felt what a
statue in a museum would feel if he suddenly came to life and
walked out into a shimmering crowd of people. Because it was
a little cold now in Calcutta, people swathed themselves in
shawls, mufflers, sweaters, coats, and several kinds of woollen
garments. The first thing one saw when one came to Calcutta

in December was a welter of warm clothes. As usual, the people of Calcutta did everything to excess; the streets had the air of a fancy-dress party as shawls and cardigans and jackets floated by solemnly. In the nights, when it became really cold, beggars set fire to old rubber tyres, and sat around the circles of slow flame to warm their hands.

The presence of Sandeep's father gave the holidays a mood of optimism and potential. They listed the things they would do and the families they would visit together. Endless questions were asked by Sandeep to which his father provided endless answers. Besides, his father would have a car at his service which they would use when he was not attending business lunches. This would be useful as Chhotomama had had to sell his car; Sandeep remembered the old, battered Ambassador and wondered where it was now; to whom did it belong? Sandeep remembered the dials on its dashboard which always showed that the fuel-tank was empty and that the car was running at twenty kilometres per hour, and he remembered the torn leather upholstery and the shuddering doors.

His father's presence also meant that this time they would be staying at the Grand Hotel on Chowringhee. The company was going to meet all the expenses, naturally. The thrill of exploring the large lobby with its mirrors and sofas, of dining at the restaurant at night while a band played and couples danced, of gazing out at the swimming-pool in the afternoon, of following the uniformed bearers with their trays, soon died out. At such times, Sandeep deserted his parents shamelessly and spent days and nights at the old house with his cousins.

Not much had changed in the old house. But the few changes that had taken place had had their effect. For one thing, the car had been sold—this meant that Chhotomama had to wake up earlier in the mornings, make a great deal more noise,

bother everyone a great deal more, and rush out to catch his bus or train with more than his usual fanfare. Around him, Mamima and Saraswati performed their old desperate dance, which was a little more desperate now, and a little less like a dance. When he returned in the evenings, he looked soiled and tired from standing in the bus and in numberless, undisciplined queues; so he had a second bath in the evening, and his songs echoed once more in the bathroom:

> *Godhulir chhaya pathe*
> *Je gelo chini go tare.*

Whenever he sang those songs, the tunes cleansed the atmosphere as the trickle of water from the shower cleansed the soil and smears of dirt from his body.

The other change that had taken place in the one and a half years was to do with Abhi. He had been transferred from a Bengali-medium school to a famous English-medium one. This would increase his prospects at the age of twenty-one, when he would graduate from college and start looking for a job. He would be what the world wanted him to be—smart, English-speaking, and brittle, like one of those ideal men in cigarette advertisements. But his prospects now, at the age of ten, did not look very bright. He was having trouble with this strange new language, English. Sometimes, when he wrote his answers in class, his teachers pointed out that they did not make sense. He would have liked to point out to them that it was the language that did not make sense. It was a riddle; it was difficult and unapproachable. At home, he had taken to sitting at his study-table with an English grammar in front of him, his eyes gazing dreamily out of the window at the palm tree in the backyard and the terrace of the professor's house. He could gaze at the

palm tree and the professor's house for hours. This habit had earned him a nickname from his friends—the Poet. Abhi, the Poet . . .

In the winter, the days ended early. Smoke rose from earthen ovens and wood fires into the air, and hung mysteriously over the lanes in the evenings. Abhi's new tutor came on these smoky evenings, every Monday, Wednesday, and Friday, tinkling his bicycle after the sun had gone down. Abhi, Babla, and Sandeep would peer from the balcony as he came in, and groan inwardly. They would recognise him at once because of the red muffler wrapped so carefully around his head—nothing was visible of his face but his spectacles. From upstairs, he looked somewhat like a burglar, a rather harmless, officious-looking burglar. He would unwrap the muffler, folding it into neat little folds; Abhi would watch in fascination, hoping the folds would be folded into tinier folds, hoping he would never finish folding his muffler. Then he would climb up the stairs calling—Aabhi. Aaabhi. Aaaabhi—the first syllable getting longer and grander all the time. Abhi would wait till the first syllable had become ominously and inordinately long, and then he would go dutifully to the stairs to greet him. If there was a power-cut, he would stand at the head of the stairs with a lantern in his hands watching his tutor grope his way up, clutching the banisters, as large shadows flickered and trembled on the wall.

While Abhi worked with his tutor, Sandeep and Babla spied on them from the corridor and made rude comments about the size of the tutor's ears. Sometimes, Abhi would take a break to drink water or to go to the toilet, at which the boys would be reunited briefly to gossip busily about the tutor and break into fits of silent giggles. They were not sure what it was exactly that they were laughing about, but this did not stop them from finding the situation impossibly funny. After a minute, the tutor

would say, "Abhi, come back to your books now," at which Abhi's eyes would become sad and pensive, the eyes of a man with many responsibilities.

When the English lessons began, the voice became stentorian and English sentences and words exploded like little bombs in the air.

— Whut ees thee name of thee boy?

— Thee name of thee boy ees John.

— Whut deed John habhfor deenar?

— John had meelk and bredfor deenar.

— *Why* deed John habh meelk and bredfor deenar?

The question was not to be answered, because Saraswati came in with a cup of tea and a plate of dark sweetmeats. "Aaah!" said the tutor, lapsing back into his mother-tongue. "Lovely tea!" It was a pleasure to hear his natural eloquence in Bengali after his brave guerilla invasion into the rocky terrain of English; silence descended as he drank his tea, no noise but that of passionate, noisy sips, and there was a temporary respite from the savage bombardment of those foreign words on this helpless, sleepy room. There was a lull, and an "all-clear" atmosphere prevailed.

CHHOTOMAMA'S business was faring worse than ever. Yet who would have suspected it? Certainly the children suspected nothing. They lived in their own world which was half illusion, because it was founded so much on fantasy, and half real, palpably real, because its tissue was wholly made of sensations. When they would grow up, and their lives and the lives of the grown-ups would be retold, they would seem like fairytales and legends. Certainly, they suspected nothing. They roamed in a silent, self-created web of sounds, smells, and colours. Once, Sandeep had woken late in the night to find

Chhotomama standing at the window near the bed smoking a cigarette. The moonlight dimmed outlines and made tangible things seem intangible, and Chhotomama and the furniture in the room appeared like figures on the wrong side of a tapestry; everything seemed to be dissolving into the smoke Chhotomama was exhaling from his nostrils. Hearing Sandeep stir, Chhotomama had turned to him and said: "Aren't you asleep, Mona? There, go to sleep now, it's very late. Go to sleep." There was affection and assurance in the voice, and affection in the touch of the hand as it stroked his hair.

IN THE winter, Calcutta was at its most beautiful. At eleven o'clock in the morning, when it was not too chilly, Saraswati brought pails of steaming hot water, which she had heated downstairs, slowly and laboriously up to the bathroom. The children were stripped naked and bathed; they gasped in pleasure and terror as someone dipped a mug in the bucket and poured great, eloquent splashes of hot water on their heads. Later, shivering and still naked, they would troop into the room and stand in a patch of warm winter sunlight in front of the window. A mother or an aunt would hold their faces firmly, imprinting, upon their defenceless cheeks, the furious marks of their fingers, and one by one, comb their moist black hair with murderous pleasure. A crow would caw in alarm.

"Ma . . . Ma . . . my parting is slightly more on the side."

"Hold still!"

A servant woman would be staring from the terrace of the next house at the brown gleaming buttocks of the children. When the little show was over, she would reluctantly tie the aanchal of her sari tightly around herself and resume her work. The crow, who had also been watching with interest, would fly away from the window in pursuit of more pressing matters.

There would be a smell of talcum powder and Jabakusum oil in the air.

In the evenings, Chhotomama would come home and have a small simple meal of yoghurt and khoi and slices of bananas, mixed together with sugar, the smallest, simplest meal a Bengali can have. As he sat in the verandah and ate this from a bowl with a spoon, the taste of it reminded him of his childhood, for he had first had this mixture from his mother's fingers as a child. Each time he put a small dollop of the yoghurt in his mouth, and chewed on the khoi patiently he tasted his childhood. It was made of the sourness of yoghurt, the sweetness of sugar, and the grey taste of bananas. Also the warmth of his mother's fingers from which he ate the mixture. It was as if his memory resided in the small, invisible taste-buds in his tongue rather than in his brain. Around him, voices rose and scattered in the lane.

Later, he went to the bathroom and began singing. Sandeep's mother and father would come from the Grand Hotel in the car; Shonamama and Chhordimoni would arrive on a rickshaw, and if it was Abhi's unlucky day, his tutor would follow closely on a bicycle. There would be a sound of foot-steps and laughter in the house, and the smell of sandalwood incense. Smoke hung over the lane, delicately bandaging the decaying walls of the houses. At the turning of the lane, boys played badminton in a small, square lawn in the glare of electric lights. The world happened in slow motion; the shuttle-cock rose and fell in slow motion.

When Sandeep and his cousins ran up to the terrace to spy on the world, they saw the moon and the great constellations in the sky. It was a clear sky, and the clouds seemed to have descended upon Calcutta; rivers of smoke and mist travelled through the streets, blurring the lights in the houses. House after house stood like a little island surrounded by smoke. This

is what it must be like, Sandeep thought, to live inside a crater, the fumes putting you to sleep, each day the last day before the eruption. When he went downstairs, and heard the grown-ups laughing and drinking tea, Saraswati closing windows to prevent mosquitoes from coming in and smoke from filling the room, and Chhotomama singing in the bathroom accompanied by great splashes of water, he wanted to tell them to tell stories all night long, because the day of the eruption had come, finally. But when Saraswati shut all the windows, he felt brightly lit room was safe, and that the house, like a patient, enduring ark built by the hands of an infinitely wise man, would carry them away over the tide. In the bathroom, Chhotomama was singing:

> *Whether you'll remember me or not, I have*
> *forgotten.*
>
> (splash of water) . . .
>
> *Moment after tiny moment, I come to your door,*
> *sing without cause.*
> *Days pass; I remain; if ever, on the road, I find*
> *myself near you,*
>
> (two splashes of water) . . .
>
> *I long to see a smile of startled peace upon your*
> *face.*
> *That is why I sing without cause.*

Another loud splash of water, then the sound of water draining away, then silence, as he dried himself, then again:

> *Spring-flowers drift to the earth; springtime*
> *comes to a close.*

> *It has filled an instant's fist; it need know*
> > *nothing more.*
> *The day will end, the light draw to a fineness,*
> > *the song cease, the instrument be silent.*
> *As long as I'm here, won't you load with riches*
> > *this mock raft of mine?*
> *That is why I sing without cause.*

The sound of Saraswati shutting the windows in the other room, the footsteps of his aunt coming up the stairs with two cups of tea in her hands, and the sound of the grown-ups talking, falling silent, talking, falling silent, like the advance and retreat of a tide.

Chapter Twelve

THE next day, Chhotomama had a heart attack. (The doctors later clarified that it wasn't an attack, but a spasm. The heart's dance has its own rules, and nuances.) At around eleven-thirty in the morning, when the children had come out of the bath, and Mamima was in the prayer-room, blowing the conch and arranging the offering of fruit and batashas for the gods, Chhotomama, who was planning to take a late bus to work, was standing by the basin, rubbing his chest and making funny noises with his throat.

"It's wind," he was saying. "What *have* they given me for breakfast?"

Everything was quite beautiful at that moment, and Saraswati was combing the children's hair. The maidservant in the neighbouring house was pottering about as usual on the neighbouring terrace. Flies were dancing gracefully in front of the mirror, and the sun kept coming out of and going back behind clouds, so that there were phases of light and shade in the world, as if a giant bird were flying across the sun, and obstructing, partially, the sunlight with its slow moving wings. Sandeep's mother was going to come from the Grand Hotel in

the car; the driver would blow the horn announcing her arrival; she would take them out to lunch. Possibly, Chhotomama would take a lift from them, and Sandeep imagined the car crammed with human beings, talking busily about trivial and exciting things.

But all the plans would have to be changed now, because Chhotomama was having a heart attack. All the plans would have to be different now. Quite unexpectedly, there he was, rolling on the bed, making an odd grunting sound, desperately trying to tear his shirt off. The buttons were coming apart, exploding like peas and falling to the floor. He was jumping up, falling back, rolling from side to side, like an acrobat doing a bizarre act to impress the children. Any moment, perhaps, he would rise and touch the ceiling. The children were staring with open mouths, and Saraswati, smiling like an infant watching a tiger at the zoo, was still combing their hair. Her hands were trembling, as if they alone understood the terror of what was happening.

"Dada . . . ," she whispered. "Dada . . ."

He roared now, and the shirt tore in his hands with a long hissing sound. Then he was silent. The comb dropped to the ground, but did not break, and Saraswati rushed forward, her white sari falling around her like a lowered flag. She called out for Mamima. The sound of the conch, the rich, powerful sound, born of human breath, that had such conviction it seemed the walls of the house would collapse, and the ringing of the bell, the heart of music at the centre of prayer, stopped abruptly. In the distance, there was a sound of a plate being upset or overturned, and the soft, hurrying patter of bare feet. At an even greater distance, on the horizon of hearing, a car blew its horn again and again in the lane.

. . .

CHHOTOMAMA did not want to go to hospital. "It's wind," he was insisting, while Mamima and Sandeep's mother shook their heads. The children floated like satellites in the distance, afraid to collide with the painful orbit of adult lives, and yet always being pulled towards it against their will. Saraswati took the company car to fetch the doctor, because the telephones were not working in the area. There was a power-cut, and Sandeep's mother began to fan her brother with a newspaper. "It's all right," he said. "Nothing's happened." He started to criticise the government for its inability to rectify the power shortage. Then he vomited, and the vomit was a small yellow puddle on the floor. "That," he said, pointing to the puddle, "that's what has been doing it." He was triumphant. "Today's breakfast." The doctor came with many instruments, siphons, and tubes. "Breathe," he said. He was pressing a kind of pump and doing all kinds of things at once. "The E.C.G.," he said. His assistant, an adolescent boy, took out a bundle of filaments which the doctor attached to Chhotomama's body. There they looked like coiled nerves that had mistakenly tapered out of Chhotomama's skin, or thin tuberous plants that had started growing from his hands and feet. Next to him a square machine hummed now and then in a bored manner. An interesting, indecipherable graph was drawn on a strip of paper which the machine stuck out like an endless tongue. Everything somehow depended on the mysterious code written on this strip of paper, which the doctor was now looking at. "The hospital," he said, when he had finished. Suddenly, the power came back, and the fan began to turn, making a peaceful, whirring sound, throwing a breeze on all their faces. When they tried to get Chhotomama into the car, they found he could not stand up. The doctor and the company driver had to help him, one of Chhotomama's arms around each neck. Mamima was crying in a strange way, pressing the loose end of her sari upon her face,

covering her mouth and nose with it like a muffler, as if she were feeling cold. Chhotomama was laughing and saying, "Don't be silly." The children were standing there, watching the faces, the clothes, the lips, the eyes, the movements that were now hurried and now calm, the tears, surprisingly adult tears, salty with unknown experience, the exact way in which they streamed from the eyes.

ON THE way to the hospital, Chhotomama had another attack. He vomited on the floor of the company car. The driver, caught in a traffic jam, shook his head from side to side. He had seen these things happen to his elder brother, who had died in half an hour. His father had died in his village from cholera, which was a different kind of disease. He began to think of his father, and those last moments when nothing could help him.

In hospital, they put Chhotomama on oxygen in the Intensive Care Unit. The relatives arrived in rickshaws, trams, taxis; some walked, some came by bus; some came alone, some in families, some with their friends. Some came with their hair still gleaming after a bath; some came unshaven with stubble on their cheeks; some came in newly pressed clothes; a few came in clothes they had slept in. Some had asked for the day off at the office; some had come without telling anyone. One by one, or family by family, they walked in and sat in the waiting room, ruminating, asking questions, speaking to each other in the dialect of their village. Later, the relatives who lived furthest away from the rest spoke about what they were doing now and what their sons were doing now and which daughter was going to get married to whom. The days were short and in a few hours it became dark, and the lights were turned on in the waiting room, where the relatives still sat talking, sipping now and then

from a flask, eating dry, crumbling sweetmeats from paper containers, shawls around their shoulders, huddled as if it were a picnic in a hill-station.

Shonamama and Sandeep's father had spent most of the time with the doctors and the heart specialist. Now they came down the stairs gravely.

"How is he?" someone asked. "Does he have a chance?"

There was something faintly indecent about the second question. Why should anyone know if he had a chance? Dying is not a horse-race. There should be no speculation about the ending, no wagers won or lost. No one need know anything but basic information provided from moment to moment.

"He's still in danger," said Sandeep's father.

As if on cue, a woman began to cry in a silly, high-pitched voice.

"Stop it!" Shonamama said. A feeling of anxiety passed like a delicate wave over the crowd of relatives. Mamima and Sandeep's mother comforted each other in whispers. Someone turned on a small transistor radio to listen to the news, and a tiny, crackling voice with a clear accent pronounced the names of different towns and different countries, and large, remote events. The mind was soothed by that great fantasy world of politics and government the radio spoke of. The children, everywhere at once, were playing among themselves, running frantically through the gleaming corridors of the hospital, imitating the busy doctors and peering fugitively at the patients, mingling with the crowds of visitors like spies. They walked to the hospital gates and made friends with the watchman with the big moustache, who was in a khaki uniform and held a long stick in his hand. In his cap and shoes, he was a commander, a glamorous emblem from a storybook. The boys roamed through the wide, well-kept lawns on the hospital grounds, and explored the shrubs and trees in the garden. With the instant

recognition of the aesthete, they realised the hospital had the potential for being an inexhaustible playground, one such as they'd never entered before. They noted the ambulances as they came in, and they played hide-and-seek in the parking lot, where cars that belonged to visitors and patients' relatives were parked in rows. Car after car after car, patient after patient, anxious family after anxious family, car after car with the windows rolled up, or the driver dozing inside, or the windshield reflecting the last rays of the sun and the images of enormous clouds passing splendidly and oceanically across it as on a screen, car after car, meditative and pensive and silent in the darkening twilight, and the children wandering between them, Sandeep and Abhi crouched in the shadows, and Babla searching for them, calling out their names hesitantly.

LITTLE by little, the relatives trickled out of the hospital and diminished into their own lives. A solitary young man among them was going to spend the night at the hospital, in case of an emergency. He sat there bravely, his shawl wrapped around him tightly, like a sari around a shy woman. Sandeep's father, his mother, Mamima, Chhordimoni, and Shonamama got into the car, the children sitting restlessly on their laps; tonight, they were all going to spend the night in the old house together.

The return was difficult and sombre, as was the adjustment to the ways of life that had become suddenly unreal. Slowly and without interest, they ate their dinner. They drank many glasses of water, however; their thirst seemed unquenchable. Later, they went upstairs, where they would lie on the beds and talk, and in the process, fall asleep, giving up their consciousness in the middle of a word.

But before they slept, Saraswati hung large, rippling mosquito-nets around the beds, because winter was a time of

mosquitoes. The room, with its ancient, brown furniture, the clothes hanging from the clothes-horse, the timeless wall-lizard, the clock and the radio on the cupboard, the photographs and portraits of grandfathers and grandmothers, surrounded them, giving them a sense of objects and things that lived always in the present; it was a relief for them that there were so many things in the room that did not possess a past or a future. The room itself was timeless, without beginning or end. The furniture and the wall-lizard symbolised another world, another order of calm, inviolable existence. Outside, rickshawallas sang tunelessly and clapped their hands in the cold, with a small wood fire before them. Their tuneless song and their clapping hands were also a part of this other existence, this bottomless being. In the city, the winter smoke hung its giant cobwebs between the houses, or stood between each house and the darkness like a lovely, protective mosquito-net. It kept the houses warm and healed the fractures in their walls and kept out the bad dreams of the night and the memories of the day. It too was a part of that other blind existence that happened around the small, painful lives of human beings.

Abhi, Babla, Sandeep, and Chhordimoni were going to sleep in the large bed. Because the nights were cold and the dawns chilly, a great soft-textured quilt, which yielded to the fingers like bread, had been provided for them. It had fresco-like patterns on it which seemed to retain a glow even in the dark. They dipped their bodies into its generous warmth, and pulled down the mosquito-net from the four poles that had been screwed on like a ship's rigging to the four corners of the bed. The quilt was like a spacious cave in which their legs roamed and scurried with the exuberance of little bears. Cold outside, and so warm inside—body rubbing against body, like triplets inside the safe obscurity of a womb. Someone turned off the lights, and the mosquito-net shimmered around them

like white sails. It had been an eventful day, but already the children had forgotten its sadness, except in a remote, abstract way. They surrendered themselves to the sensation of the present, to this ship with white sails raising its anchor and drifting towards another harbour.

Chapter Thirteen

CHHOTOMAMA did not die. The children had never expected him to, so the fact did not come as any surprise to them. Abhi and Babla knew that their father was ill, but deep down they were convinced he was immortal. So, when their faces became serious, it was less because they were worried on account of their father and more because they enjoyed imitating the serious expressions on the grown-ups' faces. It was a strange and new experience for them, this seriousness.

Of course, it was inconceivable to many of the grown-ups as well that Chhotomama should die. The doctors, at one point, had believed that he was in serious danger. But death was quite inconceivable to the relatives in the waiting room. Death was like a miracle; like the camel passing through the needle's eye. How could a flesh-and-blood human being, who had accumulated such layers of significance in the consciousness of people who knew him, suddenly disappear into nothingness through a point one could not even see? It was a miracle impossible to believe in. It is easier for the imagination to conceive of presences that do not exist—God, angels, demons—than conceive how someone who does exist can cease to be.

A trickle of relatives came in during the day and congregated as usual in the waiting room; after sunset, nearly all of them were there, keeping vigil, making themselves useful in some obscure way, or useless in a way that was oddly touching. During visiting hours, people were allowed to go into the Intensive Care Unit, but not more than one at a time, each with a small ticket in his hand. When Sandeep went in through a door at the end of two flights of stairs and a long corridor, he saw Chhotomama lying on a high bed, a sheet and a blanket covering his body. There was a faint, welcoming smile on his face; around him, there were other presences—one could call them nothing else—lying in postures of fatigue or serene relaxation on their beds. The room was cool, and dark and ordered like the inside of an office: it was as if a bizarre board meeting were being held, with directors gathered silently on beds instead of chairs. Sandeep did not know what to talk to Chhotomama about; he felt too nervous to look directly at him; he was afraid he might see a halo around his head or horns coming out from behind his ears. In fact, it was Chhotomama who had to speak to Sandeep in whispers and put him at his ease, as is so often the case; the sick man having to cheer up his visitor, instead of the other way round. He asked:

"What have you been doing, Mona?"

"Nothing."

"Have you seen any films lately?"

"No."

"Have you read any books that are interesting?"

"No." Then, thoughtfully and shyly, he added, "There's going to be a Book Fair next week in the maidan. We're going to go there."

Chhotomama smiled and looked at him from his pillow. It was so beautiful, getting to know his nephews, his sons, his brother, his sister, and his wife once again, probing them

gently with trivial questions, renewing his acquaintance with
them, rediscovering their quirks and oddities which he had
known for a lifetime, now, back from death, feeling a delicate
surge of pleasure as he recognised these little tics and jerks of
movement and speech which constituted a life.

"And what books will you buy?"

"I don't know . . . Mysteries, ghost stories . . . The ones
with the best pictures."

Chhotomama recalled the annual Book Fair which was held
around this time of the year in the maidan near St Paul's
Cathedral. He remembered the stalls, makeshift temples of
books, and the people queueing outside with a religious con-
centration and devotion. He remembered drifts of people
inspecting and sifting through books, opening and shutting
hardbound editions, cloth-covered editions, paperback edi-
tions. How often he had met old college friends and their chil-
dren wandering through the crowds. And once the fair was
over, that miniature cardboard city would be taken apart, the
books would vanish, the crowds disappear, and the maidan
would be empty, as if one elaborate mirage had dissolved once
you came too near it.

"When is your school opening, Mona?"

"School starts in two weeks," said Sandeep with an affected
weariness. "But Ma has told me we're going to be here for
another month till you get well, so I'll be missing school for
two weeks, but Baba will write to the teachers for permission,
so it's going to be all right." He said all this in a great rush, and
was pleased and relieved when he had finished.

"Oh I see," said Chhotomama. "Well you can start doing
your homework here, when you have nothing else to do."
Sandeep decided it was time to tactfully change the subject.
Lifting the small paper box he had been clutching with both
hands so far, he said:

"Ma gave you this. There's a sandesh from *Satyanarayan*'s inside, and the doctor said you could have it."

Chhotomama took the box from his hands.

"Oh sandesh . . . Very nice, very nice." He opened the box. In the centre was a single white crumbly sweetmeat, made from cottage cheese and dried milk, shaped like tiny fish with infinitesimal milky-white scales upon it. It had a little milky eye and an open mouth. When Sandeep had gone, Chhotomama ate it in the cool, dark room, and the sweet, crumbling fish disappeared magically from his fingers. Later, he disinterestedly regarded his companions, gathered in this station between one world and another, some with tubes sending a thin stream of oxygen into their nostrils. He looked down again at the paper box, and gazed at the word "sandesh" printed on its side in neat, stylish Bengali letters.

<p style="text-align:center">সন্দেশ</p>

The letters, curving, undulating, never still, curving into a kinetic life of their own, reminded him of Calcutta, of buying and selling, of people on the pavements, of office-goers in the mornings, and homecomings in the evenings, of children reading books, of arguments and dissensions in the tea-shops, of an unexpected richness in myriad rooms, all festivities of colour and light. He wanted to return to the city where all things curved and arched and danced like those letters; it exhausted him to lie in this room with these other still figures He longed to come back to life.

A FEW days later, Chhotomama was moved from the Intensive Care Unit with its sad phantoms into a medium-sized, sunlit room of his own. The doctors were satisfied, the nurses

were happy, the relatives were cautious and grateful. Mamima and Sandeep's mother were now permitted to bring him a home-cooked meal of freshwater rohu fish cooked in a table-spoon of oil, with no salt or spices, but with a hint of turmeric and a mild seasoning of black jeera seeds for flavouring and colour. The women seemed to have gained a new buoyancy and purpose in the house; they wandered about in the kitchen with the absorption and abstraction that poets and writers dis-play when they are trying to pin down a sensation into an exact formula of words without reducing its immediacy. When the faint aroma of the fish preparation drifted through the air, they breathed deeply, in a satisfied way, as if the moment of subtle inspiration had passed, leaving them fulfilled. It was pleasing to see them being themselves; in the past two weeks, they had talked only of expenses and mistakes and hopes, and, most of all, the past and the future; it was pleasing to see them once more apotheosise and transform the present. In the past two weeks, they had not been able to sleep at nights, but had lain awake, fidgeting and stirring, moving from side to side with a short clink and clash of bangles. Night had left them alone with their thoughts behind the mosquito-nets, details about a mar-riage, funny, unbearable anecdotes about a brother and a sister. But when dawn came, and the first sounds of the city, immemo-rial sounds, rose in the sky, and the sun shone on the beads of frost, and the newspaper-boy and the men at the underground resumed their work, and Saraswati could be heard tinkering remotely in the kitchen, and the crow cawed at the window, then they felt safe and calm, they slept happily in the first busy and noisy hours of daylight. The noise of the city drowned out the noise in their heads and lulled them to sleep. It had been like that for the past two weeks.

Chhotomama liked his new room in the hospital. He grew increasingly cheerful. He had magazines to read, and even a lit-

tle transistor radio on which he listened to the news and the sports commentary. In the evening, a stream of visitors came in, and Chhotomama reached new, unspeakable heights of happiness by just looking at the variousness and munificence of the clothes that people wore. After a day of white skirts, white caps, white overcoats, he found himself noticing the details of a sari or the subtle gradations of colour on a shawl, or the differences in dress between one generation and another that he had never taken the trouble to notice before. When his wife came to him, it was her Murshidabad silk sari with the wide red border that caught his eye first, prompting some faculty in his subconscious to throw up a welter of confused images from his childhood, of girls in saris returning home from school in the afternoon, and his mother bending down to water a tulsi plant in the verandah. He seemed to have become a child again, seeing things in startling and disturbing images. If a child could remember and record its first impressions after being born, the initial sense of colours and smells and faces as person after person leaned towards its cot and peered at it, scrutinised it, if it could retell its story of its first day in the world, would it be something like this?

But there were times, in the afternoon, when Chhotomama would wake from a nap and find himself facing a bright, hard wall. At first, it surprised him with its sheer presence. Slowly, he came to realise that it was his future he was looking at. There it was, bright and tangible, with the sunlight falling on it peculiarly. Year after year seemed to have passed since he left his house that winter morning, and he had ended here, facing this wall. He would have to start all over again, he told himself. With his eyebrows screwed gently, he tried to solve the problem the way he had tried to solve his first problem in arithmetic at school. All over again, he told himself, from the beginning . . . Especially for the children. He had married late, he

had begun life late. He had responsibilities to his wife, years younger than him, he had responsibilities towards his children. They were, after all, still children.

But, suddenly, the visitors started coming in, and he had no time to think, he was forced to forget. Being ill was a kind of entertainment, a communal ceremony; it involved such a lot of people. He had never seen so many people gathered in one room—three generations, at times—since his wedding or the time when he had passed his BA (Hons.) with a first class. Was he being married again, then? Had he got another degree? Was he dreaming? It was as if they were congratulating him rather than commiserating him. There was so much laughter. Yet there was grief also. There was comedy. Yet there was seriousness. It was strange how these people managed to hold both in fine balance at the same time.

Chapter Fourteen

EVERY evening, in the garden, recuperating patients were taken around in wheelchairs by their nurses, or allowed to take gentle walks, with the firm and cautious hand of a nurse on the shoulder. The patients wore loose white shirts and white pyjamas, and each walked slowly and consideringly past the trees, taking one step at a time, like a giant treading carefully between one continent and another, anxious not to trample on an invisible city or a civilisation. The children watched them in awe, and with another emotion they had not yet identified, which was pity. Each looked like an Adam who had been expelled from his sacred garden, and now, grown old, had been permitted to reenter, to relearn his old ways and his own, most simple, movements.

At night, after they had said goodbye to Chhotomama, they returned homeward through the lit lanes and alleys of Calcutta. Watching the lanes, they temporarily forgot their own lives, and, temporarily, their minds flowed outward into the images of the city, and became indistinguishable from them. Even at night, the streets were theatres full of actors and extras: reckless dogs, insufferable cows lying in the centre of

the lane, families arguing, old women gossiping, children chasing cats, rickshawallas idling, Vaishnav devotees singing religious songs for all to hear. As they watched from the car, they were charmed by the illusion, some nagging uncertainty in their minds was soothed into extinction, they briefly merged with this vague, vast enterprise in which everyone seemed to be taking part.

In some lanes, as they passed, they saw marriages. They saw cars and rickshaws with people getting out of them, people carrying gifts, approaching gates covered with intricate garlands and festoons, and the sound of the shehnai, rich, leisurely, half mournful and half serene, with the special sadness of the human voice, filling the lane with the notes of the Raag Shankara or the Raag Bhairavi. Listening, Sandeep, Abhi, and Babla fell asleep, Sandeep's head against Babla's, Babla's head against Abhi's, as if they were dreaming the same dream.

TOWARDS the end of January, the people of Calcutta celebrated the festival of the goddess Saraswati. In every house and lane, offerings were made punctiliously to the austerely beautiful goddess of the arts and of learning. Students would scribble "Nama Saraswati Nama" a hundred and eight times on a piece of paper so that they might pass their exams. Painters would say a silent prayer for their paintings, and musicians for their music. Writers would ask the goddess to bless the new book they had written: bless this book . . . bless these words. Saraswati, riding a swan, playing the veena with long, attentive fingers, would listen to everyone and promise nothing.

Mamima, too, had brought a small, earthen idol of the goddess. She was going to pray for Chhotomama's health, though this was perhaps somewhat outside the goddess's domain. Yet

surely ... The deity looked so kind and calm and generous. Her mere presence was comforting. There she sat at the end of the room, like a shy bride too diffident to converse with the rest of the family. Surely she would understand Mamima's prayer, this goddess of art and learning.

They decorated the floor before the idol with circular and geometrical motifs, using rice paste to draw the little and large designs. The women wore new, starched saris, which swelled unmanageably around them like plumage; the starch made the cotton cloth crispy, gave it the texture of a potato wafer. As they bent to make the patterns on the floor, the white paste oozing from their fingers, now stooping, now rising, the ends of their saris skimming gently behind them like wings, they reminded one of grave birds dancing in a clearing. Gazing at the white loops and spaces that multiplied in constellations on the floor, Sandeep, the ever curious, asked:

"What's this called?"

"Alpana," his aunt replied, her voice muffled and far away in the concentration of the moment. Sandeep remembered a girl he had once known, a girl who could never keep still, called Alpana. Now he knew what the name meant. He did not know what to do with his unexpected knowledge. But he felt a slight, almost negligible, twinge of pleasure, as a meaning took birth in his mind, and died the next instant.

And Abhi, clutching Saraswati's wrinkled hand, always joking at her expense, pointed at the idol and chided:

"Is that you, Saraswati? Is that you?"

"Listen to what he says!" said the old woman, shocked.

Blasphemy and tenderness mingled in the air. Mamima blew the conch, and there was a smell of sandalwood incense. The offering, made of khoi, milk, bananas, and sago seeds, was distributed in small, polished bowls and given to everyone in

the house: Shonamama, Chhordimoni, Sandeep and his parents, Abhi and Babla, the sweeper who had dropped in while passing, Saraswati the goddess and Saraswati the maidservant, and Mamima herself. In a bowl kept separate from the rest, she saved a little to take to Chhotomama in the hospital, who did not believe in the gods and goddesses, but loved the rituals and the taste of the offerings.

IT WAS the first week of February when Chhotomama was told he could leave the hospital. The doctor held a small but serious conference in Chhotomama's room, and addressed him in a priestly voice for all to hear: "Although you are returning home, you must, from the day you return, attempt to change your lifestyle." Leaning forward in the manner of an elder brother, he confided, though everyone was listening: "You are too easily excited, too enthusiastic about trivial things. You must try to be more restful, more calm. You will have to lead a more thoughtful—a more disciplined—life from now on. Certain things are out of bounds for you." He smiled. "But you will get used to it." He stopped smiling. "You will have to get used to it . . . Bed-rest for the first week at home. Spend your time reading, listening to music. By all means, listen to the sports commentary on the radio, but try not to get too excited about the result." He paused, and smirked cunningly. "Which team do you support, East Bengal, or Mohun Bagan?" "Mohun Bagan," said Chhotomama guiltily. "Well, from today, you must support *both* teams." He looked around for approval for this brilliant suggestion. The others smiled vaguely and obsequiously. He continued, "No rich food. No salt in your diet. No walking up and down the stairs. When you resume your normal life finally, you must, for the first two weeks, climb or descend the stairs one step at a time, taking a ten-second break between

each step." He smiled and slowly repeated, "One—step—at—a—time—"

In the hospital garden, the sajana tree had broken into white blossoms. In a month, the gulmohur trees would explode into fierce orange flowers, in an undifferentiated, trembling orange mass, with the effect of a volcano erupting and balancing, momentarily, the unspilled lava in its mouth. Small, green, unripe mangoes hung from the mango trees, and bees floated in the air, as if controlled by invisible threads. Between the green lanes of new, nervous leaves, the inmates of the hospital walked as usual in their loose white shirts and pyjamas. Sandeep looked at them from the bushes. He remembered what Shonamama had once told him about ghosts, how they roamed through the world, touching and observing and smelling it, themselves unsmelt, untouched, unobserved, taking pleasure in the tangible and then melting into their own afterlife.

And somewhere in the trees, the kokil had begun to sing in its clear and piercing voice, till another kokil answered its mating cry, so that a system of musical echoes, of bird calls mirroring each other, was set up in the garden as the patients walked and the children paused to listen.

> *Ku-wu*
> *Ku-wu*
> *Ku-wu*

There was something questioning and wondering about the cry, but at times it resembled an exclamation, so that it either sounded like "Ku-wu?" or "Ku-wu!"—as if a child who had not yet learnt to speak were showing an adult something, and, in this communication without language, were asking, with the merest inflection of its voice, "Have you seen it?" and then affirming, again with its voice, "I have seen it!"

But the kokil itself was invisible, apparently bodiless, for though Sandeep and his cousins chased the insistent cry from tree to tree, they found it was impossible to catch a glimpse of the bird. It did not seem to exist at all, except the cry, which rose questioningly and affirmatively again and again from the leaves. They went upstairs to tell Chhotomama about it.

"Baba!" said Abhi to his father, who was lying in bed, talking to Sandeep's mother. "We heard the kokil today. It's got a funny voice and it keeps singing all the time."

"Have you seen it?" asked Chhotomama.

"No, Baba. We tried to, but we couldn't."

"Go back and look for it," said his father. "And when you've seen it, come and tell me what it looks like."

It sounded like a directive in a myth or a fable, the old king ordering his son to bring him the fruit of wisdom, or Hercules being set his most difficult and hopeless task. The three boys went downstairs and searched in the garden. In an hour, they had completely forgotten about their mission, until Abhi saw the kokil accidentally while playing hide-and-seek—he had gone to the furthest end of the garden to find a place to conceal himself, when, looking up aimlessly at a tree, he had noticed it sitting on one of the higher branches, tearing a gulmohur flower with its beak. The tree was bare compared to the others, so that the bird could be observed quite easily: it had a slim, ink-black body, and a long, attenuated tail; it gave an overall impression of shapeliness and stateliness. Abhi beckoned urgently to the others:

"This must be it," he whispered, pointing up.

"What?" asked Sandeep.

"Look . . . ," said Abhi.

Sandeep looked up. Then he understood.

"It's as black as a crow," he said in awe. "But much nicer looking."

"It's eating the orange flower," whispered Abhi.

But it must have sensed their presence, because it interrupted its strange meal and flew off—not flew off, really, but melted, disappeared, from the material world. As they watched, a delicate shyness seemed to envelop it, and draw a veil over their eyes.

Afternoon Raag

A young man arrives in Oxford and finds himself involved in relationships with two women, neither of which is destined for fulfillment. Interspersed between glimpses of students' lives and friendships are fragmentary memories of the narrator's parents, the death of his music teacher, and the world of North Indian classical music itself.

Acknowledgements

I am grateful to the Authors' Foundation and the Kathleen Blundell Trust, administered by the Society of Authors, for grants that enabled me to complete this book, and to the editors of *New Writing 2*, where Chapter Four was first published.

Afternoon Raag

In memory of Pandit Govind Prasad Jaipurwale
(1941-1988)

The doorbell rings. The music teacher comes in.
He is smiling as usual. His body is smiling. He is
 humming a complicated tune—
outside, wind, light, and rain revolve the landscape in a
 shifting treadmill of shadow.
Inside, in the cool room, my mother and the music
 teacher sit on the carpet, as usual,
enclosed, in the drawing-room, by sofas and tables and
 paintings and curios.

My mother plays the harmonium; she begins to sing.
Her fingers on the black and white keys make, of her
 hand, a temple with many doors.
When the music teacher joins in intermittently, he
 shows what a strange thing the human voice is,
this tiny instrument in the throat, with its hidden
 universe of notes, its delicate, inscrutable laws.
A raag, spacious as the mansion the rain builds,
 enfolds—and sighs, like one of the elements.

Inside the great architecture of the raag, through the
 clear archway of notes, world without humans,
two figures sit, each alone
—my mother and the music teacher—enclosed by sofas
 and paintings and curios.

The music teacher is listless today.
He does not respond.
My mother is just a little irritated as she sings, but she
 is afraid, too, of something she does not understand.
The music teacher has merged with the sofa behind
 him, momentarily indistinguishable from the soft,
 indifferent contours of the furniture,
with the disturbing patience and resignation of
 furniture.
His wife, his widowed mother, his brother, his
 brother-in-law, his sister, his four children,
the jewelled constellation that appeared at his birth,
are moving away from him. He is alone, sitting on the
 carpet, leaning his back against the sofa.
Behind this moment of serenity in this small, calm
 room,
with its clear, cool space flowing in and out of a
 listlessness,
is something liquid and grieving, something that
 cannot tolerate its own shimmering presence,
but melts away from itself all the time, like the giant
 walls of rain, or tears, or something else.

The music teacher is dying.
He does not know it, but he will be dead in less than a
 year's time.
He will not see the rain again.

He does not know it. His ignorance of death surrounds
 him like a halo, an intimacy with God.
My mother does not know it.
The rain does not know it.
The world is being washed clean by the rain.
 Something in us, human but one with the season,
is also being washed clean, tear after tear, cloudburst
 in silence.

Nothing remains but the human voice, this tiny
 instrument inside the throat
endeavouring to carry a world inside it. Then, that too
 becomes silent.
The raag, self-created galaxy of notes, sigh of the
 elements, sighs like the rain, passes into nature.
We do not see him. My mother goes on singing, as if
 unaware. He moves further away, not drawing
 attention to himself.
We do not see him now, except as a shadow against
 the sofa,
merged with the furniture, the endless meditation of
 furniture,
his lungs filled with water, his face and feet swollen
 and his mouth smiling,
become one with the reverie of furniture.
My mother sits there, singing, the rain falls, melting
 from its own presence,
the moment perfected not by art but by mortality, the
 mortal moment, repeating and repeating its own life.

Chapter One

EACH year, in Oxford, new students come and old ones disappear; after a while, one knows the streets and by-lanes, all of which lead to each other, by heart; in the north, no one goes beyond Summertown, and the road leading to London goes out via Headington. On the first day of Michaelmas, men and women in black gowns walk to matriculation ceremonies, and at the end of the year they wear these gowns again, unhappily, to take exams; then, after the exams, the town is nearly empty, and the days, because of that peculiar English enchantment called Summer Time, last one hour longer; and Oxford, in the evening, resembles what an English town must have looked like in wartime, the small shops open but unfrequented, an endangered, dolorous, but perfectly vivid peace in the lanes, as the eye is both surprised by, and takes pleasure in, a couple linked arm in arm, or a young man conversing with a woman on a polished doorstep, and then the early goodbyes. It is like what I imagine a wartime township to have been, because all the young people, with their whistling, their pavement to pavement chatter, their beer-breathed, elbow-nudging polemics, are suddenly gone, leaving the persistent habits of an old way of life,

the opening and shutting of shops, intact, a quiet, empty bastion of civilisation and citizenry. It is because of its smallness, repetition, and the evanescence of its populace, that Oxford is dream-like.

From the window of my room I could see a library and a faculty building, and a path, curving slightly, that led to a college. Students, dressed in the oddest of clothes, in secretive overcoats, in long and black primitive skirts, men with earrings, women wearing gypsy ornaments, would gather each morning for lectures, or pass in and out of doors recklessly with books clutched to their bosoms, or sit on the steps in abandonment, as if they had forgotten their appointments. The path, which was flanked by hedges that turn bright red in the autumn, I could see far into; at one point, it ran over a canal, so that I sensed water there. This intuition of water came to me again when I was visiting Worcester College; it was an unhappy day, because I was still vacillating between Mandira and Shehnaz, falling asleep by one woman at night and spending the day with the other, but I had, for a forced, lucid period of time, come here to attend a seminar on Lawrence. On entering the first quad, I saw that the light—it was evening—behind the wall at the end of the garden was different; as if the sun had set there, so that I imagined a seashore and a horizon. Later, I learnt that there was a lake there.

Dr Mason's room was simple, with two sofas, adjacent to each other, and a study-table, next to which there was a chair on which he sat. It was a well-lit and warm room, but its colours were cool—furniture browns and wallpaper purples and magnolias and greys, the colours that create, in afternoon light or evening shadow, the abidingness of an English interior. Three undergraduates, myself, and two other graduate students sat on the sofa, while another undergraduate, bearded and with spectacles, placed himself on the window-sill and never said a

word, but listened to the others' words, seeming to weigh them, and it was his silence that I deciphered for agreement or disapproval. Dr Mason was a polite, even kind, man, a very big man, not very old, facing us in his armchair. Some students had open copies of *The White Peacock* in their hands, and as we talked of Lawrence, extolled him, applauded him, and, most invigorating of all, corrected him, it seemed both strange and natural to hear our own voices. The mind focused itself upon the sphere of the room and the table lamp, and then dilated vaguely and darkly into a consciousness of Lawrence-country, and then focused upon the room again, and this dilation and constriction went on for a long time, like breathing. An hour later, we got up to leave. There was laughter, and a relaxed certainty with which we let each other go, almost released each other, into the night. How unique student life is, with its different rooms, its temporary enclosures and crystallisations, its awareness and memory of furniture and windows and spaces.

Chapter Two

EARLY in the morning, light would frame the curtains of my
window, although at times there was only a dull whiteness.
When I parted the curtains, I would look out into the curving
road to the next college, the closed doors of the library, and the
pavements. The wind would make a piece of paper move, and,
touching the window, I would sense the cold outside. As I am
used to the sound of crows in the morning, this absence of
noise would fill me with a melancholy which was difficult to get
rid of because it seemed to have no immediate cause. It was
only when I saw students, with their odd, comical gait, and
their touchingly disguised sleepiness, walking down that road,
growing, little by little, in number as the morning wore on, that
I would feel an at-homeness and pleasure in their rhythm.
It was around this time that Shehnaz too would set out from
her college and come down the same road, indistinguishable
from the other students, but with her own thoughtful gait, a
backward-lookingness, happy in a simple way in having this
opportunity to walk to her library in Broad Street, and devote
a fresh day to copying out notes, stopping at my room for half
an hour on her way there.

She was, essentially, a lonely person searching for the right company, a wise little girl in a woman's body, dressed in black trousers, a blue top and a coat, and black sneakers. Her hair was long and striking and untidy; solemnly, she carried a file full of papers under her arm, and a clumsy, oversized bag whose significance was that there was a tiny packet of Marlboro Lights in it. She had been married once, very briefly, and then divorced; later, she had an involvement in Oxford which came to nothing. It was towards the end of this involvement that I first met her, through a friend, and then we would exchange nods when we passed each other by on the bicycle-lined pavement of a street which led to a pub and a junction. Students, drolly crossing the street, or lavishly arguing, filled out the spaces in the street and the time between one meeting and the other upon this repeated route, so that the street, with its daily, inconsequential academic excitement and drama, has become indissoluble from the inner life of our early meetings, and Oxford, its climate and architecture, seems not so much a setting as a part of the heart of our friendship.

By the time she would get up to leave, the rest of the building would have woken up and be moving about. Noises were transmitted through walls and doors: a radio; a knowing, crowded murmur in the kitchen; footsteps in the corridor; the main door shutting; the firm but almost nonphysical sound of footsteps on the gravel; there were many lives in the building made transiently one by sound. I had a feeling of being surrounded, as on a ship or a train, by personal routines and habits that would not be known again, that had their natural place in some larger, more fixed habitat, and the morning noise had about it, therefore, the concentratedness, the temporariness, and the pathos of the noise of shared travel. It was at this time, after the sun had risen, and lives, without apparent reason, once more began excitedly, when there was shouting

upstairs, windows opening, last-minute preparations, and a joy akin to that felt by passengers approaching a port, that Shehnaz would get up to leave, listening, with one ear, to the voices of other students, smiling at what they were saying. Everything they said she found worth listening to, especially if she had had a happy morning with me; she had an uncanny sensitivity to the presence of people in small spaces, in corridors, in doorways, as others have to landscapes, or to places. Being there in that corridor at that moment, as students sheepishly came out of rooms and vanished into the kitchen or the toilet, was a real experience for her.

SHARMA lived in another room in the same building. Sometimes, in the morning, he would come down in his shorts to have coffee with me. Banging on the door in a forthright manner, he would enter, and if I happened to be midway through practising a raag, he would sit quietly on a chair and nod and shake his head in vigorous appreciation as I sang. The irrepressible bodily meaning of the words "to be moved," which we have come to associate with mental and aesthetic response, was apparent when one looked at him listening to music. Sometimes he would keep rhythm to the song, arbitrary temporal divisions that he slapped and pounded on the table, and when I had finished he would still be doing this, as if he could no longer stop. Later, he would walk around the room possessively, tapping the keys of my typewriter and reading aloud all the titles of the books on my shelf in order to make himself more conversant with the English language.

Once or twice, it happened that I had gone outside, leaving my door open, and then returned and closed it, thinking I was alone. But Sharma, in the meanwhile, had come and hidden himself in the clothes closet, from which, at a given moment,

he emerged explosively. Towards the beginning of our friend-
ship, he had told me very seriously that I was to help him
improve his English. He was writing a thesis on Indian phi-
losophy, but he longed to be a stylist. I would, thus, recom-
mend to him a book whose language had given me pleasure,
and he would read aloud passages from Mandelstam or Updike
or Lawrence to me, either in the morning or at midnight, times
at which I was sleepy, he reading sonorous lines in a loud and
unstoppable voice, interrupting himself only to demand com-
ments from me that were both fair and encouraging. His
English had a strong, pure North Indian accent, so that he pro-
nounced "joy" a little bit like the French *"joie,"* and "toilet"
like "twilit." Yet this accent, I soon learnt, was never to be
silenced completely; it was himself, and however he trained
himself to imitate the sounds of English speech, "toilet," when
he pronounced it, would always have the faint but unmistak-
able and intimate and fortunate hint of "twilit." His sentence
constructions were curious, with missing articles and mixed-
up pronouns, but he compensated for these with an excess
of "thank yous" and "sorrys," two expressions gratuitous in
Indian languages and, therefore, no doubt, of great and tri-
umphant cultural importance to him. His reading practice in
the mornings, executed with the single-mindedness of a child
practising scales by thumping the keys, remains for me one of
the most relaxing memories of Oxford; me lying on the bed
and patiently listening, a time of rootedness and plenitude,
even of equable solitude, for with Sharma one is always alone,
listening to him. Mandelstam, read by Sharma, took on a dif-
ferent, unsuspected life, odd, cubist, harmlessly egotistical, and
atmospheric.

Chapter Three

MANDIRA lived in a room in college. She had come to Oxford two years after me, and I first saw her in hall. She spoke English, I noticed, with a slight American accent, talked actively at the table, walked in what is called "a brisk manner," and was surrounded by English friends. She was small and roundish, and a favourite with the porters and stewards, who would wink at her, or put an arm around her, and call her "love" or "dear," as the English do, and not take her very seriously. I did not like her, but, when I was bored, I would go to her room and drink a cup of tea. I gradually got over my tentativeness, and came to realise that a knock on her door would not be unwelcome, for she was always very hospitable in her disorganised way. The first five minutes would be spent in me settling down, after a preamble during which I decided where I should sit, on the armchair in a way that was both tortured and patient, and then open a bantering conversation with her in medias res; all this I took to be courtesy, but it made her uncomfortable, for I remember her as a compound of movement and aimless speed, putting the kettle on the boil, and then running down a flight of stairs to the kitchen for her carton of

milk. Shyness made her quick, while I, by contrast, was slow. When she was gone for that minute, I would be alone in her room, with the photographs on the wall, the secret things and cups and clothes in her cupboard, the badly made bed, the wash-basin and mirror, the textbooks on the table and the floor, absorbing the materiality of the room and also its cheerful, fleeting makeshiftness, and not knowing what to think. She was not a very tidy person, but her attempt at order and creating the semblance of a household, even the clumsy tear at the spout of the milk carton, touched me. These undergraduate rooms were larger and more comfortable to look at than the box-like, modern rooms in my building. A light hung from the ceiling, enclosed by a comical, globe-like shade, and at evening it gave a light that was both encompassing and personal. The window opened onto a path to the garden and the hall, and all day, laughter and footsteps could be heard, coming and going, and these sounds too became a part of the room's presence.

In the morning, I looked forward to the small journey I made across the road, glancing right and left with avid interest for oncoming cars, to see if I had any mail. The pigeon-holes, after the poverty of Sunday, its forced spiritual calm, seemed to overflow humanely with letters on Monday, and even if I had not got any, that small walk did not lose its freshness and buoyancy, and a tiny and acute feeling of hope did not desert me in all my mornings. From about half-past nine to ten, there was a hubbub as students stooped or stood on tip-toe to peep into pigeon-holes, and sorted and sifted letters, and the mail-room had an air of optimism, of being in touch with the universe, found nowhere else in Oxford. When there *were* letters for me—the cheap, blue Indian aerogrammes from my mother—they lay there innocently like gifts from a Santa Claus, they did not seem material at all, but magical, like signs. Then I would miss the special feeling of mornings at home, I would think

benignly of my mother's good health, and how she suffers from nothing but constipation, how for three days she will go without having been to the toilet, with an abstracted look on her face, as if she were hatching an egg. Secretively, she will concoct a mixture of Isab-gol and water, and stir it ferociously before drinking it. Then, one day, like a revelation, it will come, and she will have vanished from human company. My father, a great generaliser, collector of proverbs, shows no concern over her health, displays no bitterness.

The furniture in Mandira's room—the bed, the study-table, its chair, the cupboard, the bookshelves—was old, enduring. The armchair was solid and stoic, and seemed to cradle the space that existed between its thick arms; one felt protected when one sat in it. As I got to know Mandira better, as we became intimate and then grew increasingly unhappy, the room became her refuge, her dwelling, and when she said, "I want to go back to my room," the words "my room" suggested the small but familiar vacuums that kept close around her, that attended to her and guided her in this faraway country. Because, for a foreigner and a student, the room one wakes and sleeps in becomes one's first friend, the only thing with which one establishes a relationship that is natural and unthinking, its air and light what one shares with one's thoughts, its deep, unambiguous space, whether in daytime, or in darkness when the light has been switched off, what gives one back to oneself. The bed and chairs in it had an inscape, a life, which made them particular, and not a general array of objects. That is why, when she spoke of her room, I think what she meant was the sense of not being deserted, of something, if not someone, waiting, of a silent but reliable expectancy.

The room had other rooms next to it and other rooms facing it. Sometimes, I would come up the staircase and enter the corridor to find Mandira leaning out of a half-closed door, talk-

ing to the American girl who lived opposite, who would be standing by her own door. Even when I was inside the room, they would continue their conversation, and I would sit on the chair and watch Mandira's back; from there I could listen to the voice of the invisible girl, and to her rising peals of laughter. For ten minutes they would say goodbye to each other, until there came a rounded silence, and Mandira closed the door. What was missing was the background sound of old people and children, of babies and mothers, of families; instead one heard people running up and down the staircase, or visitors approaching and knocking. There was a toilet near the room whose cistern gurgled candidly each time someone flushed it, and a bath to which men in dressing-gowns went solemnly in the evening, and women with towels around their heads, less solemn and with an air of freedom. From the bath everyone returned radiant and clean, and slightly ashamed. As I passed to or from Mandira's room, I would encounter them but not look at them, for I had learnt that the English do not consider it polite to look at each other, but nevertheless I remember the embarrassment of the men, and the opulent towels like Moorish turbans around the women's hair.

Chapter Four

EARLY mornings, my mother is about, drifting in her pale nightie, making herself a cup of tea in the kitchen. Water begins to boil in the kettle; it starts as a private, secluded sound, pure as rain, and grows to a steady, solipsistic bubbling. Not till she has had one cup of tea, so weak that it has colour accidentally golden, can she begin her day. She is an insomniac. Her nights are wide-eyed and excited with worry. Even at three o'clock in the morning one might hear her eating a Marie biscuit in the kitchen. At such times, she moves gently as a mouse; we know it is she, and feel no danger. In the afternoons, she sleeps as a maidservant rubs cream on the soles of her feet. "My feet are burning," she says. At the base of her ankle is a deep, ugly scar she got when a car ran over her foot when she was six years old. That was in a small town which is now in Bangladesh. Thus, even today, she hesitates superstitiously before crossing the road, and is painfully shy of walking distances. Her fears made her laughable. The scar is printed on her skin like a radiant star.

Her hair is troublesome and curly; when she was young, it was even thicker than it is now. It falls in long, black strands,

but each strand has a gentle, complicated undulation travelling through it, like a mild electric shock or a thrill, that gives it a life of its own; it is visually analogous to a tremolo on a musical note. It is this tremolo that makes her hair curly and unmanageable and has caused her such lifelong displeasure. The easiest way she disposes of it is by gathering it compassionately into a humble, medium-sized bun, rendering it graceful with a final plastic hair-clip, or by thoughtfully metamorphosing it into a single serpent-like plait that looks paradoxically innocent. When the maidservant cleans the room and sweeps the dust to one corner, one may notice there, among other things, a few black strands with delicate, questioning curves that always float away with the merest breeze.

In the bedroom there is a weighing-machine with a flat, featureless face. Solemnly, in the morning, when my father is still asleep, my mother slips off her nightie, which weighs no more than a feather, and, quite naked, embarks upon the machine; for she will leave nothing to chance, let no extraneous factor prejudice its judicious needle. When she is satisfied with what she has seen, appalled or happy, she will alight onto earth again, and slip on her nightie. Then with short steps (for she is no more than five feet and one and a half inches) she will cross all the way from the bedroom to the corridor to the hall to the verandah, making this long and lonely journey in the still hours of first light; there (on the verandah) she stands with the teacup balanced in one hand, pausing now and then in her thoughts (for she is always thinking) to sip her weak tea politely, watching the lane, in which Christian men in shorts are walking their Alsatians, with a genuine curiosity. Sometimes the famous music director Naushad Ali, whose film songs we still hum in our solitary moments, can be seen walking down this lane with a cane in his hand and a companion by his side, his face wizened, almost Chinese, but humorous, gesticulating furiously

with the hand that has waved at a thousand musical instruments, bringing a loud melody to life as he passes the sleepy lane. He is old now, in his eighties, and has suffered a few heart attacks. So he is still alive, my mother thinks as she watches him. Meanwhile my father is sleeping in a most gentlemanly manner, taking care not to spill over into ungainly postures, his repose both stern and considerate as he lies on the bed with the quilt up to his chin.

After my father retired, we moved to this lane in the suburbs. Ours is the only apartment building in the lane; the rest are bungalows or cottages that belong to Christians. This is a Christian area; Portuguese names—Pedro, D'Silva, and Gonsalves—twang in the air liked plucked silvery guitar-strings. The Christian men are dark complexioned and have maternal pot-bellies, because they like drinking. The women wear unfashionable dresses, flowery purple skirts that resemble old English wallpaper, exposing polished, maroon ankles and dark knees which they cover by pulling at the skirt-ends with chaste, dutiful fingers. These women and men eat pork, and sing and dance in cottages lit with cobwebs and dim bulbs, some of which have dates upon their facades (1923), and some of which are named after some beloved great-aunt (Helen Villa), no doubt a comical figure in her time. The Christians enjoy jokes and swear-words, and the women, when they are not sullen, are gently earthquaking with laughter at what John has just said with a straight face. They are in turn friendly, talking to you in queues at banks and post offices, and short, taking offence when you innocently ask them for street directions. Most of them are Roman Catholic; when asked, they pronounce themselves "Katlick," a word that sounds both childishly mischievous and appropriately rude.

When my mother finishes her tea, she walks to the harmonium which is resting in the hall upon a carpet, covered by a

tranquil garment. But if it is not in the hall, she will ask Ponchoo, the cook, who is now awake, to bring it to the hall, and this he will do, holding it by the two metal rings on either side, anxious not to bump it against a door or a wall, transporting its heaviness with a pregnant woman's delicacy that dares not pause for breath, and with deep suspicion he will veer its precious body through the ins and outs of the corridor, and bending humbly, lay it in its place on the carpet. Then my mother will settle on the rug and unclip the bellows, pulling and pushing them with a mild aquatic motion with her left hand, the fingers of the right hand flowering upon the keys, the wedding bangle suspended around her wrist. Each time the bellows are pushed, the round holes on the back open and close like eyes. Without the body music is not possible; it provides the hollow space for resonance as does the curved wooden box of the violin or the round urn of the sitar. At the moment of singing, breath tips in the swelling diaphragm as water does in a pitcher. The voice-box itself is a microscopic harp, its cords tautening and relaxing with each inflection. My mother begins to practise scales in the raag Todi.

Morning passes. When my father used to work in the city, and we lived in a flat in Malabar Hill overlooking the Arabian Sea, my mother would sometimes go to the Bombay Gymkhana in the afternoon and settle upon one of its spacious, boat-like wicker sofas, sinking into its oceanic cushions and dozing off till my father arrived for tea. Coming back from school, which was nearby, I would see her there as a silent composition of loved details; the deliberate, floral creases of her sari, the pale orange-brown glow of her skin, the mild ember-darkening of her lipsticked mouth, the patient, round fruition of her bun of hair, and the irrelevant red dot on her forehead. Seeing her was like roaming alone in a familiar garden. In cool, strategic corners, waiters stood in coloured waistcoats with

numbered badges pinned to them; never did a name seem more apposite than then, in the afternoon, before people started coming in, when these waiters impassionedly *waited*, dark Goan men in neat clothes, inhaling and exhaling and lightly chattering among themselves. The most invigorating fact about the club was its long corridor, an avenue of light reflected off a polished floor and protected by arches. It was frequented mainly by company executives: general managers and directors. Dressed alike in tie and white pinstriped shirt and dark suit, they looked to me like angels. In the club, these managers would sit on chairs and childishly ring little brass bells to summon the waiters. With the waiters they shared a marital relationship of trust and suspicion, and an order wrongly taken could precipitate a storm and a crisis, a sudden display of emotions, shouts, and insults. Food was in abundance, from the American hamburger to chop suey to the local bhelpuri with its subversive smells of the narrow, spice-selling streets of West Bombay. My mother was always much amused by the sight of people eating around her, moving their mouths in a slow, moral way; human beings are the only creatures, she says, who eat habitually without hunger. Long-nosed Parsi lawyers stabbed their food, using knives and forks with jurisprudential elegance. Gujerati businessmen, educated in the school of life, employed fingers, holding the crispy wafer of the bhelpuri and biting it competitively, as if they were afraid it might bite them first.

Though we live now in the suburbs, habit still drives us to the city, from where my parents return at evening. My father falls asleep in the backseat of the Ambassador, this car which is now ours after his retirement, and my mother too dozes upon his shoulder. In a place near the rear window is laid out the day's shopping, curved, inanimate objects my mother loves, such as spatulas and spoons, and little oases of food. The

Ambassador is a spacious, box-like vehicle with a Taurean single-mindedness and a rickshaw's tenacity. It is known as a "family car"; on Sundays, cousins and aunts on outings will sit, perspiring, inside it; I myself associate its hot floorboards, its aching gear-pulley, its recalcitrant pedals, with domesticity and the social events of childhood. Of all cars I know, it has perhaps the most uplifting name, as if its appointed office were to, wide-eyed, bring good news to the world. Meanwhile, our Ambassador joins the long, mournful crocodile of cars from Churchgate to Linking Road, and we know we are near home when we come to the Mahim Creek, where fishermen's boats are parked upon the sand; here, even if your eyes should be closed, or if you should be entering the city from the direction of the airport, you will be woken by the smell of dried or rotting fish, a strong but pure odour blown inland, bitter and sharply intimate as the scent of a woman's sex.

When it is evening in the lane, my parents go down and walk for half an hour. Their lonely parade, their quiet ambitiousness as they walk up and down the compound, sometimes conferring, are witnessed by a watchman in khaki, sitting on a steel chair beneath blue light. This is an exercise they have rediscovered from when my father was a student in London, and my mother his newly married wife, introverted, with a red dot on her forehead and vermilion in the parting of her hair, awkward but warm in her huge green overcoat. Then, too, they would walk together the wet roads from Belsize Park to Swiss Cottage. Afterwards, they go upstairs, and my mother sits on the bed, reading *The Afternoon Despatch and Courier*. She turns first to the last page, where Busybee's "Round and About" is printed. Thus she continues this daily column about Bombay, its Irani restaurants, its post offices, its buses, its cuisine, and this man's fictional wife and his dog. Years ago, my mother and I fell in love with Busybee's voice, its calm, even tone, and a

smile which was always audible in the language. My father, meanwhile, is clipping his nails fastidiously, letting them fall on to an old, spread-out copy of the *Times of India*, till he sneezes explosively, as he customarily does, sending the crescent-shaped nail-clippings flying into the universe.

Chapter Five

THE first few weeks I knew Shehnaz, when we were still getting to be friends, were an uncomplicated time. We made appointments and did not keep them; we made appointments to discuss when we might meet; we liked each other but were occupied, like children, with other things to do. Sometimes I am nostalgic for that make-believe busyness, full of innocence, of having "other things to do," the prelapsarian background of lectures, bookshops, friends, our lives spent generously and routinely like rain-showers, stopping and starting again.

We decided to meet at the St Giles' Café near the Oxfam Bookshop. "Do you know where it is?" she asked me with a smile; these sociable questions she would invest with a mischievousness, so that they became funny and meaningful, and I would always pretend to be embarrassed answering them. I did know the St Giles' Café; it was the only place in Oxford that served a strong and dark coffee, with a scorched South Indian flavour; a white froth, almost a scum, formed on the top even before they had put the milk in it. Unlike the coffee in the Middle and Senior Common Rooms, it was hot, and one could, with a certain satisfaction, admire the steam rising from the cup

before one drank from it. The café was a small, ugly, and crowded place, full of students, and tramps minding their own business, hatted and bearded, with an unworldly look about them, like musicians. On either side of each table, there was a bench, and one had to squeeze past people to sit down, or have people squeeze past you as they got out. Thus, as one made small adjustments in position, one was always feeling grateful or obliged, strangely powerful or powerless; one shrank and hunched, and then graciously expanded again, in regular accordion-like time. Each table also had an introvert who sat in the corner throughout and looked at no one. When people were called to take their food from the counter, they were not addressed by their names, but by their orders—"Ham and eggs!" "Plate of chips!" "Bacon sandwich!"—and, calmly and without confusion, those who had been labelled so uniquely rose and walked towards the counter. Whenever the door opened, a draught entered from outside, but the baked air inside, smelling of frying bacon, cushioned us from the cold and from other influences. The paradoxical confluence of timelessness and movement in the café made it an ideal place for a first meeting between two foreign students.

Yet that meeting, comically, was not to be. It was the beginning of summer, and some girls walked barefoot that day on Cornmarket Street. There was a hustle and bustle, a festive hurry, and even Ryman's, the stationery shop, had inspired-looking customers queueing up to pay for envelopes and sheets of paper and sellotape. Sharma and I were roaming around at our ease in loose shirts, two Indians who might never have met in India, feeling at home, giving studious attention, as if it truly mattered, to shop windows and an ancient organ-grinder, edging our way towards Westgate, both of us feeling boyish, and I especially younger because I was wearing sandals. It began to thunder then, and rain very hard, as it does at home; girls

screamed in English, and people who were waiting for the bus panicked, but soon the crowds deployed themselves into neat and dripping little squadrons, cheerful and brave, and the entrance of the Clarendon Centre and the great department stores were converted into shelters with an unfussy swiftness. I had never seen it rain like this in England before; water collected in the lanes and flowed past us as it does in Calcutta; and the English were excited at first and then reasonable and collected, telling each other jokes and enjoying themselves; it was all a little like but yet very unlike the wise dailiness with which an Indian outwaits a shower. Sharma looked at the sky and felt poetic and told me how he was reminded of his village. Thus I did not meet Shehnaz that afternoon but waited outside a shop that sold shoes and saw wet and laughing people running and disappearing, and committed to memory the rare, leisurely couple who walked by, contented and soaked. Later, Shehnaz told me how she had cycled to the St Giles' Café after it had stopped raining, but had found it empty except for its owners, the stentorian callers of "Ham and cheese" and "Bacon sandwich," who were silent now, and busy mopping up the wet floors.

Chapter Six

SOHANLAL comes in the mornings. He is married to my music teacher's sister. Though he is quite short, he wears bright kurtas that come down below his knees. He demands the tablas from Ponchoo, strutting around the hall like a rooster in his early morning plumage. Then he tunes the smaller tabla with a hammer, and the bigger one on the left he booms with his fingertips. When he plays as my mother sings, his hands, which are now old, produce a pitter-patter noise. After twenty minutes, he takes a break, smoking a beedi on the verandah; and then, before he is finished, throws it away and coughs a dramatic smoker's cough. He likes doing things; returning, he takes out his handkerchief and dusts the harmonium, wiping the smooth, rectangular top. It is a harmonium made in Calcutta by Pakrashi, and he takes care to probe, his forefinger shrouded with the handkerchief, each English letter of PAKRASHI carved largely on the wood, blowing sensuously on the angular K and tracing the curves of the P and the R till he is satisfied. Then he polishes the black and white keys, and opens the cover; inside, the two rows of innumerable reeds lie bone white, each reed a delicate white splinter, with a pinhead on one

end and a flat metal strip on the belly. Sohanlal blows quietly upon them, as if they were on fire; how silent music is as it rests in these reeds, white paper-thin wands! He replaces the cover, because it is almost unpleasant to watch the inner nakedness of a harmonium. Eagerly, he moves about again, his spacious pyjamas billowing around him. As he prepares to sit, they open at the bottom like alligator mouths that have swallowed up his legs. After an hour, he glances at his wristwatch and collects his money politely and hurries out of the front door. Then next morning he is reincarnated in his fantastic kurta and pyjamas as if from a magic lamp.

It was on an afternoon in August I bought my first tanpura. We were visiting Calcutta then, and my music teacher, my guru, had come with us and was living in our house; he was going to sing at a "conference." He would practise in the mornings, and take time off to vanish to the Kali temple, returning with a tilak, a great vermilion stain on his forehead, telling my mother, "Didi, I went to see Ma Kali!" On some mornings we would sing raag Bhairav together, our two voices and styles mingling closely and floating over the other sounds of the house—pigeons, and the distracted noise of servants—his voice sometimes carrying my hesitant voice, and negotiating the pathways of the raag, as a boat carries a bewildered passenger. In the moments of simple imbibing, I would forget my voice was my own and become an echo of his style and artistry. The greater part of the unfolding of a raag consists of a slow, evasive introduction in which the notes are related to each other by curving glissandos, or meends. The straight, angular notes of Western music, composed and then rendered, are like print upon a page; in contrast, the curving meends of the raag are like longhand writing drawn upon the air. Each singer has his own impermanent longhand with its own arching, idiosyncratic beauties, its own repetitive, serpentine letters. With

the end of the recital, this longhand, which, in its unravelling, is a matter of constant erasures and rewritings, is erased completely, unlike the notes of Western music, which remain printed upon the page.

That afternoon, we took the car to Rashbehari Avenue. My guru was dressed as usual in a loose white kurta and pyjamas. It must have been six or seven years before his death, and he must have just turned forty. He was humming a complicated tune with tiny embellishments when he was not talking to me, and the oil he had put in his hair before he combed it smelled sweet. We walked to the shop, no bigger than a room, called Hemen and Co. Outside, the pavement was broken, its edges blue-grey with ash from charcoal stoves; mosquitoes hung in the air. Ascending the three steps, we saw unfinished tanpuras and sitars, long patient necks and the comical but gracefully distended round urns; some instruments hung upside down from the ceiling like bats; and a man was planing a piece of wood. My tanpura was ready with its four new strings; I remember the tentative shyness with which I touched it.

Later, we sat on the floor in my room, and my guru taught me to tune the instrument. The tanpura can be held vertically on the lap or next to the upraised knee as it is played, when it looks male and perpendicular, or laid horizontally on the ground before one, when, with the surrendering slope of its long neck and the stable fullness of its urn, its mixture of acquiescence and poise, it looks feminine. The four strings provide only two notes as a background to the song; *sa*, or *shadja*, the first, the mother-note, from which all other notes come, with which one's relationship is permanent and unambiguous, and the second note, depending on the raag, the father-note, circumstantial but constructive. To tune the tanpura, you must turn the keys on its upper end, keys which are huge, ornate, and antique, like the doorknobs of a palace. On the nether end,

upon the urn, there is a flat bridge on which the strings rest briefly, before they pass through small ivory-coloured beads that are used for the finer adjustments in tuning, and travel at last to a small plank of wood at the end, where, pierced through four open but infinitesimal eyes, they are knotted. While this painful business, this struggle, of tuning continues, four white threads are slipped beneath the strings as they lie on the bridge, and moved up and down till a point is discovered where each string loses its flat metallic note, and buzzes, a hum like that of the wandering drone, or electricity. This buzzing of the strings, this resonance, the musicians call *juwari*. That afternoon, my guru and I, like patient surgeons, tuned the tanpura till the room filled with notes *shadja* and *nikhad*.

When one remembers a scene from the past in which one is with a loved one who is now dead, it is not like a memory at all, but like a dream one is having before his death, a premonition. In this dream which precedes death, the person is tranquil and happy, and yet, without reason, you know he is to die. When we recall the dead, the past becomes a dream we are dreaming foretelling death, though in our waking moments we cannot properly interpret it or give it significance. My memory of the day I bought the tanpura with my guru is like such a dream.

Chapter Seven

BEFORE I met Shehnaz, I led a domestic life with Sharma, a warm kitchen life of teas and conversations. In this country where afternoon comes suddenly, he was a desired and happy interference, sewing my buttons, cooking daal for dinner, advising me on which clothes to wear, forcing me to buy new ones. What brought us together, among other things, was a common love for the English language. Each night, till midnight, he would recount with delight new idioms and words he had picked up during the day, and from these words he would become inseparable for about a week, using them in every context, just as a child who has been given a gift of new shoes spends a euphoric period wearing them everywhere. After lunch, we would sometimes watch black-and-white British films from the fifties on channel four, and Sharma would tell me how charming he found the rhythms and accents of Old English. He was a glum reader and connoisseur of dictionaries, an admirer of the *Collins'* and a baleful critic of the *OED*, and he had a special but clear-eyed insight into their limitations.

Chapter Eight

IN OXFORD, I would walk almost everywhere, because I had an inexplicable pride that prevented me from using buses. There were two kinds of local buses, the red double-decker and the small toy-like white-and-blue bus. When the double-deckers passed by, they looked grand and somehow inaccessible, while the white buses seemed warm and busy, with the people sitting in them clearly visible through the large windows. But sitting inside a bus was a different experience, unrelated to what one might have surmised from the outside. Once, I took a double-decker to Cowley Road. It was like entering another life, right from ascending the wide berth of the footboard at the entrance, clutching with great immediacy the pole-vaulter's pole that rose there from the floor, ignoring the stealthy staircase that crept primitively upward, to make one's way shyly inside, braving the curious but not unwelcoming glances of other people. As the scene changed from the civic architecture of High Street to the grey brick houses and Indian restaurants on Cowley Road, bodies circulated gently and continually inside, as people got in and got out; it was strangely but peacefully crowded, and one had to cling economically to a loop of

leather or a horizontal rod travelling over one's head, and sway containedly from the top of one's head to the base of one's feet, and privately regain one's balance, as the bus went on its stately but mildly drunken, intemperate course. Another time, I took a less dramatic journey on a white bus to Summertown. Everything about it was small and detailed, from the coin handed for my fare to the driver, the neat black seats, the roof lowering over my head. Behind me sat a group of chattering boys and girls, and their impudent London accent filled the bus. Only a little way away from me sat the Indian bus driver in his blue uniform, but for some reason I thought of him as "Asian," and he became for me mysterious and unclassifiable. At each stop, he greeted kindly old ladies in a hearty English manner, "Hullo, dear! It's lovely day, innit?" and later bid them inimitable farewells, "Have a nice day, dear!" but the way he was more English than the English was very Indian, and there was something surprising about his utterances.

Cowley Road was on the other side, East Oxford. Long ago I had accompanied Sharma in hope of seeing an erotic Japanese film, *The Realm of the Senses,* to the Penultimate Picture Palace. After the roundabout, three roads ran parallel to each other—St Clement's, Cowley Road, and Iffley Road. Full of spirit, we took the Cowley Road to the Picture Palace, but found, alas, that there were no tickets. The road was lined with Bangladeshi shops, and energetic little Muslim boys wearing skull-caps played on the pavement; they did not look foreign, but very provincial and East London. After darkness fell, the shops remained lit and open, and old Pakistani gentlemen in overcoats, holding crumpled carrier-bags in their hands, had a chance to meet each other inside and converse in idiomatic Punjabi. Politics was discussed; the Bhuttos; Kashmir; cowardly India; bullying India; and the Indian cricket team was dismissed, quite rightly, with a contemptuous but decorous burst

of air from the lungs. "Asian" couples with shopping-trolleys went down aisles stacked with boxes of chilli powder, packets of dried fruit, jars of pickles, and imported vegetables—roots and tubers—with the flecked soil of Bangladesh still upon them; the shopkeeper continued his conversation in full-throated asides while his hands worked at the till; and to pay him, finally, in pounds rather than in rupees was like a joke whose meaning we both shared. There was a row of Indian restaurants along the road; at six o'clock, Muslim waiters stood significantly by the windows, and at night, the interiors glowed with a lurid red light. The furniture, selected with some tender and innocent idea of opulence in mind, was cheap and striking; honest Englishmen sat being served among fluted armrests and large, mendacious pictures of palm trees and winding rivers, helplessly surrendering to an inexhaustible trickle of Eastern courtesy; everything, including the waiters, smelled strongly of mint and fenugreek. The restaurants were seedy, but generous with life; and from the silvery letters of the sign outside, to the decor within, was a version of that style called the "oriental."

Chapter Nine

IT WAS in a small geometrical graduate room, in a modern building full of other such rooms, that I lived in those days. I was on the ground floor, and could hear the doorbell clearly when it rang. It used to make me, and perhaps every other student, specially alert and anticipatory; there would be a brief heightening and then a return to normalcy. In my pocket I carried, whenever I went out, two Yale doorkeys that gave me access to the building and my own door. Each was a twin of the other, unpretentious, golden-coloured, and dignified in the way it did not draw attention to the touch; one used the keys unconsciously and trustingly after the initial uncertain period of not knowing which was for which door was over. To my door was screwed a simple hook, from which my sweater and jacket, and later, in winter, my overcoat and scarf also, hung in a warm and voluminous pile. I did not notice until much later that all the hooks in Oxford, whether in public libraries or in college rooms, were the same as the one on my door, and belonged to a great family. There were two modern, comfortable armchairs opposite my bed, but in one of them the cords supporting the seat were a little loose, so that, when one sat on it, one slipped

backward suddenly; then, after having spent one immobile and astonished moment in that position, one smiled and righted oneself. Even the good armchair was tilted at a slight, but more natural, axis, and I sat in it whenever I was tired, or had company. The armchairs, with their flat, sedentary cushions, were designed for society, but the bed was made for solitude. It had a straitened and measured narrowness, an austere frame made to contain the curves of a single body, to circumscribe it, carry it, give it a place, and when I slept at night, I possessed it entirely.

Chapter Ten

THE loneliest of occupations was taking armloads of dirty clothing, stuffing them in a traveller's shoulder bag, and walking with it to the laundry room across the road. My main ambition was to diminish each moment, to hold as much as possible in as little space, to do things with the least depletion to time and effort. I disliked portioning out the load, for instance; I crammed in more than the bag could contain, and when, finally, I could not zip it, I would push against the clothes with all my weight, repeatedly and brutally, till they had been perfectly packed in.

Or I sat in my room with Lawrence's *Complete Poems* on my lap, looking at a page on which the long Laurentian lines spilled and overflowed from one verse to the other. I hated libraries, where human beings hunched strangely over their books, behaving like birds who were not eating, but studying, their prey, in a silence where the only things that whispered were the leaves of the books. Who were these people; what did they do at night; what peculiarly displaced lust drove them to fill in order-forms and push them confidentially towards a

woman, and have a conveyor belt with a cargo of books turn endlessly in the basement for their benefit? I stayed safely in my room and tried to make sense of the beauty of "Bavarian gentians, big and dark, only dark, / darkening the day-time," or "Have you built your ship of death, O have you?" or "the fragile ship of courage, the ark of faith / with its store of food and little cooking pans," or, especially, "You tell me I am wrong. / Who are you, who is anybody to tell me I am wrong?" while the sound of someone making coffee entered my reading, and a portrait of Lawrence, gaunt, red-bearded, stared at me like a demon and kept me company.

I rented a television set for a few months, and became acquainted with Postman Pat and Blue Peter, and my afternoons were shaped by a soothing jumble of quiz shows, word games, and *Fifteen to One*. Though poor in general knowledge, at guessing synonyms, and at making sense of the teasing, child-like nuisance of letters in an anagram, my mind, for a while, joyously deluded itself that it was in a state of agile and athletic excitement, and loved nothing more than being vanquished, in the end, by a retired widow from Dorset or a stuttering unemployed electrician from Leicester, sweet and harmless-looking people who had nevertheless used their empty hours to squeeze from themselves a razor-sharp competence in these matters.

There were times when I escaped to London, and as people fell asleep on the coach, their heads nodding and chiming in unison, I had occasion to think of my parents speaking to each other in Sylheti, or the sensation of standing on a verandah on a hot day. Scenes flashed past; and they flashed past when I returned in the evening, when I would see miles of suburbia on the edge of the motorway, house after house with a fragile, liminal television aerial on the roof, beneath a sky from

which birds and clouds fast disappeared. It seemed that if extra-terrestrial intelligence had a message for earth, it would be here, among these nondescript houses, at this moment, as it darkened outside and a family gathered around a television, that they would send it, to be recognised and deciphered by, of course, a boy in shorts with dreams in his head.

Chapter Eleven

TWO sisters, Chhaya and Maya, take turns to clean the bath-
room in our house in Bombay. I have seen the younger one,
Chhaya, a girl with two protruding teeth who leaned wistfully
between chores against a door to listen to my mother practise,
or ran to snatch the bag of rubbish from Ponchoo, grow to a
young woman with kaajal around her eyes, and unexpected
breasts, two small, painless swellings. On the festival of Raa-
khi, she ties a thread around my wrist with a crazy silver flower
upon it. Maya, the older one, is silent, ebony dark, and wears
clothes made from a shimmering synthetic material with sil-
very or purple hues, so that, even while collecting rubbish, she
looks minty and refreshing.

The bathroom has a large square mirror like a window into
which my father looks in the mornings. He wears floppy,
unsmart pyjama trousers with buttons on the front which often
remain inadvertently open, creating a dark, tiny fairy-tale
entrance. After shaving, he splashes Old Spice on his cheeks,
and the skin begins to glow with a faint green light. His hair
started to grey when he was thirty, so he dyes it an unrealistic
black, leaving one white plume smoking above his forehead. In

the flat in Malabar Hill, where there was a bathtub, I used to hear him all my childhood rubbing the soles of his feet on it while bathing, making a sombre but musical sound as that of a double-bass.

In my childhood, too, my mother's enormous friend, Chitrakaki, would visit us in the afternoons. This was when we lived in a flat in a tall building overlooking the sea, the Marine Drive, and the horizon. Together they would nap, my mother's feet hidden by a cotton sheet, Chitrakaki, all two hundred pounds of her, inhabiting a loose, long gown and snoring and shuddering malarially in her sleep, both of them suspended a hundred feet above the earth without knowing it. Beneath them the Arabian Sea rushed and the earth moved, while their heads rested on pillows so soft that they were like bodies of pure flesh without skeleton. Bai, the maidservant, while she sat on the floor and rubbed oil upon my mother's burning toes, and I, sitting beside her and looking over the edge of the bed, admired the trembling and lack of composure of Chitrakaki's body, as her stomach soared and climbed and then toppled over, her head, though it was perfectly still, seeming to move animatedly behind her stomach. If Bai and I smiled at each other and passed satirical comments between her snores, she would say, in a god-like voice, "I can hear everything." She is now dead, though I remember her as before, waking from that sleep with my mother, and drinking tea, and avariciously cupping a spiced mixture of peanuts and thin crispy strands of gramflour that looked like screws or nails, and chewing upon it with an ostrich-like satisfaction in strange things. For, truly, both she and my mother loved this edible scrap, this tea-time assortment of spiced nuts and bolts; sometimes, she would bring with her a box of chakli, a savoury that is hard and brown and runs round itself in gnarled, concentric circles, and is like a coral, or the body of a sea-horse. Once or twice, we even went to a

South Indian café together, for Chitrakaki loved exploring the tastes of different regions. Here, we ate from polished Formica tables, and were served by dignified Tamil waiters who, dressed in an impeccable uniform, looked like the soldiers of an ancient army. These men emerged from hot, swinging kitchen doors with plates balanced upon their palms, and on the plates were huge "paper" dosas. These are large white cylinders made of rice paste; from a distance, they look like rolled-up rugs, and coming closer, they resemble ridiculous headdresses of vast importance; from table to table, the waiters bore them glumly, as if they were gifts.

When I think of food, I think of the cat-like way my mother disposes of fishbones, and eats the head of the rohu fish, meticulously destroying its labyrinths. Here a silent contest ensues, as she chews and bites at it from all sides, till the head disappears and the indigestible bones lie clean and polished on one corner of the plate. At dinner, our leftovers—chicken bones, ribs, the white comblike tail of the pomfret, which is simple and symmetrical—we deposit upon her beggar's plate for her to chew and gnash and then blissfully spit out. My father, the most serious person at the table, uses, unexpectedly, a fork and a spoon to eat. He cannot begin till he has been served, and till that moment, remains sombre and paralysed. Once started, he floods his plate with daal, till it has made a yellow lake with white hillocks of rice upon its banks.

Chapter Twelve

IN THE afternoon, Mohan, my music teacher's brother, and Sohanlal, his brother-in-law, ring the doorbell. Ponchoo then silently brings out the tablas and tuning-hammer from the cupboard, and the big tabla, shaped like half a globe, he balances between one arm and his chin maternally; the smaller one he clutches lightly but firmly by the strong cords of bark along its sides. Mohan and Sohanlal take a long time settling down, talking in their own language, the latter chattering very fast, while Mohan, a man of few words, sits carefully on the sofa. It is easy to see that Mohan is related to my music teacher, that he is his brother, because their faces are similar, especially the colour of their skin, Mohan perhaps even a little darker than my music teacher was. The timbre of Mohan's voice is also like my guru's, slightly husky, not loud or deep. Though he may not be aware of it, it is impossible for others not to see my guru come to life, in flashes, in Mohan's facial expressions, his turns of phrase, and his gestures. But Mohan is an unassuming man, while my guru, shorter and a little plump, was a show-off, doing astonishing feats with his voice and then chuckling gleefully at our admiration. Laughter is drawn out reluctantly

from Mohan, who I think used to both hero-worship and self-effacingly humour his brother (he told me once he had turned to tabla-playing because there couldn't be two singers in a family, and that, when they were both learning the intricacies of vocal music from their father, he found his elder brother much too quick, much too clever to compete with), while my guru, especially when singing, would laugh happily after a difficult taan, and shake with mirth when he arrived at, after much deliberately drunken meandering, the sama, bringing a small, reluctant smile to his younger brother's lips. On tapes on which I recorded my guru singing in my house, complex melodic leaps and falls performed by him can be heard punctuated by brief chuckles.

When a singer performs, it is the job of the accompanists to support him dutifully and unobtrusively. A cyclical rhythm pattern—say, of sixteen beats—is played at an unchanging tempo on the tabla, and the song and its syllables are set to this pattern, so that one privileged word in the poem will coincide ineluctably with the first of the sixteen beats in the cycle. This first beat is called the sama, and much drama, apprehension, and triumph surround it. For the singer is allowed to, even expected to, adventurously embark on rhythmic voyages of his own, only to arrive, with sudden, instinctive, and logical grace, once more at the sama, taking the audience, who is keeping time, unawares. Once this is achieved, the logic seems at first a flash of genius, and then cunningly premeditated. While the pretence is kept up, and the singer's rhythm appears to have lost itself, the tabla-player, with emotionless sobriety, maintains the stern tempo and cycle, until the singer, like an irresponsible but prodigious child, decides to dance in perfect steps back into it. Similarly, when a singer is executing his difficult melodic patterns, the harmonium-player must reproduce the notes without distracting him. The tabla- and harmonium-players behave like

palanquin-bearers carrying a precious burden, or like solemn but indulgent guardians who walk a little distance behind a precocious child as it does astonishing things, seeing, with a corner of their eye, that it does not get hurt, or like deferential ministers clearing a path for their picturesque prince, or like anonymous and selfless spouses who give of themselves for the sake of a husband. Mohan, who plays the tabla with clarity and restraint, created the ground on which my guru constructed his music, and Sohanlal, attentively playing the harmonium, filled in the background. In the care of these two custodians, my guru sang and shone with his true worth.

Chapter Thirteen

CHHAYA and Maya would spend the morning sweeping and
cleaning and collecting rubbish. Their mother, a towering,
mild woman, cleaned the stairs; sometimes, her husband, that
pudgy, well-behaved man in khaki shorts, stood in for her, loi-
tering in the compound, decoratively wielding a jhadu. This
small family, father, mother, and two daughters, was employed
by the Building Society. What they did with the implements of
their trade—bucket, rag, water, disinfectant, jhadu, broom—
was a mystery. A combination of these things did not auto-
matically add up to cleanliness. From eight to twelve, one or
the other of the sisters, bucket in one hand, jhadu in the other,
made an independent, breezy tour of each flat in the seven-
storey building.

Chhaya was the younger one, plump, extrovert, with dim-
ples and protruding teeth. She did no work, but was on good
terms with everyone. From time to time, my mother preached
to her to study hard and educate herself at the municipal school
she never seemed to attend. She was interested neither in work,
nor in studies, nor in looking pretty. The things she was inter-
ested in were my mother's singing practice in the morning, and

when I would get married. Her older sister, in contrast, was a sensitive, overweight, round-faced girl who was exceptionally dark; she suffered because of this, and worked silently, almost sullenly. She never smiled, even by mistake; she seemed to think it would make her look ridiculous. By remaining silent, she tried not to draw attention to herself, but her very uncomfortableness made one notice her. The few times I caught her eye, she did not look, but glowered, at me. Then, a few years later, after she had passed puberty, she lost weight and gained a figure. Small, dark, and round-faced, she looked pretty when she smiled, a flash of perfect white teeth, something she began to do increasingly. She had obviously discovered that she was desirable to her husband, to whom she had been married, not long ago, when she turned fifteen, a young man in the family who ran a successful butcher's shop, whom Maya mentioned casually in the same breath with the quality of mutton at the shop. Chhaya, too, began to grow up; her churidars no longer stopped abruptly at her calves, but, elegantly, came all the way down to her ankles; and kaajal appeared around her eyes. But all this, I suspect, was her mother's and her sister's doing, and was as external to her as a frame to a painting, while Chhaya, till the last time I saw her, remained the same irresponsible and talkative girl I had known when she was nine.

The principal plaintiffs against the two sisters were the other servants. Each floor had a servants' bathroom on one side and a servants' toilet on the other; by accident the bathroom came to be on our side, while the toilet was on the side of our neighbours' flat. Our neighbour, a wealthy Sindhi widow, a simple, tall, hard lady, was specially sensitive to the insult of the toilet's proximity to her flat, a flat which, with money her son sent from Dubai, had been turned into a small palace of mirrors and marble. This situation was aggravated by Chhaya and Maya, who always went about with the privileged air of

outsiders, and paid no attention to the state of that toilet. The servants complained; and, from time to time, the Sindhi lady emerged to let the two sisters know what she thought of them, and then retreated into her palace. Never have I seen people to whom a scolding mattered less than Chhaya, Maya, and their mother; only Chhaya would pretend to argue, purely for the pleasure of it, while her mother's way of showing she harboured no hurt was to, on the next day, ask for an advance on her wages.

The widow lived in the flat with her two granddaughters. While she wore her widow's white sari with a strange pride, as if it conferred on her some special distinction, the two girls wore light, flowing dresses with elegant hems and collars and button patterns. The girls bore no resemblance to their grandmother; their faces were soft and creamy and showed signs of neither anxiety nor contentment, maturity nor innocence. They were living in that formless dream world before marriage, where nothing was required of them but to look pretty and, in some subtle, not immediately obvious way, to prepare themselves for the future. I preferred the widow's hard masculinity. She was a bundle of insecurities, domineering and shy by turns, and, absented from her husband and son, a man and a woman in one. While her granddaughters watched American films on video all day, and spoke the little English they did with an American accent—a sign of both ignorance and confidence— the widow spoke no English at all; and this both put her at an imagined disadvantage and gave her a conscious uprightness of bearing in that building, where everyone was a master of Bombay English. Her face gave as little relief to the eye as the landscape of Sindh from which she came. One felt she would be leading exactly this life wherever she was, whether in her village or in New York. And yet in no way did she belong to the past.

Sometimes, in the afternoon, wearing a kurta and pyjamas, I would walk down the lane and turn into the main road. The pleasure of taking a stroll in light, loose-fitting costume, without either drawing attention to myself or catching a chill, was a luxury never permitted to me in England. The sense of time on the main road, where Ambassadors passed by, and small, silent Marutis with spiteful ease, was different from that in the lane, where minutes and hours were connected to the conclusions and beginnings of phases of domestic routine. On the main road, which was only one among a family of such main roads that had joined hands to create Bombay—not the Bombay people lived in, but the one into which people emerged every day from their houses—there were cake-shops, video "parlours," "burger inns." The names of these shops suggested the coming of age of a generation who were on breezy, unawed, and first-name terms with the English language. In the midst of all this, there was a bit of unexpected picturesque detail, an intrusion of rural India, in the magazine-stall, bamboo poles holding up a canopy of cloth, which sheltered a long sloping table whose entire surface was covered with magazines, the newest of which hung from a jute string that had been tied from one pole to another. The hawker was not Maharashtrian, but a North Indian in vest and dhoti, and, judging by his looks (though I do not recall his sacred thread) quite probably a Brahman. If there had been a magazine-seller sub-caste, as there was a priest sub-caste, a landowner sub-caste, and a cook sub-caste, he would have belonged to it, so completely and immemorially did he seem to be in possession of the lineaments of his trade. In the evening, he lit a hurricane lamp to illuminate the magazine covers, though there was enough light coming from the air-conditioned cake-shops to brighten the rest of the road. The magazines were filled with speculations about politicians who looked a little like the magazine seller, but

lacked his sense of time and place. Together, they composed an unending Hindu epic, torn apart by incest and strife and philosophy. While the political magazines were like minutely detailed family histories, there was another kind of magazine that spoke exclusively of individuals, and described a happy secular life of evening parties and personalities that seemed as remote from government as the wood-fire-lit lives of villagers. But, from time to time, the two kinds of magazine would merge into one another.

Chapter Fourteen

WHILE reading the *Times of India* each morning, my father spares a minute for the cartoon by R. K. Laxman. While my mother is, like a magician, making untidy sheets disappear in the bedroom and producing fresh towels in the bathroom, or braving bad weather in the kitchen, my father, in the extraordinary Chinese calm of the drawing room, is admiring the cartoon by R. K. Laxman, and, if my mother happens to be there, unselfishly sharing it with her. She, as expected, misunderstands it completely, laughing not at the joke but at the expressions on the faces of the caricatures, and at the hilarious fact that they talk to each other like human beings. On important days, Laxman occupies a large square in the centre of the newspaper, which he fills with curved or straight lines that strangely look like prime ministers and politicians, pursued by hairy, allegorical monsters called Communalism and Corruption. On the right-hand corner of the page, there is a smaller square, in which small-scale absurdities and destinies are enacted, witnessed through a window by a passerby, hapless, moustached, bespectacled, child-like, in a dhoti and chequered jacket, he lit-

tle knowing that millions regard him daily through this other wonderfully simple window around his world.

My parents knew each other from childhood; both were born in undivided Bengal, in Sylhet, which is now in Bangladesh. In the late forties, my father went to England, and six years later, my mother; there, in London, they were married. In those days, Indian women were still a rare sight in England, and often, as the newly married couple walked down the road, they would be stopped by an Englishman who would politely request the young man's permission to take his wife's picture. The young man would then, as he still does so often to so many things, give his good-natured and gentle assent. Prying but harmless old women would enquire, at lonely bus stops, what the red dot on my mother's forehead signified; and for many months, a picture of her hung among other photos at a studio on Regent Street. Such a good cook was she, and such an inspired purchaser of herring and stewing lamb, that my poor father, neglected and underfed for six years, rapidly gained weight and happiness after marriage. While my mother took up a full-time clerical job, my father sat for and, at last, passed his professional exams. It was while working at the India Office, and making conversation with the large fishmonger, who called her "love" and "dear," and saved the pieces of turbot and halibut most precious to her, that she picked up spoken English. Like most Bengalis, she pronounces "hurt" as "heart," and "ship" as "sheep," for she belongs to a culture with a more spacious concept of time, which deliberately allows one to naively and clearly expand the vowels; and yet her speech is dotted with English proverbs, and delicate, un-Indian constructions like "It's a nice day, isn't it?" where most Indians would say, straightforwardly, "It's a nice day, no?" Many of her sentences are plain translations from Bengali, and have a lovable homely

melody, while a few retain their English inflections, and are sweet and foreign as the sound of whistling.

They returned to India by sea, on the Anchorline First Class. Those were the last days of the world's flatness, when, as in a map in an atlas, the continents were still embroidered upon a vast blue handkerchief of water. That fifteen-day-long, floating world between two worlds—England and India—surrounded on all sides by horizon, remains clearly in my mother's mind as a brief enchantment. What marvellous food was served, both Indian and Continental, what memorable puddings! In the evening, the ladies in saris and evening dresses, accompanied by their husbands, went out to the deck to enjoy the cool air. When darkness falls at sea, and the only light is the light on the deck on which people chat with each other as if on a promenade in a town, dressed in clothes selected after quiet and unobtrusive meditation—the selection representing some solitary, individual but habitual predilection which only the spouse recognises—how unique, in that darkness of water and sky, must seem the human creation of evening! Every few days, there was a party at the dining-hall; a band played; others took part in musical chairs while my parents watched; often, classic films were shown. Such an air of celebration—its echo reminds me of similar occasions in my childhood, only I am not present. When I imagine my parents as they were before my birth, it is like encountering those who are both familiar and changed, like recognising, with sudden pleasure, children who have returned home after many years.

Chapter Fifteen

AFTER Shehnaz and I had been seeing each other for about a week, I invited her to lunch at my college hall. I waited in front of the lodge, loitering invisibly while people went about, rushing, as they always do, with a special motivated speed at lunchtime. The only thing fixed in that scene was the porter, who sat inside his lodge, in a world a little detached from ours, and ignored me stolidly. When the clock struck one, I began to walk towards the hall, and Shehnaz came from behind and caught up with me, somewhat breathless. We curved round the grassy oval patch together, and entered a looming tunnel and then emerged into the second quad, with a large square of green to our right and, to our left, the L-shaped façade of the old buildings, with their consecutive staircases and rows of neighbourly windows. It must have been a warm day, for Shehnaz was wearing a white cotton top, with a message supporting the Palestinian cause printed boldly upon it, ending in a vivid exclamation mark; I noticed then how small her breasts were, two small bumps beneath her loose top, and how bony and thin she was, her collarbones radiating delicately and

symmetrically beneath her neck, their outlines becoming clearer as she bent forward.

The hall had great length and depth, and yet, from the moment one joined the queue collecting trays and food, one failed to see it in perspective. That day I realised, with the disappointment one feels when discovering another person's hidden nature, that Shehnaz was a vegetarian. With a plate full of peas and salad, she stood waiting for me to pay at the till. Feeling ill-at-ease, we then sat facing each other at one of the interminable parallel tables that ran from one end of the hall to another. Light filled the transparent sections of the stained-glass windows. Beneath them were portraits of the dead Masters of the college, luminous presences in costume, and beneath the portraits was the table at which the Chinese graduates sat. They looked no older than boys, with straight black hair and clean, animated faces, leaning across to shout to each other in Chinese, drawing back dramatically, or lolling forward, collapsing, and settling a head upon a crooked elbow on the table. In appearance, they were more Westernised than Indians, at ease in their European clothes, industriously devouring steak and kidney pie, but they hardly spoke to the English students, forming a little island at that table at lunchtime, buoyant, and full of movement. They made a domestic noise, like brothers watching a football match on television, with sounds that signified violent disagreement, or native exclamations of astonishment, but they might have been, for all I knew, discussing mathematical formulae or their syllabus. With the Chinese table as our background, Shehnaz and I ate together, more or less silently.

When we came out from the hall, we sat for some time on one of the benches on the edge of the green square, with our backs to the library windows. From there, while we talked, we could see people who had finished lunch appearing both from

the hall and the Senior Common Room. Though I was not aware of it then, Mandira's room, which she had newly occupied, was behind us, over our shoulders. I would later become familiar with its rectangular window, whose shutter was lifted on hot days. On the roof above the room, there was a skylight, a narrow glass lid framed by wood, its simple, straight angles standing out against its darker background, and clearly discernible in this brief, summarised version from below. It was by this skylight that I would later identify Mandira's room.

Chapter Sixteen

THE road that led to Shehnaz's college passed, at one point, over a canal. Then the road became, for a very tiny distance, a bridge, and one could sit on the wall on one side before entering the college on the left.

The canal had its own life. Ducks climbed curiously onto its bank or paddled upon the water with the utmost seriousness; twigs, branches, and leaves drifted in from the south and travelled northward. Sometimes one saw a rare polythene bag or can in the water, and, occasionally, a pair of tall, unhurried swans also headed towards a destination. Such were the daily journeys on the canal, but once, I saw two men and a woman out on a punt, laughing and shouting, and as I watched from above, the brown tops of their heads, a community of legs, and the interior of the boat with its portioned spaces and shadows became, for a few moments, visible, a glimpse of dark secrecies. On the college side, the grassy bank sloped upward, but on the other side, there was a black wall, and the backyards of houses. When one entered the college, and began one's walk towards the rooms, one saw, to the right, across the canal, signs of domesticity seldom seen in these parts of Oxford, with its

student flats and old, scholastic buildings, and elsewhere in England mainly from train windows—identical square back-yards, each fencing in its peculiar organisation of clothes-lines, laundry, children, cats, and women, beginning suddenly at one point and ending as suddenly at another.

Shehnaz lived on the first floor of her building, in a room even tinier and more modern than mine. Next to her bed, which during the day served as a sofa, were several shelves with books on history and politics, a few novels, picture-postcards, and photographs of her family. The books had significant titles on their spines, narrating stories of crises in faraway countries, conjuring the exciting imaginary worlds that graduates inhabit. Yet the global concerns expressed in the titles fitted in quite unremarkably with the marginal life in Shehnaz's room, with its teacups and electric kettle, and with the green, semi-pastoral life in Oxford. Opposite the bed there was a study-table, upon which stood a lamp whose angles were always crooked; beneath it, books lay open upon their backs, with lines marked out in pink and yellow, and next to that, there was a neat pencil box with pens of different colours. The table faced the wall-to-wall glass partition that illuminated every part of the small room on sunny days, and provided a seemingly unlimited view of a wide field receding slowly towards a border of trees. When one sat inside the room and looked out, one had a sense of being surrounded on all sides by space, silence, and green-ery. Students in coloured jerseys sometimes played football in that field, radiating in various directions, as they did on that afternoon when Shehnaz lay on her bed and I unbuttoned her shirt. On such brilliant days, unusual birds could be seen run-ning on the field, especially when it was empty and hot and shadowless, and full of its own presence. Along its sides, beau-tiful English flowers bloomed in clusters, and if one walked there, one encountered small, timid creatures, shy hedgehogs

and nervous, preoccupied squirrels. Whenever I looked up that afternoon, I would become aware of the frame of the window, which created an illusory and transparent separation between ourselves and the day outside. It was impossible not to be conscious of nature and sky, not to be surprised at how incidental, like stage-sets, these rooms were, and how specific the human rehearsals within them, of love or social intercourse. Our privacy, carefully constructed in the room, lost its meaning against the background of the glass that continually let in the solitude of that landscape.

Chapter Seventeen

THE walls in Mandira's room had photographs stuck to them with Blu-tack, and posters of Great Britain, showing the interiors of churches and cathedrals, and pieces of paper that had verses typed upon them. Greeting cards from friends all over the world were arranged upon the mantelpiece, and on the wall opposite, by the window, there was a board to which was pinned an amazing array of scribbled messages, lecture-lists, and printed or handwritten invitations from acquaintances, tutors, college societies, and the students' union. There seemed to be a great crowd of people scattered through the colleges of Oxford with whom Mandira was on first-name terms; later, when her life became more solitary, more nocturnal, and was spent more upon the anxieties we created for ourselves, those letters still stayed pinned to the board, no longer representing her other life outside her room, but a forgetfulness, the dates missed, the events long over, but the lecture-lists and invitation cards remaining upon the board as a beguiling and innocent surface.

In Oxford, the modes of social existence are few but tangible. But the tangibleness of this existence—conversing at

parties, studying at libraries, going to lectures—is at the same time dreamlike. Sometimes the occasions seem like images that one has projected from within for one's own entertainment, until they fade, as they must after a certain hour at night. Night brings darkness, the emptying of the images that made up the day, so that, in the solitary moment before falling asleep, the day, and Oxford, seem to be a dream one is about to remember. At this moment, one knows that one has no existence for others in Oxford, just as others have no existence for oneself, except in their absence. Daylight and waking bring the feeling of having travelled great distances, of arriving, at last, at a place that is not home, a feeling that cannot be exactly recalled or understood later, but which occurs at the same time each morning, until one gets out of bed, changes into one's trousers and shirt, and leaves the room. To be someone's lover, to share someone's bed, does not help, but only disturbs that fragile configuration of events and meetings, that neutral and desirable intersection of public places and private ambition, that creates the surface of the dream; instead, the moments of solitariness and self-consciousness, such as before sleeping and at waking, begin to recur unexpectedly, interrupting the flow and allocation of time, of schedules, deadlines, and appointments. One begins to get distanced from Oxford; more and more, one sees it as one's own dream, an illusion or a vision composed relentlessly of others, but not shared by anyone else. This is in part an effect of knowing that one's relationship with one's lover could have only taken place in Oxford, and has no meaning outside it, and that Oxford itself is a temporal and enchanted territory that has no permanence in one's life.

Mandira lived in a college among undergraduates. The rhythms and inflections, the sounds, were different here from those of graduate life. For one thing, the internationalism of a

graduate building was missing; most of the undergraduates
were English, and, speaking in accents that belonged to differ-
ent but neighbouring localities and regions, they formed a kind
of family, constantly on the move, opening and closing doors,
engaging in interminable exchanges in the corridor, and bor-
rowing each other's provisions. There was an urgency and a
panic in much of what they did, writing weekly essays and
preparing for examinations, and tension exploded either into
laughter, or remained unexpressed as silent resentment. Men
and women mixed with each other in large, friendly groups, but
there was also a subdued tension between the sexes that came
out in their jokes, a undercurrent of signals and hidden priori-
ties that never existed in quite such a way in graduate life.
Later, I came to know that many of Mandira's English girl-
friends, whom I would sometimes find in her room drinking
tea, speaking a rapid language that I hardly followed, were
always falling in and out of love with the men on their floor or
their staircase, and a conversation with a female friend was only
a stop-gap between two sexual moments of anxiety or pleasure.
Heartbreak was usual; for about a month, one would see a cer-
tain combination of singles and couples on the staircase, the
single people in jeans and the couples often dressed in black
formal clothes for guest-night; and then the combination would
change; the male would disappear, and the woman would
return to her plain skirt and woollen jumper. For graduates,
there is no real difference between term-time and the breaks in
between; and, as most of them come from other continents,
home is too far away to go back to; so they stay on in Oxford
during the shorter vacations, going to libraries, continuing
their research. But the undergraduates keep returning home to
the coasts of England, or to the North, or to Wales, in the win-
ter and Easter breaks, home, where, one gathers from their talk,

happiness or unhappiness is a more unsurprising, everyday affair than here, home, where one speaks another language, with sister and mother and father; a simple train journey takes them there, and brings them back, changed somewhat, redder or a little less thin, or with their hair cut much shorter. When they are away, the colleges become monuments, stone passages and stairways, empty halls and gardens, a place that is something between a deserted monastery and an unused bed-and-breakfast guest-house, a world made of Latin inscriptions and dates upon walls, and neatly made beds in rooms with no one in them.

But strange things happen even in term-time. Once, I remember, someone died, a former boyfriend of one of Mandira's friends, a young man of twenty-one, a "commoner" of the college; he had died alone in his room, strangely, of a heart attack. At lunchtime, I had seen some students crying, and then, that evening, when Mandira told me the story, the correspondences began to fit. That episode, unknown to most graduates, hung over the college and Mandira's staircase for about a week. It was about at that time that things began between Mandira and myself, without either of us knowing where they would lead. She would lock her door and come and sit beside me on the bed. If one of her friends happened to knock and call out, "Mandira!" we would both be silent; we would listen to the scratching on the notepaper outside, and smile as the person walked away. She wanted very much to make love to me, and at night, after switching off the light, she would lie, small and warm, underneath her blankets. She was completely new to love, unexpectedly bold in her various pleas and demands, and ashamed at the wrong moments. Our blinded gropings were more exploratory than passionate, for both of us were inexperienced, and a little afraid of what was

supposed to happen at the end of this act. These were the only moments when we were tolerant of each other's disabilities and shortcomings. Just above the bed there was a skylight that let a glow into the room, so that we could see each other's outlines, and the reassuring shapes of certain objects.

Chapter Eighteen

AT THE end of Cornmarket Street, near the Lloyd's Bank, comes a confluence of four roads, making an irregular sort of cross which one could possibly see from an aircraft. There is no centre in Oxford, only different points of reference, from each of which the conception of the city is altered slightly. Thus one never feels completely rooted, and ascending three floors in a building of the New Bodleian Library gives one, before entering the reading-room, a view of Holywell Street from above. One senses, from that window, how distinct and well marked out each section of the city is, each partially unknown to the other, each potentially undiscovered to its own inhabitants—for, from above, Holywell Street, with its repetitive up-and-down movement of cyclists and pedestrians, the faint white fringe of its pavement, and the houses on either side appearing quite oddly rearranged from this angle, seems, in the disturbing perspective gained by height and distance, continually strange, a place that will never become familiar or old. The orderly, disappearing line of traffic, the activity on the roads, harmonious and self-dispersing, the unreality of the scene and one's relationship with its unreality, are exposed and encompassed by this

view from a third-storey window, which reveals absences between one lane and another, one house and another, untenanted, unexplainable spaces, and that absence over all these, on eye-level with the window, so that the places one has walked through or passed daily lose their known features. It takes something as small and unsuspected as this, a change of view and altitude, to bring one's foreignness to one's self, the feeling of being separated from the routines that one thought attached one to the city, of being secretly in transit. Similarly, at the junction of four roads at the end of Cornmarket Street, the minor change in gradient of one of the roads, St Aldate's, the way it dips downward, so that the line at its end is known to be a false line, a border concealing and sheltering a second and more distant border at that end of the city, marks, in the midst of everything, an unnoticed but real departure. In a city so little known, so full of such instants, such escapes, events, and the memory of events become temporary stays; Shehnaz, Mandira's room, the walks taken together, a meeting with Sharma, reassure one that one has not been in Oxford alone, that one has shared it with others, till the solitary experience of being in transit returns, and friends and acquaintances are borne away by this city, which renews itself, and becomes, once more, strange to oneself. It is the city that remains, a kind of meeting place, modern and without identity, but deceptively archaic, that unobtrusively but restlessly realigns its roundabouts and lanes and landmarks, so that it never becomes one's own, or anyone else's.

The long road adjacent to St Aldate's is the High Street. One of my earliest meetings with Shehnaz was when we ran into each other at the junction, and she was going the opposite way, into High Street, in search of a florist; I hardly knew her then, but on her request, turned back to walk with her. The florist's was closed, so it must have been evening, one of the

long, bright evenings of summer. On both sides of this road are ancient colleges, with grey steps and wooden doors and grim, outdated windows, smooth brown stone walls, clock towers, and spires. The gong of the clocks, especially the one at the Cornmarket Street end of High Street, can be heard every hour with great and transparent clarity, and at night, when I would hear the ever-increasing repetition from Mandira's room, I would become conscious of the strangeness of the place I was about to fall asleep in, of distance, and the suspension of activity. As one walks past the colleges on High Street, one glimpses, through the frame of the doorway, another frame, which marks off the end of the entrance area with the porter's lodge, noticeboards, and mail-room, broadening out into the first quad with its empty oval or square of green, its generously enclosed, yet strangely liberated, parameter of open air and space, the façade of a building, with the college chapel, behind the green, and a measured rectangle of sky. This is the abbreviated, painting-like view that passersby have of the interiors of the colleges, and the rest is hidden behind an edifice of stone that is part history and part fantasy, and has little to do with the domestic or working lives of students, and their particular slang or vernacular. Yet the students do not really matter, because within the college walls there is a world—a geography and a weather—that clings to its own time and definition and is changed by no one. In this world, glimpsed briefly by the passerby through the open doorway, a certain light and space and greyness of stone, and at night, a certain balance of lamplight, stone, and darkness, co-exist almost eternally, and it is the students, with their nationalities and individual features, their different voices and accents, their different habits and attempts at adjustment, their sense of bathos and possession of reality, who, in truth, vanish, are strangely negated, so that, when the passerby later remembers

what he saw, the students seem blurred, colourful, accidental, even touching, but constantly skirting the edge of his vision, while it is possible to clearly and unequivocally recall the dignity and silence of the doorway and the world beyond it.

A little further on, a short distance before Magdalen Bridge, are the Queen's Lane Coffee Shop and a newsagent's on the left, and the Examination Schools to one's right. On certain days in May and June, examinees in black gowns, at half-past twelve and five-thirty, trickle out, and then overflow, onto High Street from the entrance of the schools, the women in black skirts and white shirts, some jubilantly holding bouquets in their hands, the men in white shirts and black trousers, faces and outlines merging on the pavement and then separating at street-corners, a young man materialising from the crowd and awkwardly crossing the street in the midst of the traffic, sweethearts, their faces flushed with pride and anxiety, waving madly and then embracing, large groups chattering and breaking up, and other smaller groups held close in serious conference. This is one of the few occasions on which one sees something common to all these faces; before one's eyes, for the first time, a network of friendships is formed, correspondences that link acquaintances and strangers in one milling and crowded moment, that is already turning into the past, already disintegrating only to be remembered as something so immediate as not to be wholly real; for no one, later, actually knows what it was like at that moment. Common to each, as they emerge, is the nervous or successful air of opera singers; for each one has been privileged and chosen by Oxford to perform for it; and now that unique and invigorating moment, for better or for worse, is over. On the other side, life at the newsagent's goes on as before; polite people, such as those one holds the door open for, say "Thank you" and leave with newspapers and sandwiches. By chance, one might pass them on the street a month later, an

encounter that does not bring up a memory or a connection, but something in their place, neither a memory nor a connection, which causes one's identity to reconstitute itself. The newsagent's sells postcards of Oxford, small, shining squares with pictures of colleges, hidden lanes, the Radcliffe Camera, and students on bicycles. The postcards are weightless, but palpable, and when one stops to look at them, they have a recognisability that one's consciousness of Oxford lacks; they seem more real than the place one has lived in.

Chapter Nineteen

WHEN my parents moved to that lane in the Christian area in the suburbs of Bombay, I was in Oxford; I did not witness the moving. In the summer, I returned for my vacations to a house I had not seen before, but only read about in letters, a tidy flat on the third floor that was smaller than the flats I had lived in all my life when my father worked in his company.

Once, when I was sleeping late into the morning in my new room, I was woken by an insistent metallic noise, something between a hammering and a ringing. The door at the end of the room opened on to a verandah, and when I went out, I saw a rubbish truck standing in the lane, an old, obsolete truck, such as one always sees on the roads in India, with no roof except in the front, where the driver's seat is. Men who appeared to be dressed only in undergarments—vests and shorts—were clambering busily over the rubbish that had already been piled in the open section of the truck, and were now leaning in a carefree way with their elbows on one side of the truck, and looking out at the lane. The tallest man among them was standing just outside the gate to our building, and with cheeky disregard continually beating a plate with what might have been a spoon. He

stood rooted to the spot, and, because he was wearing shorts, I could see how thin his legs were, with hairless knees, bent at a concave angle because of the firmness with which he was standing. The rude noise he was making sent the sweeper-women of the building, pretty girls among them, into a panic; with worried faces, clutching large plastic bins, they were hurrying towards the truck, from which the little men in undergarments were leaning out and looking at them insolently. There was something sexual in the air, and this ritual repeated itself at this time on almost every day of the week.

I grew to love that lane. The flat was on the third floor, and its verandah brought one magically closer to its life. There was commerce between our building and the shops on the main road, from which barefoot errand boys would come carrying newspapers, provisions, videocassettes, and bottles of soda, taciturn, dark adolescents who wore T-shirts handed down by their employers, with USA, SMILE, or BEAT KING printed upon them. In this part of the city, with its small-town atmosphere, taxis were rivalled by auto-rickshaws, manic, hooded three-wheelers that were good for short distances. At the local station, these autos arrived incessantly in a cloud of dust before a queue of passengers, who, one by one, were carried off through a series of jolts and shocks towards the various roads radiating around Bandra—Linking Road, Turner Road, Hill Road, Khar. And one would come in the afternoon, every few days, to the gate outside our building, and either Mohan or my guru, or both, would alight from its tiny, semi-visible, confessional-like interior, and pay the impatient auto driver. From the verandah, their entrance into the compound was visible at close quarters, and the sudden roar with which the auto disappeared always left me unprepared.

My parents lived here for three years. During my first sum-

mer visit, walking down the parallel lanes, I found by-lanes connecting one lane to another. On either side of these by-lanes, which were like shrunken versions of the bigger ones, miniature portraits of them, there were old cottages, and, around them, a distinct island of life that had formed by itself, consisting of cats, shrubs, birds, and an absence of people. I was always grateful for, without knowing precisely why, the detour of passing through these by-lanes.

It was Chitrakaki, my mother's friend, who, having lived in the suburbs for thirty years, introduced my parents to a new family doctor in the area, someone who would make house-calls. He was a short Marathi gentleman called Dr Deshpande, long threads of black hair combed across his disproportionately visible scalp, square-jawed, stout, bespectacled, with, disconcertingly, dimples appearing on his cheeks when he smiled. Like all general practitioners who are slaves to their patients and available at their beck and call at all hours of the day, he had no degree but his MBBS; he was more a Samaritan than a doctor; his arrival was met with relief rather than apprehension. He was not consulted for serious illnesses, but for headaches, stomach-upsets, and indigestion, and for his company he charged fifty rupees less than the doctors in the city. This part of the suburbs was his natural terrain; he was linked by phone to a wide variety of sufferers, and was in demand everywhere. He usually made only one diagnosis, "There's a virus in the air this time of the year," but if one disagreed with him, he had no objection to changing it.

Chitrakaki lived not far away in a rented flat on the ground floor of a two-storey house with her husband, son, daughter-in-law, two dogs, and a cat. Once she owned a rooster which, strange plant, was convinced it was human and insisted upon being introduced to her friends. The dogs—a fox terrier that

died, a dachshund that met its end in a road accident, two hairy Pekinese—Chitrakaki and her husband loved and cared for like their own children. And they forever remained children, even when they had become old, scuffling underneath the dining-table and barking their hearts out at the wall-lizard. In other ways they were shockingly dog-like; for the mother Pekinese and her son, Chitrakaki once related lovingly, had become husband and wife, and then had had puppies. Each time, during those thirty years, when a bitch had puppies, Chitrakaki witnessed their blind, recumbent birth, and then gave them away.

She loved my mother's cooking. Whistling (she had learnt how to whistle in England, where both she and her husband had met my father as a penniless student), she would loiter carelessly in the kitchen, looking askance as my mother gave the cook instructions, vainly, and stealthily, trying to sniff out the recipe. When she tried it at home, however, it was never, never right. She was convinced my mother had cruelly held back something, a seemingly unimportant but crucial ingredient she had quite premeditatedly forgotten to tell her. My mother made things from peelings, fish-heads, dried fish. It was East Bengali cuisine, with its origins in villages on drought- and flood-hit riversides, a poor man's diet, perfected by people who could not afford to throw away even the skin of a white-gourd or the head of a fish, transformed into food by adding oil and garlic and chilli paste and poppy seed and common salt.

The people who really belonged to our lane were those who were on its margins—servants, sweepers, watchmen, hawkers of vegetables and fish who sent their cries out to the balconies and went with their baskets from door to door, even the beggars who, like the tradesmen, worked on a repeated route within a definite area. There was a Christian woman who, wearing the same tattered white dress, stood outside the build-

ing gates every week and sang a tuneless song in disjointed
English. English was spoken quite naturally here by the poor,
many of whom were Christians and said their prayers in the
language.

Gradually, the area changed. New buildings, like ours,
came up where the oldest cottages used to be, concrete struc-
tures with sequences of black holes that would become flats in
which people and children would live, the rooms, kitchens, and
bathrooms still unrecognisable, each building looking at this
stage like a huge birdhouse. The labourers sat and chipped
away at the large rocks with their chisels, while their women-
folk, with saris tucked around their knees, bent down and
scooped tiny black stones into a metal plate; some of them sat
apart, nursing babies, the breast hidden by the child's head, one
end of the sari pulled forward, held aloft, and used as a kind of
curtain to an imaginary room. The stray dogs of the lane were
friendly with the children, who would pummel them fearlessly
with tiny fists, or race them down the lane, while the dogs took
such pestering wisely and accommodatingly. This floating
community, infants and all, disappeared every year, and then
they, or another very like them, reappeared on another site.
Often, they would live in improvised shelters they had built
themselves. From the rear balcony of our flat, one could see a
building coming up in an adjoining space, where our com-
pound had ended with a wall. On this side of our house, clothes
were left to dry on the balcony, and there were garages down-
stairs in which tenants' cars were kept. The atmosphere here
was in contrast to that of the front side, where cars and people
kept coming in.

At different points of time in those three years, a maid-
servant and a cook who worked in our flat began to visit the
rear balcony in the afternoons with an aimless look in their

eyes. Both had made a long-distance, incommunicado relationship of looks and gestures with someone on the building site. There was some doubt about this at first, both on one definitive occasion, my parents were told by an informer—perhaps the sweeper-woman—that the cook (who, before she found love, was a slow-moving, turtle-like woman with luxuriant hips) had made a friendship with a Nepali watchman, a matter of waves, smiles, and glimpses, but then a serious affair of meetings when she would disappear from the house for what she thought were unnoticeable intervals. Returning, she would say she had been to the toilet. Romance was dead among the middle classes, but among domestic servants it was still a disruptive force, giving them a secret life that had the fraught emotions, the atmosphere, and the singing beauty of old Hindi films. When a servant fell in love, the implications were felt all over the house, and became a subject of conversation; my guru would interrupt his tuition to speak about these matters of the heart, glancing sideways when the servant being discussed entered the room.

Meanwhile, the new houses were completed. Each family, in those matchbox-like flats, put up paintings, placed decorations on the window-sills, hung up lamp-shades, as if life, taken out of the bundle of cloth in which it had been hurriedly wrapped, had settled down and resumed its ordinariness. As the cottages fell, and buildings came up, Hindus moved into the area to live alongside the Christians—Sindhis, a tall, migratory business people, who brought with them a passion for cars and noisy weddings, extended families consisting of grandsons and cousins, and women-folk who sang an unimpassioned, strangely tranquil version of devotionals in the evening; hovering wistfully somewhere on the border of tunefulness, it brought the quality of a faraway time and place to the area. By

the time my parents decided they could no longer live in Bombay, and in those months of waiting for the flat to be sold, until at last when they packed up everything, leaving every room with crates full of possessions, the character of the lane changed perceptibly.

Chapter Twenty

THAT year, full of those odd coincidences that brought Shehnaz and Mandira and me together, my parents moved from Bombay to Calcutta.

Calcutta is my birthplace. It is the only city I know that is timeless, where change is naturalised by the old flowing patterns, and the anxiety caused by the passing of time is replaced by fatigue and surrender. It is where my father, having left Sylhet, came as a student fifty years ago. Those were the last years before independence; and my father lived in a hostel in North Calcutta. He ate great quantities of rice in the canteen, and never left a fish-head uneaten. He was an only child, parentless, in this city where people spoke Bengali differently and more coldly than he did. North Calcutta was then classical and beautiful, with Central Avenue and the colleges of Tropical Medicine and other sciences, the imposing colonial buildings, the institutions of learning, and the roads matching the nobility of their names. And my father saw that nobility with his own eyes. In all the world then he had nobody. It was before history was born, and he himself became who he was, studying in a city that is always prenatal, prenascent. The tiny village in

East Bengal he was born in, with its village school he went to in early childhood, seems to have never existed. It is now on the other side of the border, in Bangladesh. It is as if my father came into being from fantasy, like an image, in 1923. Yet it is an image full of truth, to think of him studying in Calcutta, or taking a tram ride, one of the marginal, anonymous people who were neighbours with history, one of the millions, studying, discussing politics, listening to songs, living in hostel rooms, eating in the "cabins" of North Calcutta, who were bypassed and yet changed, without their names or the quality of those moments ever being known, by independence and partition. So India took on a new shape, and another story began, with homelands becoming fantasies, never to be returned to or remembered. What did it mean to him, then, without brother and sister, alone, to be part of so many? He loved that life. When Tagore died, millions flowed through the streets, some taking turns to be pallbearers, some surging forward to touch his feet or his body and then being left behind while others took their place, my father one of those who had momentary proximity to the dead poet, touching him before he disappeared from view, so that, whenever Ray's documentary on Tagore is shown on television, my mother leans forward towards the end of the film and peers at the screen to catch a glimpse of my father. Thousands, without name or face, but known perhaps to one other person somewhere else, appeared and disappeared around the body of the dead poet held aloft, indistinguishable from each other, weaving in and out of that moment.

Strange to think that a poet should have suddenly brought to the world's brief attention a small corner of the earth, where a rounded, musical tongue was spoken, where freshwater fish was eaten daily and its bones sorted nimbly with the fingers, where small, earnest men walked in white dhotis with tender, overlapping folds in the heat. An unknown tongue, unknown

emotions, strange, impoverished Bengal! From the dense forests and swamps of the Sundarbans, to the magical place, Kalighat, a port and a people grew, a poet and singer in each family, ideals and romance and the love of art nurtured among these frail quick-tempered people, and the wide Hooghly flowing in the midst of all this. Wide rivers, the Hooghly and the Padma, with indistinct horizons on either side, a constant thoroughfare for river transport and civilisation, with lonely passages of water and horizon where ferrymen journeyed from one side to the other.

For many years, my father's family was hardly known to me. Two portraits, of my grandfather and grandmother, hung upon the wall above the doorway to my parents' bedroom in the houses we lived in. The family had once been landowners, and then they scattered and gradually became poor, settling down in towns on this side of the border, while the great house became a memory in Bangladesh, with a few relatives still living in it. I remember in childhood travelling with my parents to a town in Assam, and being taken in a car to the outskirts, and entering a place without electricity, where people lived in a small house among other houses; we were greeted by a family: a father, his daughter, her husband, and a child, and the old man had the same surname as I. My father addressed him with the Bengali word for "paternal uncle," and they spoke in the Sylheti dialect, and fragments of that world in which the remnants of my father's family lived came alive in the light of a hurricane lamp.

My father's ancestral village was on the banks of a tributary of the Surma. To leave that village and approach the outside world one must use the waterway and the canoe, and emerge eventually into another world. Heat, mud, water, the flight of water-insects, roots holding the earth, women washing clothes, their heads covered by saris, ponds made green by

water-hyacinth, the flat, wide sails of the lotus—such images come to me of journeying down that river. It is a Bengal that missed the changes taking place elsewhere, the middle-class reforms of Brahmoism, the intellectual movements in Hinduism. More important, there, than the secular nationalist figures, Rammohan Ray and Tagore, initiators of modern Bengali culture, was a native strain of Vaishnavism, the worship of Krishna, Ganesh, Parvati, an ecstatic love of their images, sung out in unwritten songs and poems.

To that strain of worship my father's family belongs. Dispersed though they were over eastern and northern India, from Cachhar to Brindaban, rarely in contact with each other, second cousins and third cousins and uncles, some dead, uprooted from tradition, a refugee people, I would hear of singers and painters in every branch of the family, and once, on a visit to a remote part of India when I was a child, I received blessings and a book of poems from my father's aunt; it was a book she had written herself. The family, perhaps because once so rich, was little in touch with education; my father's aunt had never been to school; her Bengali was self-taught. Their love of poetry was not created by the new secular reverence for culture and literature that came with Tagore, but was an indigenous offshoot of a long line of ecstatic worship and craftsmanship. Not very long ago, in the summer, after my parents had moved to Calcutta, we made a trip to where my father's aunt's son now lived, with his sister and her daughter, in a barely recognisable lane off a small road beyond the highway at Dum Dum. They were overjoyed to see us; on the verandah to the small house, canvases rested, portraits of saints and holy men and women. My cousin was an artist, and all his paintings were devotional. On the verandah there was a table on which there were lumps of clay that looked like turds but became, on closer inspection, little animals, bulls, cows, and images of Krishna.

My cousin took me by my hand to show me these proudly. Knowing my love of music, he had taken out harmonium and tablas, and urged me and my mother to sing. Then they themselves sang with little prompting, from a vast repertoire of songs in both Hindi and Bengali, some of which they had composed themselves. An anxious, child-like joy in their own creations lived in that house. In a room at the back, my cousin was working upon a commissioned sculpture of a living saint; made from clay, to life-like measurements, sitting cross-legged upon newspapers spread out on a table, it was an ecstatic moulding for worship. Creation was worship; that family was excited and full of love for that image; they had made it together, my cousin doing the sculptor's work while his sister and her child helped him to hold it still and achieve its proportions. It was still unpainted, its colour the colour of clay, but the eyes of the saint and the expression of his face and body no longer belonged to earth and mud but to the realm of the imagination. For the first time I could see where my own private joys came from—the love of songs, of music, of pride and delight in creation. That delight is my family's gift.

Chapter Twenty-one

COWLEY ROAD, Iffley Road, and St Clement's—small, mean, jaunty families live here side by side with the Bangladeshis and Pakistanis. This is the tribe that belonged to Dickensian alleys, the aboriginal community that led its island life, its daily routines and struggles, and scarcely heard of Empire or took part in governance. For them the supermarkets were built, to work in and to shop at. Not Sainsbury's, but Tesco, with its long aisles of shopping-trolleys, sides of beef and ham, frozen chips, mango chutney, and spinach at tuppence less. Towards such centres they gravitate, living in a perpetual present, and then walk home to their houses with tiny gardens. Not for them history, old buildings, literature, but an England of small comforts and marriages, happy or unhappy. For them television, with endless runs of Eastenders and Coronation Street, showing them their lives and those of their children. There is a church here, in Cowley, for they are devout Christians, drinking Protestants, religious not in a theological but in a family way, with roles allocated to the sexes, the men believing, and supporting their football team, the women praying, and going out shopping, all of them seeming to know the words of the

Sunday hymns by heart, but blaspheming and cursing God when they feel like it. Speaking an English that is hardly spoken in any other part of the world anymore, with queer proverbs and turns, dropped consonants and vowels, turning the language like meat inside their mouths.

For them the cans of beer with German names, and black Guinness. Turners of nuts and bolts, sweepers of a clean country, the young men white and unnaturally fat on baked potatoes and cheddar cheese, still pathetically dependent on their mothers, the women wearing dresses, their feet either in high-heels or sandals in the cold, their legs unstockinged in winter, secretly shaven, with faint blue and purple veins, the older men with long, combed, wavy hair, wearing coats and flared trousers, seldom unshaven, never tying their hair in a ponytail like the students, rarely seen in corduroys, the last chain-smokers and meat-eaters of England, thin, smartly dressed, energetic, hanging around street-corners, escaped from their wives and children, looking like snooker-players, white men leading black lives. White niggers, they fought the war, sang drinking songs, married, died. Not for them cars, but the great public transport system, joining and holding communities and families together, the buses coming every twenty minutes. They are the ones who lived in a world of horrible and immediate prejudices, coined the terms "Paki" and "wog," and then lived side by side with the Patels and Muslim Bangladeshi families, and worked for their sons who look like Latin Americans and chatter in Cockney amongst themselves. For them a diet of brain's faggots and frozen peas, the middle-aged skinheads, in the nineties, become fathers with children perched on their shoulders, the punks, with their phosphorescent hair, vanished like a seasonal insect. For them, recreation is the desolately green area of the Headington Parks, pleasure a public piss in a public

toilet, and misery an hour spent in the launderette. This world is a different world from that of the University; they never meet. The state of intoxication here, broken bottles, a beggar's foul breath, is more basic than the students' social drunkenness, a state of the soul.

Whenever I have come here, it has rained. Clouds gather at this end, little England. The City centre is charming, like a picture, and the lanes off Broad Street, off Jesus and Lincoln Colleges, are romantic and small, eighteenth-century exteriors with twentieth-century fittings, romantic lamplight and mist. But here even the pubs are different. Once, finding myself at this end of town, out on an edge, I entered one; it was a weekday. It was quiet and uncrowded; people seemed to have gathered here as a matter of course, as if it were a second home; they noticed me, but said nothing. Bright wallpaper on the walls; tables and chairs; coffee was served; an old man sat in a chair by a window and the entrance, ignoring a draught, ignoring newcomers, a large Alsatian dog by his side, his only companion. It must have been nine o'clock, and yet the pub was relaxed and half empty. It had no designer photographs of old cricketers, no designer posters of old advertisements for the London Tube, for Coca-Cola, for the Festival Hall; its atmosphere belonged to itself; it was like an old house. The young men and women, couples talking with each other, looked different from the students; their hair was straight and limp; they had never been to the orthodontist as children; raised teeth, and lines around their mouths, gave their faces an odd softness. Their complexion, too, was white; they seemed like Madame Tussaud's waxworks, a lost world, remade and fixed. And yet this was their world.

Sometimes, in the evening, I would be confronted by alcoholics who, for some reason, seemed least ill-at-ease when beg-

ging from a dark-skinned foreigner. If I parted with a coin, I would receive a "Thank you, sir" in return, and if I refused, I would either be wished good luck or cursed for being in England. Once I was cursed for being a student by a beggar I had become friendly with: "There's no difference between you and me, mate, we're both dossing around on other people's money." And I remember an elderly gentleman whom I saw both in Cowley and in North Oxford, drunk every time, a myopic who wore spectacles with a strong, dark frame that gave his face a learned look which in itself is an anachronism in a University town where most students wear contact lenses.

On dry days, furniture would be piled outside the second-hand shops on Cowley Road. The pavement would be filled with wardrobes, armchairs, sofas, dressing-tables with mirrors, lampstands, in a space next to a bus stop, where a strange woman would come to a man and say, "Could you spare me your cigarette end?" Certain areas were marked out and separated from the rest by smells of Kentucky Fried Chicken. Then, at last, came the Cowley Market Hall, part hardware and stationery store, and part a derelict precursor to the supermarket, a solid, unpolished shell where couples wandered to buy things—children's toys, a hammer, writing paper, liquorice. And, as one walked on and came marginally closer to London, this would end, these lives, with their idiosyncrasies, laughter, pressures, and sorrows, portrayed forty years ago in the black-and-white Ealing comedies and dramas, no grand characters in those films, only unforgettable bit-parts, bit-characters, all this would empty out into the road turning right towards the John Radcliffe Hospital, or going straight past an elevation, green and wide and sloping upward, a public common where East Oxford seemed to vanish. *It Always Rains on Sunday,* both the title and the film itself express what goes on inside these houses, women

with husbands they both love and do not love, memories of old beaus, old sweethearts, sudden extremities, sudden panic, then routine reasserting itself, and the rain that always hangs over these streets. Then, as the film ends, so does this small world, in a great vent and opening of space.

Chapter Twenty-two

WHEN I told Mandira that "Private Shop" on Cowley Road was a sex-shop, she was curious to see it; she had never been in one before. I never took her there, though; it remained one of our many promised destinations. Anyway, it was difficult to get in without being noticed; and when one opened the door, a bell tinkled as in a drugstore in old American films. A man, pale, cheaply well dressed, one of life's jetsam, stood behind the counter, appearing to fidget busily with something, nodding and saying "Can I help?" as you entered, as if you were just another customer and this just another shop, and then, as you looked around and became briefly engrossed, he would avoid, out of consideration, looking at your eyes, trying not to appear contemptuous, but anxious to confide and be truthful when asked questions. Magazines, three for the price of one, phone numbers, giggly dildos, pink perpendicular rubber organs arranged like confectionary, brought feelings, inside one, of surprise, laughter, and embarrassment. It was because it excited the first two emotions especially that it might have been a place for a couple to amuse themselves, but when I went there, I went alone; its wonders remained undiscovered by Mandira.

There were many promises to her I did not keep, promises to go to new places, towns, sleepy English villages, to vanish from Oxford for a holiday. And then there was her wish to discover, through me, herself, for her a heartfelt but simple demand, for me, almost impossible to comply. She would have had me possess her, to commit to extinction both our selves, while I always held back, selfishly, on the brink, refusing to take refuge inside her. So it was that we lived for a time in that space in which bodies exist on the borders of each other, separated by flesh, by the life of each, which, unadmitted by both, is actually moving in its own direction, towards its own future. In this way, we teetered on the brink of each other, and her desire remained superfluous and unfulfilled.

After a spell of depression, she decided to postpone her finals by a year; in Trinity term, she moved out of the college, packed her things in two suitcases, and left while her friends prepared for their exams. She moved to a house in a blind lane off Cowley Road, a room with a wide, springy double bed, light pink walls, and tiny curtained squares that were windows. The house had a path, not more than ten feet long, leading to its door, and before the path there was a small unsteady wooden gate, of a child's height, purely ornamental in nature, which would have kept nobody out. The house was owned by an old English widow with white hair and grey eyes, a sort of harmless English witch who looked as if she practised on the Ouija board, but actually only nagged Mandira to remember to close the front door, to buy her own washing liquid, to pay her rent on time, to receive no calls after ten-thirty, and who had dinner at six and watched television thereafter. She let out her rooms upstairs to students, or to anyone for that matter, for Mandira's neighbour was a woman who worked all night and slept during the day.

Mandira then began to live more or less alone, cut off from

her old friends, her college routines, and her tutor, an old don in spectacles. The only person who visited her then, besides me, who would drop by dutifully from time to time, was a nineteen-year-old English boy from college, awkward, inarticulate, his eyes hidden by a mop of hair, who loved Mozart and Beethoven, who communicated with Mandira by simply "being around," by smiles, by listening as she talked of her problems, by nodding in agreement and uttering monosyllables to support his nods, by running her small errands, by making silent gestures like lending her his pullover. His name was Simon. He became even more silent and reserved when I was there, and remained, throughout, a witness to the precarious way in which our involvement began, and then the way it dwindled. He was one of the few English students in Oxford with working-class origins; his old parents, whose only son he was, lived in Dover; his father was a trombone-player in a four-man band. Simon was doing physics, one of those things you cannot learn, but must have an aptitude for. Of all Mandira's friends, he remained the most faithful to her, accepted her as she was, overlooked her shortcomings; towards the end, he even transmitted to her his love of classical music, and I would find her sometimes, listening, with a self-conscious expression, to a Beethoven sonata.

Then, to supplement her scholarship money, Mandira began to work in the Covered Market, part-time jobs at a florist's and a cake-shop, for which she did not require a work-permit. In the morning, she would cycle to her library. After lunch, she would walk to Turl Street, and then enter the market, and, once inside her shop, she would wear a white apron over her clothes, and a white cap on her head, the uniform at the cake-shop. Because she was so fair, she looked almost, though not quite, English behind the counter; whenever I vis-

ited her, I bought a pastry or a tart, and she could not resist smiling at the nature of our meeting, the ridiculousness of her apparition in such a uniform, for she seemed, at such moments, to see herself from the outside. The lady at the shop, as the widow whose house she lived in, would ask her occasionally, "Is he your boyfriend?" to which she would say, half pleased and half exasperatedly, "No, not really."

Through her I became familiar with the Covered Market, with the intricacy and timelessness of its organisation, its hours of business, when it served as a thoroughfare for students passing between Broad Street and High Street, its fixed closing-time of five o'clock, when the iron gates on both sides were shut and locked. Who would have thought, surrounded on almost every side by colleges, Jesus, Lincoln, and Oriel not too far away, Broad Street, Blackwell's, and the Sheldonian on the other side, that here there was a place of buying and selling, a place that both quickened and constricted the appetite? For not far away from the sweet-smelling, moist floors of the florist's were the butchers' shops with sticky larders and clotted blood, dead pheasants swinging upside down from hooks, fragrant carcasses, pigs' livers and trotters. Here, then, exposed, was the dark Anglo-Saxon love of offal which went back centuries. In another part of the market were stalls with stacked yards of silk, folded around a flat board, and the old system of measure here, and the way the shopkeepers busily touched and tested the cloth with their fingers, reminded me of the stalls of New Market in Calcutta, where people still speak of cloth in terms of the human body, and still speak sometimes of one or two "hands" of cloth. Mandira worked, from two to four o'clock, in the midst of all this activity. For that period of time, she became, unquestionably, part of that small community of shopkeepers, attendants, helpers, girls-behind-the-counter, as easily

and completely as she had been, before, one of the student community. Once, I accompanied her as she swiftly and confidently took a cardboard box full of rubbish to that special, secluded area in the market where refuse was emptied, and collected later by a truck. She was herself, and yet wholly transformed.

Strange place, Oxford, and strange discoveries one makes within it! Strange students' rooms, with their own, always slightly unfamiliar, dimensions. During that time when I was undecided between Shehnaz and Mandira, hurting them both, being hurt by both, confused as I had never been, I lived on the ground floor of the graduate building, and Sharma lived in the room just above mine; we had a floor and a ceiling in common. From the beginning, Shehnaz and I tried in various ways, in kind and unkind, in rational and irrational ways, to shake off each other; but Oxford is such a lonely place, such a small place, so few its streets and its landmarks, that those who have felt some affection for each other come together again and again. When I went missing (and sometimes I was with Mandira), Shehnaz would wait in Sharma's room for me to return. Coming back, I would hear that Shehnaz had been looking for me; going to her college, I would not find her there. For long periods of our relationship, if one were to add all these moments, we kept ourselves absent or hidden from each other. On one occasion, I remember, I had been out for several hours; she had come twice to my room and gone away. When she came for the third time, I was in Sharma's room, and we saw her from his window, coming down the road. As she rang the doorbell, entered, and then climbed up the stairs, Sharma said, "Quick, hide in the cupboard!"; it was something he himself loved doing, a bad but endearing habit, surprising me by stepping into my closet when I was not there, and then coming out and taking me unawares. Guided by him, without a will of my

own, I was led inside, to stand there among Sharma's shirts and trousers as he opened his door and asked Shehnaz in. Silent, hidden, I watched through the crack between two doors, which gave me a surprisingly wide vision, as Shehnaz, dressed in churidar and kurta, sat on the armchair and asked in a puzzled way, "What, is he out again?" and Sharma replied nonchalantly, "No, no, he is here, he is somewhere here." And yet, I did not, like Sharma, have the courage to emerge.

Chapter Twenty-three

SOHANLAL was born in a kingdom in Rajasthan and, as a boy, he became a court dancer. There were times when he had to perform before the king, when his guru would take him and another boy to dance as Radha and Krishna at the court. When the dance was over, the audience would bow before the two children as if they *were* Radha and Krishna. That world, of gestures and wonder, existing in the wide, silent margins of the land, is gone now. All has been named and brought to consciousness, the colours, the words and their meanings, but Sohanlal is one of those few people who remember the darkness of what was there before, the old language and its life.

When we were alone, Sohanlal would show me the lanes of Brindaban, sitting on the floor with one leg crossed and the other knee raised, his bare feet visible but the rest of his legs covered by the white cotton cloth of his pyjamas, the upper part of his body in a silk kurta which descended and rested calmly upon his lap like a great handkerchief. His arm would be lifted at an angle that inclined towards his head. Brindaban appeared as he moved while singing the words in Avadhi that had been composed by Bindadeen Maharaj. Avadhi, an older version of

Hindi, still spoken in the villages, is such a poetic language
that its most common expressions can bring places and spirits
before the eye, can stir love in the heart. Its discontinuous
grammar and incomplete sentences are a product of the con-
sciousness that existed before there was any difference between
the past and present. When Sohanlal became Radha, his face
would be turned away a little, in shyness and also in hurt at
Krishna's transgressions, one eyebrow raised but the eyes
averted. But when he was Krishna, he was the child Krishna,
his lips smeared with curds and butter, or dancing upon the ser-
pent's head, or swaying very lightly to his own music. Often,
women would seek out his mother to complain of his mischief,
and many times, when he stopped their path as they walked
towards the River Yamuna, they had no choice but to threaten
him and plead with Yasodha. All his excuses and alibis were
known to her, but by the time he returned it had become eve-
ning and her heart was filled with love. The lies he said to her
at that moment she pretended to believe.

When I hear the raag Maand, I think of my guru and his
brother and Sohanlal, for it bears the characteristics, the stamp,
and the life of their region. Their faces, their language, the
colour of their skin, the cotton clothes they wear, are set
and have their meaning against the same landscape. Each raag
was once a folk melody, a regional air sung, with tiny varia-
tions, to different words, by members of a community of fami-
lies before its notes were ordered and systematised into the
melodic progression called a raag. But when a Rajasthani sings
Maand, or a Punjabi sings Sindhi Bhairavi, he returns to his
homeland, which for him is a certain landscape influenced by
seasons, a certain style of dressing and speaking, a web of
interrelationships and festive occasions. Each region has its
own grace-notes, its peculiar turns in singing, and there were
some grace-notes I had to learn and relearn arduously which

Sohanlal told me came naturally and without practice to the people of his land, from temple singers to young peasant boys. Maand was a raag which, when sung by my guru or Sohanlal, revealed its airy, skeletal frame, with holes and gaps in it, its unnameable, magical beginnings, and its spirit-like mobility in covering distances, in traversing scorched mountainsides, deserts, horizons, water, following back on the route of migrations that had led away from that country. The raags, woven together, are a history, a map, a calendar, of northern India, they are territorial and temporal, they live and die with men, even though they seem to be timeless and exist outside them; they are evidence of the palimpsest-like texture of northern India, with its many dyes and hues, its absence of written texts, and its peculiar memory, so that no record of people like Sohanlal, or my guru and guru's father, exists unequivocally, or without rhythm and music.

Each raag has its time of day, a cluster of hours called "prahar," or its season. Goud Sarang and Shudh Sarang are sung at midday, while Madhuvanti in late afternoon verging on twilight, Purvi and Shree from dusk to early evening, and in late evening, Abhogi Kanhra. Midday brings the smell of ripening jackfruit, the buzz and gleam of bluebottle flies, the fragrance of mango blossoms which, Tagore said, opens the doorways to heaven. The notes *sa re ma re ma pa* of Shudh Sarang, with the sharp and yearning ascent of the second *ma*, its resolution in pancham, define the bright inactivity of midday, its ablutions and rest, the peace of a household. Twilight cools the verandah; midday's boundary of protective shade separating household from street, inside from outside, is dissolved, the sad, flat rishab in conjunction with the sharp madhyam and pancham, the notes of Shree related to each other by dancing swoops and curves, calm the mind during the withdrawal of light. No raag is so pure that it does not remind one of another raag, that it is

not, in some elementary way, a variation or version of a raag sung at some other time of day, or some other season. For instance, does not the heat and blaze of Shudh Sarang resemble, in its structure and shape, the watery gravity and plumbings of Megh? The seasons and hours have no absolute existence, but are defined by each other.

Chapter Twenty-four

IN THE last and hottest days of summer, Bombay waited for the rains to arrive. The earth hardened into brown Deccan bedrock, the black rocks by the Arabian Sea were warm if one touched them, people pulled curtains across the windows in the afternoon; it was a time of stupefying heat when reeds and grass grew long and leaned against walls, mango and jackfruit ripened, and flame-red gulmohurs lit the trees. The first drops of rain were a spray that moistened the cloth of one's shirt. This was the time when letters and newspapers arrived partially wet, the wet paper became soft, the parts of the newspaper it had rained upon darkened by a blue-grey shadow. For those who lived in houses like ours and owned a car, it was a season that brought relief; for the maidservants, sweepers, and part-time servants, who too, in a sense, "lived" in Bombay, it was a time of trials and miracles, when one side of their roof collapsed and another side of their house blew away.

In August, in the last quarter of the monsoons, there would be a gathering, in memory of my guru's father's spiritual teacher, in a small temple in old Bombay, a community extravaganza that began early in the evening and continued to the

dawn of the next day, as, one by one, musicians came and performed their piece and received my guru's family's disorganised hospitality and then left, while that family, with its grandfathers, daughters-in-law, and children, stayed wide awake through the night. My mother and I were invited to sing as well, and we took this performance seriously. So we set out in our Ambassador, with the tanpura resting on the front seat, and went down the drizzly roads of North Bombay, past eating-houses, local railway stations, old cinema halls, in search of the Ganesh temple at Matunga, which was our landmark. There, upon asking directions, the car turned into a lane, a shaded avenue of middle-class Marathi civility, where, in the houses, boys did their homework and young girls, their hair tied in a plait, studied harder than the boys and learned natya sangeet from their mothers, and, in the other room, the father-in-law, a widower, waited for dinner, while his son stood on the balcony in a vest and pyjamas. Through this lane we passed till noises were heard and lights were seen. All the family was there, in the courtyard adjoining the small temple, and already there was a singer performing inside, his voice heard and serenely ignored as it came through a loudspeaker. The women—my guru's mother, his wife, Mohan's and Sohanlal's wives—sat together in a small room with no door, to enter which one had to take off one's sandals. Distant cousins, ne'er-do-well uncles in dhotis and turbans, irresponsible brothers-in-law who were fathers to several children, hung around in semi-joyous, semi-disgraced abeyance in the festive crowd, and were always available when an extra cymbal player or tanpura player was needed. Family snobberies, hierarchies, bonds, made themselves felt from the powerful, segregated clan of elderly women to the excited children in shiny clothes. This was my guru's world, a little Rajasthani village in Bombay.

This community would rematerialise in much the same way

at funerals and weddings, and at the airport on the two occasions when my guru went to England. Then the traveller abroad was blessed by the elders, and nearly everyone was given a chance to hug and garland him, from close to seldom-seen relatives who reappeared at such moments to display family love and solidarity. This solidarity, which was a form of dependency, for the poorer relatives used this as an opportunity to ask favours of those who, like my guru, were doing better for themselves, became evident again, in all its formal comedy and transient but sincere show of love, during my guru's illness. I was then in Oxford; my parents were preparing to sell that flat in the suburbs and leave Bombay forever. My mother described it to me later; the clan, enlarged now by concerned relatives who had come down from the villages for this special purpose, rallied around my guru and made every effort to hasten his death. Some of them came and stayed in his tiny flat; for them, it was a pilgrimage to see Bombay. A few years ago, my guru and his brother had sold their "chawl" in King's Circle, and, with government loans, bought two flats, one for each brother, in Versova and Andheri. This, for them, had been like a liberation from an old and stifling way of life. Once, when my mother went to visit my guru in Versova during his illness—a recently developed area, with new buildings and roads alternating with patches of marshy land—she found the creation of a great lunch in progress, the women chopping spinach and boiling milk in the kitchen, the relatives moving about in the tiny space of the "hall," careful not to step on the small shoals of children, the aroma of food spreading through the house, an anecdote being developed and an observation elaborated, while my guru lay on his side on the bed that was next to the front door, his head on the pillow, watching all this. In Bombay, where property is sold at thousands of rupees per square foot, each inch of space is magnified; a hall is called a hall, a bedroom

a bedroom, though none of these rooms may be larger in size than a kitchen. The laughing Rajasthani women wore bright chiffon saris, draped them over their heads, and kept a small part of their faces symbolically covered with the last remnant of a veil. In all that crowded commotion, medicines were given at the wrong time, or forgotten. The fabric of an ancient hospitality, irrelevant courtesies, meaningless gestures of goodwill, all important in the creation of the decorum of that village life—and they owned little else but that decorum—this was eternal, nonindividual, it would go on; and, already, my guru was an outsider to it, he was leaving it behind. After he died, this life, as expected, continued cheerfully, divided from death only by a thin, transparent border; my guru's wife saw him in her dreams; sometimes he reassured her that he was happy "over there"; at other times, he gave her sound financial advice: "Eat chutney and chappati but don't sell the flat." Influential government servants whose daughters or wives had been taught by my guru came forward to help his widow and children; helped her to set up a small, government retail shop that sold milk, peas, and meat. Then my guru stopped appearing in dreams.

Chapter Twenty-five

THE old Calcutta airport, a dignified colonial bungalow with potted plants, is gone, but the "new" domestic airport, now proxying as the international airport, stands and welcomes arriving passengers. Most of the travellers, coming or leaving, belong to Calcutta itself, Bengalis or Marwaris with children running from the bookshop at one end to the coffee-stall at the other. Outside, in the light, a crowd of boys and young men wait perpetually to greet the passengers as they emerge, to take their suitcases, to offer them taxis. You shoo them away; you try to ignore them; and then they have already forgotten you, they have found someone else, or are quarrelling playfully with each other. But one or two of the younger ones will reappear at the car-park and run with the car and see you off for the gift of a coin.

As a child, I used to come here with my parents for my holidays; but this time, returning from England, my parents were waiting for me outside the arrival area, my father and mother standing in the light, while passengers, pursued by those exuberant, sparrow-like local boys, passed before them, negotiat-

ing trolleys. Was it my imagination, or had some of Calcutta's black vapour darkened their complexions a shade? They looked as if they had been exposed to the sun, and seemed smaller as they stood there. But when I asked them, they said it might be because they had woken early in the morning; and here they were to receive me.

The drive homeward goes past a village scene, with huts, plantains, lakes, and malnourished but energetic children. Then, without hiatus, the city begins with a great drum-roll of traffic, and one is in the midst of a marketplace of houses, tailors' and butchers' shops, billboards, and tramlines, bargaining for movement, haggling to go forward. Nothing has changed for the last twenty years. The Bengalis are like Irish families, except that they are small in height and the men have no access to drink, but the city is a mixture of officiousness and circumlocution that makes one despair. The air is awash with Marx and Trotsky; the airport, to which no international flight but Aeroflot and the Bangladesh Biman has been coming for years, is no gateway to fresh influences from abroad, but an interesting, if puzzling, building: and in Calcutta, nothing has happened after Marxism and modernism. In tea-shops and street corners, Bengali men, as ever, indulge in *adda*, a word that means both a pointless, pleasurable exchange of opinions and information, and the place or rendezvous in which it is conducted; if it were possible to say, for instance, of a certain kind of languorous conversation in England, "I'm having a pub," its quality might be approximately communicated in English.

And on the roads, one's neighbours are still Ambassadors, created by the Birlas from odds and ends—the body of a Morris Oxford and a tractor's engine—outnumbering by far any other car. Ours still has its old Bombay numberplate. On the Ambassador one finds perhaps the only doors that have to

be slammed shut, with the maximum of force, without any intention of venting ill temper, but as a perennial good-humoured habit as one gets in and gets out. Families that own them have had them for twenty years, half the duration of independence, in which time they have been repaired, repainted, sent to garages, reupholstered, and, when the owner is in straitened circumstances, left exposed to the elements. Every few years, the Birlas produce a new model at their factory, Mark III, Mark IV, which exactly replicates the previous one; for the Ambassador has remained faithful to the ideal that was perfected in the secure, organic era of the "protected market," and, in its shape, still retains that philosophical look, that aura of being cut off from the "real" world: squat, conservative, and spacious.

Cruising downtown in it, one risks the bother of paying tax to the Municipal Corporation if one parks it. The tax is collected by men who, sweating from running from car to car in the sun, slip a ticket under the wiper when you are away, and reappear punctually to collect the fee when you are back. Loafers and layabouts as described in the stories of Parashuram and Bibhutibhusan Bandhopadhaya, often charging you without giving you a ticket, they have taken up this job as human parking metres because they haven't found any other. The trouble they cause is brief, like a mosquito's sting, and subsides when one drives away.

When I arrived here in the summer, it was from an Oxford that had just gone through its annual dress-rehearsal and theatre of the exams. That was when Shehnaz finally put to use the notes she had made diligently over two years, when, after retching at her basin from nervousness, she would wear her black gown and set out early mornings through narrow cobbled lanes towards the Examination Schools, followed, and led, by other characters similarly dressed, some stepping out of the

perfectly ordinary houses along the sides of the road. It was at this time that I began to realise that we were here in Oxford less as individuals than as students, attempting, in a touchingly innocent way, to complete a course and obtain a degree that would not only please us, but our parents, whoever and wherever they were. We were children sent here who, for a period of time till the exams began, behaved and felt like adults. Once the exams were finished the childhood was over, the childhood of which even Shehnaz, Mandira, and I—the affection we felt for each other at our intersection of each other's life, and the loneliness of being in Oxford—were part.

A student fills the closet and shelves in his room with provisions that seem numerous when they are visible, but actually can be stuffed into one, at the most two, suitcases. The student takes the coach to Heathrow; leaves by air; his books are packed in a crate and shipped after him, to travel out of the country upon the old sea-routes. The student's departure is deceptively fast, while his books' is slower, more weighted and material, and will reach his country only three months later. A few things are left behind in boxes in the college storeroom, or with friends, as if there were hope of returning in the future.

That summer in Calcutta, I sat and wrote a letter to America, to Shehnaz, and never posted it. Petty details and grievances, and a contradictory feeling of closeness, came to me as I was writing the letter. I took it with me to the General Post Office, a huge building on whose steps, all day, people ascend and descend dramatically, like the diminutive, busy men in the first black-and-white films. Inside, the Bengali male, dark, not more than five feet and five inches tall, hair carefully parted at the side, can be seen among pots of glue, or queueing up at one of the many windows where an employee sits portioning stamps, or having his letters weighed at a counter, and stamped with an archaic object that looks like a pestle. By

evening, however, there is hardly anyone left, and the main room looks large and peaceful in the glow of fluorescent lights; a few employees working overtime sit behind counters, looking as porters on a provincial railway station do after a train has left, the sense of departure, of a world beyond this one, having disappeared into the ordinariness of another evening and night. I had my letter weighed and stamped, and then decided not to send it. The thin, bespectacled clerk, in whose frail hand the ancient stamp looked so heavy and powerful, said irritably, "You mean you want it back?" He explained to me the rules governing such procedures; he became, temporarily, the voice of the General Post Office; but I only saw before me a middle-aged Bengali whom, I felt vaguely, I already knew from a previous encounter. The more he sensed my frustration, the more he protracted his lecture on a higher logic that transcended personal ideas of reasonableness; and when he handed me the letter, he had me take it out of the envelope, which he tore thoroughly with his own hands.

Chapter Twenty-six

THE two of them have been sleeping on the single bed, he against the wall, and she, lying on her back, next to him. Once, unable to bear her cramped position anymore, she slipped off the bed onto the ground, her pillow with her. That was early in the morning. Now it is light. She gets up before him; she rummages among the shelves. She finds a jar of biscuits, and begins to eat them. When she peers through a crack in the curtains, she sees a hedge, and, barely visible above it, pinnacles and rooftops, the dreaming spires. Soon, outside the window, because it is summer, there will be visitors, a goose and a gander, one with pale brown feathers and the other with dark, translucent colours. Like the first tourists to discover a town, they explore the lawn together, though each, doggedly, keeps its distance from the other, maintaining a tangential, somewhat covert, relationship with the other's self-absorption, like the English couple, Henry and his wife, who are always separated by a few paces during their humdrum walks in *Monsieur Hulot's Holiday*. The days belong to these two, with their fussy, academic interests; they do not seem to be in the first flush of love, but in a period of retirement, discovering earthly wonders; and when a

window is half opened, they quack acknowledgingly, rather than gratefully, at the thrower of crumbs, but never trouble themselves to look straight at a human face.

She wears her fluffy slippers, quietly opens the door, and goes to the bathroom so as not to disturb him; she solemnly washes her face, brushes her teeth, and combs her hair for almost a minute with her head bent sideways, as if thinking or remembering. Outside, she can hear other students making their first disconnected movements, the tentative noises, like those of a musical instrument being tuned, gradually accumulating and amplifying into a larger significance. She had never thought that she would give so much of herself to that boy still sleeping inside. He makes her angry, now that she loves his college and friends more than her own, and her heart is heavy with the distance she will have to travel. They were friends at first, they took walks, and then he wanted something more—and had she, too, wanted it?—and she found it more and more difficult to say no, to make him unhappy. And when he was unhappy . . . She makes herself a cup of coffee, and takes it back to the room. She will have to go now, she says, but she will be back in the afternoon to help him pack. I'll go and start my own packing now, she says. She wears her trousers and shirt, which are lying on the chair in the shadow, and picks up her things.

Stepping outside, into the clear June day, she inhales the air and hugs herself, and, with quick steps, crosses the road confidently, missing two oncoming cars on either side. She feels relieved, as if Oxford were new to her, as if nothing had happened, and she had not known him, or any of the other people. It takes two years of rainy days, of human contact, to feel this moment of freshness. This is what it should have been like in the beginning, not the newcomer's worries and desires, lived from moment to moment, the reckless craving for companion-

ship and communication. She smiles and nods at the working men in overalls and the scouts coming in; she is happiest acknowledging people she has come to know by sight. She begins to run towards her own college, as the path curves, and students like herself come out in twos and threes from the gate, quite blind to her, and others go past singly and swiftly on bicycles. She is still running down that path lined with bicycles, where flowers have blossomed on the hedges, and the canal flows on the other side. A group of American academics wearing suits, who are here to attend a conference, emerge, unled, in an excited, bustling train from the doorway like school-children who have lost sight of their teacher. She is coming back to her college in the morning, with its comforting hive-like rooms with large windows, in which students have woken up and parted their curtains, and their study-table, books, and table lamp are visible. She must say goodbye to her scout before she forgets, and to the boy who sits in at the porter's lodge in the evening, who used to once bravely dye his hair different colours; she must give them her address. Then, if she has time, she will walk down to the Bodleian to see if that book she had ordered before her exams has arrived; she still feels tempted, as if it were the treasured vestige of a discarded habit, to take a look at it. Will that leave her enough time to meet her tutor in North Oxford before lunch—that man whose ordinary, trust-worthy name appears beneath the complicated and obscure titles of certain books she will put into her bag tonight, who used to write god-like but compassionate notes in an awesome hieroglyphic on the margins of her essays—and then come back in time to help him with his packing for the summer? The thought wearies her. The thought of parting, of never meeting again, of having to repeat to each other that they will see each other in December, of knowing that he will start again; Oxford wearies her. Just to study here, and go to the library, and walk

up the stairs and come down again to have a sandwich at lunchtime; she could do that forever. But it is never as simple as that. If she could choose, what would she choose? She is going back home to her parents and her wonderful, wisecracking sister, she will never mention it to them, and then she will get married. If she is married, she would like to have a baby in a year; it is something she has thought of, in a vague but intense way, for a long time. She will begin another life.

Chapter Twenty-seven

THE first day I arrived in Oxford, it was raining, the fine, persistent, baby-like drizzle in which no one gets wet. Propelled and navigated by my suitcases, I found myself before a window in a centuries-old building which was now run, in a mood of chicanery and make-believe, as a fully operational shelter for scores of bright-spirited graduates in sweaters and jeans. I travelled then to my room in the modern annexe across the road, but returned each day, for food and letters, to that fairy-tale site, with its series of rooftops like witches' hats, which would disappear in a mist in January, its irregular flagstones outside the steps that had iron rings like knockers upon them (as if they opened onto secret underground entrances), and its mysterious employees who had ranks that set them apart as members of an ancient English sect—"porter," "steward," "scout." On my second day, I got a glimpse of Sharma in the dining room in the basement, dressed up like a provincial colonial, walking stiffly in a black suit I was never to see later, wearing it with that exact degree of painfulness that people do in the sweltering tropics, managing to look hot in it even in a cold country. His hair still possessed that neat and combed look

imparted to it by an Indian barber, and he wore black-framed spectacles and a pencil-thin moustache, all of which constituted the cargo of his former life that he would lose accidentally, at one stroke, in a matter of weeks. But at that time, with a stern expression on his face, he resembled, with complete accuracy, the discomfited man facing the camera in his old passport photograph.

That was my second day. Even then, Shehnaz and Mandira were waiting to happen to me, for the rain and lack of sunlight had already entered me, from which I would create, inevitably, wisps of fantasy and desire that would later become flesh and bones and blood capable of breaking the heart, becoming one's own, and then, after a year, again changing into rain and grey light.

That year, I bought myself an Olympia typewriter, and tapped out, with one determined finger, essays and poems upon it. Word processors and computers were then just coming into use, but I had no patience with the idea of leaving my room and crossing the road to the other building in order to familiarise myself with this new medium. I pretended to ignore it, and with one finger leaping blindly and instinctively from one key to the other, I laboriously but contentedly typed out my first essay on the Olympia. It was a unique object, with its arms fanning out and starting up individually when one touched a letter, a strange balance of mechanical harmony and obedience, an object that in the old days men used to call a "machine," and feel unspeakably different from, a difference that produced both hostility and then later kinship. The computer is not a machine, but an equal in the marketplace, and one enters into no relationship with it, but surrenders to its strategic uses; but, in those days, I had not realised how indispensable it would become, and how its soft monochromatic hum would replace the hellish, Blakean, loud industrial noise of the typewriter.

Sharma, adept as he was at picking up new lifestyles and languages, embraced with generous openness, and without delay, both WordStar and WordPerfect. With everything that was then new to him—except with meat, for he was an avowed vegetarian—he became friendly: computer-friendly, party-friendly, library-friendly, supermarket-friendly. He was kitchen-friendly as well, and spent a good amount of time making food that emitted an aroma of spices that magnified the sense of what it meant to live in England. Demerara sugar, orange juice, nuts, a spiced lentil mixture he had bought at an Indian shop, and long-life milk were all assigned their places on the bookshelves and the window-sill in his room. "Please have some nuts," he would say in English; or, in colloquial Hindi, offer me the lentils, scooping up a handful himself and tossing them mouthward. He used to be, then, in a state of constant excitement. When he was in a mood, or under pressure with work, his mind would always be flitting elsewhere, making his movements restless and his manner infuriatingly polite; one could see that he wasn't listening. But when he was at ease, he would be motherly and genuinely caring, and exude a strength that was strange in one who was so much more a foreigner to this land than I was. The matter-of-fact but buoyant way he began to cook the evening meal, the confidence with which he expressed himself in English, dropping articles and subverting grammar, made me think that my own sense of foreignness, of loneliness, was a luxury and an invention.

In those days, I could hardly experience England without being obtruded by what I had read about it in its literature and history. And even my compulsive nostalgia for home was half imaginary. For Sharma, perception was a different thing; he discovered England afresh, and on him its impact was more direct, more immediately generous, than it was on me; and yet, outwardly, he remained untouched. He had read Wordsworth

and Shakespeare in India in Hindi translation; he loved
Macbeth, especially the scene in which Birnam Wood moves for-
ward; he was not shy of picking up English customs or making
English friends; and if he yearned for home, he did not men-
tion it. Yet he did not exchange his persona for a new one, as
many city-educated Indians do in England; he remained still
and deep. The choices that existed in my world—between
clinging to my Indianness, or letting it go, between being nos-
talgic or looking toward the future—did not exist in his. He
was from a village in North India, and it was miraculous that he
should be here in Oxford among other Indians of a different
class, and it was the miracle of being in Oxford, of knowing
Shehnaz, Mandira, of future meetings, incarnations, new faces,
that I would become aware of when I was with him.

His room used to blaze with pictures of gods and goddesses.
Each student inhabits at the beginning of the year a room with
blank walls and empty shelves, and then makes of it what he
will. Sharma stuck calendar pictures on the wall, in red, blue,
orange, Kali biting her tongue, Parvati riding a tiger. They
reminded me of roadside kitchens, of the backs of lorries, and
the small radiant picture before the bus driver's seat. With their
octopodal limbs, Kali's face faintly reminiscent of Hema Mali-
ni's, they were such good companions of the common man at
home. Although they would have had no place in a middle-
class house in Bombay, here in England, in Sharma's room,
they existed for a while comfortingly and unironically.

By our second year, books occupied every inch of available
space in the room. Sharma wished to understand the European
mind, and nowhere so clearly and accessibly was Western cul-
ture contained as in books, and it was these books—Hawking's
A Brief History of Time, *The Norton Anthology of English Lit-
erature*, Collins's thesaurus, *One Hundred Years of Solitude*—

that were placed on Sharma's bookshelf. Many of them he did not read; but even buying a book at Blackwell's was a discovery; in one book was contained science; in another, meaning and pronunciation; in another, literature. Even novels, he found, had a peculiar wisdom to impart that he was not wholly unfamiliar with, having read the ancient Hindu epics; although as a child, studious and earnest, he had never read storybooks for being too trivial.

When, after midnight, we would settle down to a conversation, it would continue to the small hours of the morning, as, gradually, the graduate building became still around us, and Sharma told me of his childhood. His village was like a fiction; it had no electricity; it was not to be found on the map of India. He confessed this with a mixture of deprecation and pride. Such was the intensity of the dark in that village that when the landlords lit their petromax lamps a mile away the shadow of that light fell on the earthen walls of Sharma's house. His mother, whose photograph now hung in his room, was a frail woman of puritan fervour and great vision; his father was an idle, fun-loving dandy who liked nothing more than a gossip with the other men of the village. These two, for the most part, treated each other like distant relatives and led their own lives. Sharma and his older brother grew up in their mother's wings in a village which, with its vain and ignorant landlords, its huddled families, its canals, fields, and thunderstorms, was a little universe. Sharma travelled outward first by foot, to a school in a neighbouring town; then, years later, on a train, he arrived at the big city; and finally, by another train, he went to Delhi. During our conversations, I grew familiar with the shadowy, marginal figures—well-wishers, relatives, friends, villains, and oppressors—who all, without knowing it, became impartial coordinates in his determined but steady

progress outward, away from them. As he spoke, I would smell chick-peas being roasted in their shells; I would wake up one morning to find the ceiling in an uncle's room had collapsed around him, barely disturbing his sleep; I would be full of revolutionary rhetoric when officials rigged the local elections; I would dress as Hanuman the monkey on a festival; I would travel sitting on the floor of a third-class train compartment to Lucknow; I would hear the roar of motorcycles and taste dust as the landlord's sons arrived at the earthen house. When Sharma spoke, reality and fancy, my past and his, became reordered in new proportions.

He was a sensitive person. A memory, a poem, or a song could move him so much that sometimes a tear, large and sticky, would roll out from a corner of his eye when he was recounting it to me. He would either wipe it away with a quick, self-conscious movement, or dab his eye patiently with his handkerchief. There were occasions when I would say something that would offend him, and we would not speak to each other for hours, or even the whole day.

One evening, he came down to my room in his shorts, with a cup of coffee in his hand. This was not unusual; it meant that we were going to be engaged in a conversation which would take us to the realms of autobiography, or throw us into an abstract discussion on religion, or make us pause over the nuances of literary experience. His face was grave, like one who has something important to communicate—perhaps a piece of bad news. "I am very happy," he said solemnly, "that you are studying Lawrence." I gave this remark its due weight. "Last night, in my room, I read 'Snake.' It is beautiful," he said. "Then I read 'Ship of Death.' It's *great* poem, it is very rich. But I cannot decide between the two."

Taking out, without further digression, my copy of the

Complete Poems, he read out loud and clear, as if he were singing:

> *Have you built your ship of death, O have you?*
> *O build your ship of death, for you will need it.*

Coming next to me, he pointed out these lines, asking me, quite seriously, if I had read them:

> *A little ship, with oars and food*
> *and little dishes, and all accoutrements*
> *fitting and ready for the departing soul . . .*

"Of course you must have," he conceded apologetically. "I believe you must have read every word by Lawrence."

Each time these lines bring to me the idea of a seascape, and sometimes other conflicting pictures, like the memory of daal and sweet potatoes being ground and mashed all day in the kitchen, then patted, shaped, and fried into pithhas, and left overnight in syrup; my mother choosing the brownest one for me, and the little less perfect one for my father.

Freedom Song

✳

FREEDOM SONG, set in Calcutta in 1993, is
about the city and two families who live there.
The first consists of a couple, Khuku and her
husband Shib; their son has been living for a
few years in America. Khuku's old friend
Mini is visiting them while she recuperates
from arthritis. Khuku and Mini spend their
time talking about family, friends, health
and, occasionally, Muslims and the Babri
Masjid. Not far away, in Ishwar Chandra
Vidyasagar Road, lives the second family:
Khuku's brother Bhola, his wife, their son
Bhaskar and daughter Piyu; a second son,
Manik, has gone to live in Germany. Bhas-
kar, much to the consternation of the family,
has recently joined the Indian Communist
Party, disappears to sell the party newspaper
GANASHAKTI (People's Power) and has
become active in street-theatre.

IT WAS a solitary voice, saying *Allah-hu-akbar* and other familiar but incomprehensible syllables. Though it was coming from quite far away, for the nearest mosque was a mile north-ward, she could hear it clearly, as if it were being recited in this very lane, and its presence filled the grey area between her sleep and waking. The singer, if one could call him such, seemed absolutely absorbed, wherever he was, in the unearthly lift of the melody, in his indecision between repetition and pro-gression, and in the delicate business of now prolonging and now shortening a syllable. The city was still—the trams, the trees whose leaves were covered with a film of dust, the junc-tions, Lower Circular and Lansdowne Roads, the three-storey houses on Southern Avenue, the ten-story buildings on Ballygunge Circular Road. Soon that machinery would start working again, not out of any sense of purpose, but like a watch that is wound daily by someone's hand. Almost without any choice in the matter, people would embark upon the minute frustrations and satisfactions of their lives. It was in this moment of postponement that the azaan was heard, neither announcing the day nor keeping it a secret.

She got up, as she had been getting up for fifty years, ever

since she was fifteen years old, and became serious about her singing, going out into the drawing room in the house in Shillong to practise, so as not to wake up her sleeping brothers or suffer their cheerful mockery. The morning today was almost as cold as the mornings in Shillong used to be; she was slower now, her hips wider, as those of a woman who has borne children are said to be, and, at this moment, a little unsteady on her feet. Solemnly, she put a shawl around herself and disappeared into the darkness of the bathroom, as if she had a rendezvous there, and, ten minutes later, emerged again. Her husband was asleep, his outlines barely distinguishable from the quilt. Her own quilt had become a bunched-up, higgledy-piggledy mess, and seemed to have a small child hiding underneath it.

When she came out of her room, she found the door to the guest room open. The curtains had been parted, and the single bed already made. As she was looking around, the knob on the bathroom door turned and Mini came out, her spectacles misted, patches of wet on her blouse and petticoat. She had always been a clumsy girl. The bathroom, whose window faced east, was flooded with light.

"What, Khuku!" she said with great surprise. "You're up already?" Then, a note of both respect and affection entering her voice, she said, half to herself, "Shib must be asleep."

"I was woken by the azaan," complained Khuku. "And, believe me, Mini, I had no sleep last night, I began to think about Bablu and I lay wide awake with my head feeling hot."

"Really!" said Mini, feeling outraged on her behalf, and seeming to speak of a group of absolutely tiresome school-children (for she *was* a schoolteacher), "They are going too far! And," she said, "it isn't really Indian, it sounds like Bedouins." With a look of satisfaction on having said this, she began to comb her hair, which was wavy, not very long, and still all

black. Then, hobbling towards the dressing-table, she stood opposite her reflection, exactly as dark and stocky as herself, and began to sort out, with both hands, the folds of a white sari with a green border, tucking it first into the petticoat that had been tied not only above stomach level, but almost approaching the chest; chin lowered, she drew the layers of the sari around herself till she was almost completely ensconced in it. "Bas!" she said when it was done. "Now we can go outside." But Khuku had already slipped out silently to the hall and was telling Nando to get up.

"Get up, you lazy man!" she commanded him. "Give us tea!"

Nando went on sleeping. She went around the hall aimlessly, like an insect exploring a window-pane, and then entered the room her son stayed in when he came back from America; the beds were perfectly made, all his books were standing on the shelves, and in the cupboards lay piled his old comic books and Tintins, and a pair of sandals. She pulled back the curtains which were drawn at night for no particular reason by Jochna before she went home. Meanwhile, Mini had settled into an armchair in the hall, and was already studying a very funny book by Bonophul, peering hard at the print through her glasses. As if out of some vestigial survival of embarrassment, Nando rose from the carpet, dragging his blanket behind him, a dark four-foot-ten-inch demon, and walked dolefully towards the kitchen.

Khuku sat down on the armchair next to Mini, who closed her book and looked up.

"How are you feeling, Mini?" asked Khuku. "Did you sleep well last night?"

"I'm much better already," she said. "Your house is so beautiful and comfortable that I have no choice but to feel better!" She laughed as she always did, her dark brown lips

parting to reveal her uneven white teeth, her head and shoulders and chest shaking together. Then, almost immediately, the sides of her eyes crinkled shyly, because she was one of those who had grown up in an age when it was believed that to laugh too hard was not proper for a woman. "In fact," she said, "the moment I'm better I'll be going back. There will be a lot of schoolwork this term."

"Quiet!" said Khuku. "I can't ask you something without you talking about going back! Will you let yourself rest for a while?"

"There is Shantidi," murmured Mini.

"Shantidi is capable of taking care of herself!" said Khuku. "She travels from one end of the city to the other!"

"She might get into a bad mood . . ." said Mini softly, staring at the carpet.

"Shantidi," said Khuku gently, "is very anxious that you get better. She'll be unhappy if you go back before you are perfectly all right."

Mini began to laugh again, this time pursing her lips and nodding her head slowly backward and forward. It was not clear why—probably at Khuku's childish insistence, or probably because she could not picture Shantidi unhappy; a little bad tempered, yes, if she could not find her sandesh mould or a hairpin. Only five days ago, when Khuku had arrived in her Ambassador to pick up Mini from where she and her older sister lived in North Calcutta, in the New Municipal Corporation Building, which was, in fact, twenty-five years old, Shantidi had been away at an acquaintance's funeral. Three years ago, recovering from hepatitis, she had gone about, somewhat tardily, with a torch and a walking-stick. Now she did not fear even trams and buses, and pushed her way inside and pushed her way outside. When Khuku was helping Mini down the dark stairs towards her car, Shantidi, after expressing her grief to a

relative, and saying with all conviction what a wonderful person was the departed, a simple and pure-hearted woman who had never harmed anyone, was eating jilepi and shingara from a paper plate, and talking about her favourite subject, politics. The caterers, in another room, were heating food in drums over open fires, and stirring the hot and bubbling mass with long black khuntis. The dead one had led a long and peaceful life, and how wonderful it was, thought Shantidi to herself, that her daughter's eyes, who was smilingly welcoming guests, followed everywhere by her small inquisitive son, should still be a little red with weeping.

Now, at six in the morning, in a house on Ishwar Chandra Vidyasagar Road, a very dark twenty-eight-year-old man was hiding, terrified, beneath his blankets. What he was terrified of was not clear, but he had slipped under the blanket as far as he could, and only his frowning eyes, his forehead, and his hair, the shorter ones of which stuck out like rays and stings in every direction, were visible. Almost everyone was awake, moving in that dreary somnolent state from wash-basin to toilet to wash-basin, except the young man. His father—Khuku's brother—who, wearing a pullover and tennis shoes, had just returned from a walk by the lake, was now climbing the stairs, singing, and hesitating between one step and the next to repeat a particular note till he rendered it as he desired. With a grunt of finality, Bhaskar threw off, in a storm, the blanket and sat upright. Then, as if he were some kind of newborn animal, he propelled himself on his bottom to the edge of the bed, his legs sticking out before him like two huge talons. "Haridasi," he shouted. "Bring tea!" Is that Bhaskar? thought his mother, downstairs. Though fourteen years had passed since his voice had changed to a man's voice, a tenth of a moment always elapsed before his mother adjusted herself to her son's grown-upness. Without a word, standing by the edge of the bed,

Bhaskar began to do a quick, abbreviated version of his exercises, recommended to him by a physiotherapist for his backache, breathing in quickly, bending hurriedly to clutch his knees, as if they were about to desert him, and then expiring in relief. Piyu, his sister, supporting her weight on one leg, was brushing her teeth furiously and rhythmically, and observing him closely; she had been standing there and brushing for a full minute, till her teeth had been lost for the Colgate foam forming at her mouth.

"Dash oh do yoo ayi goo," she said.

"What?" said Bhaskar, looking sideways from his ostrich posture, his head hanging between his knees.

She went to the wash-basin and spat, and then rinsed her mouth thoroughly, blowing her left cheek first and then her right. Returning, she repeated:

"That won't do you any good."

"You mind your own business," said Bhaskar, and bent down again.

She went away, hurt. And when his conscience was satisfied, Bhaskar rushed to the alna and began to look for his jeans among the silently hanging clothes. "Where is it, where is it?" but the clothes would give no answer. Then he found them and wore them hurriedly, clamping his lower lip with his teeth as he strove to push a button through a button-hole, but zipping the fly effortlessly. He slipped off his crumpled kurta and put on a pink one. A children's song was coming from the radio in the next house: "Sajalpurer kaajal meye naite nemechhe," sung in a ringing, girlish voice. From the walls above, the faces of his mother's parents gazed at him, she with the sari's aanchal draped about her head and smiling slightly, he serious and patriarchal in a white kurta, his skin even darker than Bhaskar's. Morning came to the house through the windows at the back of the second storey, via a school in a field and a doctor's house;

when a shutter was opened, the light found its way straight to one's eye. By this time mynahs, shaliks, sparrows, crows, had begun to echo on parapets and window-sills, and a cat had woken up and fallen asleep again.

The doorbell rang, and Bhaskar's mother wiped her brow with her sari and proceeded towards the verandah. Looking past the branches of the shajana tree, she saw Mohit between their gaps, no longer wearing shorts, but trousers, standing with his bicycle on the pavement. Four days ago he had completed his end-of-term exams, for which he used to study alone early in the mornings. Today, he had woken up at five as usual, had a bath, wished his mother goodbye, and come cycling to Vidyasagar Road.

"Ei, Mohit! What do you want?"

"What do you mean, what do I want?"

"You want to come in?"

Mohit stood with one hand on the bicycle. The road was misty behind him.

"Yes, I want to come in," he said sternly.

"Wait there," said his great-aunt, and wandered inside, smiling. "Haridasi!" she called.

"Yes Ma," came the small, childish voice from the kitchen.

"Open the door outside for Mohit."

A minute later, coming up the stairs, Mohit found Piyu standing on the first-floor landing.

"How was the ride?" she asked. After Mohit had grown an inch last year he was as tall as her and could look her in the eye.

"Fantastic! I came through the lake."

His great-aunt began to follow him around like a mendicant.

"Will you have luchi, Mohit?" she asked.

"No," he said.

"Omelette?"

"No."

"Pithha? Have a pithha. I made them yesterday."

"No," said Mohit firmly, as if he were used to warding off such requests. "In fact, I just had something before I came here." His hair was still gleaming from the bath he had had half an hour ago.

"What did you have?"

"Oof! What a question," said Mohit, looking ashamed. "Milk and toast and roshogolla," he admitted with a mixture of bravado and embarrassment.

"Would you like a cup of tea?" asked Piyu.

Mohit hesitated; for it was a sign of adulthood to drink tea, and he was tempted, in his great-uncle's house, to partake of a pleasure denied him by his mother.

"All right!" he said impatiently, not looking at anyone in particular. "All right, I'll have tea!"

When Bhaskar came into the dining-room in his jeans and pink kurta, tea was still brewing in the pan. Mohit was discussing irrelevancies with his great-aunt and Piyu, his elbows resting on the table, his legs locked around one of the legs of the dining-table. So secure did he look that it seemed no buffeting of fate could move him from his place. Pigeons, in a mire of feathers and excrement, had begun to make crowded noises in a dark foot-wide corridor by the water tank of the next house, which was perpetually visible from the window next to Mohit. But Bhaskar first entered the kitchen and said resentfully:

"Half an hour and you still haven't made it! Dhur—now I don't want it."

Poor eleven-year-old Haridasi, she took everything literally; her mouth curved downward. She stood on tiptoe and strained to gaze at the pan.

"What could I do?" she said softly. "I had to open the door

for Mohitda." She said, "Don't go, Bhaskarda, it'll be ready in a minute." The smell of tea, strong and bittersweet and a little rancid, like sweat, had begun to waft through the kitchen.

But Bhaskar had, without pause, already walked out of the dining-room, saying, "I'll be back in an hour." Piyu, still hurt from his retort ten minutes ago, decided she had not heard this. "What about your tea?" called out his mother. When he did not answer she said to the table, "Let him do what he likes." Piyu lifted herself from this scene as if it did not matter. Then Mohit disrupted the small dining-table community further by getting up and shouting, "Bhaskarmama, wait for me, I'm coming." "Ei, where are *you* going?" asked Piyu in astonishment. Deserting them, he revealed, "With Bhaskarmama!" Bhaskar's father had emerged absentmindedly from the toilet and was washing his hands with a piece of Lifebuoy soap. "Where are you going?" he asked. Running down the stairs, Mohit said, "With Bhaskarmama!"

WHEN Mohit caught up with him on the pavement, he said: "Bhaskarmama, I'm coming too."

Bhaskar put an arm around the boy, who was a little out of breath, and said, "Then come; I don't mind." Two pigeons, making rapid pistol-like sounds with their wings, took off over their heads.

Now, at half-past six, two state transport buses went down Ishwar Chandra Vidyasagar Road, blowing their loud hooting horns; they were half empty, an unusual sight. There was a small encampment of rickshaws along part of the pavement, their extended arms planted on the ground, their collapsible roofs raised, their wheels at rest; rickshawallas, heads and shoulders covered with a piece of cloth, were slapping their hands in imitation of applause and hurling tobacco into their

mouths. Retired men, as free as children, all of them dressed for some reason in white dhuti and kurta, were either creeping out of their houses or returning from a walk, with or without a walking-stick. The first to go about their business were the crows, clamorous, a little neurotic, turning up, as usual, by the tea-shop entrance (if one could call that absence in the wall an entrance), by the lane's rubbish dump, on the pavement, upon the roofs. Fog, a compound of charcoal smoke, exhaust fumes, and mist, hung in the lanes; you did not notice it at close quarters, but, a little distance away, you saw it loitering by balconies and doorways. The colours of the houses on Vidyasagar Road, pink, or moss green, or light yellow or blue, were dimmed by the mist, till they looked like the colour of old cotton saris that have been worn for many years and still not thrown away.

They came to a house. An old man was sitting on the balcony of the first floor upon a wicker stool and eating from a bowl. A woman in a cardigan leaned over the banister and looked over her shoulder and cried, "Hurry up, Mira, do you want to miss your bus?" The old man dipped his spoon into the bowl and said, "Don't scold her, Ma, she's a little slow." The mother said, "Mira—Mira? I can see the bus coming now," although the lane was still empty. The door to the room on the ground floor was open, separated from the courtyard by a porch which was a little stage that accommodated a coir mat and two or three pairs of rubber slippers. There was a message on the wall outside: C.P.I.(M.) FOR UNITY AND HARMONY AMONG ALL COMMUNITIES. A man, wearing pyjamas, a shirt, and a sleeveless pullover, came to the door and said: "You're late." "Give it to me, don't waste time," said Bhaskar. As they were waiting, Bhaskar lit a cigarette, and Mohit, still a little awed and shocked by this act, began to pace up and down the porch, stopping only to inspect a fern that had grown on one side. A small girl had arrived at the pavement in uniform, a blue skirt, white

shirt, and blue pullover, accompanied by a servant girl who would herself have been no more than ten years old. She was swinging her plastic water bottle upon its infinitely co-operative strap and standing a little way from the servant girl and talking to herself. Occasionally, she looked up at where her mother and possibly her grandfather were standing, ignoring the rest of the world, as if her imminent farewell were meant only for them. The man in the sleeveless pullover emerged with a pile of *Ganashakti* and transferred it from his arms to Bhaskar's. "Did you sleep well last night?" he said sourly. Bhaskar ground the cigarette underfoot and kicked it into the courtyard among the mournful plants and ash-grey earth. "I'll see you later," he replied. He walked out of the gate, followed hotly by Mohit.

Each newspaper was folded and tied with a jute string. "You take half," said Bhaskar. "Here." "What are you going to do with them?" asked Mohit, cradling them and laughing. "Distribute some," revealed Bhaskar very seriously, "and sell the others later." Bundled up, they were slim and surprisingly hard, and each paper could be held in the fist like a baton. They began to walk back the way they had come, to an increasing accompaniment of noise from motorcycles and cars. As they passed the houses, Bhaskar aimed his paper at one or two of the porches, where it fell on the floor with a sharp sound, or sent it flying at a first-storey balcony, a swift journey in the course of which the paper arched in midair and finally landed just beyond the flower-pots. There was a special purpose in these throws, for the readers of *Ganashakti* were fellow-travellers of the Communist Party, they believed in its necessity and its vision, and an inexplicable bond was formed between the distributor, whose every aim with the bundle seemed to be a salute, and the silent house. Mohit glanced back to see if the houses in which the readers of *Ganashakti* lived were any different from the

others, but they were the same, with the fronts of balconies and doors painted in white or green, and other parts chipping away to reveal a structure of stone and iron that was as intricate and fragile as a honeycomb. The two went on until Bhaskar had completed the round and they had come to the end of Vidyasagar Road. By now Bhaskar had acquired a small limp; Mohit said: "You're growing old, Bhaskarmama. The party must be in a bad way if they're taking members like you." "What do you think I should do?" "I think you should do yoga," said Mohit. "Buy a book and learn the asanas. Or you won't be selling newspapers for long." "I want to have some tea," said Bhaskar.

AFTERNOON saw Khuku and Mini fall asleep on the double bed, Mini on the side on which Shib slept at night. These days the fan was not switched on, and the women hugged their own bodies, a light shawl lying casually upon their feet, taking on their tender, ghostly shape, while now and then Khuku complained of the cold and shivered. She had had all the windows closed except one, which let in a smell of smoke that must have drifted, unmoored, from a distance. Because the room, without the hum and movement of the fan, was so still, the world outside seemed proportionately larger, with more space having come into existence to accommodate the different afternoon noises, of bird call and bird chatter, and vendors, hammering, and taxis. Somewhere below, cars arrived, people got out, doors were slammed one by one, or almost together: not everyone was asleep. Next to Khuku, Mini, very softly, was snoring, and on another floor, someone coughed, the little angry explosions seeming to go off just outside the window. Khuku clasped her throat with her hand and warmed it. How pleasing that sensation was, warmth, so rarely known for most of the year! Khuku began to fall asleep.

Outside, Jochna, sitting on the verandah at the end of the

hall, combed her loose wet hair and considered the city. Uma, leaning over the banister and looking unconsciously upon the tiny heads of the watchmen far below, hung clothes to dry from different-coloured plastic clips. In a slow, imperceptible way, the city swam around her, the temple with its pseudo-classical shape that was being "completed" for fifteen years, which they thought of simply as "the temple," the vacant white perfect terraces of decaying ancestral mansions, surrounded by the enigmatic tops of masses of trees, the solitary, invisible factory chimney, with its waving plume of smoke the colour of pigeon feathers, the weathered white marble dome of an ancient princely house now given out to wedding parties, shining as coldly and beautifully as a planet, and, at large intervals, the famous multistoreyed buildings with mythical Sanskrit names, all this swam around the two maidservants, Uma and Jochna, the first, who did not know her age, but looked thirty years old, abandoned by her husband, but vermilion still fresh and bright and new each day in the parting of her hair, and the other, fourteen years old, short, dark, with intelligent eyes, and slow to smile. Uma was telling her the story yet again:

"He begins to go for weeks to the other village, until I ask him, 'What do you do there?' and he tells me, 'I'm living with my wife,' and I say to him, 'If she is your wife then who am I, eh?' He was like that from the first day, I can touch you and say that. He said, 'I never wanted to marry you, it was my people who made me.'"

Jochna had other stories to tell, of her elder sister who was learning to make clothes in a tailoring class, and her nine-year-old brother who went to a municipal school. Tinkling sounds came from outside, of hammering and chiselling, as labourers worked like bees, and seven- or eight-storey buildings rose in the place of ancestral mansions that had been razed cruelly to

the ground, climbing up like ladders through screens of dust. An old mansion opposite the verandah had been repainted white, to its last banister and pillar, so that it looked like a set of new teeth. In the lawn before it, a mali in khaki shorts, alone, unaware of being watched, fussed over a row of potted plants. In another sphere altogether, birds took off from a tree or para-pet, or the roof of some rich Marwari's house, startling and speckling the neutral sky. Not a moment was still or like another moment. In a window in a servants' outhouse attached to a mansion—both the master's house and the servants' lost in a bond now anachronistic and buried—a light shone even at this time of the day, beacon of winter.

For a long time, neither of them seemed to move from where they were sitting. Then, burrowing into the hall, they lay down on the carpet between two chairs, a sofa, and a centre table, their feet, or Uma's shoulder, visible depending from where one saw them, leaving empty the place where they had been, a verandah framing a winter sky, and light, an occasional sweep of birds, and grey, thinning smoke. Now only the sounds remained, giving a sense of the city outside, caught in the light, and a mosquito, like a lost aeroplane, that had wandered in; the sound of the two voices, Jochna's and Uma's, fell like drops of water, again, and again, deep, sounding muffled underneath the sofa. The colour of Jochna's dress, with red and black flowers, reminded one of the interiors of pavement stalls on Rashbehari Avenue, with dresses folded or hung up in the afternoon, and a fist clutching forty rupees. It could have been worn by a small plastic doll. There was something of a cat's secrecy about the two figures.

In the kitchen, the blue fluorescent light was suddenly extinguished, leaving its doorway dark until a pale, undecided patch of colour appeared in it—Nando, in his white pyjamas

and shirt. On his black face, the eyebrows were knitted, either because he could not see well these days, or out of concern or puzzlement over some elusive thing.

"Hey, you," he said.

The two figures stirred as if they had been immersed in something, lifting their heads like cats raising their whiskers from a bowl of milk.

"What?" said Jochna, altering her voice to a surprising hardness and volume, for she, between the two, was unafraid of his bully and bravado.

Nando softened.

"What?" he returned.

"What are you saying?" said Jochna.

"No, I was only saying—have you washed the pans?"

"Can't you see?" She might have been addressing a hectoring child.

Nando didn't mind this scolding. As if something had suddenly occurred to him, he turned back to the kitchen. Poor man, he had probably just wanted to have a few words before going in and smoking his bidi by himself in the servants' room—because he never slept during the day. But the girls kept him out of their afternoon world, to which they had already returned, their sides and shoulders pressed against the carpet till they hurt, their breasts rising and falling lightly. They let no one encroach upon their territory between the sofa and the centre table; if someone did, they got up, flustered and serious. And Nando could not make normal conversation. He either flirted with Uma, standing beside her by the kitchen basin and brushing his shoulder against hers, or they quarrelled loudly, or made fun of each other in small, irritating, uncharitable ways. With Jochna he dared nothing at all, because she bore his daughter's name, and was just as short with him as his

daughter was; in fact he tried to please her whenever he could; but, in that frail demonic body with red eyes and tobacco-stained hands, there also existed a genuine paternal soft spot for Jochna. This was known and accepted in the household.

While these people rested at home, Khuku's husband sat in an office on the outskirts of the city. It was an old company, once reputable and British owned, called Little's, and it produced sweets and chocolates. There was a time when its oval tin—Little's Magic Assortment—was available in every shop in Calcutta, and its toffees and lozenges in cellophane wrappers stored in jars in every cigarette shop. The company had changed hands several times, until now it was owned by the state government, and, after having made losses for many years, was named a "sick unit." Its loyal machines still produced, poignantly, myriads of perfectly shaped toffees, but that organ of the company that was responsible for distribution had for long been lying numb and dysfunctional, so that the toffees never quite reached the retailers' shelves. Years of labour problems had sapped the factory and its adjoining offices of impetus, but ever since the Communist Party came to power, the atmosphere had changed to a benign, co-operative inactivity, with a cheerful trade unionism replacing the tensions of the past, the representatives of the chocolate company now also representing the government and the party, and the whole thing becoming a relaxed, ungrudging family affair. This kind of company was not rare in the "public sector"; in fact, brave little bands of men held out in such islands everywhere; but Khuku's husband, before retiring, had worked in a successful private company, where every department whirred and ticked from nine to five-thirty like clockwork, and he and his colleagues had only heard of the renegade lives of the "public sector" companies from the outside. They were spoken of as

backward but colourful tribes with a time-tested culture of tea-drinking, gossip, and procrastination, who had stoutly defended, for many years, their modes of communion and exchange from being taken over by an alien "work ethic." Little did he know, then, that, in his days of retirement, he too would end up here. It was, in a sense, a relaxing place to be in, like withdrawing to some outpost that was cut off from the larger movements of the world. The factory was tucked away in a lane on the outskirts, not far from an important and congested junction on the main road, where no one would have expected it, hidden behind stone walls and a huge rusting gate that opened reluctantly to outsiders. Once, the two-storey buildings made of red brick, with long continuous corridors and veran-dahs, with arches that were meant to give shelter from the tropical heat, would have been impressive and even grand. Now it was like a hostel; cups of tea travelled from room to room, and bearers ran back and forth in the verandahs. There was a perpetual air of murmuring intrigue, the only sign of life, until the doors and windows were shut in the evening.

Yet the employees were, in their own way, simple and good-hearted. And though Khuku's husband was only an adviser, they treated him with a bit of extra respect and sometimes as if he ran the place. "Put it back on the rails, sir," they said, "we need people like you. What a state the company's in!" And Khuku's husband came home and told Khuku these stories, his eyes shining, and felt young again. And Khuku told her brother in Vidyasagar Road, "He'll put the company right." Khuku's brother, in a kind of infatuated haze, said, "Little's—Little's will be all right again." For many days after, he would not let Piyu or his brother's children touch Cadbury, and go out him-self in search of Little's chocolates. His relationship would become temporarily strained with the keeper of the local shop,

Pick and Choose, who was always doing his accounts on a scrap of paper and was not very concerned about human beings. "What, sir, you don't keep Little's toffees—*we* ate it when *we* were young. *You* must have eaten it as well. No, this shop is not what it used to be," he would conclude, shaking his head. "What can we do, Bhola babu?" the shopkeeper would say. "They don't *send* us the chocolates," as if he were speaking of a powerful but heartless family.

Meanwhile, Khuku's husband had discovered that, in spite of their good intentions, the employees, after making their supportive and rallying statements, went back first thing to a convivial round of tea in the canteen. So he resorted to saying "Do it at once!" or "I want some order in this place!" till he knew better. A few weeks later, he met, at last, the managing director. The managing director had joined the company three months ago, but since he was a state civil servant as well, he naturally could not spend all his time here—he was merely a stop-gap before a full-time man came along. "Pleased to meet you, Mr Purakayastha," he said to Khuku's husband. "I've heard so much about you—we are very fortunate, very fortunate. We need your skills, sir. Tell me—are you happy with your office?" A new room had been refurnished specially for him, with a filing cabinet, a telephone, and a window that looked out over the wall into the lane. "Oh yes, you shouldn't have gone through the trouble," said Khuku's husband. "No *trouble*, no trouble at all! In fact, you're the one that's going through the trouble," he said, waving around him. "No, no," said Khuku's husband. "In fact, Mr Sengupta, I would like to have a talk with you." He smiled and looked seriously at the other. "Definitely, Mr Purakayastha. We are very keen to hear what you have to say. Definitely." Yet the managing director— a relatively young man—spoke like one who would not be

around for long, for all managing directors used this company as a kind of airport lounge, from where they went on to somewhere else, never to be seen again. And so it was the eager tea-drinking employees that Khuku's husband spent most afternoons with.

"REALLY? Are you sure?"

It was morning again. Khuku was speaking to Mohit's mother, Puti, in their familiar East Bengali dialect.

"Mohit told me yesterday."

Khuku laughed, disarmed by the picture that composed itself before her eyes—Bhaskar marching down the street early in the morning, brandishing newspapers.

"What will he do next?" she said.

"He should get married before he does anything."

"I hear they're trying to find a girl."

"It won't be easy."

"Oh, it won't be easy, will it?" she asked.

She cradled the receiver and curled her toes; her feet were up on the divan.

"Mashi, how can it be easy?" cried Puti. Her voice came agitated but musical on the ear-piece. "You know how long Arun took to find a wife."

"Yes, Arun," agreed Khuku. "But Arun is so . . . short."

"Arun is short but Bhaskar is dark," said Puti. "And tell me, which father will give away his daughter to a boy who has party connections?"

"Which father will?" echoed Khuku. "It's Bhola's fault. Though he's a good-looking boy in his way. I used to call him 'Black Beauty' when he was younger."

"Leave your 'Black Beauty,'" said Puti. "'Black Beauty' won't help him when his father-in-law finds he sells *Ganashakti*."

LATER, Khuku put her feet in her slippers and walked to the dining-table. Mini was wrapped in a shawl, and Khuku's husband was wearing a dark blue slip-over upon a shirt whose sleeves were rolled up above his wrists.

"It's cold," said Khuku, pulling her shawl tightly around her shoulders.

Both hers and Mini's hair were tied in buns at the back; both had wavy hair, but Khuku's was crowded with curls, with not an inch of straightness to be found anywhere, only skips and jumps and leaps.

"Yes," said Mini. "Ever since yesterday."

"You should wear your full-sleeve pullover," said Khuku to her husband.

"Where is it?" he asked, a little crossly but dreamily.

"Can't you find anything? Mini," she said, "he really can't do anything for himself, and, God forbid, if I die before he does . . ."

Mini smiled at her friend.

"Have some oranges," said Khuku to Mini. "They're sweet as sugar. Mritunjoy bought them yesterday from Park Circus, and do you know how much they cost—you won't believe me—fourteen rupees a dozen."

"What are you saying?" said Mini, looking up.

"Yes—fourteen rupees a dozen! Who said Calcutta is not an expensive city? They say that Bombay is expensive, but I

think Calcutta is no less." She said this as a complaint but a note
of pride was audible in her voice.

"Jochna!" she cried. "Give Didimoni an orange! No, don't
give it, bring the bowl here, I'll choose one myself." Jochna,
with a mysterious smile on her face, held the bowl in her hands
while Khuku delved in a hugely absorbed way into the oranges,
turning them over, till she picked one and handed it to Jochna.
"Give it to Didimoni," she said.

"Give one to Shib," murmured Mini.

She looked at her husband, as if she had just noticed him.

"Will you have one?" she said.

He shook his head, never wasting a word if he didn't have
to. As Mini, with her small dark fingers, ripped the peel, the
smell of orange suddenly burst upon the air.

"Do you know what Puti told me?" Khuku separated the
portions of the orange, which came off with white threads
hanging by their sides like bits of cobweb. Absentmindedly she
picked off some of the threads with her finger and put a piece
in her mouth. "Bhaskar sells *Ganashakti* in the morning. Mmm,
it's like sugar." She picked up another piece and sprinkled
sweet white powder upon it. "The sweeter the better," she said.
Such a sweet tooth had she that when she was a girl she would
eat handfuls of sugar, crunching the large unrefined crystals
happily with her molars, and no one would notice, for she was
a lonely child who haunted the margins of her large family.
Once she had eaten sweet Ayurvedic pills till they had given her
a stomachache, much to the disgust of her elder sister. What
was normally called "food" had held no appeal for her until she
got married.

"*Ganashakti?*" said Khuku's husband.

"Yes," said Khuku, spitting out the pips into her cupped
hands. "Mohit was there with him."

Khuku's husband shook his head, but said nothing.

"There are many boys in my area," said Mini, putting a piece of orange in her mouth, "who get so involved they don't do anything else for the rest of their lives. Many. Two boys, Anshuman Biswas and Partho Guha—good students at school—have even left their jobs." Khuku and Mini worked busily while talking, spitting out pips which were being heaped in torn pieces of the peel. They were enjoying the winter.

WHEN afternoon came to Vidyasagar Road, wet clothes—
Piyu's dresses, Bhaskar's pyjamas and kurtas, even a few soggy
towels—hung from a clothes-line which stretched from one
side to another on the verandah of the first floor. The line,
which had not been tightly drawn anyway, sagged with the
pressure of the heavy wet clothes that dripped, from sleeves
and trouser ends, a curious grey water on to the floor, and,
especially in the middle, one noticed the line curved downward,
as if a smile were forming. To the people in the house, the
clothes formed a screen or curtain which threw shadows and
provided bewitching glimpses of the speedy criss-crosses of
the grille, and through those criss-crosses bits of the balcony
of the house opposite and the sky and the shajana tree, all of
which surprised by still being there. The slow leaking of the
drops of water from the clothes and their casual, flirtatious flut-
ter with every breeze would not have been noticed by the
passerby on the road, who, if he had looked beyond the remain-
ing leaves on the shajana tree and the iron nerve pattern of the
grille would have seen them suspended there stilly, like ghosts
or patches of colour. Who had put them there? To know that,

one would have had to be present at half-past two, when Haridasi, helped by Bhaskar's mother, watched regally by Piyu, had hung up the clothes one by one, till the passerby would have seen all the figures, including Piyu in the doorway, gradually consumed by the clothes that they were hanging up.

Winter came only once a year, and it changed the city. It gave its people, as they wore their sweaters and mufflers, a sense of having gone somewhere else, the slight sense of the wonder and dislocation of being in a foreign city. Even the everyday view from their own houses was a little strange. Smoke travelled everywhere, robbing the sunlight of its fire. Afternoon, with its gentle orange-yellow light, was the warmest time of day, though the wet clothes, assisted by a breeze, dried more slowly than in the summer. And as the orange light fell on the brickwork and the sides of the houses, it was easier to tell, from the flushed rose centre that now appeared on a terrace and now a parapet, that its origins lay in fire.

On the street, Tommy the dog haunted the rubbish heap again, probing, in a concerned way, its bright smelly edges with his nozzle. When someone cranked the handle of the tube-well, it creaked and twanged like a one-string instrument. Crows, sometimes alighting on a window-sill or a banister, clamoured as usual, comforting the child in every human figure in the house, those who were half asleep or awake, bringing up memories of other human, beloved faces, or creating the expectation of homecomings. Their cries had something to do with hope and return and the continuance of human business. Bhaskar's mother, turning in her sleep, grew full with the return of her son in the evening.

She was sleeping with Piyu on the bed; her husband lay sleeping on the divan in the next room. He was snoring, but gently compared to his night-time snores, so that one would

not have heard it from the bed that Piyu and her mother were
sleeping on, but, moving closer to the doorway, one might have
been distracted by a faraway sound that was hardly a sound at
all, trapped, urgent, but private. Then, abruptly, one would
have realized what it was, and the body with its small belly and
bald patch, clothed in kurta and pyjamas, and the frowning
mouth and big nose, would have formed around the snore.

On Bhaskar's mother's outstretched hand, on the shining
dark brown skin, there was, near the thumb and the index fin-
ger, a large pink spot like a rose where the skin had peeled off
after one drop of boiling oil had leapt on it while she was fry-
ing luchis. The yellow Burnol paste that she put there timidly
and perfunctorily after stubborn exhortations from Piyu had
now faded into what looked like healing dabs of turmeric. She
was dark, and slept intensely, while Piyu, beside her, was fair
and fresh-faced, a plant that had been nurtured in this garden,
in the shadow of pillows, cupboard, shelves, clothes-horses,
untouched as yet by life. Let it always be so, the house around
her seemed to say, the four walls and the beam on the ceiling,
let us always keep her as she is. Let her not leave us. She
breathed gently. The sun came in through the clothes-line and
printed the wall and the blue bed-cover with triangles and
rectangles.

Haridasi, small Haridasi, barely four feet six inches tall, had
cleared the dining-table, first cupping her endlessly compliant
palm and pushing bits of moist rice and salt that had littered the
table into its dark cave, to rest there between her heart line and
her life line, collecting bits of fishbone as well to deposit them
there, and then curling her fingers as if she were holding a
secret and throwing the debris into the kitchen basin, though
she had been told not to. She wiped the table after this with a
wet cloth. Then she sat in one corner of the kitchen, the only
one awake in the house, a guest, a stranger, a friend, and ate

from a plate with a heap of rice and a puddle of dal and vege-
tables on one side. She was quiet as a mouse. Without being
aware of it, she tried to mix the puddle of dal uniformly with
the huge quantity of rice. She loved rice.

It was today, in the evening, that Bhaskar's mother would
take her husband to the doctor for his annual checkup. For
about two weeks she had been persuading him to go, but some-
thing else always came up instead. Now, at last, they had a free
evening ahead of them. It was a short journey by car, past the
Lake Market in Rashbehari Avenue, turning into a lane at
whose entrance wheat and grain were piled in open heaps by
the roadside. It was a lane they came to seldom, except on these
visits to the doctor's chambers, and they usually forgot where
exactly the house was, with its porch lit by one bulb and the
narrow corridor, smoke filled in the winter, that ran next to it,
inward to the green waiting room at the back. The lane seemed
far away and strange, and yet, in reality, was only a short dis-
tance from Khuku's house, and from the lane in which Bhas-
kar's mother's sister lived, and Piyu's college, and Lake Market
where, once or twice a week, Bhaskar's mother bought fish and
vegetables. Once the visit was over they immediately went to
the Fern Road Pharmacy and bought the medicines that had
been prescribed, and proceeded without further delay to a rela-
tive's house.

Bhaskar's father had a great, child-like respect for this doc-
tor. Though he was himself an engineer, the doctor was what
in his youth some of the brightest young men went on to be: an
FRCP from London. Those were the days when young men
went to England, not America, and came back with degrees and
sometimes even an English wife who wore a sari. The letters
"FRCP" made Bhaskar's father feel that both he and India were
suddenly, completely, though temporarily, young again. Each
time he went there, he signed his name on the compounder's

slip and sat in the waiting room with his wife and the other patients as shyly as if he were visiting his in-laws, flicking through, meanwhile, old copies of *Span*. Once they were inside, he loved listening to the doctor's diagnosis and asking questions about the prescription, not because he doubted the doctor but because he always wished, whenever he had the opportunity, to widen his own limited, though not negligible, knowledge of medicine. The doctor was a mild, slightly boring man whom time had passed by; he wore black-framed bifocal spectacles and had small tufts of black and grey hair coming out of his ears. He was content to see fewer patients these days and sit behind his old wooden table with its green leather top, his arms rested behind a glass paperweight with little flecks of pink and blue suspended in its strange, crystalline atmosphere, and talk in a leisurely way about his son who was studying at Caltech and, in winter, about all the marriages that were now under way in the city. Behind him, on the wall, there were two framed photographs—the class of '49 in Calcutta Medical College, and the class of '55 in London, the students mostly men, with recent, smart, close-cropped haircuts.

Now an interminable mail-train passed on the railway tracks that formed the horizon that could be seen in the gap between the houses on the other side of Vidyasagar Road. For a while, all other local and habitual noises, of birds and cars, were subsumed under the long, swelling note of the mail-train whistle, which, with its lone trumpeting, made the air vibrate around one. But yet they slept in that vibrating air. Then, when the train had gone, the air was cleansed, and the room was as quiet as its reflection in the dressing-table mirror, with Oil of Ulay, Lactocalamine, Vaseline, Pond's Dream Flower Talc, and two lipsticks arranged carefully, with all devotion and seriousness, on the shelf before it. Very slowly, like town officials who had respectfully ceased their transactions for a minute, the

crows and sparrows began again, but sounding more distant now, even chastised, perhaps in comparison to the grand inter-lude of the train whistle. In this new, petty, semi-silent, post-whistle moment came the postman to Vidyasagar Road, dressed in civilian clothes, a dark red sweater, a full-sleeve shirt whose broad collars were hidden by the sweater's neck, and black terrycotton trousers with bottoms that were wide and floppy; on his shoulder there was a hand-woven cotton sling bag such as college students swing casually and thoughtlessly by their sides, crammed with neat, though uneven, stairways of letters, a small blue aerogramme climbing up to a broad brown-paper envelope, which rose again to a disproportionately small inland postcard. This frail man, eclipsed almost entirely by his sweater and his trousers, now, retrieving more and more piles from his shoulder bag, seemed the paradigm of modest, unattractive, but real generosity, as he, without any special demonstrative-ness or affection, left at least one letter in every letter-box on his progress from one house to another. In the yellow-green letter-box by the gate to Bhaskar's house there came a wedding card with "Shubho Bibaho" inscribed on the envelope; on the card inside, embossed in fine gold lines on a red background, a wedding procession moved forward, looking as wedding pro-cessions might once have looked, with a palanquin and red-and-gold revellers in profile, wearing turbans and blowing pipes and beating drums and making an infernal racket. There was another card, announcing a funeral, with "Ganga" printed in Bengali on the envelope. Lying on it was a yellow postcard from Bangladesh, sent by a distant relative; one half of the square, divided by a vertical line from the other, had clean hori-zontal lines that had been meticulously loaded with Bhaskar's father's name and his address, and the numbers of the pin code imprisoned inside tiny printed boxes. The letter, written in blue ink, began on this side with pleasantries and general reminis-

cences and then came, in its tidy persistent way, to occupy all of the other side, ending with a plea for financial help for a daughter's marriage. Like a house which shelters sons, daughters, grandparents, servants, frustrations, expectations, a whole world under its roof, the postcard, with not one inch of it wasted, gave whatever space it could to words that expressed both necessary sentiments and urgent requirements. And there was a letter from Robi, a nephew in Pennsylvania, with photographs of his daughter enclosed, now seven. He had once lived in this house as a student. The one-dollar postage stamp, with Lincoln's picture on it, would be acquired by Mohit for his collection.

On the first floor of the house, on the double bed where Piyu and her mother were now sleeping, a grandmother had lived twenty years ago. She was Bhaskar's father's mother; of her seven children, Khuku was her favourite, but she was in those days in Bombay with her husband and a son of her own. From time to time, the grandmother's children, who were scattered with their families in different parts of India, would visit this house to see their mother, who was eccentric and did not have much to say to them anymore; she had brought them up and now her duties, she had decided, were over. Bhaskar's father, Bhola, and Khuku, who was only a year older than him, often called their mother "Goonga." The bed on which Piyu and her mother were now sleeping was her bed, her divan, her armchair, her footstool. In the morning her quilt and pillows were banked on one side of the bed, the bed beaten with a jhata by Durga, and then draped with a bed-cover. She, wearing her white sari, for her husband had died thirty years ago, sat peering at the *Amrita Bazaar Patrika* through her reading glasses, beginning at the first paragraph on the first page and ending at the last. No one dared bother her but the children, among whom she was only openly affectionate towards Piyu, who

could still barely walk, and was regarded by everyone, in-
cluding six-year-old Bhaskar, as a discovery, a curiosity, and
especially amusing in the way she imitated certain grown-up
gestures. The grandmother's lunch was laid out on a table
before the bed by Nando, who worked then in this house, and
looked much the same in his white shirt and pyjamas, his hair
oiled, and his face demon-like. "Ei Nando," she would shout,
"bring the salt and the oil!" and Nando would rush back with
salt on a plate and a bowl of mustard oil. She had died a few
years later. The pomelo tree by her window, whose fruit she ate
with mustard oil, secretly adding sugar, had blossomed again
this winter, its fruit picked and stolen by a new generation of
urchins and scallywags who looked exactly like the ones who
had climbed the tree twenty years ago. Some of her children, in
those twenty years, had grown old and died as well, leaving
Khuku, Bhola, and two more brothers, including the eldest,
who, though hunched now, and forgetful of names, still found
time to get angry about umpires' decisions in cricket matches.

It was an old house, a hospitable house. In the big room
on the second floor, which Bhaskar now had more or less to
himself, and where he engaged in animated discussions or rest-
ful gossip with comrades from the party, shy men with mous-
taches whose frail chests suddenly expanded during these
discussions—on the large bed in this room Bhaskar and his
brother Manik, who was now in Germany, used to sleep once.
When Khuku's son, Bablu, came down for the summer,
Khuku's elder sister would also have arrived from the hills of
Assam where, in a town with a funny name that sounded like
a kitchen utensil, she was head mistress in a girls' school.
Reading everything from *Beowulf* to *Puja* annuals at the oddest
of angles—for she would lie sideways and let the magazine
dangle from the fingers of one outstretched hand, moving
grudgingly only when it dawned on her that it was impossible

to turn the page without the aid of the hand that was trapped beneath her—reading everything at such angles had given her eye a squint, and her an incongruous lost and searching look. Incongruous, for, despite being widowed when she was thirty-four, she had raised her children robustly, feeding them well and twisting their ears. During those summers, on the bed on the second floor, she told Bablu and Bhaskar and Manik stories about ancient Rome, and the last days of Pompeii. At present, the bed upstairs was empty, with winter sunlight falling upon it, obstructed only by the mullions in the windows, and Bhaskar was away at the factory in Howrah—but once he had lain there on his stomach with a new book before him and seen rak-khoshes with fangs and nose-rings drink the blood of innocent kings, rakkhoshes who married female rakkhoshes and pro-duced hordes of fearful little khokkhoshes with small fangs and round eyes. Durga had told Bhaskar and Manik when to be careful of ghosts—between two and three o'clock in the after-noon, when grown-ups slept or were away at work and even real objects threw no shadows, and, at night, during the preg-nant hours that preceded dusk. If they sensed anything un-earthly, Bhaskar and Manik promptly muttered to themselves the lines they knew by heart:

> *Ghoul's my daughter,*
> *Ghost's my son.*
> *Ram's in my heart,*
> *And no harm can be done.*

The children came to the house like guests; their parents and Durga were already there when they arrived. They wel-comed them and took them out of their first wondering, semi-conscious state. Once, when Bhaskar was seven and Manik five, they saw from their bed at three or four in the morning a

woman who was not Durga or their mother hanging clothes to dry in the bathroom; then they fell asleep again. It was an old house; a family had lived in it before their parents had moved in, and Bhaskar was certain that a woman in that family had died. He hinted, but never admitted, that the woman he and Manik had seen was the same woman.

This house had been a wedding gift from Bhola's father-in-law, part of a dowry. Since then it had gone through changes, for the worse and then for the better, but its red stone floors and stairs and its bottle-green windows with slats and the small prayer-room upstairs had remained the same. The kitchen had been painted; new shelves had been fitted; and the earthen oven, dust-coloured, hollow, into whose sides Durga pushed wood and coal, had been put in the shed at the back of the house where coal and wood used to be kept. Durga herself had returned to her village.

At four o'clock Bhaskar's mother woke as surely as if an alarm clock had gone off inside her. Her eyes, in a face puffed with sleep, opened, red and unfocused. For fifteen years she would get up thus at half-past six in the morning and, with her eyes still small and red, walk towards the bed where Manik and Bhaskar were sleeping and push them by their shoulders, for they always slept on their sides, curled up, one side of their face sunk in the pillow, so that, waking up, their cheeks would be lined with pillow marks. Manik had always been shorter and fairer than Bhaskar, until, when he was fourteen, he shot up and they were both the same height, though Manik, much thinner, sometimes looked taller. And Manik, wandering joyously with his friends in the sun, grew darker, till he was brown as a roasted nut. In the morning, their mother would shake their rather bony frames (Look at them, she would think in disgust, not a bit of flesh on them, just like urchins) and say in a loud whisper, "Ei, Manik! Ei, Bhaskar! Get up! Get up!" while they

clutched their pillows tightly and grew more and more angry in their sleep. When they had any spare time, these two were always arguing and fighting, till, each wrestling titanically with the other, they fell rolling upon the bed. They were separated and brought to their senses by two sharp slaps and smart tugs of the hair administered by their mother. "You idiots! Look at yourselves! Why don't you fight on the streets? That's where you should be!" Then she would turn to Bhaskar. "And you . . . I know very well you're the one who starts it . . . this other one's an idiot, but you . . . you're a mischievous devil!" "What did I do?" Bhaskar would wail, wiping his eyes and about to cry. "And look at your face . . . Every day it's getting longer, till it's begun to look like a slipper! You don't eat anything, you don't do any work, all you can do is tease this fool!" These days the house was quieter. School had been one of the most difficult of times for everyone, getting up in the morning, coming back in the evening, and doing the homework, buying a new white uniform every year, the white shorts being replaced by trousers, Bhaskar, Manik, and Piyu swigging down glasses of Haringhata milk each morning as quickly as if it were medicine, lifting their faces from their glasses with uneven white moustaches around their lips, how their mother suffered for them, what tension, sewing buttons and pushing them towards the school bus on time, the rice still unfinished on their plates— "Tell him to wait!" Piyu would shout, rinsing her mouth at the basin, "Tell him to wait!"—while the bus engine rumbled sullenly in the lane; she—their mother—had gone nearly mad coping with it. Yet now the house was silent, lives took shape, things changed, and widened, unused spaces wandered about the house, Manik had gone to Germany, and it seemed there had been a certain innocence and neglect about that time. She wanted to witness it again, she wanted Bhaskar to marry now and have children and that whole maddening bustle to resume.

She got up and walked to the basin and sprinkled her face with cold water from the tap. She would, before going to the doctor's with her husband, prepare a snack—Chinese noodles with bits of vegetable and perhaps chicken in it—to amuse Piyu and Bhaskar and make herself happy. She called it "chow mein." Her husband would demand some, and then finally have to beg for it, but she would deny him the noodles that evening because he was putting on weight and that was bad at his age. Her children would chant "Chow mein! Chow mein!" as if the name made them hungry and also satisfied their appetites, and if her husband got a small ration upon a plate he would say that it was as good as, if not better than, what you got in restaurants. They would shovel up the noodles with tablespoons after they had put some of Han's Chilli Sauce in it, thumping the end of the bottle with the palm of their hands until their palms became red, and thick drops of the sauce, pale green, like something that flows in drains, had fallen out sluggishly. She had started making these steaming diversions—noodles and soups—playfully about ten years ago. And now she dialled the number of Mohit's house. It was picked up by Mohit's cousin, Sameer, who was three years younger than him.

"Hello!" he said, hoarse and loud. He sounded urgent and ready, as if he had been shouting all this time at the top of his voice.

"Hello," said Bhaskar's mother.

The female voice took Sameer aback. A note of wonder came to his voice.

"Yes?" he said softly (though he found it difficult to speak softly).

"Can I speak to Mohit?"

There was a stunned silence. Then Sameer found his voice; he shouted at his normal volume— "Ei, Mohit" and Mohit's voice in the background, slightly superior, and heavy after it

had recently broken, wanted peevishly to know "What is it?" Sameer was like the boy who cried "wolf" at every opportunity, and no one took his shouts seriously anymore. But this time Sameer sounded vindicated, for he had important news: "It's a girl, she wants to talk to you." There was silence again. Then, tense and prepared, Mohit's voice came on the phone; and it was easy to visualize Sameer's wide eyes, open mouth, and pricked-up ears behind it.

"Yes!"

"Can you recognise me?"

"Are you sure," said Mohit in his knowledgeable way, "that you have the right number?"

"So you don't recognise me."

"Is this a joke?" asked Mohit stiffly.

"I'm Didimoni."

There was an embarrassed sigh. Then, complainingly, Mohit cried:

"Didimoni, why didn't you say so to Sameer? This donkey said you were 'a girl.' " "Ei, Ram!" could be heard from Sameer in the background.

"Never mind that. You two come today for chow mein at my house."

So that was agreed. They would tell Mohit's mother and all three would arrive together in the evening in an auto-rickshaw.

"How's the pain?" asked Khuku.

"It's a lot less," said Mini. "Very little now."

"You should get a walking-stick, Mini," said Khuku. "It'll be much easier for you. Your leg," and in Bengali the words *tor pa* sounded so affectionate, as if she was referring to her leg as if it were her daughter, "won't have to take the weight."

"No," said Mini, in her quiet but inflexible way, for she had already made up her mind about this, "no, Khuku, I can't take a walking-stick everywhere. It's so much trouble getting onto buses. I'll only lose it."

"Lose it! . . . but what of the limp?" said Khuku. Then, "Anyway, that will go."

It was so relaxing to have Mini in the house, for it was lonely for Khuku otherwise. But having Mini there made her feel less restless, and not want to go out all the time. It was enough for Khuku to see her sitting on an armchair in the hall, reading an old copy of Parashuram or Bonophul whose binding had its threads coming loose; she held the book considerately, which, in spite of its hard cover's being out of joint, still had pages that turned like new ones. She had read these stories before, and was rereading them now, as she always did when

she had a free moment, deriving a great, calm pleasure from them—for no one, looking at the serious expression on her face, would have been able to deduce that these were extremely funny stories. The household continued in its normal way around her; and she sat there in one corner, disturbing no one, in her cotton sari, her feet in sandals, and the book resting in her lap. She had bathed and was ready before lunch, but never reproached anyone if lunch was late. It was not that she and Khuku had a great deal to talk about; but if Khuku wanted to complain about someone, or voice a worry, Mini listened, nodding her head gravely, or bursting into a short laugh, and after Khuku had finished, she would say, "He shouldn't have said that," or "Oh, don't bother about them." It was as if she understood Khuku perfectly.

They had been best friends since they were children. And, though she had married and had a child of her own, now a young man doing research in economics in California, Khuku had always been, from their first irresponsible schooldays in Sylhet, the childish one. Mini, though a few months younger at sixty-five, and by some curious distant relation a niece, had the older, calmer, more self-contained air; it was as if living alone so many years with her elder sister, teaching geography and Bengali at a school, gave her this centre of self-sufficiency which comforted Khuku. She was a judge's daughter; in Sylhet, Khuku, whose father had died early, and who was the second youngest of seven undisciplined children, used to spend afternoons sucking pickles and chattering on the porch of Mini's house: they were both given to bouts of frivolous laughter. Khuku hated boys; Mini went to sewing class without a needle. And Khuku—Khuku had gone on to become a mother, and Mini had become a schoolteacher—both facts were equally difficult to believe.

But Mini had her own shy, repressed side, which rarely

came to light. For instance, after the luxury of bathing in Khuku's house, she, in her unsmiling unostentatious way, splashed eau-de-cologne on herself; and she had her preferences in brassieres, liking those that had small coloured flowers on their cups. But all this was her own secret, for then she covered herself in a large maternal white blouse and a neutral cotton sari. More than a year ago she had got arthritis, which had worsened till, with a deep breath, she had to prepare herself for her journey every morning to school, walking, step by step, tentatively down the stairs, leaning more upon her good foot, and then limping very slowly, but in a measured, symmetrical way, past the compound, through the gates, into the lane, onto the bus, and alighting finally near the school. The children in the compound had grown used to her new walk, for all things become slow with time, and her body too had almost got used to it. But she told Khuku, "It cut as if someone were putting salt upon it, Khuku re." "There is *no* solution but complete rest," declared Khuku, saying "complete rest" in English. "And do you want to become a cripple?" "No," said Mini quietly. Thus had Mini's recuperation and long holiday begun in Khuku's house.

Khuku had her own unworldly routines. She sang, to the accompaniment of her own harmonium, and her voice was still young and as tuneful as it had been when she was sixteen. Her voice was almost a miracle. In Sylhet and Shillong, it had shone, but, for one reason or another, life had passed by without fame coming to it. She could not be bothered. Now when people who lived in that Shillong were reminded of Khuku, they said remotely: "You mean Khuku Biswas, the one who used to sing?" and they recalled a thin girl in a sari, her hair tied in a plait, standing on a stage before a mike, and outside the narrow steep hills of Shillong winding and winding, and Khasia children with red cheeks and high cheekbones sitting by the roadside. "She got married and went to England, didn't

she?" And here she was again, still sitting before the harmonium, still conscientious about her vocal exercises, though she had tired a little of the delicate beauty of Tagore songs and sang Nazrul and Atulprasad these days. Sometimes, indeed, contrarily, it seemed to her that Nazrul Islam was greater than Tagore, and she had begun to sing again a Hindu devotional kirtan which this Muslim poet had composed in a moment of ecstasy, which she had learnt as a child of seven:

> *How could I be happy at home?*
> *For if my Shyam has become a yogi*
> *Then as a yogini with him I'll roam.*

Her husband loved this song; he sat listening to it very solemnly, as if he had a hot potato in his mouth.
Then:

> *But if it's earth he wants*
> *Then I'll be the earth at his bright feet*
> *For the love of my beloved.*

Always the song returned to its first three lines, where lay its home and heart, its original question and its answer.

> *Aami ki shukhe lo grihe rabo?*
> *Aamar Shyam jodi ogo jogi holo shokhi*
> *Aamio jogini hobo.*

Twice a week, Suleiman Hussein came to play the tabla with Khuku. He was something of a dandy; he had a trimmed white beard which he dyed black before major musical performances. A slim man with a small paunch, he wore a different kurta with his white churidars whenever he could, and a black

Kashmiri sleeveless jacket in the winter; he was irritating—but punctual. "Didi!" he would cry out at four o'clock, whether Khuku was sleeping or not, "Didi, don't you want to start?" "So you've arrived exactly on time again—like Yama, the god of death." Suleiman would blink. Then he would begin to cackle with laughter, the sides of his eyes crinkling and his cheeks swelling and flushing. "Yama! Didi—Yama! He Ram, he Ram!" Khuku grew impatient when Suleiman laughed at her jokes; she waited equanimously for him to finish. Then a place in the hall was cleared for them by Jochna, and Suleiman yawned, stretched his arms, and began to tune the tabla on the right with a hammer. And Mini watched owlishly from an armchair, waiting for Khuku to begin.

THE house, if it could be called such, was a small stone struc-
ture with an asbestos roof.

They were standing before it, one or two of them leaning
against the wall that was mapped with a few discoloured
patches where the paint had come off; on a tin plate above the
door was painted a hammer and sickle in orange, and the letters
and numbers: C.P.I.(M.) UNIT 69. Sumanta Saha, a huge lumber-
ing man, had disappeared to the side of the house to urinate
into the gutter. Matches were struck against the sides of match-
boxes, they rasped, a smell of sulphur sprang into the air, and,
patiently, filtreless Charminar cigarettes were lit, and their ends
dimmed and began to burn. Bhaskar inhaled deeply, contem-
plated the distance, then exhaled a stream of smoke slowly
from his nostrils. He still found a boyish pleasure in smoking—
it was something he had discovered twelve years ago with
another group of friends—it made him feel solitary, asocial,
alone, in communion with the smoke entering and leaving
him, but it was not something he did before his parents or rela-
tives. "Ei—ei, Bhaskar," said Arun Nashkar, a barely audible
whine in his voice. "Ei—do you have one?" Bhaskar stirred
unhappily. "Dhur," he said. "You never bring your own." "I'm

trying to stop," said Arun Nashkar sagely. The other's hand vanished into a trouser pocket, retrieving something therefrom, a crumpled golden-coloured cigarette packet which he held out to Arun Nashkar. "What for?" he asked. But Arun Nashkar did not answer, for he now had a cigarette in his mouth, and Bhaskar had handed him, with the tired air of one who is under a compulsion, his own cigarette to light his with; the cigarettes kissed for a long moment, Arun Nashkar's eyes narrowed and his cheeks hollowed, and then reluctantly, heavily, they parted, Bhaskar took back his and returned it to his mouth, Arun Nashkar breathed and a mist of smoke partially hid his face.

The day was warm, and yet they felt insulated in their slip-overs. Many of them had congregated on the pavement to absorb the sunlight, their hands cupped around bhaads of tea. The meeting was over; Samaresh Hajra had made a speech about the International Monetary Fund, beginning, "Friends . . . comrades . . . our country has opened its doors to the imperialists again . . ." But now that the meeting was over the room was empty and the doors ajar. When they had come into the room, they had opened the windows on either side, easing down the locks at the top that squeaked when they were moved. Now the dung smoke that had entered the room during the meeting hung quietly in it. Mosquitoes that had drifted in during the talk still wandered about, searching a human smell. On the young party members' arms they had left tiny red pustulations; all through the talk there had been the sound of agitated slapping. And, in the poster, Lenin's eyes, above his neat beard and below the dome of his bald head, shone humorously. Here, in the deep green humid Gangetic delta in Bengal, among jackfruit trees, malaria, and bluebottle flies, was one of the last Socialist governments in the world, and here, in a lane ten minutes away from Ishwar Chandra Vidyasagar Road, was

one of its local outposts. "Ours is an economy of small busi-
nesses, small enterprises," Samaresh Hajra had said. Drama-
tically, he had taken a fountain-pen out of his pocket. "This pen
is made in our country, India. It may not write as well as a
Parker, it may not write at all after a few days"—there was
laughter—"but we have made it ourselves." What Samaresh
Hajra had told them was true—that foreign investment was
dangerous to India, though the bourgeoisie, whose needs had
made India bankrupt in the first place, were looking forward to
it. Then a head had peered in through the door. "Dada, should
I bring tea?" It was the Bihari boy who worked in the tea-shop
on the opposite side of the road. During the summer he wore
only khaki shorts, and his brown skin shone, but now his head
with its crop of dry hair stuck out from a shawl which hung
down loosely from his shoulders. The meeting had ended five
minutes later. They had trooped out through the door, onto the
pavement, cigarettes had been lit, and Narayan, who had shot
off, returned, still running, with bhaads of steaming tea on a
tray.

Dipen Mandal was a singer and the youngest of that group.
He wouldn't have been more than twenty-one years old, and
still had no moustache or beard. His mother had died when he
was a child, and he had been brought up by his father and aunt;
he loved new clothes, and today he was wearing a white shirt
with broad collars and light blue trousers with narrow flares.
He was just a boy, really, and couldn't keep his eyes off the two
sisters in saris who stood on the balcony of the house on the
other side of the road. His father, who always wore clean,
starched dhutis and kurtas, was a singer too, but perhaps better
known as a revolutionary poet who had published two volumes
of verse in his youth; both father and son had been present in
that long, winding procession pledging support to Cuba and
Castro that had gone down from Tollygunge to B.B.D. Baag

in September. Dipen was the only one among this group who didn't like tea and didn't smoke because of his voice. He was serious about his singing; he took lessons in classical music from a guru; he practised in the mornings. Sometimes it seemed that he was more interested in singing revolutionary songs than in party work, but the others in the group were indulgent towards him and treated him like a younger brother and called him Deepu. Standing on the pavement, keeping at an arm's length from the rest, he was humming a vocal exercise, *"Sa re ga, re ga ma, ga ma pa . . ."* Deeply engrossed, peacock-proud, he uttered the first line of a patriotic song: "O unlock this, unlock this, unlock this door of darkness!"

What happy times they had together! There were dress rehearsals, processions, demonstrations, street plays, adult education for the illiterate, Dipen Mandal breaking into "Sing Cominternational" on May Day to the accompaniment of his single-reed harmonium. They had all grown up on the border that separated middle-classness from a fathomless darkness, on the border where a street of middle-class houses ran out to the railway lines and the makeshift huts beyond, the fathomless cricket- and firefly-haunted darkness in which paraffin lanterns were lit; all their lives they had barely managed not to slip off from their haven of schoolbooks and exams. Samaresh Hajra had a younger sister, two brothers in school, and his mother was a widow; for the last two months he had had no job. He was the one who had spoken today of the International Monetary Fund. Only Bhaskar, perhaps, among them, could be said to have come from a family that was properly middle class; thus, there was an ineffable aura about his ordinariness—he was held in respect.

There was an old bicycle shop across the road, with mournful floppy tyres hanging like festoons at the entrance. Further on, the road bifurcated, and at that point there was a triangular

island of green barricaded by iron railings, some of them miss-ing, in which there was a bust of Swami Vivekananda, painted white. What eyes Vivekananda had—eyes of deep unwavering calm which remained untroubled by the insistent hooting of the state transport buses going past. The grass that grew around the bust had become coarse and dry, and seemed more so in the winter. Cows, spent, unworldly, idol-like, sometimes reclined before that statue. Girls and boys knelt enquiringly on the pavement, searching endlessly for souvenirs, emitting urgent cries in the dusk, snot dried around their noses. At five o'clock in January it would become dark, and the small lights glowing in windows would serve as a human counterpoint to the sun-light that scattered and spread at the turning of the road. In the tea-shop, shawls would cover the tops of the timid and cold-fearing Narayan's and Narayan's uncle's heads, two Bihari expatriates, while tea continued to brew and swirl in the black-ened kettle. But now it was bright, and Sumanta Saha, who had finished his bhaad of tea, threw it on the pavement and crushed it underfoot like an egg-shell.

"Bhaskar!" he called to the one who was still unsmilingly smoking. "Are we meeting on Friday, then?"

Bhaskar was in a dark recalcitrant mood, possessed by the kind of lethargy that people usually succumb to in the summer, or just before the monsoons, in June. He lifted his large black long-lashed eyes.

"Hu."

"Have you xeroxed the script for the play?" asked the large Sumanta in his thin childlike voice.

He was speaking of the street play they were to perform in Behala, an allegorical tale about life in capitalist Russia, called *The Fall of Ashoke*, written by the talented young man whose mind engendered almost all their plays, Arjun Dastidar.

"Yes," said Bhaskar, opening his mouth a little.

"Then I'll see you on Friday," said the big man, reassured. "I'm going home now—you know why. I forgot to bring money with me—just pay my twenty-five paisa to Narayan, Bhaskar, I'll give it to you on Friday."

"There's no need," said Bhaskar.

THAT night, after Haridasi, wordlessly and systematically, had beaten the mattresses with a jhata, and laid out the soft damp white quilts on the bed, and lit the Tortoise mosquito coils in the rooms, while Bhaskar and Piyu watched the English film on television downstairs, Bhaskar's father turned the knobs for the medium and short wave on the radio—to listen to who knows what—producing a curious but characteristic mélange of noises, strange haunting voices that would be interrupted by fading frequencies, desperate snatches of the Oriya and Assamese news, the spiritual monotonous faraway sound of a raag being sung, then being swallowed up by a whistling, humming vacuum, strains of Greek music, the nasal lisping of Arab voices: it was after eleven, and India seemed to come alive on the airwaves in ghostly manifestations, and beyond it, the world. And it was an old habit of his, going back to the first months of his marriage, to stand thus at this hour turning the knobs, allowing his soul to plunge into the vast uncharted territory that the radio so mysteriously tuned into at night. He had missed the news on television, and the English, Bengali, and Hindi news on the radio; now he was hoping that some mysterious nocturnal station would tell him what the new Indian cricket team was. "Foolish to have left Gower out," he told himself.

"We should go somewhere on a trip," said Bhaskar's mother slowly, lying on the bed. "Maybe Darjeeling."

"At this time of the year?" said her husband. "No! Do you know how cold it will be there now?"

"Somewhere, then. Somewhere in the South."

She lay there, thinking. She went on pilgrimages with her sister or with Piyu to Gopalpur, or to Nabadweep where Chaitanya had preached; they all went for picnics in the winter with oranges and flasks of tea to Diamond Harbour or Digha; and, once, over the last three years, with Mohit and Puti and others they had taken a plane—a great event—to Kathmandu, and once to the hills of Kalimpong. They had gone during the Pujas, in September, when it was hot and humid and the insects named after the goddess herself—Shyama—sought out the light bulbs and lay dead on the floor in the morning. It gave them great pleasure, in that heat, to pack up jackets and cardigans and caps, and return a week later with photographs in colour with themselves—recognisably themselves, but subtly changed as if by a magic spell—standing against a blue-and-green backdrop of hills, embarrassed or jubilant smiles on their faces, Bhaskar slouching, Piyu sullen and self-conscious, Puti glorious and histrionic, and a little frown always, always residing between Bhaskar's father's eyebrows, all of them having donned those woollen caps and cardigans. There, among those misty hills, waking to early sunrises, they made friends with other Bengalis like themselves, who too were visiting from Calcutta, and whose names they forgot once they had returned to the city. Perhaps Bhaskar's mother loved those excursions more than anyone else. For three-quarters of her life, she had never been able to leave this house and go anywhere, except for those brief pilgrimages to Gopalpur and Nabadweep. But now she wanted to go to Haridwar and Kashi on the banks of the Ganga, to the long swinging bridge in Lakshmanjhula, all the sacred places she had heard of, hidden in mountains or in

repose by rivers; she wanted to go south to Kerala, and to Cochin, and Kovalam, and Kanyakumari, the tip of India. Perhaps even to Manik, across the seas . . . She had a black spot on the sole of her right foot—she had had it since childhood—which meant that she would travel widely. She had always treated it as a kind of joke, but lately, without her realizing it, it seemed to have released its powers, and her feet were planting themselves on strange grounds she had never thought of visiting.

Her husband loved this city. He loved its fish, rui and katla and koi with black oily scales, and during the monsoons he would cry out a truism that he repeated with great ardour at this time every year: "Ilish is the king of fishes!" He was a tense man, it was difficult to discuss anything with him without getting into a serious argument—all his life he had been like that. But take him out of Calcutta, and one could imagine him becoming unhappy and quiet. Thirty years ago, he had come to this city and got married. Since then, its air had changed, till now a nimbus of smoke and dust and fumes surrounded it always. But he loved it as one who had come here and made his life here. Here he had launched his small business, here he had had his children, Bhaskar, Manik, and Piyu; they had gone to the same school and read Bengali and English and read the same subjects, and in them, in the way they spoke and in what they spoke of, he saw Calcutta more truly than in himself; they were the children of this city. As they grew up, from dark helpless bundles to two thin boys who loved cricket and feared insects, and a tongue-tied girl who made orange squash by herself with a spoon and a tumbler, to the three different beings they were now, he seemed to have seen them changing as rapidly and miraculously as if he had been witnessing a plant growing over a month, and as they grew a sense of loss came to him, a sense of distance from the Bhaskar and Piyu and

Manik that twenty years ago he had dreamed vividly they would be, though he was not sure what the dream was. But three children had become ghosts as three children had grown up, and only he, it seemed, had remained the same. Who was he? Time and Calcutta seemed to pass through him like water. He had come here and fallen in love with Gariahat, its fish and vegetable market with its shouting community of vendors and darting basket boys. That was Calcutta. Then, in nineteen seventy-one, not far away, Bangladesh was created, and the refugees who had come to the city set up their small stalls in Gariahat. It was his life; no one else would know it.

KHUKU and Mini sat side by side on two armchairs in the hall, facing the verandah.

Each day, at some point, they talked of the Muslims. They talked of how, by the next century, there would be more Muslims than Hindus in the country. Mini, being the teacher, had the facts and figures. She told Khuku that "population control" was meant for Hindus alone, and Khuku, listening to Mini, began to see Muslims everywhere. They grew excited about the azaan on the loudspeakers, and about Muslim festivals in which people beat themselves with whips and cords. Once, when talking thus, and saying, "They should change as well, not just the Hindus," they had forgotten that Abdullah the tailor, who had come to take measurements, was sitting, only a small distance away, self-consciously on the sofa, more self-conscious about sitting on the sofa than about anything the two might have said. Khuku had bit her tongue and indicated Abdullah with her eyes to Mini, and said quietly, "He didn't hear us," and then, "Even if he did, so what?"

They were both in old age, though they did not feel it. Khuku's face had a few noticeable wrinkles; and these only appeared, emphasized, when she had not slept for two nights.

Her grey hairs were camouflaged by the black, and the obvious ones "touched up" with mehndi or dye. There were days when she wandered around the house with mehndi in her hair, which smelled like mud or manure till she had washed it off. And her small body, loved in its present incarnation by her husband and child, had remained constant over the last twenty years. And Mini's even smaller body, dark skinned, the forehead glowing with the hair pulled back in a small bun, the eyes upon the face not large but frank, as Khuku remembered them from girlhood, now hidden by spectacles—she was the same Mini. The only difference between them were the marks on Khuku's belly from the Caesarean operation, for she had once borne a child, while Mini's belly, bulging with a natural plumpness, was smooth and untouched.

"BJP," said Khuku, her eyes larger than usual. "I might even vote for the BJP. Why not?"

They spoke defiantly and conspiratorially, as if they were playing a prohibited game. They would stop once Shib arrived at the house.

"In fact, it was no bad thing that they toppled that mosque," said Mini. She looked small and powerful, as if she had unsuspected energies within, and could have gone up to the mosque and toppled it herself, alone. She had quite forgotten about the pain in her leg.

"No bad thing," said Khuku, who agreed with everything that Mini said.

But Khuku and Mini did not believe in Ram or Krishna; Khuku's personal deity, which she might have created herself, or which had possibly been created by her mother, was one she called Bipad Nashini, or Destroyer of Distress, whom she saw as a maternal figure who watched over her and her family, and whose name she muttered whenever she was worried: "Hé bipad nashini, hé bipad nashini." This mysterious female

divinity resided, it seemed, in Khuku's heart, there she had her home in the world, and from there she sprang to life when her name was uttered in that worried, child-like way by Khuku.

Long before she either disbelieved or believed in things, Khuku had heard of the Muslims, or the Musholmaan, as a child. Her world was then populated by her mother, her brothers, and by a huge family of ghosts and spirits. It became dark soon, there was no electricity, and she could scarcely keep her eyes open; in the next room, her elder brothers and elder sister and mother kept on talking. In that world, her closest companions were her younger brother, Bhola, who was then no more than an idiot who had barely learnt to speak, and Pulu, who was older than her by a year. Pulu believed in the next life, and in other worlds, where daylight was a soft purple, and he was always getting cuffed on the head by his elder sister for asking so many questions and being such a nuisance. He was brilliant at arithmetic and a great crammer and knew all the tables by heart. Khuku loved him very much, and one of the first words she had ever spoken, "Dada," referred to him. It was he who first told her of the Hindoos, who were a fierce wandering tribe with swords who cut up everything in their path, as their very name, "Hin-doo," suggested, and Musholmaans, he explained, were ghosts who haunted the dark and hilly regions of Sylhet.

IN THE afternoon, Bhaskar reclined on the bed; his back had been troubling him again. He had not made the long journey to the factory because of it; instead, he had had a full meal, and now he sought the most appropriate position for his head on the pillow. In the morning, he had woken up with limbs quite frozen, and had had to ask his mother for help to get off the bed; he had hopped about like a huge injured bird. Now he lay back and sighed, with a book on yoga in one hand. The pages were light and wispy, and the paper was peppered and flecked with impurities; the Bengali print was faded. Almost each page had another page with a photograph facing it, smoky black-and-white photographs that were really blue-grey, with figures in them doing various asanas, the first two pages of photos being occupied by Surjomukhi Maharaj, who had written the text, a fat, fair, bearded holy man with small eyes and a smile on his face. The rest of the photos were of thin unnamed men in brief white jangias, immortalized in that blue-and-white world in dozens of strange postures, straining, as it were, to become something else, to fly, to be transmogrified. The text made unexpected revelations in a deadpan way: "*Muktaba-yuasana:* This is good for the digestion. Those who do this

daily will not suffer from gas or stomach problems. First lie on your back and breathe in, then slowly raise both your knees . . ." Bhaskar must have read the book more than twenty times, for he had bought it from the Dakkhinee bookshop when he was fifteen. He could only just remember the shopkeeper taking it out of the window, slapping the powdery dust off it, and handing it to him. Bhaskar had at that time been passing through a long phase of interest in yogis and Mr Universes, an interest he had passed on to Manik as well, and their hero and idea of perfection had then been Monohar Aich, the great Bengali body-builder, who had muscles swelling and hardening on every part of his body. Since he had acquired the book, Bhaskar had been much stirred by the importance of the names of the exercises—padmasana, virasana, muktasana—and had interred them as a kind of knowledge. In those days, his mother was always asking him, "Have you done your schoolwork?" and a great lethargy and reluctance filled him as he dragged himself to his textbooks. But, whenever he could, he read the articles in *Sportsweek* and *Sportsworld* about Shyam Thapa or Pelé, or flicked through the pages of the yoga book till he had become familiar with the descriptions of the asanas and those thin, bare-chested men in their state of arrested transport, with the pale luminous white wall behind them. When their mother looked at Bhaskar and Manik, she saw two wiry, restive boys, but she also saw, in their eyes, in the way they walked, in the way they spoke occasionally, what they saw themselves as— Tarzan and Hercules—and, vividly, she could see them increasing and filling out to their imaginary proportions, to their ideal, while, at the same time, being able to see them for the two thin boys they were.

Bhaskar had never been, although he was a great shirker of studies, and also a great daydreamer, a particularly rebellious boy. If his feet ever accidentally brushed against a book, for

instance, he immediately and swiftly touched his forehead and chest with his index finger in quick, absentminded repentance, and as, in those days, books and magazines that were being read by Bhaskar, Manik, or their mother would always be lying by pillows or on the middle of the bed, because the bed served as floor and bed and table at once, and because Bhaskar's normal mode of locomotion in the room was quick skips, jumps, and runs from bed to floor and floor to bed, his feet were always grazing books, and he, at least five or six times a day, was engaged in making that brief, absentminded gesture. His daydreams were the usual ones dreamed by Bengali boys of his age: of alternative lives that were much like the lives of Swami Vivekananda and Subhas Chandra Bose. At the age of seven, he had been given a thin book with broad, flapping pages called *We Are Bengalis*, with small biographical tales about Vivekananda and Vidyasagar and Tagore, each prefaced by a portrait of a serene and grave face; and some of the stories fired him with pride, and others made him cry. Once he understood what a wonderful thing it was to be a Bengali, and that he was Bengali himself, he went around the house chanting, "We are Bengalis! We are Bengalis!" and this echo, predictably, was taken up by Manik, who had no inkling of what it meant.

He had read the book on afternoons much like this one many years ago, lying on his stomach and flicking the pages. The story he liked the best was the one about Swami Vivekananda, who was once an ordinary man called Narendranath Dutta. Narendranath wanted a simple answer to a question he had asked men of several religions—Buddhism, Christianity, Islam, Hinduism—and the question was: Have you seen God? Only Ramakrishna said, "Yes: yes, I have seen Ma Kali!" Testing Ramakrishna, Narendranath placed a picture of Kali under his mattress, and the saint leapt up in agony as if he had been burned. Ramakrishna, seeing Narendranath was a great

disciple, gave him the name Vivekananda, and Vivekananda, journeying to America, homeless in Chicago, and then put up by a kindly old lady, brought glory to India by addressing the Parliament of World Religions with his speech: "Brothers and sisters of America . . ." For a long time after, Bhaskar remembered every detail of this story, and he seemed to be there with Vivekananda when he was Narendranath and wandering from temple to church, and he entered the strange world where, with Narendranath, he met Ramakrishna, and he was there with Ramakrishna as well, when he sat in a trance and saw Kali before him, appearing little by little, her blue skin, the pink of her tongue, the black of her hair, and then becoming whole, and he came back to the real world with a little of the smoke and incense and terror still upon him. Through those days, as he walked from one room to the other in the afternoon, or came out from the toilet, he wondered if it was possible to see Saraswati or Durga or any divinity by chance, for a minute, for no reason. Then, one day, he asked an older, fifteen-year-old cousin who lived in North Calcutta, "What would happen if you saw a god? Is it possible?" "A god?" said the cousin. "Yes, like Kali or Durga. Does it ever happen?" The cousin's face became suddenly sad. "Yes it does," he said. "But those who see a god invariably die."

IN BHASKAR'S mother's handbag lay two photographs in a white envelope. There they lay, removed from the sunlight, unless they were taken out and subjected to curious scrutiny. One was a girl from Jodhpur Park, twenty-four years old, in a printed sari, with a small smile on her face, her body in profile, and the other was in black and white, from Dum Dum, with studio lighting falling on her hair. Although her features were not perfect, it was the first girl for whom Bhaskar's mother had

a slight preference, and had let enter into her heart a tiny emotion, a small attachment, though it could not really be called emotion or attachment for these are things you feel for people you know. Perhaps it was because her face had a patience and tolerance, and her personality a seriousness that was emphasized, rather than diminished, by that small smile, the gaily printed sari denoting a kind of openness—but these were things she said to no one, not even to herself. The photographs were really for Bhaskar to look at, though he never did so properly, but glanced at them for a moment and put them away, as if they hurt his eyes. Then they had been carefully and judiciously considered by Piyu, and laughingly and embarrassedly gazed at by Bhaskar's father, and very seriously, and not without excitement, looked at by Puti, and now they lay in the handbag again, two ordinary objects that had unexpectedly entered their lives, two paper-thin cards, called photographs, with human faces upon them.

Meanwhile, Bhaskar went each day to the factory; at other times attended his party meetings; but most enjoyed the numerous rehearsals in the evenings for plays that would be performed on streets and even in theatres. These one- or two-act compositions possessed solemn messages, each one a parable or political allegory set in medieval India, or in an unnamed land that was sufficiently fantastic, sufficiently unreal, the citizens of this twilit world enacting events that had taken place only recently—the assassination of Rajiv Gandhi, the fragmenting of the Soviet Union, and, lately, the violence done to Muslims by Hindus. These disparate images, that had colluded somehow in Arjun Dastidar's head, were made material and brought alive in a small room with white walls in Tollygunge, with a hundred-watt bulb shining from the ceiling. Like inquisitive and loyal visitors, the sound of trams clattering back and forth outside and the spun pink-white winter smoke surrounded the

players in the room and listened to their every word and every recapitulation and revision. Tender, destitute noises, of a cat meowing, and maidservants chattering and laughing as they walked by, transfigured what was beyond the wall. To Bhaskar, as he tried on a costume, or cried out in literary Bengali, "Alas! What was my mistake?" (for their plays were full of aggrieved shouts and excited exclamations), there came back his childhood world of intrigue and assassinations, courage and injustice, and so, utterly convinced, he clutched his breast with his hand and fell. For what was creation but a great theatre, with swarga, with its deities in every mansion, and blue akaash, born of God's breath, and pataal, the deep, dark, crouching abyss below, perpetually exhaling spumes of dark smoke and protesting with many voices, and, in between, man, a tiny, wonderful, living creature, travelling in his frail craft, facing, astonished but fearless, the endless, dramatic vicissitudes of pataal and swarga? Who would remember him? Blood-curdling cries emanated from the room, followed by laughter.

Confused moths wandered in from outside and settled, becoming invisible until you saw them, a small triangular patch on the wall. When they were disturbed for some inexplicable reason, they burst into life and floated hither and thither, casting shadows much larger than themselves. The wall was always full of the shadows of faces, of bodies, of the slope of shoulders, the liquid outlines of loose clothes, of shawls, of pyjamas, a play of pictures accompanying messages conveyed from one kingdom to another, and cunning murders being committed. And who were these shadows but Bhaskar, Samaresh, Sumanta, Nikhil, Dipen, robbed of their features and invested with a curious darkness and poignance, shadows where the bright white lime-painted wall became mysteriously blue? And the moths, when one noticed them, reminded one of the alleyways, of green shuttered windows with iron grilles behind them, and

the perpetuity of habitation, where they lived with children, young men, fathers, mothers, resting on a wall next to a calendar with a picture of Shiv or Durga, or behind cupboards with piles of old shirts and saris, or distracting two boys as they sat down to study at their table. Such tranquillity they possessed— not a wall existed in Calcutta that would not give them repose!

And now a link was sought to be made between one person and another, between Bhaskar and a girl, who had been growing up all the while in this city, secretly, while Bhaskar had been wearing half-pants, and buying *Sportsweek* and reading Mandrake comics, and going to Gariahat Market with Robida to buy a water-bottle, and riding on trams, his shirt clinging to his back with sweat—someone, somewhere else, was growing up as well, in as random and unpredictable a way, in a little self-absorbed world of day-to-day desire. There were so many places it could have happened—in Mandeville Gardens, in one of the lanes that surrounded the South Point School; in a nook in Jadavpur; in the half-countryside, half-urban settlement of Tollygunge; in Jodhpur Park, past Dhakuria Bridge, by the daily swell of smoke and traffic. There she had grown up, dragging her feet in chappals, wandering indolently in the verandah, making friends with girls called Bapsi and Mintu. Now it was study time, and now it was evening, with the tube-light switched on, and, all through her growing up, the city, like a great arm, had protected her, and kept her hidden and nameless.

TWICE a week, they'd go to a nursing home in Dhakuria. It was a new place, built on a field that had once been empty. A by-lane of two-storey houses and trees led to it. Because the building itself was new, with a flat white façade that had red borders, it looked like a mirage, as all new things do in Calcutta. And then it had those tinted glass doors at the entrance that kept its interior a secret and imaged the world outside, and those new, flourishing money-plants on the porch that shone so, that they seemed to be made of plastic. Not to speak of the watchman in khaki, like a large ragged doll, the winter light falling on the stubble on his face.

"Ma Sharada Devi nursing home," said Khuku to Mritunjoy, the driver.

The words were enough to please Mini. She was something of a devotee of Ramakrishna and Swami Vivekananda; had long been one; not a formal one, but one who'd read their books, life stories, and sayings.

"Who built the nursing home, re?" asked Mini.

"I don't know," said Khuku, who'd never had much interest in facts. She relied on instinct. "It's a good, clean place," she said.

Some doctor had recommended it to her when she'd needed a checkup (both checkups and age had nudged Khuku, who felt so inwardly young, and surprised her into disbelief), and she had recommended it to Mini when she realized she required treatment. In her mind, the place had become associated with healing and a certain stage in her and Mini's lives, and afternoons when her husband was at work.

Her husband at work—seventy years old, hair half grey; yet the five thousand rupees coming in per month from a "sick" company was useful in all kinds of small ways. It needn't *remain* sick, now that her husband was in it. But lately Shib had said, sombre in his sleeveless slip-over, "I don't know why they've taken me." He'd shaken his head. "The government isn't interested in putting money into the company. I don't know if they expect me to perform some miracle and put it on the right course again." He was unlikely to make any miracles happen in his active old age presiding over this company he'd known since childhood. "I've heard that there are some people who resent that money's being diverted from a loss-making firm to pay my salary—so it's best not have any expectations."

Here, at the entrance of the lane, was a sprawling rubbish heap of an unimaginable colour—but the two women in the car wouldn't notice it. Mini was wearing a white tangail sari with a slender green border, and a dark cardigan; bent forward slightly, she was a mixture of light and dark this afternoon. Many times Khuku had persuaded her to wear brighter colours, but she had always refused; not saying why, but on the unspoken grounds of her age, and being single; it was just a preference and a belief she had.

Through traffic jams, bursts of exhaust fumes, a mad chorus of car horns, they'd come, passing the "boulevard" in Gariahat, with its tinsel and Christmas caps hanging from the stalls, and its portraits of Ramakrishna and imitation

Rembrandts, empty exercise books and jars of spices and generators; then the roundabout at Gol Park. Through all this they'd come.

The nursing home rose before them like a mirage. All the doctors attending to Mini had come to know both of them well—and addressed them as "mashima." There was Dr Sarkar and Dr Majumdar, both of them young enough to be Khuku's sons; both most courteous, and attentive to Mini, saying, "Mashima, sit here," and, "Tell me, how is the problem now?" Khuku remembered her son when she saw these two young doctors, and then she told them about him; and they seemed interested and always had five minutes to spare to have a relaxed chat with her. They'd got to know how Bablu was in America, doing a doctorate in economics, and how her husband was still working in a company. "That's good," Dr Sarkar had said. "Men age quickly if they don't work." Khuku had been pleased with this; she'd thought, Then it doesn't matter that it's not a good company, at least he's doing a job. When they examined Mini, Khuku either sat in one of the chairs in the hall, or stood in the corridor outside which received weak sunshine from the frosted window on the door at its end, the door that opened onto a dusty space at the back where the cars were parked. She thought how strange life was, that she was here and Bablu was in America and her husband in the office, and that there was a clean nursing home in Calcutta with good doctors; she was full of wonder at how one person ended up in one place and someone else in quite another.

When they'd finished they headed back the same way, but going down the by-lane Khuku was always tempted to visit the house, in one of the lanes nearby in Jodhpur Park, her elder sister had lived in. Of course, her elder sister was dead; but her daughter, Puti—Khuku's niece—and Manas, her son, were still there, living in different flats in the same house; as were her

grandchildren, Khuku's grandnephews, Puti's son, Mohit, and Manas's, Sameer. Both were fond of Khuku, their Didimoni, but of the two it was the younger, Sameer, less hard-working and mindful of his studies than Mohit, who was the more openly demonstrative of his affection towards his grandaunt, ready to melt in her arms, and who always had a kiss for her. Puti, too, after the death of her mother, had begun to see Khuku, her only aunt, in another light (although both sisters had been different in every way, including appearance, Puti's mother fair skinned with fine thinning hair, and ten years older than her sister, almost everything about Khuku these days reminded Puti of her mother). She—whom Khuku had called, simply, Didi—had died just over a year ago of Parkinson's disease. Her brain hadn't been affected, thank God; but her movements had been reduced to a minimum until, finally, she hadn't been able to get up from the bed without the help of nurses. At least she hadn't suffered terribly; anyway, it had seemed to Khuku, there was nothing Didi had liked better than lying in bed with a magazine; and this it had been possible for her to do till a few months before she had died; in this sense, it had been a happy ending. When Khuku visited her, she'd find that Didi was still eager to take part in conversations. She'd open her mouth and form a few words to ask a question, and Khuku would have a clear view of her betel-stained upper teeth, which protruded slightly; and when the others gossiped, she'd listen, her eyes moving and registering surprise, disbelief, and amusement. Thank God she had had hired nurses always attending to her—not everyone had a rich son in America to pay for their medical expenses; she might have died much earlier had she not been so well looked after.

N o w and then, their voices could be heard; not the voices in which they spoke to Khuku, but those that they reserved for themselves. They did not bother to speak softly; there was no one else in the flat. It had not been so silent since the days of the curfew.

Khuku often thought that three servants were too many to have in the house; there was only herself and Shib; and these three, for large stretches of time in the day, had nothing to do. Then they reigned like angels or demons without another habitation. They were itinerants, of course; three months later, they might not be here. Only Nando, even when he left, returned again and again.

"What do you think you're doing?"

It was Uma. Nando had reached forward and transferred an egg from his plate to hers. The egg was more than an olive branch; it was a testimony of his intentions towards her. Love, or something like it, had possessed him.

Uma had stopped eating; her right arm was poised in midair.

"What do you think you are doing?" she asked again. "You're lucky I'm not going to throw the egg into that

corner"—she gestured with her head—"because I don't want to dirty the kitchen and upset mashima. But I'll tell mashima about you."

Nando stared at his plate. Of late their quarrels always came to these exchanges. Nando was allowed an extra egg daily by Khuku, not because of favouritism but because not long ago he'd been suffering from tuberculosis. He'd contracted it during a spell of unemployment—after being sacked by Khuku— which he'd spent at home, in a basti near Tollygunge, before a reconciliation brought him back to the job.

DURING the curfew a month ago, all had been disorder and silence. Jochna, who was becoming increasingly pretty, had not been able to come to work for two days; there had been tension in her area and fear of violence. It was at such times that the sketchy unfencedness of their existence became palpable, that they must lead lives perpetually and nakedly open to duress. The Muslims had taken out a procession; at night, when usually an owl—Lakshmi's ancient companion and carrier—hooted near the railway crossing, with a tremulous sense of something about to happen, Jochna and her family and other Hindus in the basti had been moved to a nearby Christian school, while the furious Muslims apparently congregated and went about shouting and protesting. So Jochna did not come to work for two days. Ordinarily this would have irritated Khuku, but this time the atmosphere, distant but palpable, of strife precluded any response, unfortunately, except sympathy.

NANDO had spent most of his life in Calcutta; he had started out when he was a young man as an assistant to a cook in a sweet shop. He could not read a single word in any alphabet. In his own home, this small swaggering man would behave like a patriarch and a pest, something between a monarch and hapless vermin, and was considered a nuisance by his wife and even beaten by his son when he drank. He had a grandson, not much shorter than him, who was his only well-wisher; but being at home wrecked his health. Not long after she had taken him back, Khuku had heard him coughing, and saw him lying about like a sack on the carpet, utterly tired. Dr Mitra, who lived nearby, had come down to take a look at this fatigued specimen, and had advised that a test be done, for TB. Apparently it was still widespread in the bastis and areas these people lived in. "The only difference is that it's as curable as toothache today," said Dr Mitra. When Khuku had had his sputum tested, the bacillus had been found in it; but, as good as Dr Mitra's word, he was cured now (that had happened two years ago).

HALF in her sleep, Bhaskar's mother had been seeing them
going up, the collapsible gate opening, shutting, opening, shut-
ting, the voices in Vidyasagar Road coming down the narrow
passageway by the house, and then coalescing and coming up
the stairs. She needed her sleep; or else she had migraines.
From outside came the sound of the occasional bus or car pass-
ing down the road; long deafening horns. But nothing fright-
ened the crows.

The boys went straight up to the second storey, and there
began their rehearsals. Bhaskar's mother could hear their
voices, far away; she was half dreaming and half listening.
Upstairs, they were practising their lines between the bed and
cupboards and dressing-table; from time to time, one or two of
them wandering to look out at the street and the houses on the
opposite side. "Whose house is that, Bhaskarda?" asked Dipen,
clutching a mullion and pushing aside a fragment of a curtain
and pointing to the house that the window looked out upon.
"That's the advocate's house," said Bhaskar. "The advocate
died when I was ten, but we still call it the advocate's house."
"Bhaskarda! Tell Deepu to shut up so that I can say my lines!"
said Dhruba, standing in front of the bed. His "lines" were

really an inarticulate roar. A man called Mahesh in a rather dirty dhuti was sitting on the floor with a dholak on his lap; he'd brought it to beat out a rhythm during the chants. But the sounds they made were always being overpowered by the single-minded, protracted hooting of state transport buses. "We can use my house for rehearsals," Bhaskar had offered generously; and this explained their presence here.

"Okay, let's repeat the lines!"

"Dhiren, stand in place!"

"Allah-hu-akbar!"

"Allah-hu-akbar!"

And then:

"Let's have a tea break . . ."

They tried their best to simulate the feeling of performing on the streets, and the atmosphere of the street play they were preparing for, which was two weeks away. They went over their rudimentary but voluble roles with enthusiasm. They loved the freedom and heat of performing on the streets, of being uncircumscribed by the proscenium, the proximity and palpability of the houses that bordered their performance, their gestures spilling over onto the pulse of the ragged audience, the nearness of the street-sky; and they loved the exaggerated sketchiness of their own rehearsals, the lines never wholly or faithfully committed to memory.

"Haridasi!" sighed Bhaskar's mother downstairs, still lying in bed. "Haridasi!" When the girl had finally appeared, she said, her voice a decibel lower and deeper after her nap, "Take them tea upstairs." As Haridasi was turning to go, she said, "And listen! Give them some biscuits—those biscuits we bought a few days ago."

SOMETIMES when Bhaskar's mother heard them rehearsing she thought about Bhaskar worrying for the poor people in the world and she thought just how difficult a place to live in and understand the world was. Look after your own, was her own view.

And she was filled with an apprehension that couldn't be put in words when she heard their voices.

Yet he wasn't going to listen; he must give five hundred rupees of the two thousand he earned to the party.

Unlike her husband, she had a sharp business sense; but her energies must be devoted to the housekeeping accounts. These she kept with great meticulousness, and zeal, little figures and computations inside a notebook. Meanwhile, it was left to her husband and now her son to preside over the business.

She thought, at times, of the family house. During her childhood she had not known what it meant to live anywhere but in a great mansion with many rooms, so prosperous that she had not had any idea of penury.

She had left the house when she'd been eighteen, after getting married, though she kept going back to it for this or that festival. But after her father died she didn't feel the urge to visit

it as frequently as she had before; it was as if her ties had been loosened a little; even her ties to the world had been loosened slightly, and, although her ambitions and concerns for her children were still in place, it was almost as if she'd let go.

Even her children did not know if they knew her completely. Now, she rubbed her eyes absently in her half sleep. It was when Bhaskar and Manik were growing up that her life had passed through its worst phase, with Bhola's business going bankrupt. She had been, then, for the first time, full of fear.

Her innate business sense (which she must have inherited from her father, and which had never been put to use) had made her, recently, create a savings account whose foundations had been laid by a sum left in her father's legacy, and she would not let Bhola tamper or interfere with the savings for the purpose of his business; at first, she had not even told him about it. But mixed up with this hard-headed sensibleness were also shades of spiritualism, of irreducible faiths, and, thus, there hung in the big room on the second storey, above the clothes-horse, a picture of Ramakrishna sitting cross-legged, and, next to it, a picture of his wife, Sharada Devi. Lakshmi, Saraswati, Kartik, and Krishna sat in the prayer-room, in some way involved with the destinies in this house. This was one side of her that no one could plumb, where this accessible and ever-smiling woman was most herself, and where also lay, not in a rational way, her hopes and fears for Bhaskar, Manik, Piyu, Bhola, and herself, in that order.

There was a loud scraping movement upstairs, furniture being moved, and then the sound of feet running. What was happening?

She herself was a bundle of fears she had never grown out of. Doctors, medicines, TABC injections; all these things she ran from, running literally from the last, climbing up the stairs with the sari pulled round her ankles when the health worker

used to come on a visit, chased by her children, laughing and weeping at once; thus she had rarely been vaccinated, but had rarely fallen ill as well. This is what perpetually puzzled her sons: that the prospect of contracting a disease should cause her less fear than the simple pinprick of an injection. For this was the only time—the visit of the health worker—when they saw her frightened and agitated. Her general good health had been cause for some contentment. But she had sensitive ears, and they ached at times. The imbalances of the menopause caused one side of her face to swell occasionally. Her childhood had been spent in the then-prosperous area of Shyaambazaar in North Calcutta, she the third-youngest child of a family of three brothers and four sisters, her father doing a very successful business in cheap detergent soap. Her mother had died when she was six, but it was strange to think that she felt she knew her in a way; her picture now hung next to her father's in the house.

Years had passed, and she was left here, suddenly awake, half listening to the traffic outside.

She was closest to the sister immediately younger than her—Reena—and in an album there was a series of silly photographs taken on that day, one and a half years before she was married, by Chhorda ("Right, stand together, you two!") when they had dressed as men, especially for these photographs to be taken, Reena as a police inspector, wearing a real khaki uniform with a cap and a baton, she just as a civilian, both with ridiculous moustaches etched above their lips, and with serious expressions full of suppressed smiles. They, Abha (which was her name) and Reena, were sixteen and seventeen then, and neither had really known what it was to be either a man or a woman; they had posed on the terrace with the other old buildings in the area behind them. At the age of eighteen she had got married.

Ah, her youth, her youth. Her children would never know it.

Then another life began for her, in another house. She found Bhola full of opinions about what was Art and what was not, and about politics; and, vexed as she was by this man, a secret affection grew for him that was inseparable from the exasperation she felt. Life changed; their children grew up; but he did not change. And in the inconsequentiality of such emotions lay a specialness, that it did not matter to the world or to anyone else what his opinions were, as if there had been, alas, a pact between her and him to see what he was really like. Yet what arguments had to be tactfully averted! She had been a fan of Uttam Kumar, but Bhola, she found, thought he was a "bad actor" and had a "stupid face," and these revelations came as a shock and at first she could not possibly understand how anyone could think these things about Uttam Kumar. Nevertheless she tried to understand. Music he took very seriously, more seriously than she had ever seen anyone take something like music before—after all, what was it but music?—and he spoke of tunefulness and bad singing. He spoke of the great singers he'd heard when he was a child. All this to her was an alien idiom; thus she never told him, until many years later, that she had learnt the Hawaiian guitar for two years before her marriage, and could just about play three or four Tagore songs like "It Is Your Beginning, and My End" and "Are You Only a Picture?" on it.

How was one to speak to such a man? And such an impractical man: it was almost as if he'd made whatever he wanted of their lives, and she'd sat back and allowed him to do it. At first they used to have arguments. It took years to just properly understand each other. By that time, one part of life was finished.

. . .

UPSTAIRS, it was quiet again; and she wondered, for a moment, if everything was all right. But she was reassured that they were at work. Sometimes they were loud as demonstrators on the street, and at other times secretive as thieves. There was no telling when they were excited and when planning something quietly.

"BORDA doesn't live far from here, does he?"

Returning from the nursing home three days later, Mini asked this question. It was put forward shyly. For it was like something of a holiday for her, to be in the cool, neat, constricted south; these little trips to and from the nursing home were outings, and even now had the air, for her, of freedom. And each new day with Khuku was a measuring out of time; she, Mini, must go back before long, but to be in this part of the city was to explore a world and witness those who had been changed completely. And one such person was Borda.

"Very near here," Khuku revealed. "It's round the corner, isn't it?" she asked Mritunjoy. Not far away was Golf Green and that block of flats.

Mritunjoy mumbled words that sounded like "Yes, mashima."

BORDA, Khuku's elder brother, had stopped going out since last year. Any visit to the little flat in Golf Green was thus welcome. There were lapses in his memory these days. This had happened after the pneumonia infection, when he'd been on

the brink of moving across to the other world, and had just managed, in a nursing home in Mandeville Gardens, almost against his will, to come back. Thus, he might not recognize Mini when she visited him today, though she had visited him in the autumn only a year and a half ago, when he'd been healthy. So this is what it came to, those years in Sylhet. He used to wander about Sylhet town with an umbrella, to protect his complexion; dispensing with his studies, he used to gaze softly at girls, some of whom were Khuku's friends. Khuku suffered as her friends, unaware he was her brother, made satirical comments on his tender appraisal. Then he had got tired of that life, and he'd demanded of his mother when he was twenty-six years old, "Ma, can I get married now?"

But there were, these days, moments of clarity. For instance, recently, when his daughter Beena had been speaking about Bhaskar with her mother, he'd said, "What—Bhaskar? He's become a Communist hasn't he?" Then he'd gone into a sort of contemplation.

There was a time when he had a great deal of love for his nephews and nieces; but that was obscured now, absolutely, by a veil of silent but complete obsession with personal health and hygiene. A little over a year ago, his only grandson in Jodhpur Park had died at the age of six of a rare form of cancer; yet at the shraddh ceremony for the child, all Borda could worry about was whether he would be able to have his expected meal at the usual time. At times, now, he sat on his bed ruminating. A visitor, no matter who it might be, made his eyes light up with happiness. The words he said were hardly audible, because his voice had become soft. Golf Green surrounded him with its identical verandahs.

GOLF GREEN. A maze of houses, predominantly off-white and red, with scattered islands of green, dull façades, one lot of houses hiding from another. One could hardly ever quite remember the way, and Khuku had to rely on the man who had a small makeshift stall for ironing clothes as her landmark.

Very small children and cats sat in the balconies.

They came to the staircase on whose side was imprinted, in the style of graffiti, the letters by which one identified Borda's building.

The two got off from the car. Mini walked towards the staircase.

They had not been expected; Borda's wife, this old, faded woman, in fact, had just begun to prepare lunch.

He had been sitting there, alone, a faded red pullover pulled casually over a woollen vest. He happened to turn his head and was taken by surprise to see his own younger sister standing there and said:

"Khuku?"

The room was narrow. To see the familiar and the living in a moment of inattention is sometimes as extraordinary as see-

ing the dead; or perhaps that was only true of Borda. He stared
at Khuku in astonishment.

At Borda's question, Boudi came out of the kitchen. Borda
often spoke nonsense these days and she had to check if he was
babbling nonsense again.

Although she was only four years older than Khuku, she
looked several years older, partly because Khuku looked much
younger than her real age, and partly because Boudi herself had
aged prematurely. But the strange thing was that over the last
ten years she had remained the same; it was as if she could age
no more.

"Khuku, Khuku," said Borda.

"Look who I've brought with me," she said tolerantly.

"Who's that—is that Mini?" asked Boudi.

WHEN they were going back down Southern Avenue, the trees bare, children playing football and smoke rising at the back, she looked twice at Mini and saw that she was unmindful.

"When do you think it'll end?" asked Mini, her jaw jutting out slightly. For the signs of upheaval were still there, the daily killings, for here was a billboard coming up proclaiming Hindu and Muslim amity.

"You mean . . ."

"I mean you'll never be able to appease them," said Mini.

What if one mosque had gone—for hundreds of temples had been destroyed before. She could not understand what the fuss was about.

By the lakes, the trees with outspread branches were bare. A few boys were playing football; further away, someone had lit a fire and a funnel of smoke was rising from it.

Promises, always promises. No sooner had the mosque gone down than the government had promised that it would be built again.

"Who'll rebuild those temples?" she asked.

"That's right," said Khuku. "No one talks about them."

They turned left into Gariahat.

EACH day the azaan rose in the morning. Over the alleyways it rose, and the tramlines, spreading for a radius of over a mile.

This winter had not been a particularly cold one; it had been diffuse and gentle and chilly rather than crystalline in the mornings.

Meanwhile, the muezzin went on praising the virtues of Allah in syllables that sounded like *laillallah rasulallah*, and Allah was great, Allah was good and glorious.

The government did one thing today and another tomorrow. Today they said they would rebuild the mosque, and the next day they failed to honour the statement.

Some people thought they'd been too tolerant in the past.

Some people thought that the whole conception their country had been based on was flawed; so they must start again. Speeches were expended on the "idea" of the country and what the meaning of that idea was.

The word "fundamentalism," travelling everywhere and belonging nowhere: people tried to understand what it meant.

They appealed for the razed site to be left as it was, as a memorial to an event. Let the rubble stand.

In one newspaper, a Muslim writer said, "The heart of the parrot of Hindu fundamentalism beats in the giant of Muslim fundamentalism. Kill the giant, and you will have killed the parrot."

AT HALF-PAST ten, a lemon-coloured Ambassador arrived to pick up Khuku's husband. This was a government car. It waited downstairs as Shib wore his trousers and shoes and wound a tie around his collar.

This lemon-coloured car might thus be considered one of the perks of working at Little's. It had a young long-haired driver at the wheel who talked indefatigably and had grown rather fond of Shib, and who took him to the office each day and brought him back. He was, naturally, one of those who'd lose his job if Little's ever ceased to exist, as there seemed every possibility it might; the driver, however, appeared untouched by this possibility, which was more remote to him than his fantasies. "What was it like in Bombay, sir?" he'd ask; for he was endlessly curious about Bombay. Last week Shib had been to the Writers' Building, to the third floor, where the department that dealt with "sick" companies was. The department had a resonant name: Industrial Reconstruction Department. Under its purview fell a number of companies, although the larger firms which were once impressive but now a liability, prehistoric dinosaurs that were in a museum that was constantly being added to, like Indian Iron and Steel and

Bengal Potteries, had been bought over by the central government; their lives were governed from Delhi; they were maintained like tamed and exotic pets. Infrequently a sincere effort was made to have them privatized and release them from the imprisonment of an artificial existence into a normal life; but immediately the local trade union resisted the move as a betrayal that might cost employees their jobs. The state government took over smaller companies; it watched and waited; and when a company had ceased performing indefinitely it bought its shares, as it had bought Little's.

Mr Seal of the department had been instrumental in employing Shib, indeed tempting him to employment. "We'll see if it can be done, sir," he had said six months ago. He was referring to the task—not always mentioned—of reviving the company. "If anyone can, you can." He had wiped his forehead and Shib had sympathized with him inwardly. "If it can't be done, we'll let it go." "How can you just let it go?" said Shib. "That is what I was coming to," said Mr Seal. "Because we don't want to take a 'negative attitude' at the outset."

However, after the meeting last week—if one could call that conversation in the warmth of a late January morning across a stack of files a meeting—it had begun to become clearer to Shib that Seal could not back up his words. Perhaps Seal was beholden to someone else; there was always someone invisible in the background who tied your hands down; at any rate, there was always someone to pass the buck on to; Mr Seal seemed reluctant now, and a commitment could be drawn out of him only with great persuasion. But he would not let Shib go; "Mr Purakayastha, be patient with us," he said; it was as if he were waiting for an intervention to set things right.

For now what he had suspected all along became apparent to Shib, that there had been no change of heart, that the government would rather pay the salaries of the employees of

Little's until they ran out of spare money than allow the company to stand on its own feet, for which of course funds were necessary. And as for Seal and himself, they were divided by a common language; they spoke reasonably enough with each other, but seemingly without any intention of arriving at an understanding. It was the sort of dialogue he'd never taken part in all his working life.

Later, these meetings depressed him; left him a little tired. He waited outside the Writers' Building for the long-haired driver to spot him and pick him up.

In Little's history, in fact, the history of Calcutta could be seen to have been written. First the company created by the Englishman of the same name eighty-five years ago; then the buying over of the company by an enterprising Bengali businessman of the name of Poddar; then the death of Poddar after Independence; quarrels and disputes between his sons; the company gradually going to seed; the takeover of the company by the state government in 1974; and what it was now, something that had a kind of life and breath, an existence, but not a real one.

SCHOOL had begun again, the first troubles were behind them, and, in addition to the faint moustache that had formed on Mohit's upper lip and proclaimed his gradual farewell to childhood, the educational system had thrown further responsibility on his young shoulders, forcing him to study each day for the finals one and a half years away, giving him a seriousness beyond his years. After that, a brief respite, and then the upper matriculation, the Joint Entrance . . . Only ten days ago he'd been cycling from house to relative's house in the morning. Now his eyes were a little red, because he'd been studying late into the night the past few days. All that had happened before—the end of the tests, the curfew, the troubles far away in Ayodhya, the visit to Bhaskar's house—seemed vague and dream-like, and the days now, taken up with work and preparation, seemed like a world of perpetual wakefulness. And yet sometimes he smiled to himself and said softly, as if addressing an audience, "Comrades, we have before us . . ."

He was an only child; as was his cousin Sameer. That was neither an accident nor a coincidence. Their parents had planned it this way. No more large untidy families like Bhola's; they would devote all their attention to their one child.

Khuku said to Mini: "I've never seen anyone who studies quite so hard as Mohit. He wakes up at five in the morning . . ." She shuddered, because she'd hated studies at school; but Mini, being a schoolteacher, looked impressed.

Puti would converse with Mohit as if he were a grown-up. And in some ways, he was—with his father away on tours he often substituted as the "man" in the house. And yet he was shorter than he should be at his age, and was any day expected to shoot up.

"Why not?"

"Do I have to answer that? You know that next year is your 'final' year."

The year of the "final"—it had been waiting for him, it seemed, like a mythical mountain, always there, but coming nearer and nearer; and now it was in sight.

"And time will fly."

"I couldn't study the way he does," said Khuku to Mini after a few moments. "That boy is ambitious and knows how to look after himself. Unlike that other idiot, Sameer . . ."

Last year his grandmother—Khuku's elder sister—had died. (That had been a few months after Bhaskar, to the bemusement of all, had joined the party and even Mohit's grandmother had heard and whispered her disbelief.) There had been a sleepless air at home as she had lapsed into a coma, then passed away, then been taken away to the crematorium. It had been something like it was now, with the exams coming up—the confusion of a proper sense of time, the feeling that someone familiar had suddenly gone away, the strange sense that the absence was temporary. It was still strange that his grandmother, who had hardly moved for the last two years of her life, should have left and never returned. Meanwhile, he swotted for his exams and his eyes hurt. A year ago, his mother's eyes had become red with a brief but intense burst of

weeping when his grandmother had died, but he had been unable to shed a tear.

But now he was bargaining for something else, something of possible interest; his Bhaskarmama had asked him to come to a rehearsal, probably give them a hand; "We're busy and we need some help," he'd said in a way that made Mohit feel an old tenderness towards him, "and we need to get a message across." And of course it was a message of great and pressing importance. This feeling of tenderness, which might turn into something more serious, even a commitment, was precisely what his mother wanted to preclude; moreover, there was no time now for anything but studies; second, there is no doubt that the young are impressionable at certain moments in their lives, although his mother had every confidence in her son's essential, practicable level-headedness.

Yet this city that Mohit had been born into seemed sometimes like a bad dream to Puti, with posters, and endless peeling political messages on the walls.

He was still awkward with girls. But he would not be here long. Little did he know that two years from now he would be in America. Around him, the city decayed. This boyhood, of private tutorials, practising math questions from past question papers, of being on the school quiz team (only the other day he'd represented his school, with three others, at Don Bosco), of playing football in the parking-lot on the corner, of visiting Bhola dadu's house and eating pittha, none of it would last long. It would give way to a brief adolescence and then he would be gone to America, where his uncle was. Before long he'd sit for his Scholastic Aptitude Test.

Childhoods were terribly brief these days.

OFTEN, when Mini sat late in the afternoon on one corner of the sofa, and she shut her book and looked up, facing the verandah, she would see the sun setting in the right-hand corner. The sky glowed red, as if at the slow aftermath of a conflagration. These, the last days in Khuku's house.

Almost as if she were exploring a house she did not know very well, she got up and began to walk—she came out into the space of the dining-room, and went past the table.

Khuku must be sleeping inside. Any moment she would be out here.

The doctor at the nursing home (what was his name—Sarkar?—he wouldn't be over thirty) had told her, without force, but not without a doctor-like gravity, she should begin to do some exercises immediately. ("Just once or twice a day, mashima," he'd said.) It was a matter of how best to treat this leg, newly healing: it was almost as bewildered, tentative, and overconfident as a child, and she must give it rest but it must learn to walk again as well. She was going nowhere—just turning round the dining-table and returning to where she had started.

The pain was gone; she noticed this. It was almost gone.

She was lulled by a vortex of calm, the familiarity and spaciousness of Khuku's flat. And yet this flat, full of pretty things and tinkling curios, was both a second home and a cave of wonder to her, so unlike any other place in Calcutta, so that sometimes it seemed to her she'd suddenly woken up to it, to a brief sojourn, had been borne here in her sleep without being conscious of the journey.

She continued walking, as the sun ebbed outside.

MINI had suddenly come to Khuku's mind last month, in December; like a sudden pressure on Khuku's conscience; a few days, as it happened, after the troubles in Ayodhya. Mini had explained to her on the phone that she hadn't been able to go to school for two days because of the pain from her arthritis.

And she'd temporarily become preoccupied with the idea of bringing her to her house; till in a few days she succumbed to the pull that her friend was exerting on her unconsciously.

"Let me bring Mini here," Khuku had said to Shib. "And then I can look for a doctor. I think the main problem is that she doesn't get a moment's rest and," she smiled slightly, "she's really past retirement age despite what it says in her documents. She's younger than her real age by five years in her documents."

"How do you know?" Shib couldn't remember what her real age was.

"She told me herself, of course. It was done years ago. I think she's forgotten herself that she's older than she's supposed to be."

"See if you can persuade her," he had replied at last. For he too was fond of Mini; he'd known her when she was a girl in a frock.

Persuading Mini was never easy; it was like a gentle but strenuous tug of war.

"No, Khuku."

"But I won't hear of anything else."

For Khuku could be stubborn as well, and Mini discovered she had no answer to that stubbornness.

THAT had been a particularly empty time. For the seven days of the curfew the country had been like a conch whose roar you could hear only if you put your ear to it.

"DO YOU know that Sabita lives here in New Alipore?" said Khuku, after they'd talked about her absent son for about twenty minutes. "I just spoke to her on the phone the other day. She's put on a lot of weight. Hers is a sad story. Her only son is divorced."

"Divorced?"

"Yes," said Khuku, "his wife left him for his own cousin. Strange things happen these days."

"What of Anjali?" asked Mini, ruminating.

"I haven't seen her myself. I heard she lives in an ashram in the South. You know she took to wearing saffron and became a sanyasini. Apparently she still remembers me."

"Of course she would," said Mini.

In the afternoon, they'd begin discussing their school again, and their head mistress and deputy head mistress (the one who dressed strangely, because she'd been to England)—"and the head mistress always loved me," said Khuku, "she was always throwing me out of class"—while their conversation meandered and began again. For the twenty-five years in Bombay

and Delhi she'd lost touch with most of her school friends. Now, here they were, in Calcutta. And when the conversation went on for too long, and the plot grew too complex, Khuku would fall asleep. Sometimes Mini would doze off first, and Khuku would say, "You're not listening!" and she would wake up with a start, good-naturedly.

AFTER Vidyasagar Road had curved right and moved towards the house where *Ganashakti* arrived for distribution, and after the small barricaded grassy triangle, there was a by-lane on the left.

In this nameless thoroughfare the boys had begun to set up mikes and wiring, and often at different times of the day stealthy electronic static buzzed and disturbed the lane beneath the other noises. No one knew for certain yet that it was in this by-lane that the performance would take place. But they'd begun to make a stage.

Then a voice said, "Hello, hello," and Bhaskar's mother heard it as she was folding a sari. However, she paid it no heed, was not even conscious of it as a separate thing.

This voice continued to say, "Hello, hello." The next day it began to say more words, too garbled to be understood from a distance: "Announce . . . country . . . a few days from now."

TWO of the men, Jodu and Pyari, had remained silent throughout, notably shy unlike the others; they had been enlisted seemingly at random from the adult literacy class; one was a

carpenter and the other worked in a cement factory. They looked quite tired. "Everyone must take part," they were told; for they were all in their way ranged against one nameless enemy. "What do you think?" they'd been asked; they were approached with a mixture of admonishment and cajoling. "Dada, will we be able to remember our lines?" said Jodu, the more vocal of the two.

"It's not Tagore you have to memorise," admonished Bhaskar, and went on to other things.

Gradually they overcame their shyness; convinced themselves they didn't mind at all as long as their wives weren't there to watch them. Jodu was the short one, the one who had more confidence. He took the lead and Pyari followed. It didn't bother them too much that they didn't know what the play was about; these young men came one day, as if in a dream, and told them it was in a good cause, and they believed them. They told them that this letter was pronounced "kaw," and this one "khaw," and they repeated the letters after them.

INSIDE a room on the ground floor of a house, Bhaskar and his friends—Sumanta, Nikhilesh, and Mahesh—went over their lines and actions; a few others were drinking tea. Outside, someone kept saying, "Hello hello check one—two—three—" while inside the flame of socialism burned and dimmed and burned brightly again; the last of the sunlight fell on the road through a congregation of roofs and solitary antennae; a dog ran swiftly across and crickets began to sing. The proximity of the houses and the little street weighed in on them; this was their poor, true theatre. But, alas, they did not have the ability to concentrate for very long; they drifted out of the play into their own lives. Someone said, "Bring me some tea," or "For God's sake, light a cigarette!"

THEY woke, slept, talked. They eked out the days with inconsequential chatter.

Rumours of atrocities in other cities came and went around them. Meanwhile, Nando went out to the market and came back, having pocketed a rupee and fifty paise for himself.

Until one day Mini persuaded Khuku that she could no longer leave Shantidi by herself, and to reassure her she said, "As you can see I'm almost a hundred per cent better, Khuku, it's true; I feel stronger than I have in months." And she gesticulated with an arm, emphatically, to convey what was an essentially incommunicable truth. She gazed at Khuku, to gauge her friend's response from her face.

Earlier that week, she'd been to the nursing home again. By now she had become familiar with the corridor that led to osteopathy, and the waiting room in which she and Khuku sat until she was called in. People milled around under the signs saying OSTEOPATHY and RADIOLOGY and CANCER DETECTION for apparently no purpose, coming and going until they sat down on the chairs: middle-aged women in saris, men in spectacles.

She and Khuku had grown used to its faint electric lights, its air of being cut off. And the treatment had cost Mini only thirty rupees a visit. Half an hour of the infra-red had soothed her arthritis and numbed the leg into the sweetness of acceptance.

EARLY in the afternoon on a Tuesday they set out for Madan Chatterjee Lane, where Mini's house was. By half-past three Mini had worn a fresh sari for the journey; folded and put her things into her bag.

Khuku was feeling drowsy because she hadn't taken her nap. "I'll make up for it in the car," she said. "I'll doze off for twenty minutes." For no reason that could be clearly identified or named, Khuku felt the infinitely reticent and light touch of a sadness, something to do with journeys and roads and people, which she used to experience not infrequently when she was a girl, except that it, and life itself, was much more real then.

No sooner was she in the car than she closed her eyes. She sat in the car, her chin drooping, while the car turned near the corner of a pavement. Fifteen minutes later the noise of the traffic woke her; she said: "We're still in Beckbagan!"

It took them forty-five minutes to negotiate Lower Circular Road, Chowringhee, the junction before Bentinck Street, and finally to pass Mahajati Sadan and to arrive at the small lane on the left. By then, they felt like they'd come to what was probably another city. Just on the right what looked like a deep ditch had been dug in Central Avenue, where actually unfinished

work for the underground had been begun and then interrupted. Although the ditch looked almost fearful, there were in fact two children playing and rushing upon it, climbing from one side to the other and disappearing again.

NARROWLY the lane opened; only just enough space, like arms reluctantly parted, leaving no room for an embrace to the bosom. Yet the car moved forward into this narrow space, obstructed by handcarts and men, going more and more into the interior, towards the heart, towards a home in the heart.

MUCH would change in the next few months in subtle ways, but much would seem to remain unchanged. And the change was probably only a phase, a development as short-lived as anything else; while what seemed to be in a condition of stasis might actually be shimmering with uncertainty and on the brink of extinction.

And Mini's departure created a gap, a hiatus, that would take time to be replenished again. She had left a vacancy in Khuku's flat, a vague but living memory of her sitting upon a sofa, reading, and it would take time now for Khuku's life to reassert itself. Later, Khuku would hear of Mini's being restricted to her home because of Shantidi's accident, a fall down the stairs and a minor but troublesome fracture. Winter would end, and Mini would be circumscribed by teaching during the day and returning home. It was as if life, or history, were a spirit that kept transforming its features, discontented to be one thing at one time.

The change in the weather from late January to early February was small but palpable, a fractional abatement of the dawn's and evening's chill. The winter, crystalline at dawn, smoke filled in memory, was ending. Then there were the other

changes, the larger ones; as the country altered, gradually and almost imperceptibly, from one kind of place to another. Memories died and new ways of life came into being.

Then, in February, Bhaskar's parents began to look for a bride for him in earnest, surreptitiously almost, neither advertising in newspapers nor telling relatives, but sending out signals discreetly.

ALTHOUGH he knew now that they wouldn't make his plan for Little's work, Shib kept going as if nothing had happened. Once he was in his office, accountants came into his room to ask him to clear up some problem they were having or simply for some advice, and he would help them out—almost minister to them—wondering what his role here was supposed to be. But no real work had been done for days.

His youthfulness (though they knew he was a retired man) had moved the rest of the staff from apathy to something approaching constructiveness. He had come in like a spirit in transit. And he still walked more quickly than most men forty years younger than him.

Again the feeling of peace returned. He could pick up his telephone and ring Khuku if he wanted, but he didn't feel the need to.

He sorted out his files gravely. He was used to being alone, inhabiting his own world: for he was an only child whose mother had died when he was two. Moreover, he had completed a lifetime of looking after others and fending for himself; even Khuku, when he'd first married her, was in many ways

helpless; and he had been a sort of shade-giving umbrella to his son, who'd had a happy and extended childhood.

When he'd first come to Calcutta he'd been a young man, twenty years old, and he'd put his name down, Shib Puraka-yastha, in a register in Calcutta University.

He smiled. Is there an alchemy for making the old new?

"Tea, sir?"

He smiled and shook his head at the man who had asked the question.

The man withdrew.

Two months ago it was that he'd considered with an employee, a marketing manager in this company whose prod-ucts seldom infiltrated the market, the idea of putting in a fresh advertisement for the company. "But where?" There was, for instance, a seven-year-old poster with LITTLE's printed upon it in large letters under a railway bridge in the South—day and night the trains rumbled above it and the bridge shuddered— whose paper had peeled off almost entirely, leaving behind, miraculously, only the LITTLE's at the top.

SOMETIMES this man, who had just asked him if he would have tea, brought him lozenges in their new wrappers with "Little's" printed on both sides. He had ceased to wonder about this company, or what he really did here, or where his salary came from. And Shib had asked to see the lozenges because he was interested in assessing the "standard" of the product; he'd taken them home to his wife, surprising her by giving her a small full packet. For the story of a working life is also the story of a marriage. She'd put one to the test immediately.

"But it's wonderful!" Khuku had said, absorbed in the

flavour of the lozenge; it reminded her of when she was a child, for the flavour, as it was then, came back to her unchanged; she'd tasted them in Shillong as a girl; and she grew puzzled and anxious trying to understand the reasons for Little's decline.

EACH time a state- or government-supported company closed down, it was like a death-knell that no one heard. And Shib heard it these days.

It was only after months that people realized that a company was gone. A product disappeared from the market, or it might be bought over by a Marwari businessman and sold as if nothing had happened. And as if removed from all this, in a constricted space, the office window looked out onto the stunted outgrowth of Dum Dum.

BUT in his spare time, Khuku's husband had decided to put aside some money in shares; he had a premonition that there was a change at hand. All his life, he had worked in a company, and had had no taste for business or speculation; he had been a cautious and qualified professional. But now, four years after retirement, some demon seemed to have seized him; when he was not watching television, he wore small, focused reading glasses that sat low on the bridge of his nose, and fussed over papers and forms. Now, with economic deregulation and a freedom that, in theory, had never existed before, there was the

prospect of a rainbow deluge of collaborations and all kind of opportunities coming to the surface. And Little's would then be a thing of yesterday.

Cautiously he decided to invest some money in the mutual fund and uncharacteristically to buy a few shares in a company that made biscuits, and in another one that made shoes. Now, in the last quarter of his life, a business acumen and speculative curiosity, long suppressed in the interests of his managerial skills, began to come into play, and also a silent, watchful interest in political issues, and he began to peruse the papers with more than usual thoroughness. His gaze and concentration as he absorbed the curve and emerging shape of the time were intent.

All was silence around him. At odd moments lost in thoughts on these matters he could be found humming to himself. No one but Khuku, and Bablu, who was not here, knew that he sang. From what little could be heard of that singing voice it would seem that it was a small, high-pitched one, at variance with the quiet dignity of his persona, not very sure of itself. It skirted around the difficult portions and paraphrased the tune rather than sang it; but it was a strange, lonely rehearsal to itself (often in response to a song that Khuku had just sung) rather than meant for others to hear. When Khuku overheard him, she would say to her husband—"What? What? Are you singing? I see you're not lacking in courage!"—and discouraged, he would stop.

WOMEN'S memories of their husbands' working lives are radically but subtly different from their husbands' own, and the same must be true of their retirement. It's like seeing something from the other side. Of course, Khuku felt lonely when Shib was in his office; and always had done. But, then, during the curfew, when shops and offices and everything else had been closed—ten days of nothing happening—she'd had her wish come true, and Shib at home with her for twenty-four hours of the day.

It had been a mixed blessing, this enforced, artificial reunion. It was as if a train they'd been on had halted somewhere unexpectedly and they'd been forced to take a holiday. She'd found that he wasn't interested in discussing what was happening at all—the riots, the anger; more interested in rereading old copies of the *Statesman* which he'd accumulated during the last week in a drawer. How little concerned he was about the silence outside, in which the sound of a single car horn became disconcerting, as he sat all morning reading! Neglecting to shave, even; a grey stubble appearing on his cheeks.

The truth is, he was not used to being at home. And with Bablu away they were less like a couple than a pair of lodgers.

Then, gradually, the heap of newspapers by his side of the bed had grown, the small alley by the bed littered with papers, as if he were undertaking some sort of research. And his going to the toilet three times in the silence of the night, the sound of the flush nudging her deep in her sleep; she'd begun to worry whether there was anything wrong with his prostate. Any sign of abnormality made her worry and wonder, and this new silence outside and proximity within brought to her awareness what she probably hadn't noticed before. She listened to him breathe at night. Many nights she spent not sleeping, but thinking and awake.

Once the curfew had ended he'd gone out into the world and bought oranges. But it had been a great blunder. On returning home, Khuku pointed out that they were, from the way they peeled and tasted, those terrible sour mutations that resembled oranges, kinoos. She derided him for his lack of discrimination. "What!" Shib said. "But I *told* him I want oranges!" Indignation, however, could not change the kinoos into oranges. Life had begun again.

A ND then there were only two days left for that performance.

"No, it's not a *famous* group; I've never heard of them before. But it's a nice name. You feel you *must* have heard of them."

"That's right."

The two, aunt and niece, were desultorily discussing that frayed but bright entity, Bhaskar's theatre troupe; for this late manifestation of the artistic bent was worth commenting on. Yet one of Khuku's elder brothers, now dead, had written poetry, in rhyme and in blank verse, in twelve-line sonnets, in a marvellous phase between the age of eighteen and twenty, and had even had one poem published in *Desh*, and that copy had been circulated in at least five houses.

A NOTHER brother, Pulu, had done a stage adaptation of an unadaptable Sukumar Ray poem when he was a young man in Shillong, using all his four- and five-year-old nieces and nephews and his sisters-in-law in the cast (that was when Khuku was in London, rainswept and with six hours of sunlight, with Shib, who was still a student, and it had been

described to her in a letter; and she'd known the strangeness of being in another country that she could not recognise if she looked out of the window and have the sense of her own country return to her from a description).

AND it was now, a few days before this street play, that it occurred to Khuku that her family had always been full of ne'er-do-wells, each one doing exactly what he pleased, and if Pulu hadn't been brought to England in 1959 with Shib's help he'd still be wheeling and dealing in second-hand cars in Shillong (which is what he'd been doing when he'd had that play enacted—a major success—when her nephew and niece Moni and Beena—Borda's children—and India itself had been ridiculously, helplessly young). These ne'er-do-wells were somehow provided for by Providence. And she thought of that family and realised that the bonds of relations surrounding it, radiating across and scattered through this city and elsewhere, were finally coming to an end, and she unexpectedly grew absorbed in its memories.

"AND they're just a handful of boys," said Puti. "I wonder how Bholamama copes with them."

"He's indulgent—towards all his children, I'd say."

"But too much indulgence isn't good, is it?" said Puti, mother of a son, Mohit, who was so responsible at fourteen that he sometimes even gave advice to his parents.

At this moment, Bhaskar was witnessing the construction of a stage in a by-lane off Vidyasagar Road.

They'd arranged about seventy-five chairs, in rows.

. . .

BORDA'S elder daughter in Golf Green was among those that had heard of the performance. She, Beena, lived with her parents, and went to work each morning with the air of one about to perform, once again, an indispensable task. The rest of the family almost forgot about her at times, as they forgot those with less than ordinary fortunes; until they thought about her again in a wave of passing sympathy. She was planning to go— "Dear Bhaskar's play": she could not miss it.

For she was something of an enthusiast of the arts herself; taught Tagore songs rather tunelessly but insistently to small children who lived in her block. The small children, whom she gave lessons at no fixed time of the day, quite adored her singing. Her surname was Mitra, a word that had come to have sad, paradoxical music to it (she had decided not to change her husband's name, from whom she had separated eleven years ago). Fortunately she earned a small salary teaching at the primary level at an orphanage in which she taught English to thirty destitute children in a class. In her more lonely and sentimental moments she often felt that these children were like the children she didn't have; but who, having seen her as a young woman of twenty would have suspected that her life would take this particular shape when she was forty-five? Bhaskar's own cousin, Khuku's and Bhola's niece, she was no longer noticed, a shadow, like other shadows, enfolded within this city.

THE sound of the radio came from outside; and from a side-table Mini picked up her spectacles; it was morning and the moment of waking; the consciousness which meant a return to these sounds of the building and further away the noises of Chitpur Road.

Splashes of water fell upon the hard floor; Shantidi was in the bath; they fell, again, and again. And here was the day's paper, lying on the floor, by the door. And in the cupboard next to the door was a small container with plastic boards with dates upon them which had to be reshuffled every day; Mini would pause and change the date by hand as if not entirely convinced that it was another day until she had done so; then she would bend to pick the paper up.

FIVE sisters and brothers in that family: Mini and Shantidi, and the three brothers, Shyamal, Chanchal, and the eldest, whom they used to call Dadamoni. They had grown up in a place called Puran Lane in Sylhet, a flat area with a longish lane of houses, not a great distance from a market, and which must

have been on the east of the town since the sun seemed to rise on that side.

Their father had been a soft-spoken nondescript man; where he came from was no more clear; the circumstances of his marriage to Mini's mother too were now forgotten. What was remembered was his conversation and his uprightness, and the walks he used to take to Khuku's mother's house from time to time, and how she, widowed, would turn to this gentle man for advice. He—there were thousands like him—had died at the age of fifty-eight, which at that time was considered an acceptable age for death; Mini was sixteen years old. Their mother had gone back to the village a few years later and died there. Their lives existed only in their surviving children's memories and sometimes not even there; it was as if they had been banished into some darker place or retreated there of their own will; and their presence had been so subtle in life, so unremarkable, that words could no longer translate them into existence. They were gone, but would return, without questions, to their children's minds repeatedly. Then, after the mother's death, Mini's elder brother had taken on the responsibilities of the family in an ordinary but god-like way. He, "Dadamoni," had looked after them as if they were his children; like Shyamal and Mini, he wore spectacles, and like them he had a hoarse voice.

Then the upheaval came, and friends, brothers, teachers, magistrates, servants, shopkeepers, were all uprooted, as if released slowly, sadly, by the gravity that had tied them to the places they had known all their life, released from an old orbit. They had awaited it with more than apprehension; but when it came they hardly noticed it. The votes were counted after the referendum; their country was gone; first they went back to the village where their mother had died. After two months they packed their things and took a train to Guwahati and then a bus

to Shillong, the landscape, over six hours, changing slowly from plains to hills.

Later, Dadamoni came to Calcutta with his brothers and sisters and rented a flat not far from where they were now; and took a job as a sales representative in a chemicals company. They'd lost their home; but there was the silent, incommunicable excitement of beginning anew in what was now their own country. When they walked down the road and saw a large hoarding advertising Dutta Chemicals, they felt proud as if at a secret knowledge. (They hardly remarked later on the demise of Dutta Chemicals; it had gone out of business in the seventies, but their lives were so different by then they had hardly noticed it.)

When Khuku spent three days in Calcutta on her way to England in 1955, to marry Shib, Mini'd been living in a lane with Dadamoni, Shantidi, Chanchal, and Shyamal in the rented flat. Khuku then told Mini how beautiful the city seemed to her, for this was her first visit here; and urged Mini to marry. She had someone in mind, she said, a young man called Kalidas Sengupta who worked in an advertising firm. For those three days she pursued the subject of Mini's marriage, to Mini's slight embarrassment. Then she was gone for six years.

Shantidi came out now, half blind with the bath. She was cold.

When he was only forty-two years old, Dadamoni died. The day before he died of a heart attack, he'd had a meal of ilish fish, a noble specimen caught from the Ganga whose virtues he commended as he slowly sorted the bones in his mouth. Later, when the pains had started, he'd thought, at first, that it was indigestion. And in less than two years, Chanchal, who was running a catering business, contracted tuberculosis; and tuberculosis was still incurable in those days. With Dadamoni's death (his photograph hung on the wall in the

smaller room) everything changed with a slow momentum that they did not fully grasp; and their destinies turned out to be different from what even a year ago they believed they might have been. The possibility of Shantidi's and Mini's marriage became more remote; and then, they did not know exactly when, it no longer remained a possibility. For who would marry someone from a bereaved and hardly well-to-do family unless the woman was exceptionally beautiful? In a way they were left innocent, like children, never to know what one part of life was, not particularly worried by their ignorance, with an inexhaustible core of freshness and even romance, touched and changed only by time's attrition and the uncontainability of their own affections. They gradually stopped thinking and talking about it as one stops thinking about things whose meaning one outgrows or transcends. Meanwhile, Khuku and Shib returned to Calcutta from England as, strangely, touchingly, husband and wife, Shib armed with rare and desirable qualifications of which Khuku was proud as if she had taken the exams; and their first and only child was born in a nursing home in South Calcutta. Everything had happened in Khuku's life at an abnormally slow pace: married at the age of thirty, she was giving birth to this son after years of trying. Khuku was thirty-seven years old, and Shib forty, his hair already half grey, but his face strikingly young.

A sound from outside, like something beating against metal. There it was, again and again.

Mini would sometimes remember the two years they'd spent in Calcutta after returning from England. Bablu learning to walk, taking his first steps in the courtyard of their house in New Alipore; Khuku become plump and motherly compared to the thin woman she'd been before leaving for England, her hair dark and thick, fanning out behind her unmanageably; proud of her husband's new job in a company that made bread. She

was still singing of course; she was looking for a music teacher to teach her new songs not in her repertoire. And Mini was working in the school. She still wore almost the same kind of saris as she did now, pale, with a thin coloured border, and tied her hair in a bun.

Other noises flowed in, between the metal being beaten, as if all material things in the neighbourhood were gradually being transformed into sound.

Then Khuku and Shib had moved to Delhi, and, for twenty-five years, Mini would see Khuku only when she visited Calcutta once a year, usually in the summer.

Not long after Dadamoni's death, they'd been allocated this flat in the New Municipal Corporation Building.

Mini walked towards the table in front of the fridge and poured herself a glass of water.

At one end was the small kitchen. In the centre was a space where the table was kept, and a clothes-line hung from one end to another; and to the left was a window covered by a wire gauze. The walls enclosed a medium-sized space that was partially filled with light.

The obscure lines of the gauze had become dark and sometimes a feather which had been stuck there might remain there until it had been worn away. That window opened onto the intricate jumble of lanes and terraces of North Calcutta, receding and approaching, mirroring and leading toward each other, and toward Girish Park and Vivekananda Road.

Although Mini's age was reduced by five years in her documents she was due to retire in about two years.

The two sisters were tenants here, although there had been talk for some time (always listened to with interest, always exciting a small ripple of speculation) that people who had lived in their flats for more than fifteen years would be given ownership. Among the tenants themselves there had been a

tentative self-appraisal: "Yes, I've been here for seventeen years"; or "It's nineteen years this year." The numbers were like a revelation. Time suddenly seemed to have passed quickly, even forgivingly. Each year for the last five years an official said: "It'll be this year."

UNTIL nine years ago Mini and Shantidi used to lived in this flat with their younger brother Shyamal and his family. He used to work as a junior manager in a small company; all three of them going out each day to work; reuniting at tea-time in the afternoon; Shantidi and Mini beginning to cook a meal in the kitchen at seven o'clock. Then his sisters began looking for someone for him to marry; they discovered Lalita, younger daughter of a Professor Hiren Shome of Sylhet, who was beginning life as a schoolteacher herself. Shyamal and Lalita were married, and she moved into the tiny flat, and the second room on the right, near the kitchen, became their bedroom. A few months later, a trivial incident caused a misunderstanding between her and Mini and Shantidi. There was nothing unnatural about that: for they had to live, eat, cook, and breathe and the newlyweds lead their married life in the same small space. Yet that was Calcutta then, and everything was possible and probable in their lives; and they were grateful for the flat. While Mini went out to work, Shantidi made sweets, boiling and condensing milk, frying things. Then Lalita had two children, both boys; but the quarrels between their mother and their aunts continued. The quarrels did not affect the boys' relations with Mini and Shantidi; they loved and harassed and disconcerted the two women who were gradually aging. And it was lovely to have children growing up in the flat, with tricycles and Ludo boards coming in the way, and rubber balls bouncing off beneath the bed.

Nevertheless things seemed to go on indefinitely with their portion of affection and unpleasantness and joy.

But what was begun in a certain way never arrived at its expected conclusion. So there was almost no surprise when ten years ago Shyamal and his family moved to a house in a different part of the city. And the two sisters were left to lead their lives in this building.

"DIDI, I'm off," said Mini, before setting out for the school—matter-of-factly, as if she were off to attend a political rally.

She was wearing a fresh sari; her small handbag and a cloth bag hung from her shoulder.

"I might go out myself," called Shantidi. "I'm waiting for that girl." A part-time maidservant came every day at about eleven o'clock to cook meals.

Mini went down the badly lit stairs and emerged then into the bright compound and faced the old building opposite hers, such a faithful mirror-image of her own and yet strangely different; the small first-floor flats with clothes-lines by their windows, the windows covered with a wire gauze, the pipe running down one corner of the wall. It took her about two minutes to get to the main gates and leave the buildings behind her.

As she approached the gates she was greeted from behind a gauze net by a woman with a child in her arms on a ground-floor verandah.

"Minidi, when did you come back?" Her smile was partly obscured by the gauze, and then she emerged into the open part of the verandah, almost becoming another person, the baby unconcerned in her arms, staring tranquilly at the sky between the tops of the buildings.

"How is little Bijon?" asked Mini, her slight smile echoing the woman's.

She had held so many children in her arms, here, in these buildings, and they had gone. This, these buildings, was home and not home; the country she'd left behind in her youth was home and not home; where you went later was not home either; the baby, though it did not know it, must end up making a journey, must end up somewhere else. Her feelings about home must remain painful and blurred to the end of her life. She took the child in her arm, unprotesting, then gave it back. "It seems longer than it has been really. But," her voice half concealed by sounds around her, as if all you could do was become a voice among other voices, "I had a rest and lost track of time."

"We were wondering," said the woman, "but I can now see it's done you good. There's a shine on your face; I know."

Pigeons rose suddenly into the sky between the buildings; their conversation evaporated rather than ended; the child began to make sounds as if it had had enough.

And now, with enough time still on her hands, she stepped into the lane.

HINDUSTANI and Bihari tradesmen lived here, on the left of the gates. They did not notice Mini as she walked past. They were like a tribe that clung to its own impenetrable rituals, curiously unconcerned by the public gaze; their forefathers must have moved here a hundred years ago; it seemed they hardly slept; late into the night, sometimes, one could hear the men singing devotionals, and they must be the first humans to be woken by the sunlight at dawn. The lane moved on to the right of the gates of the New Municipal Corporation Buildings and, after dissecting, at right angles, the narrow lane that led out to Central Avenue, proceeded towards an old "palace." Between shops there were landlords' houses, ornate husks, in which no one lived. But no, someone *did* live in there, for there, across

the enclosure of the courtyard, surrounded by the theatre of balconies, doors, and rather beautiful, shadowy stairwells, was the mundane parabola of a clothes-line with washing left out to dry. There were little goats in the lane, and, by the side of families, children who were older than babies but not quite teenagers sometimes turned erratic cartwheels, as if they were celebrating something.

As she approached the corner of the small lane, she passed the sweet shop in which business would swell noticeably in the afternoon, before four o'clock, before tea-time, when the daily cargo of sweets and savouries came in. And then their vivid smell would overwhelm the other smells in the immediate proximity of the shop.

BEENA had gone to see the play being enacted; Khuku couldn't go. That evening, it was suddenly done. With the performance of the street play over—however it might have been tangential or in the background—and the set dismantled, the larger family shattered and became, temporarily, little islands, each with its own memories and pastimes. All that joined them tenuously in their different places were the rumours of something like war. They read the headlines each day, in newspapers that were already old when they'd finished reading them, of a country that had turned upon itself, without really being able to take them in: "Where Hate Comes in a Communal Garb"; then the smaller headings: "Seven Killed in Violence"; or the same sentence, with "Eight" substituting for "Seven." Was it really as bad as that? There were these small eruptions and they would hear of them and feel an almost unseemly thrill. There would be a photograph sometimes, of people sitting in a railway station, under a roof like an immense tent, with their children and possessions, a child half asleep, looking like the nomads of old, suddenly uprooted, without an address, waiting to depart from the city.

Sleepy-eyed sometimes, sometimes wide awake, they, espe-

cially Khuku, would spend the morning reading. They did not know what the appropriate reaction should be: shock; a certain sense of being vindicated; or a lingering sense of unpleasantness. At times Khuku would surprise herself by thinking of Mini and wonder how she was.

Here, a Muslim butcher had been found near the bypass with his skull shattered, blood on his forehead and face. No one knew why he had been killed; there had been a quarrel, a group of people. There was silence while the police looked into it. The man's face appeared in a photograph, dead, his eyes closed and lips parted, part of his eye and cheekbone obscured by blood.

He seemed to sleep uncomfortably, his lips parted and eyes closed.

But there were always minor surprises. In the personal column, under "Death," next to "Mrinalini Choudhuri," was "Passed away peacefully on 19th January, at the age of 77, mourned by two daughters, Priya and Tuktuk, son, Bimal, and daughter-in-law, Soumya, as well as grandchildren Joy and Sharmistha. Ceremony on Tuesday 22nd. All welcome."

Khuku hadn't noticed this; but Shib saw it. The little obituary, meaningless to almost everyone, a coded message to the few it would nudge towards recognition, signified a pause before the year set off confusedly again in a predetermined direction.

"Mrinalini Choudhuri—that name sounds familiar," said Shib, ordinarily so bad with names.

"Obviously it's familiar," said Khuku, preoccupied but peremptory. "It's Banidi, that's who it is, Didi's friend in college; oh, Banidi, don't you remember!" becoming impatient.

Names; one name suggesting another. As the mist began to clear the shock sank in. Mrinalini Choudhuri was Banidi; she had come to their house last year with her younger daughter

who was in her forties, saying to Khuku, as if it were a great joke, "Khuku! I haven't seen you in *years*!" No doubt a little pleased that she'd outlived her friend, she still lovely like a long-living creeper that had coiled itself around the earthly and thrown up in the evening a new blossom. And she spoke to Khuku, her friend's younger sister, about ten years younger than her, as if she were a girl: "No, no, I won't hear of it, let's hear that song, Khuku." Inexplicably they'd lost touch for twenty years and thus there was that breathlessness on seeing each other again.

"It must be Banidi; who else would it be? We used to think she was quite pretty when she was young, you know; dark, but pretty. Why do you ask?"

"WHAT will it be today, Didi?" Suleiman asked, as he sat down to tune the tabla. Yet something about his manner always made her impatient.

She decided to sing a love-song she had learnt as a child.

> *The moon smiles without a hindrance,*
> *Light overflows.*
> *O flower, O tuberose,*
> *Pour forth the nectar of your fragrance.*

The nectar of your fragrance—the swooning perfume of an imaginary tuberose! But the song and its words had the innocence of an alphabet, learnt when only sound, and before meaning, had entered the consciousness. She no longer remembered who had taught her this song (the tabla rang, bell-like, as Suleiman struck it with his fingertips); it might have been one of her elder brothers, or a relative, or she might have picked it up from a record. Songs were common currency in the small towns, and in Sylhet they travelled from radios into the interiors of houses and people used to learn them by whatever means possible. Sometimes they would hear a visiting relative singing

them in the bath and they had the gift, almost a desperate one, of remembering a tune from these audible snatches. Songs were meant to be stored and collected; people had a large or small "stock" of songs.

> The blue sky's forehead
> Is smeared with sandal,
> And the pair of swans that belong to the forest
> Of words have spread their wings.

She sang these lines again, for she hadn't got them quite right the first time. After their father's death, their mother had sold the gramophone while she was selling other things that belonged to them. Later, whenever they wanted to listen to the gramophone, they would borrow it from Shib's family, who were rich landowners who did not keep too close a track on their belongings, and they would keep it and a stack of records with them for days.

It had been a strange, an impossible, childhood. Their father dead, their mother trying to look after them all, and they—the three youngest ones, Pulu, Bhola, and Khuku—brought up, in effect, by the older sister, who had died last year, an older brother, who had died in Shillong two years ago, another older brother, who had died more than sixty years ago, when he was only thirty years old, of an incurable heart disease—three tyrants—and Borda.

Khuku had longed to sing as a child; but it was Bhola who was always singing when they were children. So Khuku waited shyly in the background as a girl should. Their elder sister bought Bhola a harmonium, but Bhola was too impatient to sit and play it; and it was Khuku, not Bhola, who learnt how to play.

It was an L-shaped house, whose inner and outer dark

declivities were indelibly etched within her, to which they'd moved a year after their father had died, their mother taking charge of everything, and there she would often practise in the verandah. But she began practising seriously only when she was in Shillong, sometimes early in the morning, going into another room so as not to wake the others, and her brothers would tease her and call her "Bijonbala Ghosh Dastidar!" Yet she had an intent and determination that seemed to see far into the future.

Almost no one had the privilege of listening to her these days except her husband and Suleiman or those who happened to be near, including Jochna and Nando. Not infrequently her old records were played on the radio, and that voice ringing as it used to be would fill the air.

WHEN she finished the song, she began another one immediately, almost impatiently. And all at once she noticed Suleiman before her.

All of last month had been an embarrassment to him; as if he'd been transformed into a creature of peculiar and noticeable appearance. And it was as if he was surprised that he was still here, leading the same life he'd led before in Park Circus two months ago.

As for Khuku, she was often in a state of irritation. Only recently she'd been woken up again by the azaan, and at first she had thought it was a mosquito humming near her ear. It grew louder, and then faded, and then grew louder again; its note swelled faintly and then diminished, just as when a mosquito hovers above one in indecision. Then she realized what it was. Where is it coming from? she wondered. It must be Park Circus, from one of those lanes above which the minarets rose. It reminded her that there were altogether too many Muslims around her. Sometimes, in the afternoon, the sound hovered in the middle air, and, if she was passing by in the car, she could hear two different voices at different pitches; as one came closer, they filled the air.

"Is it necessary for all the world to hear it?" she had asked later.

Suleiman had explained himself and his faith apologetically, the tablas balefully silent before him. "It is the word of God," he said, shamefaced and tender about this perpetual nuisance.

See how stubborn they are, she thought; and just the other day they were quaking with fear.

It was more than three weeks since that conversation had taken place.

"Which song, Didi?" he asked.

She did not answer; not because she did not mean to, but because she was asking precisely the same question of herself, and thus had not heard him. She began a familiar song:

> *Lost heart*
> *On a narrow road*
> *I gather strewn flowers*
> *By myself*

Park Circus; Shamsul Huda Haq Road. A pharmacy and a sweet shop at its entrance. Only a twenty minutes' walk from Khuku's house.

During their festivals, sweets made of semolina were left in platters and distributed; they prayed here; marriages were made; they had their own butchers' and tailors' shops. They had their own school for the blind and their madrassas. Children and women in saris and in burkhas, maulvis and music teachers and private tutors and businessmen all mingling under storeys that were heaped one on top of the other.

IT WAS not many days after the performance and already a meeting was arranged between Bhola's family and the Duttas. "The Duttas are a good family," said Bhaskar's mother, though she did not know the Duttas. The Duttas had a daughter. When, at the end of the month, the meeting with the "girl" and her parents was set to take place at an open-air café near Salt Lake, Bhaskar, oddly, seemed both indifferent and co-operative and full of nimble self-assurance.

That very day, however, he'd said he'd have to go to a meeting. Bhaskar's mother had met this observation with coolness. "Go, then. We'll be able to make another arrangement." The café was new and appeared largely unfrequented and lit by large lanterns and set against a lake. Had it been designed in its flickering anonymity specifically with meetings such as this one in mind? Bhaskar wondered. The bypass leading to the airport ran next to it; and at this time the bypass was illuminated principally by headlights. Bhaskar's mother, her sari drawn around her to protect herself from the breeze that blew towards them from the dark, asked for Gold Spot (because it was a fairly long time since she'd had a soft drink); so did Piyu; but Bhola and the girl's parents said "Thums Up" to the waiter. The darkness

that surrounded them had in the morning been water and land and a fragment of sky. The drinks eventually came towards them on a tray and gravitated above the table. There were no other customers except a couple in the distance, who had no doubt come here for their own reasons, looked recently married, and kept glancing, whether with curiosity or displeasure it was difficult to tell, at the two families. Suddenly, taking Bhaskar aback, Bhola offered that Bhaskar and Anusuya, for whose sake this rendezvous had been arranged, sit at another table so that they could "talk amongst themselves." Heavily Bhaskar got up; lightly Anusuya, though she was overweight, got up; and made for the neighbouring table, as if they would become invisible to the others once they sat there. Bhaskar had decided that he would not, could not, marry this girl. She reminded him of a schoolfriend he used to have, a boy called Anilesh. But he was determined to be polite, as polite as he ever was; and he almost felt a surge of affection for her when she asked the waiter for ice-cream. Bhaskar sipped Thums Up noncommittally from a straw. They must have grown up simultaneously, in schools not far from each other; and now they were both in the twilight world of being unmarried. They seemed resigned and happy to be enjoying their orders.

"What do you think?" asked Bhola on the way back.

"What should I think?" said Bhaskar. "We didn't speak. She was busy eating ice-cream."

ΑND Bhaskar, after a gap of five days, resumed going to the factory. He left agitated and late in the morning after a meal of fish and rice.

The factory—time had not dulled the route to it nor made it easier—took an hour and a half to get to by car; it meant crossing the Howrah Bridge; then passing through places that were neither towns nor outposts, but that had names; and negotiating a bad road. Neither tree nor bird in sight, nothing but the little stalls one left behind with pictures of Krishna in them; this was the road to Howrah. By train, it took a little less time.

This was the journey his father had made for the last twenty-five years, the journey he'd made when Bhaskar and Manik and Piyu were at school, their heads bent separately over books, and their mother at home. Its frequency and purpose had, by now, after all these years, diminished, the trip almost become ordinary, a repeated ritual rather than an ambition. And Bhaskar too had now embarked upon this sketchy but indelible route.

Part of the reason for the aggravation of Bhaskar's back-

ache, it had to be admitted, was the jolts and bumps of the drive. The Municipal Corporation, it seemed, had no money to repair these roads and would have none in the near future. The interconnected, anonymous roads, adorned at small intervals by small tea-shops, one half-defined vista giving way to another, shrank at last and resolved themselves into something concrete and real and small, into this factory that had always been there. Its gates presented itself along a lane only wide enough to accommodate one car at a time.

The larger companies around it had left, but it and others like it had remained and made of this place their special habitat. It was Lord Vishwakarma who looked after this company and the cranes that it made and who looked after its neighbours and their small range of products.

And yet of late Bhola and Bhaskar had been discussing in a slightly emotional way the effect liberalization would have on their company. For new times bring new and unforeseen exigencies. "It'll be difficult for us to survive," said Bhola with satisfaction. "The big ones will go in for collaborations and mergers. And the small ones will be pushed out by multinationals." They made gloomy and extreme predictions.

HERE South Calcutta receded; homes, children, mothers, servants, were replaced by men in dirty overalls wandering about in the workshed. Without explanation, the machines hummed and rattled. In other factories nearby, machines hummed and rattled as well for the purposes of a tiny but persistent line of production.

There was a calendar on the wall of the "office"; an old map; near the workshop, a small shrine.

Bhaskar oversaw what everyone else was doing; checked if

any fresh orders had come through; dialled several phone numbers for fresh orders.

"The whole world's in a recession," he said. And indeed it was.

Then he made a few more phone calls.

THIS company had been founded by a group of friends, some of whom, like Bhola, had given up jobs to pool their resources into the business, others who had been waiting to make a beginning in some sort of enterprise. That was a time when many middle-class people decided to start small businesses. All of Bhola's partners lived, as it happened, in South Calcutta, not far from each other.

Then the daily journeys began, exultant at first, routine later.

As a business grows or fails, the families of its employees and owners live out their separate destinies. Children grow up over a time that seems longer than it will in retrospect; wives age subtly; they seem young and unchanged for a considerable period of time; men visit the factory and the business enters the bloodstream.

TWO years after his marriage, Bhola had decided to leave his job and put the money he had received as a gift from his father-in-law into starting this business. His father-in-law himself was an inspiration; a stern man who, through acumen rather than sophistication, had made his enterprise a success; and there was no reason why Bhola and his partners couldn't do what his father-in-law had done. The father-in-law (dead for thirteen years), whose name had been Radhanath Das—all his products

bore the legend "Das"—had personally been aghast at Bhola's decision.

The partners had intended to contribute something to the country: cranes, and other nuts and bolts of the manufacturing industry. For they were civil engineers, not Marwaris and traders; the country needed them; and there would be big money in it and great demand for it; the country needed dams, bridges, roads, and pylons as it grew . . .

The name they came up with for the factory, Goodforce Literod, was a judicious composite of English words; and "Lite-rod" became the brand name of a pulley they manufactured.

They produced calendars every year, simple dignified squares with a sheaf of dates attached, and the name "Good-force Literod" imprinted upon them, the calendars as much announcing this name as the year they were produced in. Each year, the calendars and that name had their rebirth. It was as if the calendars, whose pages so quickly became ragged, gave the company a legitimacy.

It was during the years of the Naxals that the company went bankrupt. A protracted abeyance began, in which the business brought in nothing, no income, and when it became a symbol of some specific but not easily grasped meaning; it was at this point that the business finally became more than a business, and became a way of life, a definition of the existence of the families that had invested their lives in it. Each morning Bhola's children saw their father going to work, wearing a shirt, trousers, and shoes, although something in them knew he was not going to work.

Yet the name—"Goodforce Literod Ltd."—still possessed its music for the children.

Most of the partners had died over the last fifteen years. The factory remained a husk of its first intentions.

Naturally it did not seem that Manik, Bhola's younger son, would ever return to Calcutta and have anything to do with the company. Recently he'd written from Germany that he wanted to study management in America once he'd graduated, which was a very wise thing to do.

Yet—unexpectedly—the company had been functioning for the last two years with a tepid body warmth, something approaching a normal temperature: and no one knew or could explain why. It was as if the dead partners had, from another world, bestowed their hopes and benedictions upon it.

And each year there was the Vishwakarma Puja. And all members and friends of the family who'd been invited would set out in their cars, after filling the tanks with forty litres of petrol, towards Howrah. Though the last cook, whose fragrant preparations of goat's meat and fish-head dal were well known, had died two years ago of cholera, the present cook too had a reputation. For an hour and a half they would travel, to go to the factory in Howrah and eat at the Vishwakarma feast.

But Bhaskar's joining the factory had been seen by others with bemusement and surprise; for it was not as much an entry into the world of business as an escape from it. Why should a young man, unless he had no serious ambition in life, or no choice, want to join a company that was already a ghost of itself? His parents tried not to have to think about the answer to this question. But for Bhaskar, who, after graduating with a second-class commerce degree, and rather desultorily, for a period, studying cost accountancy—for Bhaskar, who, afterwards, had moved restlessly from job to temporary job, it had meant a familiar place to go to; it meant not being swallowed up in the orbit of temporary sales work for large companies; and, most important, his pride would not be challenged, for he

would not work under anyone except his father and with his father's old friends. He gave himself, thus, wholeheartedly to securing fresh orders. He went off to meet Marwari traders; he went to Ranchi to confer with representatives of small companies. He tasted the food in various small towns.

WHEN Bhola came back to India from Germany he was only twenty-eight years old; he had no idea then he'd go into business. He had gone on a course of technical training; and he was married within a year of his return, when he was twenty-nine. Bhaskar's mother was nineteen years old then, barely a woman, and she was still—it was heard—studying for her BA. But her student life ended next year, the first year of her marriage, when she found she had failed her BA because she hadn't worked hard enough for her English exam; tears flowed down her cheeks. And Bhola patted her lovingly on the back. The English language ever eluded her and then, graciously, came to bother her not at all.

Thereafter, on failing her BA, she, who had little interest in books, would devote her sporadic but avid reading habits to women's magazines, and, as she grew older, to Ramakrishna's *Kathamrita* (which her mother used to once read) for its queer parables and homilies; for she often found her mind turning to things that were holy. She had married Bhola solely because her father had decided it should be so; a German-trained engineer counted for a great deal in those days. Bhola's family was secretly disappointed, although Bhola's wife came, as it turned

out, from a rich business family; but they would have preferred a background with more pedigree, and perhaps a fairer bride. From Assam, Bhola's elder sister, the one they called Didi, came in a train for the wedding; Khuku came in a plane from Delhi.

DURING the first two years of his married life, he and his wife quarrelled frequently because they often misunderstood each other. But he had a job that was secure, a furnished flat; he had a good beginning in Calcutta.

It is useless to speculate what his life and the lives of his wife and his children might have been like had he kept his job. But he had left it one day on an impulse, ready to listen to no one else, and they vacated the apartment, and moved to a small flat on Swinhoe Street. From there, later, they went to Fern Road, where, probably, Bhaskar was conceived. Below their flat, two doors away, there was a jeweller's, with a collapsible gate and a fat man in a dhuti and cap leaning behind a counter. Finally, they came to Vidyasagar Road.

After Bhaskar's birth (his eyes were so large and dark that they seemed to be outlined with kohl), his mother suffered from a brief but acute spell of depression, such as is common to women after the experience of childbirth. She even wanted to go home; it seemed, strangely, that she could take no more of the marriage. A few days later the depression disappeared and she never spoke of it again.

Such were their lives' inconsequential beginnings.

AND they had social obligations that kept them all occupied early that February. It was a dance with complex steps; they went to a wedding; they had to go to Banidi's funeral, she who had died unexpectedly; they visited one of Bhola's friends, whom he'd almost lost touch with; a meeting was arranged with a family in a little flat off Lansdowne Road, to see another "girl" for Bhaskar. Her father was a widower: her mother had died of cancer.

Bhola had decided secretly that he must not dwell on Bhaskar's politics or even politics at all (a difficult renunciation) during the meeting for the sake of a smooth passage to marriage. Possibly he was going to be a little disingenuous, but a little disingenuousness didn't count.

Bhaskar would put on some weight after these visits; for he ate whatever was offered to him. It didn't matter whether he was hungry or not; he believed he should profit in some way from these occasions; it was a habit he'd had since he was a child.

. . .

FOR many days now, Bhola had been trying to arrange another meeting with a "party," but Bhaskar had lapsed easily again into a state of indifference. They showed him photographs; but he was never at home! When they put their questions to him directly he mumbled his replies. It was not that he didn't care; he was twenty-eight years old; and he experienced an acute absence at times by his side. But it was as if his recent eloquence on politics had left him inarticulate about personal matters; and he had a profound fear that he would not find a bride to his liking. Which girl would marry someone who did not have a well-settled job with chances of promotion in an established company—at the very least? It was to conceal these fundamental and unspoken doubts that he commanded his parents, "Do what you want, then. And don't wait for my permission. Frankly I have nothing to say on the matter; and when have you listened to me, anyway."

THEY had gone to the house in the lane off Lansdowne Road early that month. They consulted a shabby calendar, saw that the date had arrived. Bhaskar hadn't returned home yet; they panicked briefly. No one remembered, later, how this meeting had been arranged. The door of the flat was open; a corridor led to the sitting-room; here, a neutral pattern of furniture awaited them, and Bhaskar and Piyu and their mother seated themselves.

Dr Ghosh sat joyously upon an armchair facing them. Without delay, he embarked upon an explanation about how his two children, his daughter, Sandhya, and his son, Bipul (the younger of the two, studying management in South India), had grown up looked after by him, because his wife had died twelve years ago of cancer, as if he were recounting an old instructive

parable. Over the last five years, the daughter, he confided, had taken over the household.

"Coughs and colds and diarrhoea I can take care of," he said, "but not food." He taught medicine in a college.

"Where is she?" asked Bhola, smiling.

"She's in the kitchen," said the doctor, too young at fifty to be bereft of a wife, "making tea. She'll be here in a minute."

"And what does she do?" asked someone.

"She's doing an MA in sociology, but she's an interior decorator as well . . . *That,* I would say"— he smiled—"is her first love. Everything in this house was decorated by her . . ." They looked around them with awe at the prints on the walls, the lamp shades, and the decorations: wooden Kashmiri miniatures, a picture of a yak and a Tibetan herdsman done with coloured threads.

"It's very quiet here," said Bhola, "in spite of being so near the main road! You're lucky to have a flat here, Mr Ghosh." This congratulatory observation mildly embellished the air of what was a modest but neat flat with breezes circulating in it.

SANDHYA came out from the kitchen with a tray full of tea-cups and five plates of sweets; they sat up as if they'd been ordered to, and Dr Ghosh said, "No, you must have something." She had a peaceful face; she was dark, and wore glasses. No one could decipher from her serenity that she had already seen in the same capacity a cost accountant, a marine engineer, and a lecturer, and been seen; today she had been informed she was to see a businessman's son. No, she was, admittedly, not particularly beautiful, but youth—she was twenty-four—has its own beauty wherever it resides, like a rare flower in a wilderness even in a city as large as Calcutta, an apparition

before its bloom fades. Everyone was made speechless by her and Bhaskar glanced at her quickly. They were filled with wonder for a stranger.

"*You* must have one," said Dr Ghosh to Piyu. "What's your name? A very pretty girl . . ."

"Say something," said her mother.

All her life, except between the age of one and five, when she had been garrulous, albeit with a limited and repetitive vocabulary, she had found talking difficult before strangers, as if she were hiding the best for another encounter, or person.

"Piyali," she said at last, after a long time.

"We call her Piyu," said her mother, as if by imparting this fact she had sealed a special pact between them.

"TEA?" asked Sandhya suddenly.

So easily these crucial meetings could lapse unobtrusively into boredom!—but this did not happen now. Once Sandhya had poured tea, they considered the sweets and weighed them figuratively. "The size of these langchaas . . ." said Bhaskar's mother. Bhaskar said nothing. "They're fresh," said Dr Ghosh, as if he were speaking of children he had delivered. "They come to the sweet shop every evening—I went and bought them an hour ago." As they ate, he, without undue emphasis, began to ask after Bhola's company. "We manufacture cranes," said Bhola, "and other kinds of engineering implements." Bhaskar opened his mouth once or twice, cleared his throat— and said nothing. He put a roshogolla whole in his mouth.

"I SAW you devour those sweets," said his mother, "you can never resist them"; but that night, when he ate very little at the dining-table, there was palpably some other reason for his loss of appetite.

"What did you think of her?"

His mother put this question to him a few days later, deliberately absentminded, as if she were questioning the air. A mongrel's bark followed the silence.

She had this evasive way of putting things. Bhaskar knew the question did not need to be answered; that it was a way of postponing what was to and must happen.

"Um," he said.

Sometimes, when she and Piyu stood together, they, though unconscious of the fact, almost looked as if they came from different families. Piyu was fair; her eyes and forehead were larger than her mother's; but her mother's nose was thinner, sharper, like something she had kept to herself—Piyu's ended in a sort of pleasant, slightly extroverted roundness; light and shade, the future and past, a family's destiny and its inescapable inevitabilities and individualities played around their features,

as fate often lights up the moment of a photograph. Manik's face was dominated by his father's, not so much by his features as by the vestiges of his personality. Only with Bhaskar, of whom she was now asking this question, was there a noticeable, fragile similarity of appearance.

WINTER was about to end now. The winter had made it seem possible that loud choruses and a few clenched fists raised together in the air would delay, perhaps even permanently remove, the prospect of liberalization; would punish the fundamentalists. But as time passed, distractions arose; as February approached March members of the band of players began to drift apart; one person had passed his medical entrance examination; another had got a job; the more serious of the members got more involved in professional theatre and joined professional theatre troupes; the small band broke up.

Now, instructions were issued at the local unit of the party that cadres must get down to other business: assessing the needs of the locality; assessing its problems; preparing slowly for the next local elections. Whenever Bhaskar thought he would go for a rehearsal he was pressed by some senior cadre to attend a more pressing matter at hand. The streets that used to see the erratic and unexpected outbreak of street plays were temporarily quieter and bereft of their message, at least as far as one group was concerned. There was also a contradictory rumour in circulation these days that the "higher-ups" in the party had, in secret conferences, been forced to reconsider their attitude to liberalization and that at the source of this change was the highest authority himself; reluctantly they began thinking about China on the one hand and Russia on the other.

And the large damp white quilt that had been taken out from a cupboard in the second storey in Vidyasagar Road every November was now, as it grew warmer, folded and laid to rest on the shelf it stayed on in darkness for the rest of the year.

WHEN Mini returned home in the afternoon she found Shantidi in bed in a somewhat odd position, while Anjali the maidservant was sitting and fanning her, shaking her head. As she had come to the staircase she had encountered the familiar damp silence, almost a presence, unkindled by sunlight, but as she had climbed she had sensed subtle signs of disorder she could not quite identify.

"She fell down the stairs, mashima," she said. "I had to help her upstairs."

"But how did you fall?" asked Mini.

Shantidi had slipped two months ago when getting down from a rickshaw in a lane near Chitpur Road but hadn't seriously hurt herself.

"There was something on the stairs," muttered Shantidi. "I think it was water . . ." Later, she fell asleep.

I knew this would happen, thought Mini.

Mini thought of the dark stairs and of Shantidi always hurrying, hurrying, towards an unspecified destination.

· · ·

NEXT day the pain remained; she woke up with it, found it difficult to move. The pain, just above the thigh and below the hip, distracted Shantidi, but the drama of the situation appeared to amuse her. The drama almost anesthetized the pain. But soon she grew impatient with her circumscribed condition and struggled briefly with herself, with undescribable movements, because she wanted to resume the daily routine with which she occupied herself, but whose nature very little was really known about. Mini propped her up on the bed and gave her a cup of tea and a Marie biscuit which she dipped cautiously in the tea for it to become soft and red.

It was the flat really, or perhaps just her nature: she could not stand being in one place for too long.

Later, Dr Chakrabarty came and said it could quite possibly be a fracture and that an X-ray would have to be taken.

"Will I have to go to hospital?" said Shantidi. She was like a child about to be shown a new place.

"I think so," said Dr Chakrabarty. "Is there no one to help?"

Two sweepers were hired, to their reluctance, from the building (but made more eager by a promise of twenty rupees), to put Shantidi into a chair and then carry her downstairs into a taxi. The two men in khaki shorts proceeded delicately, their knees trembling with the strain, while Shantidi gripped the chair with both hands; and Mini waited to take out twenty rupees from her purse.

That month she spent in journeys to an X-ray clinic, a small hospital with a garden not far away, and in bed-rest in the house. Shantidi had taken the chaos almost jubilantly; then, as naturally and inevitably as a seasonal moon passing into a different phase, but unnoticed, she slipped into a deep depression. Mini did not sense it; all her life, Shantidi had been excitable,

easily irritable, but intrinsically detached from the frustrations of existence.

She'd retired fifteen years ago for, it appeared to Mini, no good reason. While Mini went to school, Shantidi travelled around most of Calcutta and did not restrict herself to the north. She would turn up at the most unexpected time of the day at people's houses. She'd sat in buses and looked at the workers on Central Avenue and Chowringhee; she'd dozed in traffic jams. Sometimes it was because she had an impulse to see someone; sometimes some child had passed an exam. This was what her early seventies had been like, a simple time of unimpeded, almost incorporeal, mobility.

One day, she said to Mini:

"You're going through a lot of trouble because of my accident."

"What do you mean?" said Mini, keeping her exercise books on the table. "*I'm* going through a lot of trouble!"

Then, another day, she said:

"Who's going to look after us, Mini?"

Mini sighed. "Who's looked after us so far?" she said. "If you look at the way other people . . ."

"But things don't always stay . . ."

"What is it you're trying to say?" said Mini. "If we have problems," she said very practically, "we'll have to see about them when they come."

She stayed in school till the afternoon.

"It must be very hot outside," said Shantidi, ten minutes after Mini had come back. For the door to the small balcony had been shut to protect the room from the heat.

"It *is* hot," agreed Mini.

"You must be working very hard, Mini," said Shantidi. "Especially after I fell."

"What nonsense!"

Sometimes Mini would come back from standing in a queue at the bank, or from the market, and find Shantidi staring, as if she had quite forgotten the numberless tiny routines that made up each day and each week, as if the world had ceased to exist outside the parameters of her home. Mini counted silently the years since her elder sister had retired, and then how many years it had been since she'd had that liver problem—three—but could come up with no solution. A few days later Shantidi observed, "I've become a burden on you, Mini." "In what way?" Shantidi looked at Mini reproachfully, as if she'd been deceived. "Because I do nothing. And now I've been laid up in bed," she said. "You have to work for both of us, and you're not even well. It would be easier for you, I think, without me," she said.

Within the flat the heat was bearable. Sometimes a breeze entered the room, but intermittently, because of the block of flats opposite; that building was an obstruction. Yet the walls were cool; it was a flat that became damp during the monsoons.

THE bombs exploded in Bombay.

The day after the explosions no one wanted to go out but found themselves at work anyway, the usual noises surrounding them.

Mini phoned Khuku.

"Mini?" said Khuku. "You've come to school?"

"What was I to do? I felt I had nothing to do at home." She began to laugh, then.

"Nothing to do at home!" said Khuku. "Here was a chance for you to take a day off."

She herself was planning to leave shortly for the market with two hundred rupees in her purse. There was a pleasurable and wholly fictitious feeling of doom around this simple expedition; it touched everything about her life at the moment.

"Let's see what they do!" she said. "They won't be able to harm me," as if she were speaking of a gang of half-wit miscreants to whom it would soon be proved that she was unassailable.

She said then, conspiratorially:

"Suleiman came yesterday . . . He looked quite pleased."

This mood lasted all day.

THERE, near Mini's house, near the sweet shop with its heavy smell and the decrepit landlords' houses, birds rose almost peacefully into the air.

Thus they would rise habitually from this most ancient part of Calcutta, shriek, and then return a few moments later to balconies and cornices.

In the south, a rather mournful looking red flag went up by an excavated ditch in the middle of the road. There was no breeze these days, except the slightest one, which caused the flag to flutter.

TOWARDS the end of March, Bhaskar went to see a girl who lived in Jodhpur Park. This meeting was reported to Khuku by Puti, her niece.

"She sings, mashi," came Puti's voice on the ear-piece. "So of course Bholamama asked her to sing. Then he sang a couple of songs himself."

"Really?"

"Yes." Puti's laughter filled the space of the ear-piece momentarily. "But you know Bhola mama, mashi."

Apparently they had liked the family—it was strange how all the families had been likeable; this particular father occupied a respectable position in a fairly well known company; and the daughter, "although no beauty," had "personality."

"Is she not good-looking?" asked Khuku.

"Mm." She thought for an instant. "They said she has sharp features—a little too sharp, said Abha mami. She's neither dark nor fair."

"What does Bhaskar think?"

"Bhaskar wants to marry her," said Puti. "He liked her very much."

"But I thought he was going marry the other girl—the one whose mother died of cancer?"

Puti lowered her voice thoughtfully.

"I think Bhaskar likes whoever he meets," she said. "Now the first girl is too quiet for him. This one is more talkative."

THREE days after the meeting, the father rang up Bhola: "Mr Biswas, she's our only daughter; our only child I mean. And to tell you the truth, it's my wife who's a little unsure . . ." The wife, who'd been so welcoming, so enthusiastic! And was the telephone the right place to vent these misgivings? "No, I can see why, Mr Lahiri," said Bhola. He had half expected it. "But," said Mr Lahiri, "if it's not a serious thing—his commitments I mean—because we liked the boy very much . . ." But Bhola could give the gentleman no such assurance. "Mr Lahiri," he said, suddenly moved, "my son is concerned about things affecting each one of us today . . . But I can say that his political ideals don't affect his work or his family life." "I quite understand," said Mr Lahiri.

A DECISION *just* had to be made; would Bhaskar marry, or
would he wait? He'd come to set his heart in secret on the last
girl, but that now seemed out of the question and the desire
almost faded. He had waited; he had waited for a reply that did
not come. Then he thought impulsively, "I must not prolong
indefinitely what is after all a wearisome business." Yet he
couldn't bring himself to utter the final syllable. The second
girl was what remained; he couldn't recall her face for the
moment; but did that matter? "Say yes," he said in his own dark-
ness, addressing himself, "we cannot control our own fate."

After a few days, Bhaskar agreed to marry the second girl
he'd met.

So it was that the match was decided with hardly any of the
other relatives knowing about it; they went, ignorant and
happy, about their own ways; and even Puti who had a way of
hearing about things long before others did remained ignorant.
The others who would have heard were kept from this news for
about a week; of this union between Vidyasagar Road and a
lane off Lansdowne Road.

· · ·

THE girl was two years younger than her son; she's dark, but so am I, thought Bhaskar's mother.

And it'll do him good, she thought, to have some responsibility on his shoulders at last; for I think he still depends too much on his father. His father's growing old; it had hardly occurred to them, because time seems not to affect the people one is closest to; they have a living but transcendental existence in those who love them. He needs to grow up; he's still such a boy; and she thought of him tenderly, in her mind's eye, with a *Ganashakti* in one hand. They all had dreams, but Bhaskar's mother's was practical rather than grandiose; for she hoped, no, she believed, rather calculatingly, that the marriage would divide Bhaskar's energies and weaken this attachment to politics; while Bhaskar's dreams, they were another matter, they were the nation's dreams, or so he believed . . .

There was a plan in her mind, quite cunning, and probably all the more effective because she wasn't entirely conscious of it. She had expected, in truth, it would be a year, even more, before Bhaskar found a girl. But it had happened uncommonly quickly, as if fate itself had decided it should be so and that the problem should be dispensed with. She herself—Bhaskar's mother—remembered when she'd seen her husband's photograph for the first time, when she was eighteen, and hadn't liked him particularly because he was balding.

AND thus it happened that the date for the marriage was fixed after Bhola said yes to Dr Ghosh. The parents acted with undue haste, wanting to get it over with as soon as possible, before the two concerned had had a chance to change their minds. And the summer had only just begun to get unpleasantly hot.

The venue for the reception had now to be fixed; they gravely consulted the calendar with "Goodforce Literod"

printed on it; and they decided it would be convenient to have it in a house located five minutes away, across the main road and the tramlines, which had been renting out its ground floor for weddings ever since they could remember. Of course it was a house like any other, but noticeably at certain times of the year it was transformed and almost made unrecognisable by lights. Then, later, it returned to being just another house, but never completely lost its aura of being a house where weddings were held. Even dates in the summer for this house were in demand, for people were always getting married whenever there was an auspicious day in the almanac; thus the seventeenth was already booked, so was the twenty-first, and so was the third, leaving only the twelfth.

THEY began writing names on envelopes, names of people who lived in other parts of Calcutta, and in Pennsylvania and California and England, people who wouldn't be able to come to the wedding, and might have even forgotten what Bhaskar looked like; all their names were written in the heat, and the cards put inside the envelope.

"YOU haven't called Minidi and Shantidi yet," said Bhaskar's mother.

Bhola looked up.

"I will of course," he said, and admitted to himself that he'd forgotten. How could one possibly remember everyone? And this was a time that memory played tricks with you.

Since moving to Calcutta, they had seen each other every year except this one. For Mini and Shantidi used to come religiously by bus once or twice a year to Bhola's house with a pot of sweets from the north in their hands, their exultation far exceeding the occasion; and this was before the roads became bad and when they themselves were untroubled physically; before their brother had moved and they became overwhelmed

by the weight and pressure of their sheer everyday existence. On those visits, they had seen Bhola struggle with his business; seen Bhaskar growing up and Piyu cram for her exams; seen Bhola's mother as an old and absent woman, and then heard of her death; seen Manik go abroad; been present, in other words, in the semi-lit, casual backstage and dress rehearsals, the unconscious, helpless putting on and putting off of different selves and incarnations, of their lives.

IT WAS afternoon. And in a small lane, in front of a pavement, with the movement of a wrist, something like a curve began to appear, it was not clear what pattern was forming, then the letter D appeared upon a the wall of a two-storey house, in black paint, and then U, and N, until DUNKEL had been formed, in the English language, which seemed to blazon itself for its curious purpose; then it began again, and I and M and F began to appear in another corner. Afternoon; no one saw them; it was too hot; on the main road cars went past, up and down; a few people rested; they had eaten; beggars dozed, blind to the heat and shadows, their heads bent to their stomachs. Others on the pavement on the main road, who lived near shop windows or facing tramlines, were still finishing their meals on their plates. Now a picture was forming that would multiply, like an ornate decoration, in different parts of the city, a decoration mirrored, yet seen by almost no one, glanced at perhaps as other thoughts occupied one's head, background to people waiting for buses; yet it told a story. Gatt had been ratified of course; the whole matter had been done with and it had left a wound; yet they went on with these slogans as if they knew something might still come of it. Gradually, on the perfectly good whitewashed wall, there appeared a tiger with the finance minister's turbaned head, a man in coat-tails, a hat that had stars and stripes drawn

on it, with a hoop in one hand. The minister, who was, after all, three-quarters tiger, seemed to be polite and full of pleasant intentions but compromised by some invisible fact; he hesitated a moment before he leapt. All else, the figures in the background, the man in the coat-tails, waited; the music had stopped. Only a crow, unseeing, inadvertent, unmindful of human beings, hopped on the pavement again and again, as the spectacle, frozen, unfolded, appeared to be both searching for, and avoiding, something. Silence echoed all around; even the crow neglected to caw; what would the next action be? Again and again the human-headed tiger seemed to be about to jump but did not. Nikhil, standing and watching, wanted a cup of tea.

WHEN Mini woke up, she reached out for her spectacles. For without them she suffered a temporary darkening of vision.

And then she saw her sister. There was Shantidi, already awake, wandering about in the balcony.

Although Shantidi was better now, and her mild fracture had healed, she had changed to a new, intractable sort of introspection and stubbornness. She would not leave the house.

"What's the matter," asked Mini finally, "isn't it tiresome for you to stay here all day? Why don't you start going out a little?"

Shantidi laughed. She shook her head.

"There are things you don't know," she said. "There's a reason I don't go out."

"And what is the reason?" asked Mini.

"You are too trusting, Mini. There are people with their eye on the flat."

"On *our* flat?" asked Mini, incredulous but nevertheless agitated, her heart beating, with a logic of its own, a little faster. (For over the last two months she'd understood that they could

just barely make do on about three thousand rupees a month, but fell short if there were emergencies or accidents. And for the first time the idea came to her, the idea of them living in an old-age home, and that it might be the best future they'd have.)

Shantidi shook her head solemnly. Outside, there was the high-pitched call of a bird that seemed unused to these surroundings.

"Not only our flat—any flat! If the corporation thinks any flat has been left empty, they will take over it and sell it. And there are people over here in the building who are ready to buy another flat to add to their own property. You know that families keep growing." She gestured around her. "Besides, there are people living here who have connections with the corporation—what if they go and tell someone?" She spoke with great, knowledgeable practicality, as she always had.

For many years they'd had no one but each other, and sometimes when they spoke they just became two voices, speaking to each other for the sake of speaking, and when they were silent their surroundings became audible.

And Mini wondered where she'd got all her information— she who had almost broken her leg and had not stirred out of her home for more than a month. She's beginning to have delusions now, sitting here with almost nothing to do, she thought; this is a new development, she concluded interestedly.

"Who told you?" she asked.

"I've heard—" Then, as if to redeem this generality and strengthen her case, she said, "Mrs Roy told me as well." And suddenly she looked alone.

There was something in Mini's presence, even as she stood there, small and silent, that imparted peace. It emanated and touched those who were around her.

"But you can go out for a few hours. No one will take possession of the flat if you're away for a short while."

"Oh no no! You can't say!" said Shantidi. "These corporation people are capable of anything! And they keep track! They might knock on the door when both of us are away, and say, 'Write it down, this flat is empty.' "

THERE was a by-lane off Central Avenue, on the corner of which there was a shop that dealt in osteopathic aids and implements, part of it facing the main road. Some of these implements were curved and bent fluently, so that they looked like limbs themselves, on the verge of moving, except that they were sturdy and shone, metallic. It was strange the way you might not have seen the shop for years and then one fine day you noticed it. But when someone at school mentioned it to Mini she already knew the place. She thought she might look in and consider buying a special stick of some sort. For actually the pain, which had disappeared almost, was gradually coming back.

AND now Bhaskar wore his white bridegroom's topor; and Bhola first wore his own dhuti and then tied one around his son. But Bhaskar's fluttered in secret as if he was nervous before a performance even as outwardly he managed to appear uniformly either bored or harried; and he had the merest premonition of coming happiness, so natural a state that he would already be unable to remember any other that had preceded it.

All that month Piyu, at her study-table, had read for her tests beneath the light of the table lamp.

The frightening and exhilarated sound of ululation rose over the other sounds in Vidyasagar Road; it disturbed some of the children rapt in their textbooks in the other houses. A wedding was not unusual in the evening though it might be unexpected at that time of year. And it reminded one of other things which the city usually kept secret. People on balconies watched as a car came to pick up Bhaskar; darkness had settled on almost everything; a small group of relatives formed temporarily outside the gates of the house, deterring passersby. They were patiently waiting for Bhaskar; he'd gone to the toilet; they noted that it was twenty-five minutes to the auspicious

moment, the lagna, and hoped he wouldn't be long . . . but here he was! Then they got into the car; Bhola, his heart in his mouth, and other relatives would follow in their cars through Vidyasagar Road and Ashutosh Mukherjee Road.

It was a little after sunset that it had begun; now it was, to all purposes, night, but a stream of commerce and transactions between human beings continued in aggregations of localities, oblivious to everything else. Some people had come all the way from Shyambazar and Paikpara, with children who had their heads stuck out of the car window most of the way and had to have their hair combed before they got out. Later, there would be people whom no one recognised eating at the tables.

THE slow but by now palpable approach of Bhaskar's car set into motion a small, wing-like flutter of panic among the waiting children, cries of "Here's the bridegroom!" and much tripping on the folds of the unfamiliar garments they were enveloped in. Once more that unearthly ululation was heard, like nothing issuing from the voices of humans. In Sandhya's father's heart, as he walked forth swiftly, there was a stirring, like a stab of pain, for his motherless daughter. And in Vidyasagar Road, Bhaskar's mother, who would arrive later, sat alone with herself as company, become a shadow in the house she'd come to so many years ago.

And when Bhaskar saw the priests, he was startled and mystified. For he had forgotten the sacredness of the enterprise, the pact with ancestry, caste, and divinity which the two priests would make on his behalf. And they would evidently be his wayfarers and guides for the next hour or so.

Both of the priests were touchingly and shabbily self-conscious on the occasion, as a recently married couple might

be caught waking up at home. One of them had hair that was oiled and combed back; and the other one, when he opened his mouth, revealed he had a couple of teeth missing.

"I'll take the Gold Spot!"

"Would you like a Gold Spot, Uncle?"

"Bring one here!"

The children were fighting to serve soft drinks.

"It's not quite a bourgeois affair, is it?"

"I suppose not. What can you say about weddings, though—our mothers and fathers did it the same way."

"Our parents did a lot of things that . . . ask that boy for a Gold Spot."

Two party members, in somewhat loud clothes, unusually happy, talking above the music, were inhaling the perfume of sandalwood in smoke and exploring the territory.

HE HAD to look at Sandhya and she at him; the division—a white cloth—was removed. His relatives were teasing him and he had begun to be irritable; he remembered that one meeting they had had, and that he had not dared to look at her properly then, and this seemed to him almost a continuation of that very meeting. "Ei, look at him," cried her cousins; and she did finally, and smiled, as if at a private thought.

After an hour they both got up at the priest's command to walk seven times around the fire. When he sat down again, he thought he would open a conversation and say, "It's hot, isn't it?" but did not. When Mohit and Sameer and his cousin Arnab approached him to speak to him, as if he had been smuggled into another world but could still communicate in monosyllables with this one, he answered over the droning of the priests with a casual smile and murmur. His nostrils were full of smoke and, now and then, the smell of sandalwood. She seemed quite

stoic and self-assured, wiping away the perspiration from her forehead. It was a moment of great loneliness for them, as they sat there, not understanding the mantras; what seemed to be boredom in them was actually an odd, vacant melancholy; but, meanwhile, the photographers craned over each other, bumping into relatives, while the flashbulbs went off.

They had been asked to repeat their own names; their parents' names; each other's names; they had been wished well, in a Sanskrit they did not understand, and a happy married life by Tradition, in the person of these priests. Then one of the priests said, "It's finished," to Bhaskar as he rose, surreptitiously, as if imparting a bit of taboo information before leaving. For they had been asked by Bhola to complete the rituals as quickly as they could and had managed to abbreviate a few things and skim guilelessly over others (and dilate a few stanzas, since they were being paid by the hour) and they had finished in just under two hours. The wedding was over, and, though no one appeared to have noticed and they themselves were almost ignorant of it, the two—the young man, who evidently had a backache, and the young woman—were now married. They were at a loss as to what to do now; they had the puzzled air of people who'd just knocked on a door and were on the verge of turning round without having heard a reply from within.

B U T it was difficult to come to terms with how ordinary it was. The new dhuti was already crumpled; and Bhaskar was wearing his kurta again, shyly.

A bed had been made for them, and complex garlands and tassels of flowers, painstakingly created, hung on all sides around it to enclose the two, at some future moment, in privacy. When they would go, eventually, to Vidyasagar Road, this bed

would go with them and climb lightly up all the stairs to Bhaskar's room.

A ND after another three days, when Bhaskar had brought his bride to his house and promised, at a ceremony, to provide her with food and clothes for the rest of her life, he grew drowsy; he had spent three days eating.

In the evening, Sandhya took off her wedding sari and went into the bathroom—an interval passed in which her absence was not noticed—and she emerged wearing a red cotton sari, her hair wet. She folded the Benarasi she had been wearing and asked Bhaskar's mother, "Where should I keep this?" And it was as if a new way of life had been inaugurated in this house.

THEY were in the large room on the second floor, where Bhaskar used to sleep alone. That night they sat on the bed, with gifts on every side.

She seemed reticent.

"That light is so bare," she said, pointing to a light attached to the wall, "it should have a lamp-shade."

He looked at the light.

"Were you tired today?" he asked without sincerity.

"No—were you?" she asked, folding handkerchiefs that had been received as a gift.

"Not really," he said, suppressing a yawn. "Though I *am* feeling a little sleepy." They spoke as if they'd known each other for years, while Vidyasagar Road unfolded before them, invisibly, as if it had never changed. He immediately regretted saying this, because he wanted to talk to her; but his eyes were red and tired.

Later, he went and changed into his kurta and pyjamas and returned and lay upon the bed. Sandhya came out of the bathroom wearing a nightie, tying her hair into a plait. Her shadow hovered upon the wall, trying to find its home here.

"Where does Piyu sleep?" she asked thoughtfully.

"Downstairs," he replied.

She considered this silently. Entire childhoods had passed in this room, like a light going out, that she could only sense unclearly. He didn't know what to do next. As she sat on the bed, he turned around again; he glanced at her narrow back, at the dark skin above the neck of her nightie, the colour of her shoulders. And he wondered why she had decided to marry him; it was probably some entirely trivial reason, something he should be able to imagine but couldn't. Plausibly, almost touchingly, there might be no good reason: how mysterious the world was at every moment, the birth of love and generations. The nightie, starched cotton, was a pattern of pink flowers with white borders, almost like a curtain, probably made recently by some tailor or chosen from ten nighties that looked nearly the same at some shop; and when she lay down beside him, he scratched his arm and pretended to be tired. But he also felt the guilty, obtrusive stirring of desire; he kept it to himself, instinct or some genetically inherited knowledge instructing him that there was a decorum about these things he must observe. They still had a few of the ornamental marks that had been made along their faces and foreheads, which hadn't come off with soap; Sandhya's having been made by an aunt, widowed, forty-two years old, watched by her two twelve-year-old daughters (they were twins). But Sandhya had never known before now, the eve of her wedding, the minor artistic accomplishments this aunt, who lived on Vivekananda Road, possessed; actually, she did not know her very well; but she had, with a clove dipped repeatedly in sandalwood paste, made, with every tiny pinprick impress, those subtle marks on her forehead. If there was one thing she would have liked to keep from that day it would have been these patterns.

"I have to wake up early tomorrow," he muttered, waiting to see what she would say. But she didn't protest; she had wavy

hair; he saw that she had dark lips; the calm sound of the fan repeatedly filled the silence. "Are you missing home?" he said, turning on his side and letting his hand fall near her shoulder; he had acquired a small belly, and she seemed thin in comparison to him. This morning, she had cried when leaving her house. "No, not really," she said, quite gravely, like a child who has had a new experience. It was strange; they'd spoken with each other at length two nights ago in the rented room in that house in which they'd been married; and they had forgotten, for the time being, what they had talked about and would almost have to be reacquainted with each other. Bhaskar switched off the light and they tried to fall asleep. He had not known before how shy he was with the opposite sex. It was an uncomfortable night; whenever a car passed through the lane, its headlights lit up the wall of the room, and towards dawn, a kitten mewed and sounded like a child crying. Each sound set the tympanum in the inner ear vibrating.

Towards dawn he awoke and gazed unsurprised at her as she slept, her eyelids momentarily parted to reveal the blue-grey light in her eyeball. But she was not awake, and everywhere there were only the merest signs of life; the blue dawn; a reticent vibration from the tramline; the early insistent cry of a shalik; her breath; in each of these life resided on the edge of itself. Meanwhile the fan lulled them.

When Bhaskar woke up again, he found she was not there. He was surrounded by the sound of crows and buses and rickshaws and the tube-well and schoolchildren, all things apparently in perpetual transit. Going down, he saw to his disconcertment that she had joined his parents and Piyu for breakfast in the room where they all ate.

"WHERE should I put these?"

Sandhya was holding a chain from which a golden locket hung. She held it, weightless, in her palm.

"Let's put this one back in its box," said Bhaskar's mother. They bent forward like two conspirators. Light glinted and scattered.

It was one of the things she had given her. Last month she had taken a bus and gone to the jeweller's and had had a necklace and a pair of earrings "broken" and converted into this longer, this more beautiful piece. And she felt a strange tenderness towards it that was not unconnected to loss, for what was once hers had become something else and someone else's.

Her youth lived on in the forms these jewels took. And whenever Bhaskar's mother felt that familiar boredom coming on with a piece of jewellery, she would take the piece, like a child with a toy, to the jeweller who had first made it and describe in words the new design, and leave the piece with him as if she were lending it to him; and he would give it back to her made "new" in five days. Sometimes, when the piece was not very old, one suffered a small loss, for the jeweller subtracted about a tenth of the gold as part of his fee.

When she was young gold had been cheap, and she remem-
bered those beloved thick bangles and that floral necklace she'd
got when she was married.

After Bhola had left his job and embarked upon his busi-
ness, Bhaskar's mother had been protective and uncompromis-
ing about one thing: her jewellery. She was wise; for it was
instinct rather than experience that told her that once he started
using her gold to cover his business losses, it would happen
again and again. But it had to be admitted that he had never
made such a request. And this disinterested emblem of beauty
and desire, the soul's continual yearning for celebration, so
removed from the everyday, which would one day belong
entirely to her children, to Piyu or to her sons' wives, remained
untouched.

TWO days later they stripped the bed of its floral covering;
some of the flowers had dried and fallen to the floor, from
where they were swept away by Haridasi. For Haridasi,
Bhaskar's wedding and the bride's arrival had been events
touched with wonder. It had certainly been the biggest change
in the household since she'd come to work here. She had
looked carefully at the bride, and thought she was graceful, if
not beautiful. And the bride too had glanced at her once or
twice.

BHASKAR'S father-in-law began to visit late in the morning.

"Come in, come in," Bhaskar's mother would say from the
verandah when he rang the bell. She would feel strangely
embarrassed, as if she wanted to keep something hidden from
him. During the wedding, under the artificial canopy, the world
shut out, she'd had trouble recognising him; there they were,

like two actors from separate plays, having met in a strange place, hot now at the end of it, he poised, she uncomfortable and glowing with the heat. Twice since the wedding she had seen him in dreams, in the first one arriving at their house bearing gifts and in the second inexplicably displeased about something. Ever since then her vision of him had been oddly prejudiced, as if she, to her discomfort, knew something about him that no one else did.

Sandhya would race down the stairs barefoot from the second storey.

"It's terrible out there," he would say, coming up.

Bhaskar's mother did not quite know how to take him. And she was wearing a green sari which she wore when doing housework.

He didn't seem to notice.

"It is easy to see," he would say, "that this is a house which a lady takes pleasure in keeping tidy."

From his second visit onward he would go straight up to the second storey; there he would sit talking with his daughter for an hour. On his way out he would shout a farewell to Bhaskar's mother.

He would come at all times of the day, but mainly in the morning.

What do they talk about? she would think.

"ARE those your parents, Ma?" asked Sandhya.

There were two pictures on the wall on this side of the room, one of Bhaskar's mother's father, another of her mother. Like them, she too, the new bride, did not feel that she as yet fully existed in this house. They considered this world from the hereafter with a certain immediacy; they both had daubs of vermilion on their foreheads that looked like they still hadn't quite dried. Outside, a summer that distributed, unequally, shadows and heat had settled down on Vidyasagar Road.

"Yes," said Bhaskar's mother. "And those are Baba's mother and father."

A smell of cooking drifted up stealthily from downstairs. And she, the newly married one, turned her eyes towards a large framed black-and-white photograph of an old woman in a white sari, sitting on what looked like a chair, and another of Bhola's father's wearing a moustache. The tops of the frames had become brown with a kind of fine powder as if they hadn't been dusted for weeks. These photographs had been hanging there for almost twenty years; and now their eyes gazed upon this couple each morning. She—the grandmother—had come to Bhola's father as his second wife, after the death of his first

one, sixteen years old at the time of marriage and only thirty-two when her husband died. Only her children remembered now that she had had a gift for mathematics and had won a gold medal at school, but had forfeited her studies after marriage, much to the disappointment of her schoolteacher, an English-woman, a disappointment that the sixteen-year-old herself couldn't understand. Along the wall, all the parents were joined together in eternal life, and a peripatetic gecko was known to live behind these portraits, curved, alone, arbitrarily moving from one frame to another. And Bhola's father was a mystery; no one in this house had set eyes upon him because he had died a few months before Bhola's birth. In that death lay the key to this family's early misery, and their subsequent search for order and balance.

And now they said he had been a King's Commission Engineer, one of the "heaven-born." But, after he died, the family had been left with nothing; and later he had become this portrait in this house on Vidyasagar Road gifted to Bhola by his father-in-law, now confronted by Sandhya. Something of his aptitude and perhaps the romance of engineering had been inherited by the family, shaping and influencing lives that were generations removed from him; generations to come that had never known him; for Borda's younger son was an engineer; Bhola had tried to cast himself in his father's mould and become a civil engineer, and created Goodforce Literod Ltd.; even Manik was studying engineering in Germany. In this way the grandfather that no one knew had lived on in his children's and grandchildren's lives.

SUMMER was everywhere. Meanwhile, Sandhya began to embroider a piece of cloth and make a doll's dress inside her room. She was always making things; now a bangled hand

pushed a thread through a needle. One shoulder leaning on an elbow, her sari's aanchal falling abstractedly from her back she pursued her handiwork.

Bhaskar was still something of an enigma in her life; she hardly knew him at all; and he reappeared in the evenings after his long journey from Howrah, tired. Then he would wash his face and feet beneath the tap in the small bathroom and there would be a faraway rush of running water. Emerging, he would quickly survey his reflection hovering darkly in the bed-side mirror. One evening, lying on the bed in the glare of the electric light, he asked her:

"What's this?"

For he had picked up the small shiny blue dress that had been left inadvertently next to a pillow. It was as if some tiny, subtle spirit that had perhaps visited this room had divested herself of her clothing before disappearing.

"Oh, that . . . that's something I made over the last two days when I had nothing else to do," she said, raising her face briefly.

He lifted it nakedly up to the light.

"It's a little small for you," he said, indifferent.

SHE knew very little about the company, too little; nothing but seeing Bhaskar become each morning a person who wore pleated trousers and a shirt and shoes before disappearing to a factory that made cranes. "Take me to it one day," she said, without meaning it.

And he knew nothing about her. In marrying each other they had in effect embraced the unknown and the inconsequential. To look at, she might have been anyone; sometimes he would notice how her shoulders looked tenderly hunched and rounded when she was sitting down; the next day he checked to see if it was still true, as if reality could not be relied upon not to change at short intervals; during this time everything he saw in her he saw with a child's guilty and inquisitive eye.

But she and her husband hardly had any time together. They met in the morning at the dining-table as acquaintances would, the reverberations of night-time already having faded and left them almost more distant from each other. Bhaskar did not look at her in the presence of others; he as good as pretended she wasn't there; and then he was gone for most of the

day. The first days of their marriage was a time of trust in the unproven and of unspoken longing.

Having grown up elsewhere, she had no friends in Calcutta. A few relatives lived on the outskirts of Calcutta, and others even further away. Now and then her brother appeared, dark and bespectacled and much like her to look at, and then disappeared again. And for the first month and a half of their marriage, Bhaskar took her quite for granted.

At night their fingers and hands crept towards each other, in the greed for closeness, and for those sensations, only incompletely experienced so far, of something between pain and satisfaction, concealment, and happiness.

Upstairs was where their new life began, beneath the photographs of late and ever-present grandparents. Where Bhaskar's and Manik's and Piyu's childhood had begun and evolved and come to a conclusion, where they'd slept together on the bed in often anarchic and filial positions, played between and under their beds and bruised themselves, another existence began at last.

SHE had become used to the lane which, at first, had kept her from sleep.

Early in the morning, when it was not quite light, she sometimes sensed him going out; it was inexplicable; she sighed; and then once or twice she saw him return with a pile of newspapers, the *Ganashakti*. It was a paper she'd never read; but Bhaskar insisted to her, with what seemed to be an excessive and uncomfortable advocacy, that it contained all the real and important news and all that was really worth reading. She didn't believe him; for *Ganashakti* was a paper that no one she knew read; it was, as far as she knew, used to make cartons

and containers in the market; and its pages were swept away in lanes and alleys. These early morning excursions of his became indistinguishable to her sometimes from the intense dreams she had before waking.

She kept herself to herself and still hadn't quite made friends with the family. During her solitary explorations, she found old comic books, toys, beneath the staircase to the terrace. And she discovered near a doll with an arm missing and a Ludo board a set of tiny pots and pans—kitchen utensils. Though they were old now, they must have once been used by Piyu to cook make-believe meals for an imaginary husband and family, or probably just for the sake of imitating the motions of cooking. How possessive children are about their imaginary homes!—almost as proprietorial as they are when they grow up and have real ones. Sandhya found them when clearing away piles of other things that had been dumped beneath the stairs to the terrace (she was beginning to rearrange this floor which would be her household), their small but exact shapes lying overturned, but still intact.

AND then she put artificial flowers and leaves, imitations of tulips, roses, in two vases. She had loved these so much, almost as if they were alive—she had bought them from a small stall in Gariahat and carried them back crowded in her arms. They, however, turned out to be a less than perfect replica, the edge of the leaf frayed, with a few short strands of loose thread hanging from it.

"Why don't you get real flowers?" asked Bhaskar one day.

"If I have real flowers," said Sandyha, "they'll die in a couple of days—and then who'll give me the money to buy new ones: you?"

"But these will get dirty in a week," he said.

"They won't," said Sandhya, aware of some protective magic which would keep the dust from getting to the flowers; and with such conviction did she say it that for a moment Bhaskar was convinced as well. Thus the perennially blooming flowers, cheap, bright, immortal blossoms, remained.

THEY had still not been on their honeymoon; and the crows made an unbroken, troubled din outside and hopped about relentlessly. But they'd put all the cheques they'd got as wedding presents into a bank account; part of it they'd use for their trip. And as they spoke, weighing the size of their budget against their expected expenditure, India, in their imaginations, became a series of small hotels, connecting routes, different climates existing at once, peculiarities of cuisine.

She'd always wanted to go to Kashmir. And yet that paradise had been poisoned. How wonderful it was to wander through India with your parents as a child (she blurrily remembered travelling to strange places—this was such a large country—when her mother was alive; there was no death then, nor destiny), then to forget most of it, except a stomach upset that had made you sick or a sari being bought by your mother in a shop or the paleness of a white hotel façade, and then have a sense of it come back to you many years later as you prepared to make the journey with another person, almost a stranger.

. . .

FOR a few days, they—Bhaskar's relatives—had been waiting to see if Bhaskar, upon getting married, would gradually relinquish his commitment to the party and take up a more respectable form of existence. The party was spoken of as an illicit but persistent liaison.

"But I don't think Sandhya will allow him to continue for long."

Someone else said, "She's a hard-headed sensible girl after all."

"Let us see."

They waited. But married life and its responsibilities seemed to leave Bhaskar unchanged. He was still selling *Ganashakti*; and, even now, he would, vociferously if necessary, and for as long as he could, marshalling an array of facts and arguments, criticise the new and sinister global order, the present government that was governing shamelessly from the centre, illegal bargains between nations and business houses, and every relative, cousin, or uncle who happened to disagree with him.

CRPF soldiers; three months ago, and before then, they'd appeared when the roads were silent, waiting for riots to break out in the city though they eventually hadn't. Sleepy-eyed, waving at the children. As if they were passing through, a peacekeeping force on their way elsewhere.

And yesterday, going through Ballygunge and Park Circus, a truckload that not everyone noticed. These sleepy, sometimes smiling men. Although they were so still now, they could be cruel. Waiting patiently in the traffic jam like the others, their job probably long done . . .

THEY—Bhaskar and the wife he hardly knew—made preparations for the journey, preparations to be absent from the house for five days. From responsibilities and business partners, parents and parents-in-law, the meetings in the evening, they decided to take a train to Siliguri, and from there a bus to Darjeeling. People had taken the route many times before and many had it by heart; it was like a well-known line of poetry.

They passed roads that had been made by the British, connecting Bengal to the rest of the country, and which were still more or less unchanged, passing the dirty ponds and warm villages of Bengal, hungry children and women with their heads lowered, bulls sunning themselves; INDIA IS GREAT said the message that disappeared between two places; Bhaskar saw these things as a husband and a holiday-maker rather than one who'd become involved in the struggle; they were accompanied in the train by a Bengali family, by old women, and children with colds; they had with them two suitcases, a flask, and a tiffin carrier.

. . .

ALL works of art are illusions, for the worlds they portray do not exist; but some forms conceal that fact less than others, because they are replete with the shape of real people and real streets, almost in spite of themselves. Street theatre, for instance; the imagination of the playwright only comes into play when fantasy overlaps with and moreover reveals the actual living places he's surrounded by. Rummaging upstairs for something else, Bhaskar's mother discovered, grown damp with moisture, photocopied manuscripts among a heap of discarded desiderata and wondered what they were, for without the actual scene of the enactment—the crowded backstreets of the city—the words, in themselves peculiar and forced, made no sense to her.

"When he's back," she said when two days had passed, "I want him to see the doctor again."

"Why? Does he still have that backache?" asked Bhola.

"I think so. It's the way he bends at times. He does it slowly and hesitantly, as if it's a luxury."

AND Khuku lay on her bed in the afternoon. Although her eyes were closed, she was wide awake, she could hear Nando quarrelling, and she wondered if it was good for Shib to be in that office in this heat at his age: she didn't like it. Outside, in the blank heat, the sun pulsed like a star that could not be seen.

Oh, men must work; nothing else makes them as happy. But she lay there, cross, unable to sleep.

THERE was movement in the clouds outside, and lightning; it stirred the air. Shib came back to her as he used to be when he was a boy, when he visited their home so often that she was hardly aware of him, but unaware of him in a different way from her unawareness of him now; a different way of taking someone's presence for granted. How like a ghost that boy was, both in his paleness and in the strangeness his memory had assumed. He was her brother Pulu's best friend, a boy whose quietness was deceptive because he noticed more than he appeared to. He was wavy-haired, as he was now, and used to be unusually fair skinned, more so then than he was at present. He had no mother; she had died when he was two years old,

and he'd never had any memory of her. He used to be shy when he came to their house, and her own mother had a special fondness for him because he was motherless and an only child. Thus there was that lost quality about him, even though he belonged to one of the most well-to-do families in the town.

Unanswerable, obsolete questions glimmered in the flashes of lightning. What would have happened to Khuku if Shib had not married her? After school, Khuku's family had stopped her college education because they said they could not afford it; it was probably true. "But Khuku was never interested in school-work anyway," her brother said in explanation. She had cried for a week, for herself and in forgiveness. A vacancy opened up before her as one kind of life receded from her permanently, the world of exams and preparations and the panic of examination day, now only to be known in other people's lives. Then she had stayed at home and practised on the harmonium. She had read new novels, and entered into an imaginary world. Characters in stories became as real to her as people; like Khenti who loved pui leaves, and tender-hearted Goshtho didi in *Mahasthabir Jatak*. Years passed. She read; she waited; she waited silently for some change. She knew, instinctively, she wouldn't end in the place she'd begun in. They grew up— brothers, sisters, friends; Khuku, Bhola, Shib, Mini, not know-ing where they would live, what their children would look like, who their spouses would be, in what way their lives would be different from each other's, or what incarnation the world would take fifty years from now. At the beginning, they'd moved blindly from birth into the unknown, from darkness into the world; the passage into life, as the one through it, is a journey, and they, unlike the ones who had died in midlife or as children, had been deemed to complete it, to live out their days in the world.

She hadn't even realised that Shib thought of her in a par-

ticular way. (Shib said that it was her singing that had decided him; and this alarmed her; what if she had not been able to sing?) But Khuku's elder sister, that stern woman and tender romantic, would always say later, "I knew it. When Khuku pinched Shib once, and I saw Shib blush, I knew it." Khuku herself had had no idea. When he first proposed to her, in a roundabout way, through her mother, she refused without hesitation. "But I don't think of him in that way!" she said. "He's more like a brother to me . . ." Her mother had said, "Think again. You won't find another like him." But Khuku hesitated; she was certain she was in love with someone else. How intense and chastening those emotions seemed now! On and on one goes, gradually to become a stranger to oneself, but never completely, and never knowing what it is that pushes us in one direction and not another . . . And how deeply they believed in romantic love in those days: it was all those long novels. She procrastinated; she said neither no nor yes. Then one day, after she had finished singing a song, she saw a kindness on Shib's face she had not noticed before; it had always been there, but she had not seen it; it was as if she'd suddenly recognised who he was. Soon after they were engaged, and Shib went to England; and, after six years, she followed him there. It was a few years after Independence; Shib's father had died; he knew he would never return home. Their marriage was thus a marriage of childhood acquaintances, of two people who had known each other when they had hardly mattered to one another and who had grown one day into their shared life without hardly being aware of it; only slightly embarrassed when that awareness came. And their new life, under some nameless star, began with each other.

THEN she remembered her friend's arthritis, and the pain, persistent, monotonous, as personal as something imagined, which was born of neglect and carelessness. Yet the thing about arthritis was that you didn't know why it happened to one person and not to another; there appeared to be no clearly identifiable cause; it was yet another mystery that governed and left its casual and even heartless impress upon existence. It's four months now, she thought, and recalled that Mini should have been back in three months for another checkup. And yet the thought of Mini, whose every trouble filled her with a sense of responsibility, also, contradictorily, brought to her a feeling of happiness and excitement.

The last time she'd called her was when there had been an explosion in Central Avenue, not very far from Mini's building; and they'd trembled and thought that the troubles had begun in Calcutta. But no, to their relief, but almost to their disappointment as well (for they succumbed easily to excitement), it was the arsenal of a local hoodlum that had blown up by accident.

I wonder how she is, thought Khuku (for Mini came back to her as a person in a dream), and dialled the number of her school. "Hello?" she said. "Can I speak to Supriti Biswas?"

The person at the other end seemed to weigh this question and consider its merits. Supriti Biswas. In a voice that sounded slightly put out, the person eventually relented and said, "Hold on a minute, please."

There was a gap of five minutes. She heard the voices of children, random and happy, in the ear-piece. Then a voice she knew well said, "Khuku?"

LATER she grew sleepy; the talk had relaxed her. The light of oncoming dusk played and scattered on the large windows. It scattered and seemed to vanish but remained like a glaze. A thought came to her: I'll go there tomorrow; she said she'd be at home.

She'd fall asleep now as usual in the middle of the afternoon and wake up unable to tell for how long she'd slept, whether it was ten minutes or half an hour or more. Why, sometimes it seemed to her she'd fallen asleep as a child and woken up to find that most of her life had passed by; she was here.

A visit to a friend's house has its own secrecy. Sometimes it seems that there is no reason, except a slight sense of boredom, a hint of life's emptiness, a memory of familiarity, and a promise of pleasure. Half asleep already, she prepared herself for the journey.

Five years ago, after her husband had retired, she'd come to this city with some trepidation and uncertainty to make her home here in old age. The young leave this city if they can; the old, it seems, return to it; and this had been the incentive for coming here—the possibility of experiencing, in early old age, the buoyancy of visiting known houses through these roads, of watching the old apparently arrest and embrace time as children and grandchildren grow taller and older, surprising one.

And there were friends, which she hadn't thought of then. Every time she went to the New Municipal Corporation Buildings with their strange E-shaped block of flats off Central Avenue it was as if something had changed slightly from before and she couldn't put her finger on it. The route was familiar, though, the dust and reconstruction and disrepair. It was not so much a return to childhood for her as a contact with something she'd known for a long time, in conditions neither she nor her friend could have foreseen. And now, very lightly, like a merciful gift of remembrance, obliterating as it engendered, it began to rain. It fell on the graffiti on the walls inside lanes, the hammer and sickle that multiplied everywhere, and the pleas for family planning, the advertisements for companies; it first rained on South Calcutta and then moved towards the north, the clouds prefiguring, and desultorily washing, the route Khuku would take.

I'll take a flask of tea and some sweets from Mahaprabhu, she thought.

For she didn't want Mini or Shantidi in the kitchen once she'd arrived.

Must tell that rascal straightaway, she decided, thinking of Nando. Of course, if I tell him now he'll forget about it tomorrow.

She must remind that shirker to put the tea in the flask the first thing the next morning.